SLAIN

LIVIA HARPER

To Dave, with all my love.

SLAIN

LIVIA HARPER

"It's so often true that Christians are one army that kills their wounded. And we don't…we don't try to nurse them back to health."
  - Pat Boone, Christian Entertainer

CHAPTER ONE

"Let me hear it if you're fired up for Christ tonight!" Pastor Pete, the youth pastor, says into the mic like it's a megaphone at a pep rally.

There are hoots and hollers from the pajama-clad, Red Bull-buzzed crowd in front of us. I try to concentrate on what I'm supposed to do, instead of my little secret, buzzing inside me like a lightning bug. Okay, maybe it's a big secret. Huge. Am I grinning too wide? Knock it off, Emma.

"All right. Let's do this thing." Pastor Pete strums his guitar to start an amped-up version of "Our God is an Awesome God." He looks like Hipster Jesus: thick beard, plaid shirt, worn denim, long hair. I sing harmony just behind him, a fly girl for the Lord.

The other teenagers sing along and clap—more than three hundred of them tonight in this too-bright basement. We're at a youth group lock-in at Summit Christian Fellowship, where my dad, Frank Grant, is head pastor. I am head pastor's daughter—it's not an official position, but it should be. Tonight I'm up on stage in the Youth Center, singing with the worship team, where I am every Sunday morning, every Wednesday night, and other nights too, so many they all blur together like a photograph taken too slow. Tonight is Friday, nearly midnight. We're locked in until ten tomorrow morning for one big, holy sleepover.

This room is like a concert hall: stage, lights, bright colors, polished concrete floors. The whole design is supposed to be trendy and youthful: Loving Jesus is what all the cool kids do!

1

But the modern hardness just makes the room reverberate with echoes, like everything we're singing is being sung back to us, louder and slower and ten times over.

The song changes to something softer as I stare out at the sea of teenagers. They stare back, waiting.

I paste on a smile and do what's expected of me: a little game of follow the leader, though they'd never admit it, not here. I force my hands up toward the cold basement ceiling; force my body to sway to the music that is the same, same, same as always. My forehead screws into the perfect picture of reverence. I've had lots of practice.

After my hands go up, theirs do too. Not all at once. They stagger it, pretend it's their idea, pretend they've just-right-this-very-second been moved by the Holy Spirit. Some of them get their tongues going for God, a cartoon speech bubble from their mouths, *habadah-shebada-bah*.

I used to think my going first gave them the courage to do what they were straining to do already. Now I doubt it. I'm just their Taylor Swift in this tiny, stupid little universe.

Six more weeks until graduation and a plane to New York. Six more weeks.

Someone shouts, pulling me out of my daydream. At first I think it's a prophecy, another so-called gift of the Spirit, but this is fast and shrill. I don't understand. It takes the band a minute to stop playing. Then Beth and Amy are at the door. Amy's crying, hysterical.

"Somebody come! Please!" Beth cries.

My blood runs cold, but everyone else laughs awkwardly. Beth is the head of the drama team so they must think this is a skit. Pastor Pete always puts on these wild skits, full of demons and desperate people making poor life choices. But I've memorized the schedule for tonight, and this isn't on it. Did they see Jackson?

Once she's got our attention, Beth turns and runs.

I'm out the door then. Others follow me down the hall, chasing Beth's back as she screams. Someone behind us, an adult voice, yells at us to stop, but I don't. I have to know if they saw him when he left.

We race down the hall and up the stairs, my dark hair flying behind me like a flag. We run through a long corridor full of

Sunday school rooms, then past the Connections Café, past the Rock Auditorium, and past the Devotions Bookstore. We run through the massive lobby and right into the main sanctuary, empty and dark and big enough to hold five thousand. The sound of our breathing disappears into the air above the rafters.

June is lying near the pulpit, her body sprawled, her sundress fanned out like she fell backward and never got up. And her eyes are blank. Not fake, come-to-Jesus-lesson blank. Empty. And there's blood all over her front. Only it smells like copper instead of corn syrup and her chest isn't moving and there's no way she can hold her breath that long.

Something that was sweet inside me shatters to dust, a butterscotch candy on train tracks.

No, no, no, no, no, no, no.

It can't be real, it just can't.

"June?" I ask, my voice cracking. There's no answer.

Someone screams and turns away. Others hold their hands over their mouths in shock. Then there's a panicked clatter of questions, Pastor Pete telling us all to go back downstairs.

Then a noise. A door opening. The lobby? Slam. Click.

"What was that?"

"I saw someone!"

I'm barely breathing. I can't breathe at all. The whole world splits into before and after this moment, and I'm stuck on the wrong side: an hour ago, yesterday, last summer. The first time I saw June, soggy from the rain. How she looked both fresh and dirty at the same time, like a daisy still upright after a mudslide. And then tonight, before everything else happened, June worried and wanting more from me like always. But then everything else did happen.

And I forgot all about June.

CHAPTER TWO

A FEW HOURS AGO

The wooden cross on my shoulder is hollow. It thuds against our bones as I and four other girls carry it through a crowd of candle-lit banquet tables toward the dance floor in the center, our matching white tulle skirts swishing against our calves as we walk in perfect step. There is a line of twenty more girls behind us, but only the five of us are carrying the cross. Girls as young as six, as old as twenty-three. Our fathers and brothers, dressed up for tonight in tuxedos, stand at attention at the tables, watching our little procession: a rite of passage.

We're in the auditorium of the church, which, unlike the larger sanctuary, only holds a thousand when the chairs are in rows. It's used for special events so that the main sanctuary is always available for regular church services. Tonight the chairs have been cleared to make way for banquet tables and a dance floor. The event sells out its 250 tickets every year.

The cross on my shoulder bears wear marks from where girls have carried it into this room, this same way, for fifteen years. Seven years' worth of the marks are mine. I've attended every ball since I turned eleven.

The girl next to me is crying. Fat tears tumble down her pretty cheeks as her blonde hair sways against her back in wispy waves. Her name is June, and this is her first Purity Ball. I try as hard as I can not to roll my eyes at her. I guess I cried at my first one too, but things were so much different back then. I still haven't decided if they were better.

"You okay?" I whisper as we approach the center of the

4

dance floor and lower the cross onto its stand. Paige, my best friend, eyes us to stop talking as she reverently drapes white chiffon across the short arms of the cross and hangs a crown of thorns over the hilt. She really believes it all, and is maybe the one person here who makes it hard to think they're all faking it.

"It's all just so beautiful, Emma," June says. "I wish. I just wish—"

But then the music starts, and it's time to dance. We whirl away from the cross, spinning and raising our arms daintily. Our Worship Dance Team leader, Miss Hope, calls it ballet, but no one who actually does ballet would call it that. It looks more like what toddlers do in princess dresses in their backyards.

As the music finishes up, we all bow dramatically toward the cross like broken swans. I look over and see that June is still crying, harder now. Part of me wishes I could be as moved by this as she is.

But I can't anymore. I just can't.

"If I could ask my daughter, Emma, to join me up front please?" I make my way to the podium where my dad is standing, his dark hair combed back in a slick wave, his tuxedo perfectly tailored, a soft smile on his face. He's not the kind of preacher who booms. He's the kind of preacher who whispers and makes you feel like it's a boom.

Since our little opening dance number, a formal dinner has been served, and I've had a chance to change. All the dancers have. Now we wear white ball gowns like debutantes even though the whole thing is pretty much the opposite of being a debutante. Instead of coming out, we're being shoved further back in.

But the dress part? That I'm on board with. Mine is a vintage silk fit-n-flare with a v-neck I had to argue with my mother to keep. I love this dress. It makes me feel dangerous and sexy, like a chestnut-haired Marilyn Monroe. I feel like a movie star, especially with the diamond earrings my Grandma Wellington sent me for Christmas.

When I arrive at the front, my dad takes my hand. "Fathers, before we begin the pledge, I'd like to take a moment to bestow a blessing upon my own precious daughter." His voice is soft and open, like a waterfall far away, its collection of crashes combined and muted by distance. He takes my face in his hands and stares into my eyes. I try not to fidget. I try not to think about everyone else's eyes on me: the other girls, their fathers, and many of the boys too. Even my sorta-boyfriend, Mike, is here tonight.

"Emma," my dad says, "you are so beautiful, both inside and out. God has blessed you with grace and wisdom and a servant's heart. He has made you a shining light to your peers, an ambassador of his love and his generosity." He closes his eyes and moves his right hand to palm my forehead. I close mine too, and bow my head as expected. "I ask tonight that God bless you with the strength and courage to set aside your own desires and let Him work through you to His glory. Proverbs 16:9 says, 'A man's heart plans *his* way, but *the Lord* directs his steps.'"

Real subtle, Dad. This morning I bring up the idea of going to New York University instead of Bethany Bible College, and all of a sudden my "blessing" is to be strong enough to want what I don't want. How convenient. I wonder what he'd say if he knew I've already been accepted, that the conversation was just me testing the waters about how to break the news to them. I wonder what he'd say if I told him the other, bigger news—that I'm not a Christian anymore.

He'd probably send me off to some wilderness camp or something, like Lily Vincent's parents did to her after she had sex with that guy at Youth Convention two Thanksgivings ago. Which is why I'm waiting to tell them. But I'm going no matter what they say.

My dad keeps talking. "I ask Him to help you set aside your pride, to quiet the demands of the world as you learn to listen to His, and only His voice, and thereby grow to be the strong, Godly woman He has called you to be."

And now, of course, everyone's going to be wondering what I did, sneaking little looks at me and whispering in each other's ears. Fantastic.

He turns back to the crowd. "Amen."

"Thank you, Daddy," I say, pasting the sweetest of all the sweet smiles on my face. I lean in close enough for the mic to pic up my words. "I'm so lucky to have a father like you."

He hugs me and kisses me on the forehead, then turns to address the crowd again. "Daughters need to hear that, don't they? They need to hear that they're beautiful. And if it's not you telling them, dads, then someone else will. I promise you that."

There are solemn nods from the men in the crowd.

"At this time, I'd encourage you to take a moment to bless your own daughters. Tell them they're beautiful, tell them they're loved, tell them God's special purpose for their lives."

There are soft murmurs across the room as other fathers do the same, speaking to their daughters in hushed, private tones, holding their faces close as they hover over dirty plates scattered with remnants of prime rib and mashed potatoes.

All of this used to make me feel so special, so important. But now? It just makes me feel manipulated. If the church itself is a lie, then my parents are biggest liars of all.

When the murmurs quiet, my dad speaks again. "And now for the part of the night where we, as fathers, make a promise to God to protect the purity of our daughters. Please take your pledges out and stand with me."

He shuffles a piece of paper, the purity pledge, to the front of his notes. "Fathers, please repeat after me with the names of your daughters. I, Emma's father…"

Everyone looks toward us as the crowd echoes him with a cacophony of names.

"Pledge to Jesus Christ our Savior to be the shield and caretaker of my daughter's purity until her wedding night."

Their eyes soak into me as they speak, and it makes me want to squirm. How many people are thinking about *my* purity? I have to force myself not to crawl underneath the podium.

"I pledge to lead and guide my daughter by being an example of purity in my own life."

The faces of the men are so serious they could be going into battle.

"As the high priest in my home, I will pray a covering over my daughter…"

I imagine them at war with a swarm of penises, and have to sneeze to keep from snorting. My dad shoots me a look, and I put on my Very Serious face again.

"That she may, with my blessing and authority, have the

7

strength to be righteous before marriage."

I mean, what are they gonna do? Build a moat around our crotches? It's all such a joke.

But do I really believe that? That all this is a joke?

I know the answer as soon as I let myself ask it. I do believe it. This, along with everything else, means absolutely nothing.

So if it means nothing, Emma, if it really means nothing? Then maybe it's time to prove it to yourself.

"God bless you as you seek to provide protection to your daughters. Amen," my dad says. Then his voice turns official, "Brothers In Christ, please assemble your swords for the Purity Processional."

Brothers In Christ is sort of a Christian version of the Boy Scouts for teen guys who want to spend their Saturday mornings learning survival skills, studying the Bible, and marching around with guns. Which, around here, means almost all of them. Mike, of course, is their current captain.

I hadn't noticed until now, but the guys are already assembled at the side door. They march in, military style, Mike in the lead with two rows of five boys behind him.

When Mike reaches the cross, he commands, "Detail. Halt."

The guys stop.

"Center. Face."

They turn on their heels toward the center.

"Officers. Present."

They pull their swords from scabbards held by red sashes looped across their tuxedos, each embroidered with a gold cross.

"Arch."

They lift their swords to form a tunnel.

"Blades to the wind," Mike says, and all their blades flip toward the back door.

My father turns to me. "At this time I'd like the young women to follow Emma to the back of the room, while the fathers join me at the cross."

I walk to the back door, toward my mother, Gloria, who's standing beside a vase of tall white roses on a small table. More than one person at church has uttered the comment, "*a modern-day Jackie-O!*" when they encounter her. So many people, in fact, it gets old. She's always well put-together, yes. And poised. But my dad isn't exactly the freaking president.

She hands a rose to each girl as she arrives, squeezing my hand and smiling as she hands me mine.

"Good job, sweetie. You did great up there."

"Thanks," I say.

Then she tugs up the straps on my dress so the neckline doesn't go as low.

"There, that's better," she says.

The other girls crowd together in the back, waiting. As each girl's name is called by her father, she walks through the tunnel in her white dress and lays a rose at the foot of the cross to symbolize her decision to remain pure until marriage.

Finally, it's my turn.

My father stands next to the cross. "Emma Grant, my lovely daughter, how do you answer God's call to remain pure?"

It's a good question, isn't it? What do you believe, Emma? What do you truly believe?

"If you pledge to be a temple of the Lord, a pure soul until marriage, please step forward."

I walk through the tunnel like a bride, slow and solemn. What other choice do I have?

As I pass Mike, bearing a shining blade above my head, he nods to me in approval, and pride too—that I'm his, that his girlfriend is among the chaste, the pure. A prize among women. *His* prize. Like he's responsible in any way for who I am or what I do.

I wonder what he'd do if I didn't want to stay pure? The way he kisses, sloppy and urgent and needy, the way his hands roam, waiting for me to stop him, keep him in check, I doubt his resolve would last more than thirty seconds. Everyone thinks we're going to get married someday. Everyone is wrong.

I arrive at the front, my toes brushing the pile of white roses resting there. As I place mine at the foot of the cross I decide it will mean something different this time, something completely different.

As soon as I can get away, I find a dark corner and text Jackson:

North Doors. 10 p.m.

CHAPTER THREE

I CHANGE INTO REGULAR clothes in the choir room with all the other girls. The place is strewn with curling irons and makeup cases and dress bags. It looks like a hurricane touched down at a beauty pageant.

The Purity Ball is over, and our parents have gone home, but it's only the beginning of the night. Soon the entire youth group is meeting downstairs in the Youth Center for a lock-in. There will be games and movies and a midnight worship service. Boys are included, but their sleeping bags will be dutifully segregated. They're calling it, "A Night of Pure Fun", because of course they are.

I let my dark hair out of its prim bun, and it tumbles past my shoulders in long waves as relief tingles through my scalp. I like it so much better this way, swingy and free. My hair is really my only good feature, so I wear it down whenever I can.

I take off an earring as Paige walks up to me. She and I have been friends since we were babies. Our parents have known each other since Bible college, so we've practically grown up together. Paige's dad is the assistant pastor, which basically means he's second in command to my dad. And her twin brother, unfortunately, is Mike. It's part of what's making things so complicated to break up with him. I've tried three times, but something always goes wrong.

Paige hasn't changed yet and still looks amazing. Her springy brown curls are piled on top of her head behind a glittery tiara. Her dress is a full-length lace column, sleeveless to show off her athletic arms. I won't say Paige is vain exactly, but she's totally buff and wears sleeves less often than anyone I've ever met.

She hands me her Red Bull. "Here. Drink."

"Thanks," I say, taking a swig.

"No problem," Paige says. "You kinda seem like you need it."

She thinks I'm tired. I'm not. I'm terrified.

He's coming. Here. Tonight.

"You're gonna have to take off the tiara sometime," I say with a grin, changing the subject.

"I really don't know what you have against tiaras." She laughs and sits down next to me. "Look at what it's doing for my neck. I totally have a neck now."

"You've always had a neck."

"Not, like, a real one. Like Audrey Hepburn. That girl was gorgeous. She had a neck for days."

"Coveting someone's neck is a sin," I say, faking serious.

She sighs dramatically. "I can't help it." She gets a little closer and whispers, "Hey, did you see June bawling?"

"Yeah. What was that all about?"

"I think maybe the Purity Ball came a little too late for her."

"With who?"

"Not Nicolas. Before. Like, before she became a Christian I think."

"I guess it's not the worst thing that could happen to a person," I say, dipping my toe in the water.

"Well, maybe not the *worst* thing, but it is kind of sad, don't you think? I mean, how would you feel if Mike wasn't a virgin when you guys got married?"

My heart folds in on itself, just a little bit. I'm dying to talk to her about all this, to tell her everything that's really been going on with me for the last year, longer than that really, but how can I? Every time I've tried she's had the same reaction. "Paige—"

"And don't say you don't know if you're going to marry Mike, because *I* know you're going to marry him. Otherwise, how are we gonna enact *the plan*?"

"We made that plan when we were nine."

"And it's still an excellent one," she says. "Step one: become real sisters. I hate to say it, but that's where Mike comes in. You're gonna have to take one for the team on that one. Step two: buy houses next door to each other. Step three: have babies together. Step four: our babies get married. It's very simple, Emma."

"Cousins can't marry each other. I've told you that, like, a million times."

"In Colorado they can," she says. "I checked."

"What?"

She wrinkles up her nose, equally fascinated and grossed out. "It's true."

"Well, maybe it's legal, but it's also disgusting."

Paige opens up her mouth to argue but stops to stare at something. I turn to look just as June herself walks up to us.

CHAPTER FOUR

JUNE IS RED EYED and frail looking. She's still wearing the dance costume so she must not have changed into a gown after our performance. Maybe she didn't have a gown to change into. She doesn't seem to wear a lot of new things. I guess it's not a big deal, but with her cry-rubbed face and pale skin, the overflowing layers of tulle seem like they could swallow her whole.

"Can I talk to you guys about something?" she asks.

"Yeah. Of course," I say, even though I really don't feel like handling her right now. I never know how to talk to June. She always seems to be in her own world. I'm only really friends with her because I'm not allowed to not be friends with anyone here. It's one of those unspoken pastor's daughter duties. I should really be on the payroll.

"Sure," Paige says, her face immediately concerned. "What's the matter?"

"It's just…I, well…I was wondering—"

"Ladies," Miss Hope, our dance leader, calls from the doorway. "Gather up please."

We stop our conversation and make our way to the center of the room to face her.

Miss Hope shifts where she stands, stretching a foot inside her ballet flats. She's trim but sturdy and nearly six feet tall. I've never seen her wear heels, probably a habit formed because she'd tower over any of the eligible men her age. The idea makes me sad for her. Happy, too, that she found Pastor Pete. Their wedding is only a month away. Everyone's talking about it like it's Kate and Will.

"I just want to say that I'm so proud of each and every one of you for making the commitment you did tonight."

She's wearing white just like us, but her look is simpler— an empire waistline in floor-length chiffon with a square neckline and sheer three-quarter sleeves. Her dirty-blonde hair, as always, is cut in a blunt bob at her chin.

"As many of you know, I too chose to commit my purity to Jesus when I was a young lady. And I'm thankful to say that my first kiss, my very first kiss, will be at the altar on my wedding day."

She's beaming like she wants us to clap or something, but we just stand there, quiet. There are maybe a handful of us who haven't ever kissed anyone, most of whom are in the homeschool crowd. The rest of them? Sure, they're saving *it* until marriage, but kissing? That's definitely happening.

"Now I know that a commitment like that isn't possible for everyone, but that's what I felt the Lord called me to do. And with His strength, and the guidance of my father, I've done it. If any of you are interested in that path, I'd be happy to share my experience with you. Even if you might think it's already too late, it's not. It's never too late to live up to the standard God has set for you. There's no such thing as physical intimacy without consequences, but it's about making the best choice today, and every single day after that."

She smiles sincerely, taking a moment to look at each of us individually. I cringe under her gaze. Am I really ready for this? Ready to go to a place there's no coming back from?

"But whatever you decide, I charge you to guard your hearts and save them for the man Jesus has hand-picked to be your perfect match. I know I'm glad I did."

It's a beautiful idea. Romantic and sweet as a fairy tale. I have to remind myself that fairy tales rarely come true.

"Now chop-chop, ladies," Miss Hope says from the doorway. "I want everyone ready to go down to the Youth Center in five minutes. The activities have already started, and I know you won't want to miss anything. I've got lots of fun stuff planned for tonight."

We rush around, grabbing the things we'll need for the lock-in. Everything else is staying up here until morning. I've got my sleeping bag and a backpack with my PJs and toiletries ready to go when June finds me again.

"I don't mean to bother you, but—" she says.

"Don't be silly," I say. "Why would you be bothering me?"

She gets this smile on her face, grateful, like me saying she's not bothering me is a big deal. She's like that sometimes, and it always makes me feel bad, like I'm royalty and she's this lowly peasant or something. June is a nice girl, but the kind of too-nice that makes you reach for something sour to balance it out. I should make more time for her, I know, but the truth is that this place is full of Junes, and there's only one me.

"Thanks," she says. "I just really need to talk to you about something. You always know exactly what to say to make me feel better."

"I'm glad to hear that," I say.

She takes my hand in hers and squeezes it. I see Paige looking at us from across the room, painfully curious, grabbing her stuff fast and making her way over.

"I really think of you like a sister." June says "I mean, I know we're not really sisters. But if I could pick anyone in the world to be a sister, it would be you."

"Thanks. That's really sweet of you," I say, not saying that I don't really know her that well. Certainly not well enough to say the same of her. "So what's going on?"

Paige pops in to our conversation. "Hey guys. What's up?"

"It's Nicolas," June says, to both of us now. Nicolas, her boyfriend and my ex. I'm the one who broke up with him, but it was still a little weird for me when they got together. She was the first girl he dated after me.

At first I didn't quite understand what he saw in her, but then it clicked. Looking up at you with those pale-blue eyes, asking you to love her back, love her the best, save her from her loneliness? She's the epitome of that One Direction song, "That's What Makes You Beautiful", which is such a guy fantasy to have. She makes Nicolas feel like a superhero, which is something I could never do. She makes all the guys feel like that.

"I just thought, since, you know…you used to date him, maybe you could give me some advice?" June says.

"I don't know if I'm—," I say

"You're not breaking up, are you?" Paige asks. "You guys are, like, the cutest couple."

Tears spring to June's eyes. "I, um—"

"Come on, girls," Miss Hope says from the doorway. "Time to go."

"Oh no," June says, giving us a desperate look. "I don't have my stuff."

"Later, okay?" I say. "Find me downstairs. I'm sure it's nothing. We'll figure it all out, I promise."

She nods, then races off to a corner to cram her things into a backpack. She still hasn't changed from her ballet outfit, and there's stuff strewn everywhere in her corner. Miss Hope is giving her a stern look from the door.

Paige whispers to me, "Maybe you could get your parents to adopt her. Then you'd really be sisters."

A laugh spurts out of me before I can draw it back, and I immediately feel guilty for it, so I elbow Paige. "Be nice. She's harmless."

CHAPTER FIVE

JUNE AND I DON'T get a chance to talk. Pastor Pete and Miss Hope have every minute organized to keep us busy, too busy for idle hands groping in dark corners, or in my case, too busy to talk to June.

It feels like I've played a million stupid games with the other kids by the time I finally feel the phone buzz in my pocket just before ten. It's him.

I'm here.

Adrenaline spikes through my body, a heady mix of danger and power. My fingertips jitter with it. I type *"I'm crooning"* instead of *"I'm coming"* and send it accidentally. Who cares. He'll understand. I don't want to take the time to retype it. I want to see him now.

I run over to where I have my sleeping bag setup and grab my purse. My plan is to tell the chaperone at the door that I'm not feeling well, then disappear farther down the hall when they're not looking.

"Emma?" Nicolas stands in front of me, looking both concerned and confused. "Have you seen June? I can't find her."

"No. Sorry," I say. "But if I do, I'll tell her to find you."

"It's just—I haven't seen her in a while, and I'm a little worried."

"How long?"

"I don't know. Twenty minutes? A half hour maybe?"

My eyes nearly roll, but I manage to keep them steady. He's worried about her after twenty minutes? It's exactly this about

Nicolas that makes me glad we broke up. His protective vibe is nice, but he can really smother a girl sometimes. "I'm sure she'll turn up," I say. "She's probably gabbing in the bathroom with Ruth or something."

"Yeah, probably. Thanks," he says, looking around the room as I walk away, clearly still uneasy.

When I'm nearly to the door, there's a burst of laughter behind me, and I look. Chuck Rand is bent over, Bic lighter to his butt. A huge burst of flame shoots out. Some girl I don't know screeches in delight, and Pastor Pete is on them, taking Chuck by the arm and leading him toward Miss Hope. They talk, and Miss Hope scurries over to me.

"Emma, could you do me a favor?"

"Umm—"

"The pizza will be here any minute. I just need you to go up to the cafe and bring down a few more cases of soda from the pantry. Maybe another two hundred cans? We're running low down here. There's a dolly in there that you can use to bring it down. Can you do that?"

"I, ah—" My mind is scrambling for a reason to tell her no, but I'm going blank. I can't think of a single thing other than the truth: I have to meet a boy.

"Thanks. I really appreciate it," she says.

And with that, she hustles to the door where Pastor Pete and Chuck are waiting.

Paige walks up to me. "What was that about?"

"Could you do me a favor?" I ask.

"Sure."

I dart out into the hall and see Pastor Pete, Miss Hope, and Chuck going into the stairwell up ahead. I catch up fast. When we get out of the stairwell on the main level, I head toward the South Wing, opposite of where I want to go, just in case they're watching.

Our church is built on the top of a hill and laid out sort of like a compass, with the sanctuary in a circle at the center and wings at every point: north, south, east, and the overpass to the church's school on the west. The West overpass is technically a little more northwest. They made it that way so the school's three large buildings (elementary, middle, high) wouldn't obstruct the mountain views from the back wall of the sanctuary, which is all windows. During church, you can see them through the glass, majestic and purple, towering over the athletic fields at school. Some people come to the Sunday evening service just to see the sun set.

Pastor Pete, Miss Hope, and Chuck are headed toward the North Wing of the church, the top two floors of which make up the administrative halls where the pastors' offices are. It's also exactly in the way of where I need to go. I get to the Connections Café but I don't go to the pantry. I wait there, in the dark, until I hear their footsteps disappear, then race back the other way.

I look, but I don't see anyone. It's dark. I open the door a crack. They have all the lights off outside because the youth group are the only ones here, and we're supposed to be confined to the Youth Center. My eyes adjust. There's nobody there.

"Jackson?" I whisper. Then I see movement. He peeks out from behind the wall, guitar case strapped on his back, those big dark eyes and wry smile shining out beneath his hoodie. He has the best smile. If a birthday present could be a smile, his would be the one wrapped like the thing you want most, its shape so distinct you're 90 percent sure what's inside, but still have to open it to see.

He saunters up to me, tall and broad chested and so handsome it makes the breath catch in my throat.

"Hey gorgeous," he says, then wraps one hand around my waist and the other behind my head to pull me closer. He kisses me like he doesn't care who's watching, like he doesn't care about getting caught. *Oh. My. God.*

They always tell us that you can't use kisses to judge a relationship, because everyone can kiss. Maybe everyone *can* kiss, but not everyone can kiss like him. When he finally pulls his lips from mine I have to stifle a giggle, stuck between giddy and scared and, well…*excited.*

He twirls a finger through my hair, slowly twining me closer to his face. "God, I missed you," he says. It's been eight days since I've seen him. Too long.

"Me too." I kiss him back.

I think I see someone in the parking lot then. A dark

movement among the cars. I tug him away from the glass doors.

"Come on," I say. "We better hurry. I have to be back before the midnight service starts." I grab Jackson's hand and pull him with me as I run.

We race down the South Wing and into to the south stairwell. We go up two flights. This floor is used for our theater and media teams. Half of it is dedicated to theater practice space and storage. The other half is all film and sound production. We have a full recording studio where we record choir music and inspirational spoken word. We also have a small sound stage that produces weekly video content for the website. It's mostly just the pastors speaking, or promo videos for whatever they're going to be preaching about next.

I take him to the recording studio. It's locked, there's a lot of expensive equipment in there, but I nabbed my dad's master key for this very purpose. Inside, Jackson's eyes go wide.

"I can't believe this. In a church? Holy shit." Jackson pulls out his guitar.

"Told you."

"You sure this is chill? You're not gonna get in trouble, are you?"

"It's good." I smile. I've been counting the minutes. He will play his guitar to moaning, and I will sing lyrics that have nothing to do with Jesus, and we'll bring the demo with us out to New York, where we've both been accepted at NYU. We will live in a city full of music, full of art and energy and little bars where we can make our own kind of famous. Me a softer, indie version of Katy Perry and he a modern James Dean.

And tonight—maybe, hopefully, oh god—will be the night that I finally give myself to him. If, of course, I have the guts to go through with it.

CHAPTER SIX

SO HOW DID A girl like me get involved with a boy like Jackson? A boy who's not in my church? A boy who doesn't even believe in God?

The truth? It was like magic.

I know everyone says that, but for me it was true. It was like he materialized out of thin air once all my questions about God turned into answers, like he was waiting for me all along.

We met last October, at a football game.

"Go, Warriors!
Go, Go,
Go, Warriors!
We're num-ber one,
And we know it!"

I force the cheer out with the other girls, but my heart's not in it. I'm sitting on Katie's shoulders, holding up the left side of the banner. It reads *If God is for us, who can be against us? — Romans 8:31*. Homecoming is against a public school this year, Arvada High. This message is for them. Apparently, God takes sides in high school sports now.

My fellow cheerleaders seem to think so. But it feels like a taunt to me, a jeer, not a cheer. It's mean spirited and unsportsmanlike, even though we pride ourselves on our morality.

I've been noticing a lot of that lately. Not just with the cheerleaders, but at school, at church. How, even in stuff like this, we create ways to make ourselves believe we're better than everyone else. It's different than holier than thou. It's my house is bigger than your house, my car is better than your car, my God is better than your God. For winners to exist, there have to be losers, and we love having the losers around. We don't actually care about saving souls, we want people beneath us, a crowd of them, the bigger the better, like a pretty girl who only wants ugly friends.

I'm ashamed to think I've been standing right alongside them for so long. Last year at this time, I was the one making the banners.

The boys barrel through, ripping it to pieces. The remnant left in my hand only says, *If God*, which seems like the whole question lately, not just a piece of it. If God loved me… If God is omnipotent… If God exists at all…

They're private questions, not ones I can talk to anyone about. And honestly? They're not even really questions anymore.

Katie launches me off her shoulders, and it's time to scream and kick. Finally. This is the part I can do. I jump and race along the field, hands up, waving at the crowd, revving them up. It gets me going too. I feel better, glad to give my body over to the movement of it.

Then I see him, or feel him maybe, because I turn to the opposing side. And he's looking at me, helmet in hand. Only me.

His gaze frightens me it's so intense. Dark eyes like mirrors, reflecting the arena lights straight back toward me. I feel locked in his crosshairs, afraid to turn my back. I only realize I'm standing still when Katie yanks my elbow to get moving. Another cheer has already started. We race to the sidelines, late.

I don't see him again until halftime, when he's heading toward the locker rooms and I'm lined up just off the field for the homecoming court presentation, Mike on my arm in his football uniform.

"Good luck, gorgeous," the boy says as he passes, a cocky grin plastered on his face.

I can't help but grin back, even though Mike is standing right there. My face blossoms red.

"Excuse me?" Mike says.

But the boy just keeps walking.

"Jerk." Mike says, then turns to me. "Don't worry, he's just trying to get in my head."

I wasn't worried.

On the field they announce I'm homecoming queen and Mike is king. Of course we are. I'm probably the only girl in the universe who wishes she wasn't homecoming queen. It feels like a burden to smile and wave and pretend I'm surprised and demurely accept Mike's cheek peck so the crowd can roar.

I resolve again to break up with him, maybe after his birthday next week. Or is it the week after? Either way, I'll do it. I will.

The other cheerleaders and I do our halftime routine with the band. I swear, as I fly up and spin through the air, I think I catch his eye again. But when I land and turn around to look, I don't see him anywhere.

It's me, not him, who, after the game is over, finds a place near their bus to hang out. I check my phone, as if I'm there by accident. It's forever I'm standing here. The girls are texting me, trying to find me, but I don't text back. I have to see him again. I have to give him a chance to see me.

He doesn't come. Other boys straggle on the bus, freshly showered and dressed in clean clothes. They're sullen, licking their wounds from the loss, a good school but not as good as ours. I wish for them we hadn't won. And maybe for me too. I wish they'd made our banner a joke.

The bus leaves without him, which I don't understand. Whenever we travel, we have to go as a team on the bus. It doesn't make sense. How did I miss him? Maybe he wasn't real.

I make my way to the locker room to get my stuff. When I come back out, Katie and Angela and Erica and Paige are hanging out in the hallway.

"Emma!" Paige says. "There you are."

"Hey." I say.

"Where have you been? We've been texting you," Katie asks. Her voice is irritated. I've forgotten I'm their ride to the after party.

"You have?" I pull out my phone. "Sorry, my ringer's off. Ready to go?"

But before they can answer, my phone is snatched out of my hand.

"Hey!" I say.

He's standing there, punching in numbers, his dark eyes twinkling, that same confident grin.

"Emma, I'm Jackson. Nice to meet you." He hands my phone back to me, and walks away backward. "I'll call you." He turns and jogs out.

We're all standing there, speechless.

What can I say? He's a guy who knows what he wants.

"What was that about?" Katie asks, her eyebrows raised. She'd love to catch me doing something wrong. She's always had a thing for Mike.

"I have no idea." I say.

Paige catches my eye. She raises her eyebrows, a gentle warning. She's the only one here who can read my face. I may be just as surprised as they are, but I liked that, and she knows it.

She didn't like it. I'm her brother's girlfriend. Despite our friendship, I need to watch myself.

I wipe my face clean of it, tuck away the moment for later.

"Was that the same jerk from before?" It's Mike. I didn't see him come out of the locker room. But here he is. He must have seen the whole thing.

"Who knows?" I say. "Just some random dude." I tap my phone awake, roll my eyes. "I'm deleting his number right now."

"You want me to talk to him?"

"No, that's okay. Let's just go to the party."

We go to the party, all of us together, and we laugh and play board games and eat pizza and do everything we always do. But the entire time all I can think about is the number burning a secret light in the center of my phone. The number I most certainly did not delete.

CHAPTER SEVEN

THERE'S DANGER COMING THROUGH my voice. It's wretched and lovely, my heart scraping down a chalkboard.

It's for him. Just Jackson and no one else. His eyes lock on me through the glass. *I am my beloved's and my beloved is mine.*

I keep going until the end. The last, long note of it is strangled from my throat like the dying embers from a campfire. When it's over, I am empty, breathless. I gave all of myself to it, and there is nothing left.

"That. Was. *Legit*," Jackson says, his voice piped into the sound booth from a mic on the control board. "Seriously. We have it. I've never heard you sound so good."

"You think?" I say.

"Yeah. Let me run to the john then we'll listen to it together."

He's grinning ear to ear as he takes off his headphones and darts into the hall.

I absentmindedly curl the mic cords back into place. I catch a glance at my reflection in the booth and run a brush through my hair. I slide a fresh coat of lip gloss over my lips and straighten my shirt. I breathe against my hand to check my breath and pop in a mint. Am I going to do this? Am I really going to do this?

By the time he comes back, I still don't know.

"Ready to hear this sucker?" he asks.

"Like, so ready," I say nervously.

He presses buttons, then plays the mix, coming into the booth to listen to it with me, where the sound can fully envelop us both. The strain of my voice against his guitar is lightning on skin, the branched brand it makes when it strikes flesh. We've made something together, something only the two of us could make.

He loops a finger through my jeans, tugs me close. He smells like cinnamon and soap, and all I want to do is inhale him. I run a hand up his chest as he kisses me. Jackson's kiss is a challenge, a dare. So I kiss him back, hard, until I can breathe his air into my own lungs. I could disappear into that kiss.

He brushes my hair away from my ear. "I'm going to kiss you here," he says. And he does.

Then he runs his thumb across my clavicle. "And here," he says, as he leans down to kiss me in the soft dip at the base of my neck.

"And here." He traces lower, between my breasts, and kisses me there too.

Then his hands are on me, everywhere. He isn't fumbling and clumsy like Mike. He isn't tentative and searching like Nicolas, not weak. This boy doesn't care about respect. He's in total control. He's picking me up and setting me on a stool, and my legs are around him and my hands are on him too, searching, hungrier this time.

He can feel it, the difference in me. He catches my hands in his, looks me in the eye. "You're not saying no," he says.

"I'm not saying no."

"You sure? Like, for real?"

I close my eyes, try to flush my mind of everything I've heard tonight, everything I've heard my whole life. "I'm sure."

"You don't have to. Not for me. Not if you don't want to."

"I know. I—" But suddenly I'm tired of words. Instead of an explanation, I kiss him, hard enough to convince him, to convince myself, that I know what I want.

"Okay," he says, his breath coming rough. "Okay."

We fumble our clothes off, my T-shirt catching on my nose as I pull it over my head, probably making me look like I have a pig's snout. Jackson doesn't seem to notice. He reaches for the button on my jeans, unbuttons them fast, then pulls down until I'm standing in front of him in just my panties.

I turn away, embarrassed, but he grabs me close and lifts me against him. And then we're on the ground, and my panties are off, and I'm closing my eyes, self-conscious and not used to not knowing what to do.

"Open your eyes, Em," he says.

So I do. I open my eyes and look into his. It's like staring off the edge of a cliff. If I jump, will I be able to fly? Or go crashing into the rocks?

I have to do it. I have to know which it will be.

And then he's there. And it hurts a little at first. But his eyes are locked on my eyes, and the pain passes, and before I know it the heat of him burns up all my promises: the purity pledge I signed in the sixth grade, the promise ring Mike gave me on my birthday, the vow I made with the other kids in front of my father tonight, until there's nothing left but white space and the sweet sigh of relief that escapes my lips.

I can fly.

CHAPTER EIGHT

WE'RE TANGLED ON THE floor together, an awkward mess of angles that somehow fits together just right. My face is nestled into his chest, covering the tattoo of a flock of swallows flying across his heart, wild and swirling and free. He's never told me much about that tattoo, just that he got it after getting released from juvenile detention a couple years ago. It's amazing how far he's come since then, working hard enough to get accepted at NYU right along with me.

"Don't go back down there tonight," he says, toying with my hair as he talks. "Let's go somewhere. Right now."

"Where would we go?" I giggle.

"The mountains. We could stay there all weekend."

"And what? Live off the land?"

"I know this guy with a cabin."

"You're serious?"

"Maybe. Come on, Em. There's so much more out there than this place."

"Jackson," I say, my voice saying no even though I wish I could say yes. I *really* wish I could say yes.

"Come on," he says, smiling. He flips me onto my back and presses my hands against the floor. "I could wrestle a bear for your dinner."

I just laugh. "You're completely insane."

"Am I?" he says with a twinkle in his eye.

He lets go of my hands and goes for my stomach, tickling me until I can't breathe and have to beg him for mercy. Then pulls me close again, my head back in that perfect spot on his chest.

"How are you?" he asks. "Are you okay? With all of this?"

I take a deep breath, letting it all soak in. Do I feel different now? Has anything really changed? There's a smile in my heart as I realize the answer is both yes and no. No, nothing has really changed. I don't feel guilty, don't feel wrong, don't feel devastated at the mistake I've made. Nothing as beautiful as that could be a mistake.

And yes, because everything is different. The whole world. It's bigger than it was before. More beautiful.

"I'm...fantastic," I say.

He laughs, the boom of it in his chest almost concealing the noise.

The noise.

What was that?

Then there's another sound, and I see it too late. The audio recording light mounted on the ceiling, switched on, red and blaring, one here, and a matching one in the hall to ward off intruders who might inadvertently ruin a take. It's not capturing anything, but it is a beacon of our presence. How did I not think of it?

That sound was a door. There's someone here; I can feel it. I push Jackson away. He doesn't understand it at first, thinks I'm teasing again, and pulls me closer to him.

"I heard something."

He lets go, and we both leap up, scrambling for our clothes. My T-shirt is back over my head, and my jeans are on, and I'm out in the hall in a flash, looking to see who it was. Praying that no one saw me. Saw us. But they must have.

That sound. What was that sound?

But when I tear open the door to the studio, there's no one there.

"Are you sure you heard something?" Jackson says, right behind me.

"I don't know," I say. "I thought so."

He jogs down the hall, looking, but comes back to me shrugging his shoulders.

"I didn't see anyone."

"Are you sure?"

"I looked everywhere. All the doors are locked along the

hall."

"Okay," I say, even though I feel anything but okay.

"You're probably just nervous, babe. Your mind's playing tricks on you."

"Maybe," I say. "But I should get back anyway. It's nearly midnight. The service is about to start."

"Okay. You go ahead. I'll clean things up here."

"You know how to get out, right?"

"Yeah, no problem."

I kiss him goodbye.

I race back toward the Youth Center, piling my hair into a bun to mask how messy it must be. There's music blaring from the room, so loud I can hear it the minute I open the door to the stairwell.

As I run through the hall, I see a spirited game of basketball in the gym. And then another game of Red Rover going on in the Youth Center. Red Rover. Anywhere else it would be a game for kids. I'm not sorry I missed it.

The whole thing is a cacophony of bouncing balls and shouting teenagers and Christian rock anthems everywhere.

Paige catches me at the door as I enter.

"Where did you disappear to? I was starting to get worried."

"I've been around," I say, breathless.

Paige smirks. "By "around" do you mean off in a dark corner with my brother?"

"I—"

She puts up her hand. "Nevermind. I don't actually want to know the answer to that question."

"Fair enough," I say, relieved to not have to lie to her. Paige still doesn't know about Jackson. I don't know how to tell her, but the conversation is unavoidable. I have to tell her about it, and I have to break up with Mike. Now.

It's not the first time I've tried, but this time I'm going to have to stand my ground. And when I do, Paige will have to know why. I resolve to find Mike tonight, to talk to him as soon as the service is over.

"Oh hey, where's your earring?" she asks.

I reach to my earlobes and feel a diamond on the right but nothing on the left side. Crap. It's probably in the recording studio. Hopefully Jackson will spot it and take it with him when he goes.

Paige raises her eyebrows and grins. "Maybe you can get Mike to retrace your steps."

"Paiger, we should talk. Want to get a coffee tomorrow or something?"

"Okay," she says warily. "What's going on?"

But then Pastor Pete cuts the music and the chaperones are shouting to the crowd that the midnight worship service is about to begin. The kids from the gym shuffle inside to take their seats.

"Later," I say to Paige. "Tomorrow, when we can be alone."

"Okay, whatever," she looks concerned but doesn't press it further.

I take my place on stage behind a mic, and Paige sits down at the piano.

"Let me hear it if you're fired up for Christ tonight!" Pastor Pete says.

CHAPTER NINE

"INSIDE. NOW," PASTOR PETE shouts. He holds open a door to one of the prayer rooms, and we all run in. I swallow the tears down my throat, my sadness replaced by fear.

The room is off the main sanctuary, one of many places where people who need prayer during a service can go for more one-on-one attention from one of the members of our Prayer Ministry. The room is simple—no windows, a small table, and four chairs. And now us. Me, Pastor Pete, Chuck, Amy, Beth, a boy named Brian who's in Brothers In Christ, and another boy named Sam who I don't know very well.

"Guys, help me get this table against the wall," Pastor Pete says. They rip the chairs away and tilt the table on its side across the door, then pile the chairs against the table to make a barricade. The church has an "active shooter" emergency plan that everyone in a position of authority has to be trained on. I'm pretty sure Pastor Pete is following protocol here.

"Okay, okay," Pastor Pete says, clearly nervous. He runs a hand through his hair. "I need everyone to line up against that wall." He's pointing to the same wall the door is on. "It'll give us the best chance if anyone comes in."

Oh god. Oh god, oh god, oh god.

Jackson. Did he have enough time to go? What if he's still here? I pull out my phone to text him:

Hide! Shooter in the church.

But I don't get a response before Pastor Pete sees me typing.

"Emma. Call the police," Pastor Pete says, as he pulls out his own and dials. "Tell them we have an active shooter situation."

"Yes, sir," I say.

"Everyone else who has phones turn them to silent right now and stay quiet."

They all obey.

Beth and Amy huddle together, crying. How could they not be thinking of Columbine? Of the Aurora theater shootings? Of the shooting at a local high school just before Christmas break? All stuff that happened here. Are we the next tragedy on Colorado's list?

As my phone rings for the police, I can hear Pastor Pete on his phone, warning someone downstairs to secure the kids in the Youth Center. Then he switches off the lights, and everything goes dark.

"Nine-one-one, what is your emergency?"

I can't believe the words as they come out of my mouth. "Hello, I'm at Summit Christian Fellowship on Westlake Road in Denver? We have an active shooter in the building."

As I'm telling them everything—where we are, where the others are, what we saw, what we heard—my phone buzzes with a text:

Holy shit. Already gone. Is this a joke? You okay?

And a little part of me, a small part, relaxes just a little bit.

Ten minutes pass. Then forty. Then an hour.

I hear nothing but the whispered prayers of the others in the room, and I can't help wondering if all this is a punishment from God for what I did tonight.

Could you be more self-centered, Emma? Seriously. Someone died.

June died.

I try not to think about it.

Beth interrupts the silence with a whisper. "I just don't understand why someone would do this to us. At church. I mean, all we ever do is try to help people."

"It's probably somebody who hates God," Brian says. "Probably hates Christians too. Lots of people do."

"I don't know man," Sam says. "I think it's gotta be a psycho. Like that weirdo in Aurora."

"Hey, guys," Chuck says, a tentative grin in his voice. "How does a crazy person get out of the woods?"

"How?" Sam asks.

"They take the psycho path."

A snort escapes my nose. It's a dumb joke, and totally inappropriate right now, but I can't help it. Chuck may be kind of annoying sometimes, but you can always count on him for a little comic relief.

Sam chuckles too. So does Brian.

"Okay, guys, that's enough," Pastor Pete whispers. "We need to stay quiet. Why don't we spend a little time in prayer?"

We all sober up, bow our heads.

"Dear Jesus," Pastor Pete whispers. "I thank You for keeping us safe in Your care tonight. We pray that You would cast Your protection around those who are downstairs right now. Keep Your shield over their heads and guide the police to—"

BANG BANG BANG BANG BANG. Someone pounds on the door.

"Denver Police Department. Is anyone in there?"

The police hustle us out of the building, then direct us across the street where the parents are assembled in the cafeteria of Summit Christian High School. All the other kids, the kids from downstairs, are in there already. I spot Paige and Ruth and Nicolas huddling with their parents. The police must have evacuated the larger group first.

I try to look for June's parents, but realize I wouldn't know them if I saw them. We've never met. I didn't even notice her with her dad tonight. They probably have them somewhere more private anyway.

"Emma, baby," my mom says through tears as I crash into her arms. "I'm so glad you're okay."

She's not usually a hugger, but I guess tonight is different.

My dad appears at our side, looking ashen and empty. "Emma, thank God." He hugs me tight, my mom right along with me, then says, "What happened in there? The police are saying—"

"June's dead," I say, feeling empty. "June's dead."

None of it feels real.

It takes the police two more hours to clear the building. They find nothing. No shooter, no gun, no sign that anyone broke in.

Whoever it was got away. Whoever it was probably wasn't an active shooter at all.

After the building is fully secured, we stay in the cafeteria as detectives take down our information, releasing families one by one. There are whispers everywhere that God was surely protecting us, and that's why the killer got away. I'm not so sure that June's death constitutes a major victory for Jesus.

Jackson has been texting all night. But with 911 on the line, there wasn't a chance to text him back. The first chance I get, I sneak into the bathroom to send off a quick text, but as soon as I turn on my phone, it dies. I've been using it all night, and the battery is empty.

After that, I mostly just try to help my mom keep things under control. It's she who takes charge, not my dad—making sure kids are able to contact their parents, calling in helpers from the congregation to bring coffee and donuts for everyone, getting a list for the police of every kid and adult chaperone who had been there that night. I've never seen my dad look so useless. He's usually such a commanding presence, but I guess you never expect something like this to happen to your congregation.

Finally, the detectives make their way to me. With my parents obligated to stay anyway, I'm the last kid they talk to. Everyone else is gone.

"Hey there," the woman says. She's square shaped, like a Popsicle, with a stout middle and skinny legs. "I'm Detective Shonda Boyer."

"Emma Grant."

"Looks like you're missing an earring, Miss Grant."

My hand reflexively reaches for my empty lobe. "Oh, yeah. I must have lost it somewhere."

"That's a shame. Mind if I ask you a few questions?"

I go through the basic events of the night, telling her everything I can remember about how we found June.

"And then we saw she'd been shot," I say.

"Did you hear a shot at any time during the night?"

"No, ma'am," I say. "It was really loud downstairs, and the sanctuary is kind of far away from everything else."

"Mmm hmmm. And do you know of anyone who had a reason to hurt her?"

"I don't. I'm sorry. She was—she was a really sweet girl."

"Okay. Can you tell me the last time you saw June alive?"

"I'm not sure. I know I saw her when we were changing after the Purity Ball, which was just before nine, but after that I can't remember, I'm sorry."

"Okay, thanks." She says, flipping her pad closed. "Oh, one last question."

"Yeah?"

"You guys weren't planning to go swimming later, were you?"

"Swimming? No."

"And you hadn't gone swimming earlier in the evening? After the Purity Ball?"

"No, why?"

"Don't worry about it. It's probably nothing. Thank you for your time, Miss. You've been very helpful. We'll be in touch if we have any more questions."

CHAPTER TEN

I DREAM OF A crow pecking at my bones and startle awake. There's a tapping at my window, not a dream but real. Someone's there. My heart stops for the moment it takes to realize who it is: Jackson?

I leap out of bed and cross the room to open my window. And there he is, hovering on the roof that juts out below my window, his dark hair messy from the breeze. How he got up there, I do not know. He's never done that before, never been here before.

"What are you doing?" I say, still groggy. "You can't be here. My parents—"

"You weren't answering your phone. I've been going crazy." He leaps through the window sill and crushes me against his chest, his muscle-heavy arms burying me there. As soon as I feel his touch, I relax and collapse into it, wrapping my arms around him too. He takes my face in both his hands and kisses me. I taste cigarettes on his breath, and a minty cover-up that's too weak to fool anyone. He's been smoking again, which I thought he'd given up months ago.

"Jesus, Emma. You should have called," he says. "They aren't saying anything on the news. Just that a girl was killed. Not when. Not how. Nothing. I didn't know—fuck."

"I saw her," I say, June's image flashing in my mind, the flowers on her sundress soaked in red. "I knew her."

And for the first time it hits me that it's all real. The whole, awful mess is real.

June is gone.

I tuck my face into his bulk and cry while he holds me, even though it feels wrong for me to cry. It feels unfair that I can cry and she can't. It feels selfish. It feels like I don't have the right to do it, that I wasn't close enough to her to cry like this, that I'm a tagalong to her pain, a footnote in her whole life.

How many tears are we allowed when we know someone who dies? Is there a right amount, a ration, a sliding scale based on how much we loved them? If so, I don't deserve any at all.

"I'm so sorry, baby," Jackson says. "I'm so sorry."

I'm sorry too. For everything, June. I'm so sorry I wasn't better to you. Nicer. I'm sorry your life wasn't longer. I'm sorry you didn't get a chance to do all the things you wanted to do. I'm sorry I didn't even know what those things were. But mostly, I'm sorry I wasn't there, not really, not when you needed me.

It's moments like this that I wish there was a God. No one understands this, how much I wish it was all true. How much I long for it in the sad moments, and the happy ones too. Losing the idea of God was like breaking up with the most incredible man you've ever met. It wasn't some boring teenage rebellion. It was devastating.

I wish there was a God so bad right now. But there isn't. Praying would be a lie, a betrayal of myself and everything I've discovered. So instead of talking to God, I let myself cry.

When I've finished crying, at least for now, I leave Jackson in my room and tiptoe down the hall to make sure my parents are still asleep. Thankfully, I can hear the rumble of my dad snoring behind their door, punctuated by my mom's gentle wheeze. Sure they're asleep, I make my way back to my bedroom, locking the door behind me.

Jackson wanders, taking everything in. Everything suddenly looks so dumb: my cheerleading trophies, the worn stuffed tomato on my bed from when I was a baby, the shelf full of Bibles—one for every birthday, and the verses taped to my mirror that I haven't yet taken down.

"Nice place," he says. "Is that your own bathroom?"

A fresh wave of embarrassment washes over me. Everyone in his family shares a single bathroom, but our house has one for every bedroom, plus two more. It's too much for just three people, and the thought of how wasteful it is makes me cringe.

"Yeah," I say.

"Fancy," he says, but there's a hint of disapproval in his voice. He'd probably use the words "bourgeois" or "McMansion" to describe my house. I would if I were him.

"Are you hungry? Or thirsty or anything? I can sneak down to the kitchen."

"No. I'm good. I just want to know what happened last night."

We sit on my bed, and I tell him everything.

"I thought they might have caught you inside the church," I say. "That's why I ran up there in the first place."

"I think they almost did. I was about out the door when I heard all this noise, somebody screaming. I thought you guys were playing a game or something. I had to hide behind that statue of the angel."

"You did?"

"But then it sounded like a whole bunch of people were headed my way, so I just ran."

"It was you." I say, realizing, my throat tight. "When you left. Everybody thought it was an active shooter, but it was just you trying to get out of there."

"They thought I—?"

"Thank god you made it out." I hate it when I say "thank god," but it's a hard habit to break. "That could have been—oh my god Jackson—that could have been bad."

He looks up at me, fear behind his eyes because of his record, because of going to juvie last year. It wasn't for anything really bad, just shoplifting and a couple fights, but compared to the kids at church, he'd look like a psychopath.

"Please tell me no one saw you," I say.

"I don't think so. Jesus, I don't know," he says. "Did anyone say they did?"

"Not that I heard. No one in my group got a good look," I say. "Everyone was so panicked."

"But still, my fingerprints are all over the place."

"Along with a lot of other people's," I say, holding his hand tighter, trying to reassure him even though I'm not totally sure myself. "Hundreds of people went through those doors last night."

"But I'm probably the only one of them with a record. What if the police figure out I was there? I have to talk to them."

"And say what, exactly?"

"Don't worry." The tone in his voice is angry, gruff. "There were a lot of kids there. They don't have to know you were with me."

He stands up and heads toward the window. I follow, grabbing his hand to stop him. "You think I care about that? Because I don't."

The look he gives me, it almost breaks my heart. Eyes wary but a flash of hope behind them that disappears the moment I spot it. Sometimes it feels like he won't let himself believe that anyone could love him.

"I don't care if they know we were together. In fact, I'd prefer it," I say. "No one else saw you there. You'd have no alibi without me. If you're going to the police, I'm going with you."

I release his hand and grab the jacket hanging over my desk chair. By the time I turn around, his face has softened a bit.

"I can't let you do that, Em. What about your parents? What about New York?"

"It's better than you getting locked up for something you didn't do."

He balls his hand into a hard fist and stares out the window. "I'm sorry you even have to worry about this."

"We'll figure it out, okay?" I say, looking into his eyes. "This isn't going to change anything."

"You know that's not true," he says. "It'll change everything."

I sit down on the bed again, and he joins me. I'm the one to break the silence. "Then maybe we don't say anything."

"I don't know. I don't like that at all."

"Someone killed June. The police are bound to find them soon, right?"

"Maybe. But what if they don't?"

"Just hear me out, okay? You getting out before everything happened was lucky. In so many ways. The worst thing that could happen now is that they find out you were there and I tell them we were together. Why tell them if we don't have to?"

"I don't know, Em."

"I'm the pastor's daughter. It's basically the most solid alibi you can get. Yeah, I might get expelled, but what could they really do to us? I think it's safer, at least for now, if they don't even know you were there at all."

He stares into my eyes for a long moment. "Okay," he finally says, though it still doesn't sound like he's totally comfortable. "If you think this is the best way to deal with it, that's what we'll do."

We sit there in silence for a moment, me hoping I'm making the right decision about this. But it has to be this way. It's just too scary to think about Jackson getting torn to shreds just because of his past. I can't be responsible for that. He's not the person he used to be. He deserves a second chance.

As I'm thinking, Jackson pulls something out of his pocket and hands it to me: the CD. Of course. In all the confusion of the last twenty-four hours I nearly forgot about the demo.

"I know it's kinda stupid now, but I thought you might like a copy."

"I do. Thank you."

I take it, hold it in my hands. It flashes in the sunlight from the window, as bright and gleaming as our future. This is the second chance, for both of us. And I'll do what I have to do to protect it, to protect him, to protect us both.

"I might not be able to see you for a little while," I say. "My parents are going to be paying closer attention, there's going to be a lot to do. Texts are okay, but I don't want them seeing me answer any calls. So if you need to talk to me, just text or e-mail, okay? Let me figure out a time when it's safe to call you back."

"I hate this."

"Me too, baby. But it's safer for both of us this way. If we need to see each other we can meet at our spot."

He nods, his face cloudy. "This is so fucked up."

"I know."

CHAPTER ELEVEN

I WATCH JACKSON SCURRY through my backyard and out the side gate before closing my window. I'm still exhausted and tuck myself under the covers to get more sleep just as I hear my parents stir and head down to the kitchen for coffee.

Usually on a Saturday we'd be at church by now. My dad would be in his office, busy prepping for the night service, the first in the succession of identical sermons that begins Saturday night and ends, after the fourth repetition, on Sunday night. My mom and I would be helping out with whatever else was going on. There's always something on a Saturday: men's prayer breakfasts, SonShine Kids troupe meetings, Brothers In Christ meetings, community Bible study groups, Women's Ministry outreach programs, missions training. A couple weeks ago the whole place was crazy, prepping for the Easter service, which is always a big production. This year Pastor Pete played Jesus in the Passion Play, and when he rose from the dead, they flew him from the stage all the way over the audience. The seats were packed.

But there's nothing happening there today. No church planned for tonight or tomorrow, just a vigil tomorrow night in the parking lot. Everything else was cancelled.

As of today, the police are still there, collecting evidence. But since they realized that June was the sole victim, that it wasn't an active shooter, they seem to have limited the scope of their search. My dad expects to be able to open the administrative offices on Monday for regular business. And even with the cleanup once the police are finally gone, they're thinking the church will be fully open by Wednesday for June's funeral. June will be eulogized in the same room where she was killed. I try not to think about how messed up that is.

There's a knock on my door.

"Come in."

The knob jiggles, but doesn't open, and I realize I forgot to unlock it. I dash out of bed and open the door, trying to think up an explanation.

"Em-bot?" Paige is standing there in her sweats, eyes red-rimmed, her curly hair mashed into a sloppy bun on top of her head.

"Paiger." She attacks me with a huge hug, like the time when I was five and came back from visiting my grandparents in Texas for a month. She knocked me over with that one.

"I had to see you. I tried to call, but no one was answering," she says, still clutching me tight, tears in her voice.

"We've had it off the hook. All the reporters."

She finally lets go, wipes her eyes. "I figured. Our house is the same." Of course it would be. The press is probably working their way down the staff list.

"And my cell's still at church," she says. "Did you get yours?"

"Yeah. I had it with me, but it's dead." We drift over to my bed and sit down.

"How are you? Have you been okay?" she asks.

"Yeah, I'm okay I guess. You?" I ask.

"Honestly? I'm kind of freaking out. This is all just so insane."

"I know."

"I feel kinda bad," she says.

"About what?"

"Just...she always wanted to hang out, but I was always too busy."

"You were nice to her, though," I say, half to her and half to myself.

"Yeah. To her face. But that's not the same as being someone's friend, as really, truly caring for their soul."

I lean my head over until it's resting on hers. "We promised her we would talk to her that night."

"I know."

"But I completely forgot about it. I totally blew her off.

Maybe if I hadn't…"

Paige sits up, looks me in the eye. "Don't think like that."

"I can't help it."

"If it wasn't for you June wouldn't have had any friends at all. And, more importantly, she wouldn't even be a Christian."

That's right. I had forgotten.

"You led her to Christ, Em. If it wasn't for you she might be in hell right now."

Or she might not have stayed at our church, never been shot.

"I mean, at least we know, no matter what," Paige says, smiling through her tears, "…that June went to heaven."

The thing is I don't know that. What comforts Paige doesn't comfort me. I don't know if heaven exists at all, so all I can think about is how unfair it is for her life to end so quickly. So completely.

"Do you really believe that?" I ask.

"Of course I do. Don't you?"

"Yeah, I guess so," I say. This isn't the right time. And maybe it's not a conversation I'm ready to have with her even if it was.

Paige stares at me. She's wearing that face that she gets sometimes when we play tennis. Paige is the best at tennis in our whole school, better than all the boys. They won't play her anymore because she destroys them. I'm just about the only one left who will, and I only do it because she's my friend and because she lets me win a lot, and because she's just that amazing to watch. In every game she gets this look on her face. It's the moment when she's decided whether to win or lose. Only I never know which it will be. I can only see that she's decided. She has that look on her face right now.

"What were you going to talk to me about the other night?"

"Hmm?"

"Before everything happened? You asked me to get coffee, said we should talk?"

Mike. He hadn't even crossed my mind until now. I was going to talk to her about breaking up with Mike.

"Honestly, I can't even remember," I say. Everything is so different now. It hurts to even think about it, but I can't break up with him anymore. Not yet.

"You're not having doubts are you, Emma?" she says.

"No. Of course not," I say.

44

She pauses for a minute, then lifts herself up on her elbow and sighs, and I know she's letting me win. "What if...," she says quietly. "What if *I* was?"

I'm so stunned I don't even know what to say. A glimmer of hope fires in my chest. What if she's feeling the same way I am? "What do you mean?"

She looks up at me, and her expression completely changes. She rolls her eyes and crashes backward into the bed. "Stop looking at me like that, weirdo. I'm not about to go all atheist ninja on you or something."

My glimmer dies out.

She continues, "I've just been thinking about, I don't know, the way we do things around here, I guess. Sometimes I just...I have questions."

"Like what?"

"I don't know. A lot of things. It's not really important."

"No. It is. Tell me."

She nibbles on her cheek, takes her time before she speaks. "Like, for instance, June the other night? She felt so bad about her past, and it sort of feels like we were all responsible for that, the way we talked about, you know, *sex* around her. I hate thinking that she died feeling like she was less than anyone else."

I grab her hand and squeeze it. "Yeah. I know what you mean."

She squeezes me back. "I wish I could think about her any other way, but all I can picture is her crying. I wish I could just see her again, happy, like she usually was."

Suddenly I realize I might be able to help. There is a way to see her again. I grab my computer.

"What are you doing?" Paige says.

"Remember when June gave her testimony?"

"Do you think it's still up?"

"I don't know."

I bring up the church website and navigate to the youth group page—Elevate Youth Ministries. And there it is, under a heading that reads "Meet our Youth"—June's smiling face, blonde and sweet and tissue-paper delicate.

We shift until my head is leaning against the headboard, Paige's head on my stomach and the laptop in my lap. We've watched a million things together lying around like this. I click on June's video, and Paige grabs my hand.

June is on stage in the Youth Center, her dress faded and dingy, like it had been worn a thousand times. She takes the microphone from Pastor Pete and blinks, unaccustomed to the bright lights up there. It's a Wednesday night service. I can just make out the shape of my own head in the audience, center section, third row, Paige on one side of me, Mike on the other. The date below the video says it was shot on February 26, just over a month ago.

June takes a deep breath and exhales it right into the microphone. The sound of her breath is a thundercloud across the space. Then she speaks.

"My sixth birthday party was at Six Flags. My birthday is on June first in case you want to buy me a present. It's easy to remember because it's my name too."

It's hard to hear her, so Pastor Pete motions for her to tip the mic closer to her mouth, and she does, but this time it's so close it fuzzes her s's so all her words feel cloudy. She doesn't seem to notice.

"I can't remember having a birthday party before that one, and I can't remember having one since. My parents kind of do things all the way or not at all. But this was one of those times when we had money, so I knew it was gonna be amazing."

She stretches out her left hand, working out the nerves.

"It was my first time there, so I was really excited. My sister had been once, and she told me all about it. I didn't sleep the entire night before, but I wasn't tired at all. The air smelled like funnel cake, and I was wearing my favorite pink dress, and there was a blister on my heel from my brand-new sandals. We rode so many rides and ate cotton candy and played all the games, and I remember I won this pink piggy at that one where you use a water gun to race horses on a track?"

Someone coughs, and it seems to throw her off. She looks confused, and pauses for a moment before starting again.

Paige is crying next to me on the bed.

"Everything was perfect, except for two things. The first is that I was only six and too short for a lot of the rides. The ride I wanted to ride most was that big, old-fashioned swing that raises up into the air and spins around and around. But I was way too short."

"The second thing was that my dad was supposed to be there, but it was getting late and he hadn't shown up yet because he was working. I could see it was making my mom mad every time I asked. I mean, what could she do? But I really wanted him to be there so I kept whining about it. She got so mad she shoved me and my sister off on our own so she could smoke with her friends."

She stops again, looking a little stricken, like she hadn't meant to say the thing about her mom smoking.

"I started to cry because it was getting really dark, and I knew we were gonna have to leave soon, and my dad still wasn't there, and we had ridden all the kiddie rides a hundred times, but all I really wanted to do was ride that swing. I think I had gotten it into my head that if my dad showed up he could do something about it. So my sister came up with this plan. She was gonna distract the ride operator so I could sneak over the fence and get in."

"I don't know what she said to the operator, but it worked. I climbed over while she was talking and got a seat."

She closes her eyes, shutting us all out, gathering her thoughts. You can see the concentration tightening her forehead. June wasn't exactly a showy person. She could talk your head off, yeah, but not in front of everyone. The fear she must have felt being in front of all of us like that must have been intense.

Her silence goes on so long that Pastor Pete finally speaks up, "You're doing great, June."

She looks up at him and smiles that too-grateful smile of hers, then looks back to us. "Once I sat down the best thing happened! My dad sat down right next to me! We were so busy hugging that the ride operators didn't even notice my height. They just hooked me in and started it up.

"I remember the ride spinning, then going up and up and up. I loved it so much! It was just so beautiful. I leaned my head back and watched the stars blur to streaks. My hair flew behind me like I was flying, and it really felt like I was. The wind pricked up goose bumps, and they felt like magic on my skin."

Pastor Pete coughs, probably bothered by the magic comment and wondering where the story was going. We all were. You can see people shifting in the audience, losing patience.

"Then I did this stupid thing. I lifted my little pink piggy into the air, to make it fly. And it slipped out of my hands. And before I realized what I was doing I lunged for it and the swing twisted under me. I tried to wiggle to steady it, but my butt ended up slipping through the chain on the side of my seat."

The room gets really quiet. People stop shuffling. I remember being there. In an instant, she had us all perched on the edge of our chairs.

"I don't know how far off the ground I was at the time. But I was barely holding on. I was folded over in half, my head and hands and feet were still in the seat, but my bottom was dangling out like I was sitting inside an empty bucket."

"I remember being scared and sorry and embarrassed that everyone could see my underwear. Which was stupid, because I was about to die, but I was six, so I guess that's what you think about when you're six."

Next to me on the bed Paige's breath hitches in her throat, and I know what she's thinking because I'm thinking it too. It's like June was doomed, destined in some way for tragedy.

"I remember trying to scream but not being able to. It seemed like my breath got caught in my throat for what felt like forever."

Was that what it was like when she died? I'm crying now too, right along with Paige. I had just wanted to hear her voice, but this is too much.

"And then I remember my dad swinging over and grabbing me. First my ankle, then my hand. I remember him holding on to me so tight I thought my bones would break right off."

"What I don't remember is landing. I didn't black out or anything, I just don't remember it. I remember the moment after we landed, though. He pulled me out of the seat and held me really tight. He was breathing really hard, and his body was vibrating just like mine. But, somehow, we were both okay."

Paige sniffles, wipes her face. This was harder to watch than I thought, but there's only a little left. And June looks so alive, so normal. If I turn it off she'll be gone again. Paige tucks her face into my stomach, and I put a hand on her head, gripping her close.

June keeps talking, "I know God sent my dad just in time to save me that night. God saved me before I even knew about Him, so that I could live long enough to meet Him."

She looks stronger now. The color is back in her cheeks, and her voice is full and confident.

"Jesus had a plan for me. He had a plan for me to find this church and find Him and stand here tonight a whole person. So even on hard days I think about that night, and I remember God's plan, and I remember that my future is in His hands too and that if I trust Him He'll never let me fall. Thank you."

She lowers the microphone, and the room explodes in applause and a chorus of hallelujahs. A smile runs across her face. She's beaming, so happy to make us all so happy, so moved by her words. I decide to remember her exactly like this.

"Thank you," Paige says. "Thank you."

CHAPTER TWELVE

ON SUNDAY MORNING, THE police call and ask me to come in to answer more questions about the lock-in. Now my parents and I are sitting in a small beige conference room at the police station, just big enough for a table that seats all of us: my family plus the two detectives—Detective Boyer, the one I spoke to that night, and her partner, Detective Bud Simms, who looks like he could be a hundred years old.

It smells like armpits in here.

"So you used to date June's boyfriend, Nicolas?" Detective Boyer asks.

"Yes." I say, worried about answering questions about him. Of course he'd be their first suspect, but there's no way I'm going to help indict him.

"Were you upset when he broke up with you?"

Her question is jarring. Why would they care about how we broke up? "He didn't break up with me. I broke up with him."

Detective Simms perks up at that. "Oh? Why?"

"Because I wanted to date someone else."

"Your current boyfriend, Michael Kent?"

"Yes."

"Is all this personal information really necessary?" my mom asks, giving the detectives a smile that, if they knew her, they'd know wasn't a smile at all. "With all the attention that comes from our work, we do our best to keep our daughter's private life private."

I have to keep myself from laughing. The only things sacred about my life are the things they don't know.

"Exactly," my dad pipes up. "I thought you needed Emma to help out with information about the lock-in because of her unique position in the youth community."

"We're just trying to get a clearer picture. Get to know everyone. All of this is helping a lot," Detective Simms says, scratching his nose with the wrong end of his pen and accidentally drawing a blue line down the crease of it.

"So you broke up with Nicolas to date Michael. How long ago was that?" Detective Boyer seems to be in charge of asking the questions. She seems to be in charge of everything.

"Last spring."

"When last spring?"

"Maybe April? It was before prom."

"You don't keep track of your anniversary?"

"I'm no good with dates," I say, smiling.

Detective Boyer looks over to Simms with a frown and rubs her nose to let him know about the line. He rubs at it, but doesn't get it off, leaving a blue smear where it used to be. Boyer seems annoyed but lets it go.

"Okay. Let's talk about that night," Boyer says. "When was the last time you saw June?"

"It was like I told you. I can't remember for sure."

"Give us your best guess."

I sit up straight, fold my hands. "I know I saw her in the choir room after the Purity Ball. After that, I lost track of her."

"Why weren't you hanging out together? You were friends with her, right?"

"Yes, I guess so."

"What do you mean by that?"

"I didn't really know her very well."

"Is that so? A lot of other people thought you were one of her best friends."

"She liked to tell people that, but like I said, I didn't really know her that well."

"So why would she think you were such good friends?"

"I tried to be nice to her, I guess. She's new to the church, and it can be hard to make friends."

Detective Boyer leans back in her chair with a wry smile. "So you're saying the church crowd isn't too friendly?"

My dad frowns, glares at her. "We accept everyone equally,

Ms. Boyer, which is why Emma was extending a kindness to the girl."

Detective Boyer nods, but the look on her face seems to say, "Yeah, right."

"I'm sure you can understand how certain people have a tendency to get overly attached to someone like Emma," my mom says.

Detective Simms jumps in. "Let me ask you something else, Emma. We're estimating the time of death between ten and eleven," he says.

Ten and eleven? I had assumed that June was killed just before we found her near midnight. But if she was killed between ten and eleven, that means she'd been lying there for nearly an hour, all alone. It means she was killed while Jackson and I were together.

"Can you tell me where you were during that time?"

Oh god. What do I say? I can't tell them the truth. Not with my parents here. Not with Jackson's criminal record. I don't know what to do. My heart races until it feels like there's a base guitar strumming inside my throat. I panic. "I was in the bathroom. I wasn't feeling well."

"Which bathroom?"

"Um, the one upstairs. In the Kid's Korner." As soon as it comes out of my mouth I regret it. It's a totally stupid thing to say.

The two detectives exchange a look.

"Anybody with you?" Boyer asks.

"No, I was alone. My stomach was upset."

"I'm sorry to hear that. Sounds awful," she says, and the way she says it makes me feel like a jerk for complaining about an upset stomach when June was murdered. Especially when it's not even close to true.

"Do you remember seeing June anytime after you guys changed?" Simms asks, but all I can focus on is the blue on his face, now glistening from getting mixed up with the oil on his nose.

"I'm sorry?" I say, not remembering the question he just asked.

"Do you remember seeing June anytime after you changed clothes?" he asks.

52

"I'm not sure. There were a lot of people there."

"Three hundred and fifty-six," Boyer says.

"Okay," I say.

"There were 356 people there, Emma. Ten adults and 346 teenagers. And the thing is, we seem to be able to pin down where almost everyone was around ten thirty when June was killed. But we're still not sure about you."

"I told you. I was in the bathroom. I wasn't feeling well." My voice sounds more defensive than it should.

"Hold on now." This time it's my dad. "Do we need a lawyer here?"

She doesn't answer him. "Which bathroom again?"

"The one upstairs. By the Kid's Korner."

"Why didn't you use the one right next to the Youth Center? It would have been much closer."

"I don't know."

"You don't know? You skipped a bathroom that was thirty feet out the door, a big bathroom where several other girls were already inside, changing into their pajamas. And then you went up two floors, alone, past the main level where there are at least three adult bathrooms, to use a bathroom where the toilets are child-sized? And you don't know why? Can you see how I don't understand?"

"I guess I wanted some privacy." I pick at my cuticles. "Like you said, it was crowded in there, and it had already been a long day and I wasn't feeling well."

"If you wanted so much privacy that night, then why did you even go?"

"I go to everything." Pastor's Kid Obligation #3,872.

"Is Emma a suspect in all this?" My dad again.

"We haven't named anyone as a suspect yet. Like I said, we're just trying to get all the facts," Detective Simms says. He's so bland I want to gag.

"Well it certainly seems like you're going in a direction that I'm very uncomfortable with. Emma is a good girl. I won't have you accusing her like this."

"Like I said, Mr. Grant, this is all just routine," Detective Simms says.

Detective Boyer pulls a baggie out of a file folder and pushes it toward me. "Do you recognize this?"

I stare at the baggie, tilt my head until my eyes can see past the glare on the surface from the overhead light. Inside is a diamond earring. My diamond earring.

My heart drops into my stomach. How did they get my earring? Why do they have it now, sealed into a little plastic bag like it matters?

"That's enough," my dad says, standing up.

"We found it underneath your friend's body. Any idea how it got there?"

Underneath June's body? Then it's not just my alibi they're worried about. They think they have proof.

"I, I, I don't—," I stammer.

"Don't answer that, Emma," my dad says. "We're not continuing this without our lawyer present. Come on, girls. We're going home."

CHAPTER THIRTEEN

"WHAT WAS THAT IN there?" my mom asks, fuming, all her fire in my direction. "The way you were acting…I wouldn't be surprised if they thought you were guilty."

We're in my mom's brand-new Mercedes ML350, in the parking lot of the police station. They're sitting in the back to talk to me, one on either side, while the SUV idles, driverless. My dad just got off the phone with a lawyer, who we're meeting in an hour.

"And that business about the earring?" she asks. "My mother gave those to you. How could you be so careless?"

"I don't know. I don't even remember when I lost it. I guess it could have been while I was dancing. Maybe June found it and was holding on to it until she saw me."

"Of course she could have found it. There are a hundred reasonable explanations," my dad says. "The police are grasping at straws."

"She had them on during the processional. I distinctly recall seeing them on her."

"Wait! I do remember. I took an earring off while we were changing. I was going to put it away so I wouldn't lose it, but then I must have forgotten about it when June came over to talk to me."

"So you just left them out where anyone could take them?" my mom says.

"I guess so."

"You guess so. Perfect." She shakes her head, irritated.

"Those detectives would just love it if it was her," my dad

says. "It's a shame what lengths some people will go to in order to discredit believers."

"Which is why you have to make an extra effort to be flawless, Emma," my mom says. "You simply cannot make mistakes like that. It reflects very poorly on the church."

The church. They're not worried about me at all, they're worried about themselves. My parent's love is a shallow sort of love, a supposed-to love that I didn't really understand until I felt how Jackson loved me. To them, I'm like a handbag or a designer watch, the perfect accessory for the church power couple. Perfect grades, perfect smile, perfect me.

It's easier not to say that, though; always has been. "I'm sorry," I say instead.

"Is there anything else we need to know?" my mom asks. "Before we talk to the lawyer?"

"It's very important that you tell us the truth right now. If you were in that bathroom like you said, then fine. We'll figure out a way to deal with it. But if not, it's important we know. There's nothing you could do to make us stop loving you."

I'm pretty sure there is. I'm pretty sure there are a lot of things I could do, one of which I've already done.

"I told you everything," I say.

"Good," he says. "Don't you worry, honey. We're not going to let them treat you like this. Our Heavenly Father entrusted us with your care, and we take that very seriously," he says. Sometimes my dad forgets that he's not on the pulpit. I wish, especially right now, that he'd drop the act.

"I know," I say. It's too warm in here. I want them to crack the window, but I don't ask.

"Why don't we pray?" my dad says.

We close our eyes and bow our heads. They put their arms around me, and I want to push them off but I don't. I count the seconds instead, count the fingers on my hands, count the whorls in the walnut console.

"Dear Jesus, we ask You to guide the detectives in their search. We ask You to bless them with Your infinite wisdom, that they may first cast out the beam in their own eye before attempting to remove the mote in another's. We ask You to reveal to them the true devil who entered Your house, oh Lord, that he might see Your justice. And we ask You to protect our baby girl. Cover her with Your love, shield her with Your mighty presence. Turn the swords against her into plowshares and show her, through all of this, that You are always by her side."

I wish he was sometimes, I really do.

"You don't have anything to worry about. The way I see it, they're fishing." The lawyer's name is Terry Graham. "The girl herself had access to the earring when they were changing. She could have taken it. And there were a lot of people who could have gotten into the choir room."

There was no question about who my parents would call. Mr. Graham is lean, but has a face like a pit bull. He reminds me of a British movie gangster, only without the accent. We've known him forever; he's on the church board, and his grandson, Andy, goes to elementary school at Summit Christian, where I'm a senior.

We're in Mr. Graham's office, which is modern and covered in sleek wood paneling. Where there's not wood, the windows overlook the streets of downtown Denver from twenty floors above, the mountains hovering in the background like sentries.

"I called my guy in the force. All they have is opportunity and a very, very weak motive. They don't have any witnesses. They don't have a weapon. They really have nothing, which is why I'm guessing no one's been formally charged."

"Can they do this, then? Treat her like this?" my dad asks. My mother reaches out for his hand. I don't think she's eaten much of anything since June died. She's always been thin, and now she's starting to look drawn, like a guitar string pulled to snapping.

"Unfortunately, yes. This is the way it goes. They're pressing everyone extra hard, not just Emma. Sounds like this Detective Boyer is known as somewhat of a bloodhound. They say she's pretty relentless."

This is not making me feel better. Maybe I should tell them everything. Now, before this goes any further. Then I think of Jackson. I told him I wasn't going to say anything, and I have to stick to that, at least until I speak to him first.

"She's already managed to narrow down the suspect pool considerably. It looks like there were only seven other people not in the two main rooms at the time of the murder: Chuck Rand, Pastor Pete, Hope Crowley, Paige and Michael Kent, Nicolas Lawson, and June herself."

"They don't seriously think it could be someone in the congregation, do they?" Mom asks. "Especially one of the kids?"

"That detective, that Boyer woman? She has a chip on her shoulder about religion. I can tell you that," my dad says.

"I'm getting the same sense about her, Pastor. But there were no signs of forced entry. So whoever did it either had a key, was already there, or got let in by someone who was."

"What about picking a lock?" Dad asks. "I've heard about some very sophisticated devices out there."

"It's possible, but they're not seeing any signs of it, so they're pursuing what they have. Which leaves us with that list. Everyone else at the lock-in has multiple witnesses for their whereabouts because they were in groups, some playing basketball in the gym and the rest either playing Red Rover in the Youth Center or watching it."

I remember coming in at the end of the game, racing in feeling like I would burst with happiness. By then, June was already dead.

Mr. Graham says, "Pastor Pete, whom I've spoken with personally, was disciplining Chuck about some disturbance he had made shortly before."

"He lit his fart on fire." It sounds stupid once it comes out of my mouth, and totally the wrong thing to say, but it's true. They stare at me, not sure whether to chastise me or let it go. "Sorry. It's true. I saw him do it. Then Pastor Pete and Miss Hope took him out."

"Yes. They took him to Pastor Pete's office, after which Chuck and Pastor Pete had a discussion about his behavior, which each of the three verifies." It was a dumb thing to do, but Chuck is always doing dumb things like that. I'm surprised he's not caught more often.

"There's also Nicolas Lawson, the girl's boyfriend. He says he was looking for June, whom he hadn't seen since ten or so. Several witnesses report him asking about her whereabouts, but none can pinpoint exact times so he hasn't been totally eliminated. However, I know the Lawsons personally, and I think it's unlikely the boy is responsible."

Everyone who knows Nicolas would feel this way. He may be a little on the know-it-all side, but he's farm-boy innocent and soldier honorable, the kind of guy older girls want to mother and younger girls want to be protected by.

"Which leaves Paige and Michael Kent, who were together getting cases of soda from the coffee shop pantry on the main level."

Paige. I didn't even register her name on the list. And the fact that it is on there? It's totally my fault. I'm the one who asked her to do that. Then I remember something else.

"The police kept asking me about whether or not we were going swimming later," I say. "Did your contact say anything about that?"

"Yes. He did. Apparently the girl was wearing a swimsuit when she died."

"But I saw her. She was fully clothed. She was wearing a sundress and tennis shoes and—"

"The swimsuit was under the girl's clothing," he says. "They're not sure what to make of it. She may have been using it as undergarments."

Was she? Do I remember seeing her in the changing room? I can't be sure.

"But that's for the police to figure out. What's important right now is that we get all the facts. "He gives me his most stern look. "I understand you were alone at the time of the murder? In one of the Kid's Korner bathrooms?"

"Yes."

"Now, Emma, this is the time for complete honesty. And I'm sorry, but that just doesn't make any sense at all."

"But it's true." I'm defensive because it's not true, not at all. If I admit I lied about this, it will make me look so much guiltier. It feels like he knows I'm lying so I stick to the lie harder, force him to believe. I can see it's not working.

"Why would you do that?"

"I just…," I sniffle, for real, frustrated with all of this. I had nothing against June, and I had nothing to do with her death, so why should I have to explain myself like this?

"I get overwhelmed sometimes. And I was feeling sick because I ate too much at the ball and then slammed a Red

Bull. It had been a long day, and everyone was there, and I just wanted a few minutes to myself. Sometimes I go up there to be alone. No one's ever there during youth group stuff." Some of this is true, and I'm hoping it will make the not-true bits sound true too.

"The thing is, and they haven't made this common knowledge just yet, but they think they have you gone from the party for more than a few minutes. They think it was nearly two hours."

"That can't be right," I say. It is right.

Mr. Graham seems to soften a bit. "I think I understand, but do you understand how it looks to the police? What would help, what would really help, is if you saw anything while you were away from the Youth Center."

"I can't think of anything."

"Any weird sounds or lights on where they shouldn't be? Anything out of place? Any cars driving around in the parking lot?"

Then I remember the noise. I remember feeling like someone was there, watching me. Watching us. But what can I say? I was supposed to be across the entire church from where I saw them. What if I said something about it and made it harder to find who really did it?

"No. Nothing."

"This is ridiculous," Dad says. "Why should Emma have to defend herself here? It's like they're not even considering her as anything but a suspect."

"At least she's still a minor," Mr. Graham says. My birthday is on May 31, five weeks away. "They can't question her without your presence until she's eighteen, which is good. You did the right thing calling me. I don't want you talking to anyone about any of this without me there. Anyone, okay?"

I nod.

"No texting, no calls, no friends, no outside family, no teachers, and especially no police. They show up for 'just a quick chat' you call me, got it?"

"Yes, sir." I can see that he likes it when I call him sir. He was worried before, but now I'm the girl he always thought I was. Polite, contrite, spotless.

"Your job is to stay quiet until this all gets cleared up. Keep your normal routine, though. We don't want you to look like you have anything to hide. Go to school, go to church, then go home."

"Yes, sir," I say. He beams.

"We're not going to let anything bad happen to you, sweetheart, okay? You're a good kid, and everybody at church knows that. You have nothing to worry about."

Only I am worried.

CHAPTER FOURTEEN

AT SUNDOWN THAT NIGHT is June's vigil. There are over a thousand people there, holding candles in silent respect of June. Most of them I don't know. There are a lot of reporters, a lot of cameras, and a lot of what I suspect are strangers coming out to gawk at tragedy. They all feel like intruders, like gossips holding cups to our door so they can listen to our pain and feed off it.

I look around until I spot the people I do know. Mike and Paige are standing near the front, where someone has set up the cross we danced around at the Purity Ball. It's right on the front lawn, buried in flowers and teddy bears and florist balloons printed with *We Miss You* and *Rest In Peace*. There are drawings too, and pictures. Someone has put together a collage of photographs, most of which I've never seen before, but all of which seem to have been taken at various youth group activities.

And around it all, on the lawn, her name is spelled out in candles:

JUNE

Glowing. Flickering in the darkness. Her name.

The sight makes my throat thick.

Paige spots me and waves. Mike nods to me too. I haven't talked to him since that night, though I've been meaning to call, because it's what I would do if I was really his girlfriend, in my heart. It suddenly seems strange that he hasn't called me yet. But he's probably been as sidelined by this as everyone else has.

All the other kids are here too: Chuck, Ruth, Ben, Angela,

Erica, Katie, and Nicolas (June's boyfriend). I walk over to them and join their ranks. I've grown up with these kids. I may not believe the same thing as them anymore, but they're the only ones I want to be with right now. None of them know what the police are thinking about me, and not one of them would believe it if they did.

Paige hugs me when I walk up to her.

"Say something, please," she says through her tears. "The adults aren't saying anything, and her parents aren't even here, and all this silence is killing me."

I look up and see Angela nod to me, Chuck too.

"Please," Paige says. "You knew her better than anyone but Nicolas, and he's mess." I look over to him. He's totally destroyed, barely standing he's crying so hard. I've never seen him like this before. The sight of him so broken breaks us all a little bit more, I can feel it.

"What am I supposed to say?" I ask Paige.

"I don't know. You'll figure it out. You're good at this kind of stuff."

Angela speaks up, "Do it. It would make everyone feel a lot better."

Then Ben chimes in too. "Come on, Em."

And Chuck, "Yeah. Say something."

My hands are shaking as I leave their circle and take a few steps toward the cross. Maybe I shouldn't do this. Maybe this is a bad idea.

Once I'm there, everyone stares at me expectantly, at least everyone close enough to see. I clear my throat, trying to think of what I should say, but nothing's coming. Nothing at all. What can I say about her? That she was sweet? That she was brave? That she was loved? I don't know, not really, if any of that is true. What I know of her seems so small compared to what her entire life must have been made up of. Who am I to say anything at all?

The only thing I can think of, the only thing playing though my head, is the song I sang at my Grandma Betty's funeral: "It Is Well With My Soul."

I don't have anything else, so I sing.

"When peace, like a river, attendeth my way,
When sorrows like sea billows roll;"

The crowd, all of them now, turns their attention to me. My voice quavers, but I keep going, letting it swell and rise with the melody.

"Whatever my lot, Thou hast taught me to say,
It is well, it is well with my soul."

I take a breath to calm my nerves, then move on to the refrain.

"It is well…"

And I hear it then, the words sung back to me as they are when it's sung in church. The echo is from my friends. Paige and Angela and Ruth and Katie, joining in so I won't be alone.

"It is well," they sing.

"With my soul," I sing.

"With my soul," they echo in response, the boys coming in now too. Ben's deep bass and Chuck's shaky baritone. Then all of us together, and someone from the crowd joining in with a harmony.

"It is well, it is well, with my soul."

I move on to the last verse, and now they're all singing with me. The whole crowd, at least the ones who know the church, who know the song. You can tell the intruders by their silence, but the rest of us are singing it out into the night, together. Which is good, because the tears are coming again, too hard to stop, and I wouldn't be able to do it by myself, not without them.

"And Lord, haste the day when the faith shall be sight,
The clouds be rolled back as a scroll;
The trump shall resound, and the Lord shall descend,
Even so, it is well with my soul."

It seems right somehow, this song. Perfect. Not in the way it's meant, that Jesus is coming one day to show himself as God. But in the spirit of it: *the faith shall be sight*. The whole idea of being steady in the storm because the truth will come out. Someday we will find out who did this to her. And I'm going to do everything I can to make that day come as soon as possible.

I get my breath back, and sing the last refrain in full voice.

"It is well,
            It is well
With my soul,
            With my soul,

64

It is well, it is well, with my soul."

I don't have to start the next song, or the next. They seem to spring up spontaneously after that. We sing more, and cry more, and hold each other's hands and hug until there's nothing left inside any of us. Eventually, people start to leave.

By nine thirty, it's just the core group left. We convince our parents to let us to stay out late so we can meet at a diner and talk. School has been cancelled all week, so the parents give in. I think they know we need to be with each other right now.

"Why don't you ride with me?" Mike says. He seems tired, drained just like we all are.

"Okay," I say. "Sure."

We walk toward his car alone, Paige having agreed to ride with Katie so Katie wouldn't have to drive by herself in the dark.

We get to Mike's car, but he doesn't unlock it. Instead, he comes around to my side, steps close to me, then reaches past to open the back door.

"I got you something," he says, pulling out a dozen roses, but not yet handing them to me. He just stands there with them. It seems like he's trying to say something, but can't get the words out.

"What are those for?" I ask.

In that moment a vision flashes in front of me of what my life would look like with him: married at nineteen, chained to the house with a string of babies, an endless series of "Yes, dears" and bland dinners and doing laundry, and never doing anything for myself, just because it makes me happy, ever again.

"I wasn't sure I was going to give them to you," he says. "But what I saw tonight made me believe in you again."

"What do you mean?"

He steps close, and instinctively I back up a step until my back is against the car.

"I mean that these flowers are a gesture. Something to tell you…"

He takes a deep breath.

"…to tell you that I forgive you, Emma."

"Forgive me for what?"

"I saw you," he says, the words twisting a knife inside him. It flashes on his face, but just as fast he buries it. "The night June was killed? I saw you with that guy."

CHAPTER FIFTEEN

My heart plummets to my stomach. Mike was the noise. He was the one snooping around in the dark. And if he wasn't with Paige, then he could have been anywhere.

I squeeze out past him into the open space of the parking lot, which is now empty.

"I thought you were helping Paige with the soda."

"Is that all you have to say?"

"Why weren't you with her? Tell me, Mike."

"This was afterward. We couldn't find the hand truck, so I borrowed one from upstairs. When I went back to return it later I saw the light on outside the studio. And what do I find? My girlfriend, naked, *fucking* that guy from the football game last fall, like a *fucking* whore."

I've never heard Mike swear before. Not once. The words sound so off in his mouth, so wrong.

He takes a deep breath, calming himself. I see a piece of him loosen, then pull back together, rearing forward toward his goal. The way he does when he's blocked playing basketball, not the lithe player but the powerhouse, shuffling his feet, barreling his bulk past the opposition, his eyes never leaving the hoop. There's a fine line between being persistent and being stubborn.

"But like I said," he says slowly, regaining his control. "I forgive you. I want to make things right between us."

"Mike…" I don't know what to say. I think he wants me to break down into tears so he can pick me up and put me back together again, Humpty Dumpty style. It pricks up my anger. But he keeps talking, totally unaware of my feelings.

67

"You're the one I want. I'm willing to put the past behind us and move on." This line sounds practiced. I wonder if he's been repeating it to his image in the mirror.

"I don't get it, Mike. Why?"

"Why what?"

"Why would you still want to be with me after this?"

"Because I'm not a quitter. And I won't let you be one either."

It's the kind of thing coaches have been saying to him in locker rooms his whole life. It should make me feel good, but it doesn't. It's bullshit. Mike doesn't care about me specifically, he just doesn't want to lose.

"Well I'm sorry, but I don't think it's quitting to break up."

"Don't you see, Emma? This is exactly the kind of moment we've learned about. Churning through relationships like this? Hookup culture? It's all just practice for divorce."

I almost roll my eyes, but I don't want to get him pissed off again. It's such a joke. The whole idea that dating a lot makes you more prone to divorce is insane. How am I supposed to figure out what I like if I don't date? All anyone has ever told me is to find a good Christian boy who doesn't pressure you into sex. Don't worry about looks, just worry if he has a heart for God. Those are the only requirements. But what about everything else? How am I supposed to figure out the rest of what makes someone a person, and especially a person I want to spend the rest of my life with? What if I want someone daring or ambitious or strong or, god forbid, good in bed? Doesn't that matter at all? The whole thing sounds like a system designed to make me set my standards low, and settle for being miserable with whatever I get. I'm done acting like it makes any sense.

"I don't want to be with you, Mike. And yes, I went about it in a really shitty way, but—"

"Nice, Emma." It's just like him to scold me after he was the one who dropped the f-bomb twice.

"— but that doesn't mean I'm obligated to stay with you."

Mike is flustered now. There's a crease of skin above his nose. It's the same thing he does when he's taking a test. He can't figure this out. He can't figure me out.

"I gave you a promise ring, Emma. That means something to

me. I thought it meant something to you too. God spoke to me, and I don't take that lightly. He told me you were going to be *my wife* someday."

"I'm not marrying you, Mike. I'm just not. We're not good for each other. And as of now, we're not together anymore. Honestly, it's kind of a relief you saw what you did."

"A relief?"

The roses are squeezed near snapping inside his meaty palms. He doesn't know it, has never asked, but roses are my least favorite flower. They're a boring flower of street-corner salesman and Walgreens refrigerators, something women are taught to want and never question if they truly love. I'm an orchid girl. If Mike knew that, there's a chance I wouldn't be with Jackson at all.

CHAPTER SIXTEEN

So if I was so unhappy with Mike, why didn't I just break up with him a long time ago?

It's not a simple question to answer, but it boils down to this: I wasn't always unhappy with Mike. There is a before and an after, but in between there was love, or at least something that wanted to be love, and isn't that almost the same thing?

As far as church guys go, Mike is a prize. He's a pastor's son, a natural leader, a spiritual force. Not to mention the whole athletic, dimpled, Superman good looks thing he has going on. I guarantee there's a girl right now scribbling *Mrs. Michael Kent* a hundred times in her notebook, dotting the "i" with a heart and wishing I was dead in some tragic, senseless way that would leave him consolable. Probably Katie Reed. Definitely Katie Reed.

The thing is, I never really saw him that way, not for a long time. Sure, people always thought we'd get together. But to me, he was just Paige's annoying twin brother. He was the boy who always called shotgun first, the boy who stole our teddy bears for target practice, the boy who outed us for sneaking the first Harry Potter book from the library and devouring it like it was our last meal (which, as far as Harry Potter went, it was.) He was the boy who pulled my pigtails and elbowed me in the ribs and chased me with two handfuls of baby garter snakes out on his grandparent's ranch the summer we were ten. As most sisters do, Paige despised him, and we were fiercely loyal to each other, still are. So it was either Team Paige or Team Mike, and I was Team Paige all the way.

The time he stole our Barbies and chopped their hair? We cut his hair in his sleep, Delilah-ing him into an emergency buzz cut on picture day in first grade. We got grounded from each other for a month for that one.

In second grade, he lifted up my skirt to show the playground my underwear, and I slapped him right in the face. The teacher saw it and made me write a hundred times, *I will not hit boys*. Not *I will not hit*, but *I will not hit* boys. He received no punishment, just a warning not to do it again.

In retaliation, I made him an apology hot cocoa and peed in it. Paige and I nearly busted open laughing when he took the first sip, even after he spit it out and threw it all over us. We were wicked little things back then, before we had the wicked pressed out of us by the expectation of sweetness and light.

But we grew up. Mike got handsome, and I hit puberty, and we mostly ignored each other because it was just too awkward to think about at first.

Then at some point I started to notice Mike's intense passion for God. There was nothing false about it, nothing forced. He simply loved Christ. Our junior year, Pastor Pete started to create nights at youth group for students to preach. Mike was the first to sign up. He spoke about being on fire for God, and it made us all on fire too. Mike only has two speeds: sprint and stop. His sermon was no different. All that intensity showed up there too, and it woke something up in me. It made me hope that everything I'd had doubts about could actually be real after all.

By then he was playing big brother to me and Paige about everything, even though he's the same age as us. He drove us to school. He hovered close whenever we were dating anyone. Of course in private he criticized all my love interests, and I pretended his opinions didn't matter. Only they did. I don't know how to explain it, but I wanted his approval because I wanted the relationship with God that he had, or that I thought he had at the time. He was doing something right. I wasn't. So when he hinted he was interested, I broke up with Nicolas and said yes to Mike.

Everyone was so excited for us; we were like church royalty. But as far as my spiritual life went, nothing changed. There were no revelations, no new understandings. Just the same confusion as before, but with the added pressure of making it seem like we were equally yoked.

And all that spark we brought to our fights? It didn't transfer to our relationship either. But by the time I figured that out, it was too late for an easy exit. The thing about great battles is that eventually someone has to lose, and that's what it was like to date Mike. As soon as we got together, he won and I lost.

CHAPTER SEVENTEEN

"A RELIEF?" HE SAYS again. He's huffing in the moonlight, pre-Hulk mad, humiliated by my refusing his generosity, and maybe fixing to teach me a lesson. Pastor Kent has always been very pro-spanking. Paige doesn't talk about it a lot, but I'm pretty sure she still gets the belt. Mike has a look on his face like that's exactly what he'd like to do to me right now. I try not to remember how big he is, how quickly he could snap me in two with those fingers if he wanted to.

"You need me, Emma," he says.

"Really?" I say.

"You think I don't know what's been going on with you? That the police are looking at you for June? Terry Graham tells my father everything."

So much for attorney-client privilege.

"So what? You suddenly have some sway over the police? You're just gonna barge in there and tell them to back off and everything's gonna get better?"

"I might not be able to make things better, but I could make them much worse. I wonder what the police would say if they knew Jackson was there that night."

Did he just say what I think he did?

Jackson.

I heard it come out of his mouth, clear as ice.

How does he know Jackson's name?

"Number seventy-seven? Jackson Thomas? From what I hear he's quite the bad boy. Did you think I wouldn't look into him after that stunt he pulled giving you his number?"

"What do you mean?"

"I asked around. Apparently, he has quite a reputation. I hear he's even done some time, which I'm sure the police would find very interesting."

"He was with me the whole time that night," I say. Well, almost. He did go to the restroom once, but Mike doesn't need to know that.

"And I bet you're just dying to tell everyone all about how he was with you."

"You can't say anything, Mike, you just can't. That stuff is all behind him now."

"You make me sick, you know that?" he says. "You should be begging me for my forgiveness, begging God for *His* forgiveness, but instead you're wasting your breath defending someone who took advantage of you."

"You think he took advantage of me? Because he didn't. I wanted him, Mike. I still want him."

"Fine. I'll just call the police right now then."

He pulls the phone out of his pocket.

"No! Stop!"

He puts the phone down.

"Are you ready to stop talking and listen for a minute? Your dad was right, you know. You really need to work on putting your pride aside."

His words snarl my anger, but I can't lose control again. I have to protect Jackson. "Fine, okay. Let's talk. What do you want?"

"First, you completely break off contact with him. If I hear of you seeing him, or anyone else for that matter, even by accident, even from a distance, even at a baseball game or something, I go straight to the police."

Life without Jackson? Not possible.

"Second, you have to make an effort to make things work between us. We go out on Friday nights. We sit together at church. You go to prom with me." The problem to Mike isn't whether I love him or not. It's whether other people think I love him.

"For how long?" Am I considering this? Am I actually considering this?

"For until I say how long. You're not exactly in a position to negotiate here." He stands up straighter, crosses his hands over his crotch like he's in the military. "So that's the deal. Take it or leave it."

"I can't," I say. Can I?

He looks at me, shocked. "Think before you talk for once, Emma. Think very hard."

"I didn't do anything wrong." It sounds whiny, like something a child would say. I know the minute I say it that it doesn't matter. Right now the truth doesn't matter at all.

"Tell that to the police," he says.

"Just let me think about it, okay?"

He steps back, considers.

"You have until tomorrow morning, or I call the police."

CHAPTER EIGHTEEN

I DECIDE TO WALK home instead of going with Mike to meet the other kids. It will take me an hour, but it's better than sticking around. I need time to think. I make my way across the parking lot and toward the streaks of cars on Westlake Road.

Mike left Paige while they were getting the soda to find a hand truck. *And* he was on his own when he returned it. He could've killed June at either point. He had the time. The police don't know it, but he did. Do I really believe he'd be capable of something like that?

I don't know. Looking at his face tonight, red and fuming, I —I don't know.

Maybe. Maybe under the wrong circumstances. If he was provoked, angry, if he lost his temper. Maybe we're all capable of something like that if we're provoked. But what could June have possibly done to provoke him? He barely knew she existed. I can't think of a single reason Mike would have to hurt her.

I shiver. The spring hasn't yet given up to summer, and despite the sunny days the nights are see-your-breath cold. I have no jacket; it's still in my mom's car. Surrounded by all the others, I was perfectly warm. But alone out here is different. I pass under a street light and see that my fingernails are blue. It's an effort not to give in to the shivers.

There's a Starbucks a few blocks down so I go inside, order a tea, and warm up in a corner near the fireplace. Eventually, the tea heats me from the inside out, and I start to think more clearly.

All I want is to see Jackson. It's a bad idea; I know it is. Mike might still be watching. Besides, we agreed not to see each other until all this blows over. But I need him right now. So much has happened, and he knows nothing about it. I might not get another chance to tell him for weeks.

I look around, glance out to the parking lot to make sure I don't see Mike's car, and pull out my phone.

"Can you come get me?"

It only takes Jackson fifteen minutes to get here. I'm waiting outside for him. It feels like I haven't seen him in weeks, and I want to wrap myself around him, feel his arms around me, but I don't do it. What if Mike is hiding somewhere out in the shadows?

Jackson leans in for a kiss when I get in, but I stop him.

"Don't," I say. "I'm sorry. I'll explain later."

"God, I've missed you."

I clutch his hand. "Me too."

"Where are we going?" he asks.

"Our place? I've got at least an hour."

He smiles that smile. Jackson, my Jackson, the boy of all boys. The rest of me, the part the tea couldn't reach, is warm again.

"So what gives?" he asks. "Are your parents letting up already?"

"Not exactly. I needed to—there are things you need to know." I tell him everything. The police, the lawyer, and eventually…Mike.

"You've got to be fucking kidding me," he says. His jaw sets; his eyes turn to laser beams. He crosses two lanes to u-turn, head back the way we came.

"What are you doing?"

"Where does that asshole live?"

"It doesn't matter where he lives."

The car speeds forward.

"I dropped you near there once, didn't I? When you were spending the night with Paige? Over on Elm?"

"He's not even home right now."

"Then we'll wait until he is."

"Baby, please. Turn the car around."

"It's not okay, Em. He's totally manipulating you. And using you. And just being a general dick."

"I know, but he kind of has all the cards right now."

"He's just trying to get you back. He's not going to talk to the police. He's full of shit."

"You don't know him like I do. He'll do it. He's not going to give up on this."

"Guys like that don't deserve to—"

"Jackson, stop the car right now. I'm serious."

He turns toward me but doesn't slow.

"Let's at least talk about it first, okay? After that, if you want to go over there and punch him in his stupid face I won't stop you."

Jackson takes a deep breath and pulls over to the side of the road. "I can't stand this," he says. "All this secrecy and sneaking around? It's not worth it."

"I'm just trying to protect you," I say.

"I don't need to be protected." He looks right at me. "I can take care of myself."

"You scare me when you talk like that. I don't want you falling on a sword for me. That would only make things worse. How do you think I'd feel if they found out you were there? You were there because of me."

"It's not your fault, Emma. You didn't do anything wrong. And neither did I."

"But that's not the way it would look to them. You weren't supposed to be there. None of the other kids in the church have a record like you do. I lied to them. We had plenty of time alone. It's gonna look bad for both of us. Really, really bad."

"So we just give in to his demands?"

"Look, I don't want to play his little games any more than you do. But if he goes to the police, we could be in serious trouble. One of us, maybe both of us, could go to prison for the rest of our lives. We might never see each other again."

He shakes his head, looks out the window.

"But if we do what he says?" I say. "It's just over a month until we graduate. I play nice for the police until they figure out I'm innocent. Then we go. I have enough saved up to get us through the summer. And once we're gone who cares what he says? They'll probably find the real killer by then anyway."

He seems to be calmer, listening.

I take his hand in mine. "So the real question is whether we can risk never seeing each other again in exchange for the possibility of a few more weeks together. That's the only question."

"I hate this," he says.

"Me too," I say. "But honestly, has anything really changed? It's basically the same situation it was a week ago, only now he knows."

"Things are different now, Em, and you know it. Before, I don't know. I never liked it, but I tried to be chill for your sake. But now? I can't stand it." He grows quiet. "I don't share."

"Hey," I say, catching his eye. "Neither do I. I'm all yours, okay?"

He turns to me, nods, but I can see he still doesn't like this. I don't either. I can't stand the idea of not being with him for even a day. Or of giving Mike exactly what he wants. But what else can we do?

"Will you take me to our spot?" I ask. "If we're not going to see each other for a while, I'm going to need a proper goodbye."

Jackson drives me home. We take a lap past the house to check. There are no lights on. My parents aren't home yet. They probably went out to dinner with some of the other parents.

Jackson drops me off a couple blocks away just to make sure the neighbors don't notice. I kiss him through the window before he drives away. My whole body feels emptier when he goes. Who knows when we'll be able to see each other again?

Inside, the house feels colder than usual. I turn on all the lights in the kitchen and pump up the thermostat. Then I realize how hungry I am and make a sandwich. As I finish eating, I pull out my phone and text Mike the only two words he really wants to hear:

You win

He must be waiting for it, because I get a text back right away.

Glad 2 hear u came to ur senses

The whole thing makes me feel dirty. I put my dishes in the dishwasher and head upstairs to my bedroom to take a shower.

I try to picture Jackson as I take my shirt off in the hall, try to imagine him here with me, to remember the way he touched my skin tonight.

I don't see it until I'm already through the door.

Cold air twitches the curtains. My window is wide open. The room is destroyed—mattress tossed off the bed, drawers emptied onto the floor, the contents of my closet strewn everywhere.

Someone was here. Or still is.

I hold my shirt against my chest and peer into the shadows, but I can't tell what's really there and what my mind is making up. There's a shape in the corner. A man crouching with a knife?

I back up, slowly, toward the door, fingers vibrating with fear. I flip on the light switch and jump from the shock of it.

The man in the corner isn't a man at all. It's a pile of stuff, pulled out of my closet haphazardly. What would someone want in my closet?

The realization strikes me. My savings. The cash we're using for New York. I hid it under my bed, along with my acceptance letter and a course catalogue from NYU. Nearly five thousand dollars, saved from birthdays and Christmas and Easter cards, and an early graduation present from Grandma Wellington. It's absolutely every cent I've gotten over the last year.

I scramble to the floor and dig out the shoebox. Something clunks, loose inside of it.

I open the box.

And there, instead of my money, instead of my papers from NYU, is a gun.

CHAPTER NINETEEN

I DON'T TOUCH IT. I've made a lot of mistakes, but I'm not that stupid. I leave it in the box where my fingerprints can't mark it. I peek inside again to make sure my mind isn't playing tricks on me, but it's still there. A gun, a real gun, with something screwed onto the end of it. A silencer?

This can't be just any gun. It must be *the* gun.

The thought of it in my room, in my hands, pricks my skin with a thousand needles. I'm alert, aware of every part of my body. But not in the good, present way. I feel my bones stretching like they're too big for my skin. Adrenaline pumps into my too-small heart, beating it to wildness like horses spooked by a rattlesnake.

I hear a creak and jump.

Then the familiar whir of the garage door rising. My parents. They can't see this.

But where can I put it?

I only have seconds, moments, before they're inside.

Where won't they look?

I throw my shirt on and race downstairs, down to the storage room in the basement.

The old toy chest.

I hurl it open, shove the shoebox under dolls and puzzles and stuffed animals, then slam the lid shut.

I run back upstairs, just in time to see my mother walk through the mud room into the house.

"Didn't think we'd beat you home," my dad says, right behind her.

But my mom has stopped. She's reading my face. There must be terror written all over it.

"What's going on?" she asks.

"Somebody broke into the house."

"Are they still here?" my dad asks, fear in his eyes.

"I don't know."

"Gloria, go outside and wait in the car. You too, Emma."

"Come on, honey." My mom leads me back to the garage. I look back and see my dad pulling his hunting rifle from the hall closet.

"Go on, Emma. Outside with your mother," he says. "Everything will be fine."

In the garage, Mom fumbles with the key fob, then beeps the car awake. We sit inside, doors locked, garage open, waiting for my dad. She takes out her cell, dials.

"Yes, this is Gloria Grant at 227 Hawthorne Lane. We've had a break-in." Even in a panic, her tone is even, controlled. Only someone close to her might notice the slight waver.

"I don't know," she says. "My husband is checking now."

I hear talking on the other end, then she turns to me, "Did you see anyone when you came home?"

"No. I don't think so."

"You don't think so or you didn't?" she asks.

"I didn't," I say.

"She says no. Yes, thank you." She turns back to me. "They're on their way."

When the police finally arrive, my dad has let us back inside, claiming the house is clear. The officers, young guys that look like they're not much older than me, ask us to stand outside and wait while they check the house again, and dust for fingerprints.

My heart stops as I watch them. The housecleaner was here yesterday afternoon, and I know she gave my room a good wipe-down, but what if they find Jackson's fingerprints? He was here just yesterday. But my worries are warrantless. They find nothing. Even I haven't been in there long enough to leave a mark.

And the only thing missing is my stash of money and NYU papers, which I can't exactly tell them about. Soon we're all huddled in the living room, Mom bringing us hot tea and coffee, while they ask their questions.

"So you came inside. Then what?"

"Like I said, it felt cold, so I turned up the thermostat, then ate a sandwich and went upstairs."

"And then?"

Before I have a chance to answer, there's a knock at the door, and it opens. Detectives Simms and Boyer step inside without invitation. I'm actually glad they're here. Maybe they'll finally understand that I have nothing to do with this.

"Hi, folks. Sorry to hear about your troubles tonight," Detective Simms says. Boyer is silent, taking in the scene, the usual scowl twisted on her mouth.

"Officer Handler? Could we speak to you?" Detective Boyer asks.

The officer who was talking to us goes to them.

"Excuse us for a moment," Simms says.

They step outside. Bits of their muffled conversation seep through the door. ...and you don't think?, ...okay, sure, ...any signs of?, ...what about? Puzzle pieces drifting in the air, but no picture to match them against.

Finally they're back in.

"Could you show Officer Handler and myself the room, Mr. Grant?" Simms asks.

"Of course," Dad says, and the three of them go upstairs. What if they had found it? What if they had seen that gun under my bed? I would have been arrested tonight.

"I know you've gone over this already, but if you wouldn't mind, I'd like to hear it straight from you." Boyer says, straight-faced and unsympathetic.

"Do you think this has anything to do with the murder?" Mom asks.

"It might." Boyer says. "You got any more coffee back there, Mrs. Grant?" Boyer asks.

"Certainly," Mom says.

When she's gone, Boyer turns to me. "So you're the only one home when, suddenly, somebody breaks in?"

"That's not how it happened."

"Okay, how did it happen?"

"I think they were here before me. I think they left before I got home. I don't know. I didn't see anyone."

"Neighbors didn't see anyone either. You close to your neighbors?"

"Sort of. I don't know."

"How about security? You know those guys? The ones your parents pay a fortune to patrol around their little gated community?"

"No. I mean, I've seen them before, but I don't know them."

"Cause they didn't see anyone either. Seems weird to me that in a neighborhood like this no one sees any sign of an intruder, don't you think?"

"Not really."

"Also seems strange all this happened when your parents were out."

"We were at the vigil. Tons of people saw us there. The guy would have known we'd be out."

"What makes you say it was a man?"

"I don't know. Nothing, I guess."

"So this man breaks in, messes up your room, and only your room, but leaves no fingerprints and takes nothing, right?"

She's looking at me like she knows about the gun. How could she know?

"I haven't had a chance to really look."

"But your computer's up there, your jewelry, your TV, your iPad, correct?"

"Yes."

"Okay, so I'm a thief, right? What kind of stuff do you think I'm after?"

"All that stuff, probably, which is why I don't think it was a thief."

"Who do you think it was?" She leans in, pretending to be interested.

"I think whoever broke in is the same person who killed June. I think they were trying to hurt me too." I say.

Boyer leans back like she's blown away by what I said, then she crosses her arms over her chest.

"Do you think someone has a reason to want to hurt you?"

"Do psychopaths need a reason?"

"So a random psychopath killed June, then broke into your bedroom to try to kill you too?"

"Maybe."

"If that's the case, Emma, then why didn't they stick around to finish the job? You were all alone, right?"

"Maybe they got spooked. Maybe they didn't know I was alone. Maybe—"

"You want to know what I think?" she asks, even though it's not really a question. "I think after you walked home, alone, you came in and did this yourself." Her eyes fix on me, examining my reaction.

I try to keep a straight face, but I'm panicking. Did she say I walked home? Could they be watching me?

I try to focus on what she didn't say. She didn't say Jackson dropped me off.

"How do you know I walked home?" I ask.

"That's not important right now."

They must be watching me. They must. But she isn't saying anything about Jackson. Does she know? Or did they only see me once I got home? Maybe they've only been watching the house.

It must be that. It has to be. If she knew about Jackson, she'd definitely be asking about him. No question.

"Why would I mess up my own room? That's the stupidest thing I've ever heard."

"I think you like attention, Emma. I saw that clip of you on the news tonight, singing your pretty little song at the vigil. You're real sweet when the cameras are on, aren't you?"

"That was—I was just trying to help."

"I also think you're scared. Scared people do stupid things, and at some point those stupid things put them behind bars. I always find the evidence, Emma. Always."

It's the closest thing to a threat I've heard her say out loud. But it's refreshing in a way. At least I know now she has her mind made up about me.

"Get out of my house," my mom says.

I don't know how long she's been in hearing distance, but she looks mad. Boyer gets up to leave just as my dad, Detective Simms, and Officer Handler come back downstairs. Mom turns to Dad.

"This woman is harassing our daughter," she says.

"I think we're done here, gentlemen," Boyer says, then turns to my mother, "But you might want to ask your daughter why she was lying to you about getting dropped off by her boyfriend tonight."

"What is she talking about?" Mom asks.

I stay silent. Boyer's got a cocky smile on now. Her words are directed at my mother, but her eyes are on me.

"We had an officer driving by the house who saw her walking up the block alone. I had a daughter, I wouldn't want her walking around alone at night."

"Emma?" my mom's face has gone white.

"Have a good night, folks." Boyer says, and leaves. Detective Simms and Officer Handler follow her out. The door shuts behind them.

"What was she talking about?" Mom asks.

"I walked home."

"From the diner?" She asks.

"From church. Mike and I got in a fight. I didn't want you to worry."

My mom looks at me hard and long. She can feel it, that there's something off in my story. "You can't do that, Emma. It's too dangerous. Especially after what's happened. We have no idea who's responsible or where they are or anything."

"Your mother is right," my dad says. "If you need a ride, you call us. Period."

"Okay, I'm sorry."

"But what I'm more concerned about is how that Boyer woman keeps turning the littlest thing into some major strike against Emma." My dad shakes his head. "This whole thing is getting ridiculous. I'm calling Terry."

He heads out of the room, down the hall toward his study.

My mom is staring at me again. "Are you telling me everything, Emma? Because it feels like I'm missing something here. Why not call Paige for a ride? Or Katie? Or any of the other kids?"

"I just needed time to think, okay?" I say, irritated.

"This is very serious, Emma. If I find out you're lying to me, there will be consequences."

"I'm not." I practically spit the words out at her as I race up to my room, feeling just as crappy about lying to her as I do that she's doubting me.

CHAPTER TWENTY

I CLOSE THE DOOR to my bedroom, half relieved that the police are gone, and half terrified.

There's no question about where the gun came from. It can't be random. My earring near June's dead body could have been a coincidence. But hiding the gun in my bedroom, trashing the place so I'd call the police and they'd find it? That was deliberate. Why would someone do this to me?

There's only one answer: whoever killed June wants me to take the blame.

I'm scared. Scared and angry. Fist-through-a-wall, kick-you-in-the-face, scream-'til-my-throat-rips-open angry. Some asshole wants to have friends, fall in love, make their own plans while all my hopes fly away. No. I won't let that happen.

I start to clean up, throwing stuff back in my closet, shoving things back into drawers.

I have to do something about all this, but what? First things first, I have to get rid of that gun. I consider the options.

I could keep the gun here, but that's asking for trouble. Who knows how long I have until there's an anonymous call to the police and they search the whole house? I got really lucky, finding it so fast. I don't think the murderer wanted me to find it. Why would he? Unless he wanted me to touch it, transfer my fingerprints, but then why would he have put it inside the box? No, I wasn't meant to know it was in my bedroom until the police found it there. I'm lucky they didn't use the burglary as an excuse to search the whole house. Every moment that passes is one moment closer to the police banging my door down. I have to get rid of it soon. Tomorrow.

There's the police, but that option seems even more ridiculous. I try to imagine how the scene would play out. *Hey, officers, funny thing, but I found the murder weapon in my room. Wasn't there before, I swear!* If Detective Boyer thinks I'm guilty with no concrete evidence, if she thinks that I faked an intruder to get attention, then she'd be downright orgasmic if I told her about the gun. There's no way.

I could bring it to my parents, but my stomach clenches at the thought. I imagine their eyes broken immediately by my guilt. Maybe they'd believe me. But then what would they do? They'd make me take it to the police.

Which leaves only one option. I have to get rid of it. But how? That car driving by the house when I came home couldn't have been the coincidence they made it out to be. They must be watching, probably closer after tonight.

I've seen police officers go through a suspect's trash on TV. That has to be based on something real, right? They're probably monitoring everything that comes out of our house, looking for something just like this. They'd definitely notice if I just happened to stop by a dumpster on the way to school.

I can't give it to a friend either, or it would put them in just as much danger as I'm in right now. I can't even tell anyone. All my friends would just tell me to go to my parents or the police. And if I didn't? They'd tell my parents themselves, even if they thought I was totally innocent, just to protect me. I would if I were them.

And then it hits me. I know exactly what I'll do.

CHAPTER TWENTY-ONE

THE NEXT DAY, AFTER my parents leave for work, I dig the shoebox out of the toy chest and open it up. Gingerly, using a towel to avoid leaving fingerprints, I lift the gun out and put it inside the backpack. Every twist and jostle of it makes my nerves twitch. I've never held a gun before, not once, and don't know much about them. Is there a safety? Is it on? I can't tell. If I drop it, will it fire? I'm extra careful just in case.

I take my loaded backpack and drive straight to the church, slowing at every bump and stoplight. What better place to find the murder weapon than in the church itself?

The main entrance is still closed, so I go through the administrative entrance. Mindy, the receptionist, greets me with a concerned smile.

"How are you holding up, sweetie?"

"Fine," I say. It feels like there's a sign on my forehead that says GUN! GUN! GUN!

"Well, me and Tom have been praying for you and your family every night."

"Thanks," I say. I shift my backpack nervously, trying not to fidget more than normal, but not remembering what normal is, like when you stare at a set of letters so long it stops being a word.

"It's such a tough time for everyone, but especially your dad. The burden on those shoulders, I can't even imagine. We are so lucky to have a strong man of God leading us, especially at a time like this."

"Yeah," I say. I know my dad has a lot on his plate right now, but the hero-worship stuff gets old fast. I've seen my dad, grouchy every day before he gets his coffee. I've smelled his disgusting morning breath from across the room and heard him fart just like everybody else.

"I hope you're taking special care of your daddy right now. He needs it."

I paste on my good-girl smile and say, "I sure am. In fact, I better go check on him right now. Nice to see you."

I walk past her into the stairwell. The backpack jiggles on my shoulder with every step, making me feel like it could explode any minute.

I don't go all the way up to the staff offices, where my parents are. Instead I walk straight through the administrative hall, stealing glances at all the people working in their offices. I'll have to stop in to see my parents later, just in case anyone mentions they've seen me.

I make my way to the stairwell at the other end of the wing, then downstairs again, through the building, walking by the police tape in the lobby, and down toward the Youth Center. I expect it to be empty, but there are people in here—the Cleaning Ministry, a group of volunteers who cleans the church regularly. Today the group is bigger than usual. I guess there's a lot of work to be done after everything that happened. A glance around shows there are still sleeping bags laid out, still backpacks everywhere and abandoned plates of pizza and cans of soda. I haven't been in here since running out and seeing June's body. Apparently, no one else has been back either.

"Hey, Emma, whatcha doin' here?" The voice is from Rick Rasmussen, the church's only staffed janitor and the leader of the Cleaning Ministry. "This part of the building isn't really open yet."

My heart stops for a nanosecond. But then he smiles, and I relax a little. He's got a smile so wide that the skin around his eyes is permanently crinkled.

"Nothing. Just wandering around," I say.

He fishes a hard candy out of his pocket for me, something he always does, which makes all the kids love him. "Well don't you work too hard now," he says, then grows somber. "Life's too short."

"You're right. Thanks."

I leave the Youth Center and decide the next best place to hide it is in one of the adult Sunday school rooms. I find the biggest one, the one lined with couches and armchairs. Carefully, making sure to only touch the parts that are still wrapped in the towel, I pull the gun out and slide it underneath a couch, snatching the towel back at the last second and letting the gun land with a soft thud on the floor.

My heart races my hands to shaking. I've done it.

There are still major problems to deal with. But this one, this neon sign of danger, is solved. I feel lighter as I walk up the stairs to check in with my parents. So light I could float balloon-high.

It's gone. The gun is gone.

The downside is that it might not be discovered for a long time. How often are those couches moved? At least whoever finds it will probably be an adult who wasn't even there that night. No one will be hurt by this action, especially not me.

The best part is that it will be found eventually, and maybe there's a clue with it. Probably not fingerprints; the killer has been too careful. But maybe DNA, or fibers from their shirt, or a tiny hair from their dog—something that will tell the police who actually did it. Something that will tell the police it wasn't me. I have half a mind to phone in an anonymous tip, but it's too risky.

As I walk out onto the top floor, someone calls my name.

"Emma!"

It's Pastor Pete. His face lights up to see me. That's one of the best things about him. And it's not just me, it would be the same reaction for anyone. He's genuinely happy to see people, especially teenagers.

He waves me over from his door. Well, one of his doors. Pastor Pete has two sides of his office. The office side, where his desk is, and a lounge side, with beanbag chairs and games and toys and stuff so students can hang out and talk to him.

"So, what're you doing here today?"

"Nothing," I say, which is universal teenager language for something.

"Wanna hang out for a minute?" he asks. "I could use a little break"

"Sure," I say. Visiting Pastor Pete is as good a reason as any for being here.

"Awesome sauce," he says. It's an expression he uses a lot. I think he thinks it makes him sound cool.

He opens the door to the lounge side, and we go in. He goes to the mini-fridge. "Want something to drink?"

"Water?"

"Coming up."

He hands me a water, and we settle into beanbag chairs.

"I really appreciate what you did at the vigil the other night. Several people mentioned how special that was."

"I'm glad to hear that."

"So how have you been holding up with all this?" he asks. He's the first person who seems genuinely concerned about me, and it feels nice. I wish I could tell him everything. Or maybe I wish telling him everything would lead to a solution.

"I don't know. It's been hard, I guess," I say.

"It's rough to lose a friend."

"Yeah. I guess so."

"But?"

I sit there for a moment, thinking. Maybe there's a part of this, a small part, that I can talk to him about.

"I don't know how great a friend I really was to her. It feels like I could have done something to save her. Like I should have been there for her more."

"I think we all feel that way. I know I do," he says. "It's natural when something like this happens, but I don't think it's actually the truth. It's just our minds trying to make sense of something really hard."

I look up at him.

"I saw how great you were to June. You invited her to really be a part of things around here. And she was." He looks at me with a keep-this-between-you-and-me sort of look. "You and I both know that she needed a little extra love and patience sometimes. You gave that to her. That's an amazing gift."

"But I should have been with her. And I wasn't."

"I know it's tough to hear, but God has His own plans that we don't always understand. And that night those plans didn't include you getting hurt too."

"I don't know," I say. "I really don't."

"What do you mean?"

I hear the truth coming out of my mouth before I can stop myself from saying it. "It sounds like something we say to make ourselves feel better. If it's part of a plan that's bigger than us, then it's a lot easier to deal with. But I just don't get how this can be something God wanted to happen."

He sighs. "I get it. I really do." He leans back in his beanbag, propping his feet on a puffy footstool and folding his hands over his stomach. "Those are some tough questions, and I won't try to bullshit you with simple answers." Every now and then, Pastor Pete swears. He's careful about it, though. He never does it around adults, or kids prone to tattle. What I can't decide is if it's an old habit he can't break, or a new one he's using to relate to us.

"You want to know a little secret, though? You wouldn't be a real Christian if you didn't struggle with those questions sometimes. I think God likes us to ask tough questions. I don't think He wants a blind follower. I think He appreciates someone who comes to Him after they've been through the desert of their doubts. I think asking makes you a stronger believer in the end."

I want to spout off a hundred verses that disagree with that particular idea, but I don't.

He scoots forward, and the awkwardness of it, his navigating upright in a beanbag chair that wants to suck him under, helps me quell my desire to argue. The action is nearly as useless a fight as my arguments would be.

"The important thing, though, when you're asking, is to make sure you listen too. As long as you do that, He will show you the answers, or at least give you enough peace to handle the uncertainty. Can you promise to do that for me? Just keep listening?"

"Of course," I say. Of course it's my fault if I don't hear something that doesn't exist.

"Let me pray with you?" he asks.

I nod yes.

He finally maneuvers the mass of the chair to his favor. He leans forward and takes my hands and prays. The words brush my ears, but I don't absorb them. There's nothing he says that I haven't heard a thousand times before. Circles and circles and circles of logic that always eat their own tail.

"Amen," he says.

"Amen," I say.

"How about I give you a minute?" he says. He does this every time, with everyone. He prays with you, then lets you have time to pray by yourself. It has happened so many times I've lost track.

"Okay," I say, knowing prayer won't help and wishing I could leave.

After he goes, I wander around the room, staring at the posters on the wall, at the collection of toys on the table, looking for something to fidget with. There's Chinese fingercuffs, one of those triangular board games with the pegs, and a handful of bouncy balls. On the shelves is his collection of figurines and toys, each one in pristine condition. Some are even still in the box. There's a Luke Skywalker, and a plush chipmunk with giant felt teeth. There's a collection of Pokémon dolls and a stuffed pig.

Something about the pig pricks at a little pocket of my memory. I pick it up and try to remember what it was. The pig is soft and bright pink, its tiny paws a furry white on the bottom.

Then it hits me. June's testimony. The story about the toy slipping out of her hand and her dad saving her.

There's a gentle knock as Pastor Pete comes back in.

"Looks like you've been acquainted with Mr. Wiggles," he says with a smile. "That was my favorite toy growing up. I carried it everywhere until I was six."

"Oh yeah?" I say. "It reminded me of June."

He tilts his head, confused. "Why is that?"

"Her testimony. I watched it online with Paige the other day. Remember that story she told about riding the swings at Six Flags and losing the pig?"

A look of recognition dawns on his face. "Yes. That's right." He shakes his head, deep in thought. "What a miracle."

I was thinking something else. I was thinking that if there was a God, it seems like he had it out for her, even back then.

When I get home, there is an e-mail from Jackson. I open it, and a picture of Central Park fills the screen. Green trees frame a stone bridge that stretches over a lake. A boat floats beneath it, carrying lovers who gaze at each other as if they are the only two people in the world.

Below it, his message:

> *I'm going to kiss you here.*
> *Love,*
> *Jackson*

Despite the day I've had, my heart soars. How does he always do it? Remind me that the world is bigger than this moment? Remind me that we have a future together, no matter how hard things might be right now?

I type a message back to him:

> *And I'm going to kiss you back.* ❤
> *Miss you like crazy. So much to tell you, but not safe to meet yet. I'll let you know.*
> *Love,*
> *Emma*

CHAPTER TWENTY-TWO

Wednesday morning comes too fast. We arrive at the church just in time to open the doors for the men delivering June's casket. She's in there, inside that box. The thought thins the air around me.

Paige and Mike come in a few minutes later.

"I hate funerals," Paige says. "Don't let them give me one, okay? Just burn me and dump me somewhere pretty."

"Don't talk like that," I say.

"Yeah. Don't be stupid," Mike says. "Of course you're having a funeral. Everyone has a funeral."

"Not if she doesn't want one," I say.

He glares at me. Apparently, he expects me to agree with him about everything in addition to pretending I don't find him disgusting.

"Whatever," he says. "Ready to go inside?"

"I guess so," I say.

Mike grabs my hand, so hard it feels like it might break. His palms are sweaty, and it makes me wish there was a condom for hands. We find a seat together, me sandwiched between both him and Paige. Whenever we're in regular service and not youth service, the youth group kids sit together in the section farthest to the left side of the stage. We've been doing it so long I don't remember when it started.

All the other kids join us as they filter in: Ruth, Katie, Ben, Chuck, and all the others. Nicolas is here early too, but he's not sitting with us today. He doesn't even say hello. He's sitting in front, staring at the casket like if he stares hard enough she'll be alive again. His mom holds his hand, and his dad drapes a supportive arm around his back.

Soon, the five thousand-seat church is packed with people who barely knew June. Except for the kids in the youth group, maybe ten of the people here have had more than a five-minute conversation with her ever. Reporters take up a whole section marked for the press. Our own media team has the cameras going too, like they always do. In such a big space, people spend more time watching my dad on the three jumbo screens than they do watching my dad. The word spectacle was made for moments like this, and it makes me mad on June's behalf.

"I can't believe this, can you?" Paige says.

"No. It's ridiculous."

Paige looks at me funny. She likes it that so many people showed up to mourn June's death.

"Just, all these people didn't even know her."

"I know, but she would have loved this."

She's right. June would have loved it. She always seemed so awestruck every time the audience clapped after a dance number. So seeing everyone here, just for her? She would have been bowled over. And here I am, getting defensive.

"There she is." Paige says, her voice cracking a little as they open the casket for viewing. "She looks so sweet."

June's coffin is up at the front, surrounded by flowers and propped wide open. There's a big photo standing on an easel with her smiling in it, broad and hopeful. I'm pretty sure the picture was taken before one of our dance performances, because she's wearing what looks like our white costume, the one we used to play angels at Christmas, but without the wings.

Paige pulls me up with her as she stands. "Come on," she says.

I'm scared to get closer, scared to look over the edge, but there's no getting out of this.

"Coming?" Paige asks Mike.

"I'm fine here," he says.

We get in line, Miss Hope and Pastor Pete just ahead of us. Miss Hope is crying softly, leaning on Pastor Pete's shoulder for support. He drapes an arm around her shoulders and gives it a squeeze. It's actually a little weird to even see that. They're always careful about PDA around us, even though they're engaged. But today no one is going to call it inappropriate.

"How are you girls doing?" Miss Hope asks. Her eyes are red, and the tissue in her hand is crumbling.

"Okay," I say, though my voice says I'm not.

"I still can't believe it," Paige says.

"It's tragic," Pastor Pete says. He looks gray and empty, like an old balloon deflated and stretch-marked on the sidewalk.

Miss Hope hugs us both and sobs into our hair. It sets Paige off crying too, but I feel too empty to cry. Miss Hope finally lets go and kisses both of our foreheads.

"You call me if you need anything, okay?"

"Okay," Paige says, and they turn back around.

The line moves too fast. As we get closer all I want to do is bolt.

June's mom sits in the front row, at least I think it's her. I've never met her. She's crying a lot, and loud. A woman next to her, maybe June's older sister, holds her hand but seems irritated with the crying, like maybe she wants to crawl under her chair. I would be too. I wonder how the church found them. As far as I know, June is the only one in her family who is a Christian.

Dad said the church is paying for everything. The only thing I really know about June's family is that they're really poor. She never wanted to say so, but you could tell. I think, more than anything, June just wanted us all to believe that she was just like us. Only she wasn't. Nobody was like June.

I take the last few steps up to the stage, Paige's hand clutched tightly around mine. And suddenly June's there, and my throat closes up. She's beautiful, but not the right kind of beautiful. June never wore makeup, but they have her painted like a beauty queen, too glossy and too perfect. She's wearing a sky-blue silk dress I've never seen. It's brand new, the kind she never had. Somehow that look of a lost little girl is gone. She looks too grown up, too generic. She could be any one of us, even me. And it makes me sad, because that thing that wasn't like us, that thing that made her June, is gone.

I wrap my hands around my middle and try to make the tears stop, but my body is shaking and I can't move away. I know I'm taking too long. I can feel their eyes on me, the cameras fixed on the sobbing girl who said she was June's friend but didn't mean it. The girl who should have been with her instead of shoving her away. The girl who should have stayed with her all night.

I want to go, but my feet are locked up and I can't. I just can't. Maybe if I stay here I can save her for real this time.

"Come on, sweetie," Paige says, and my feet start to move again.

After June's burial, everyone comes back to the church for the reception. The sound of people munching on sandwiches and slopping cold casserole onto their plates feels so wrong. It seems like we should be able to think of something better to honor a life than: A girl died—here's some Jell-O salad.

I make my excuses and go home.

Paige calls as I'm throwing on clothes to go for a run.

"Hey," I say, before I hear her crying. "What's the matter?"

"Come over," she says. "I found something."

CHAPTER TWENTY-THREE

PAIGE MEETS ME AT the door. Her house is a sprawling ranch with six bedrooms for four people in a gated community down the road from my own. I want to ask her if Mike's there, but I can't. She's so upset, swiping at her eyes with her sleeves. She's the toughest person I know, and it makes her look like a little girl.

"Look at this," she says, holding her phone out to me. "I didn't get it back until today when we were at church. And I totally forgot I took it."

The phone is paused on a video, the image too blurry to make out. There's a shuffling, and I look up to see Mike standing in the hall outside the living room, skulking in the dust-moted mid-afternoon shadows.

"Hey," he says as he walks toward me and kisses me on the cheek. I try not to flinch. "What are you doing here?"

"Paige called," I say.

"Oh," he says, disappointed. He must have thought I was here to see him.

"Yeah," she says. "And I have dibs on her right now, so back off."

"Fine. Geez," he says, rolling his eyes.

Paige yanks me by the elbow toward her room, calling over her shoulder, "Geez is short for Jesus, you know. It's disrespectful."

Mike shakes his head and saunters off.

Paige shuts the door. "Sorry, but I don't want him seeing this until I figure out what to do about it. He can get all vigilante sometimes."

"It's fine." I don't tell her I'm relieved.

We sit down on her bed, which is covered in a pink eyelet bedspread. For being such a killer athlete, she's super girlie.

She presses play. There's laughter and shouting. The image is temporarily blocked by the back of people's heads, but Paige, the one holding the phone, seems to elbow her way through the crowd as the camera twists and blurs. I think I can make out the red-on-wood stripe of the church gym floor.

Then Paige gets to the front and steadies the shot, and I see that the camera is pointed at me. I'm sitting in a chair blindfolded, with four other kids sitting next to me in a line, also blindfolded. It's the night of the lock-in, maybe around nine thirty. We're all in the gym, separated into groups of ten or so, going around the room in a circuit of games. I think we were split into teams? I can't remember.

Miss Hope sets a small box on my lap. Then she gives similar boxes to the other kids. You can't quite see it in the video, but it's an old Kleenex box, wrapped in black paper, with a sign that says: *BATTERIES*. The other kids' boxes say: *SPAGHETTI, GUM DROPS, COTTON BALLS*.

"Okay, everybody quiet down. No hints. No talking." Miss Hope says to the crowd. Then she turns to us. "On your mark, get set, GO!"

We dive our hands into the boxes, feeling around. Chuck's hand shoots up into the air in an instant, and he screams "Noodles!"

"Gummy Bears!" Ruth screams.

"Almost, guys," Miss Hope says, jovial. "Almost!"

The look on my face is confused. I wasn't even close. I'm terrible at this game, and I wasn't exactly concentrating. I was thinking about Jackson, wondering when I could check my phone next to see if he had texted, to see if he was still coming.

"Um, um, spaghetti!" Chuck shouts.

"We have a winner!" Miss Hope says. I remember being glad Chuck won. It saved me from the embarrassment of having to guess. I had no idea.

There's a swoosh of the camera down toward the floor, and the video ends. I turn toward Paige, confused.

"Didn't you see it?" she asks.

"See what?"

Paige presses play and the video starts up again. She scrubs forward to where Chuck shoots his hand up. "There." She points to the corner of the image.

Against the wall, to the side of all the action, June is standing with Nicolas. She has her arms wrapped around her body, the way she sometimes did. They were thin and long like a ballerina's, and she could wrap them around her stomach so far that her fingers nearly met behind her back. The only time I ever saw her like that was when she seemed to be upset about something.

Nicolas reaches toward her, but she twists away. Then she runs out, leaving him standing there alone. Then Paige's grip on the camera shifts slightly, and I can't see Nicolas in the frame anymore.

I look over to Paige. She looks away, chews on the inside of her cheek, then looks back at me. "Can I tell you something?"

I nod yes.

"It's probably nothing, but then I saw this. And now…I don't know. I can't stop thinking about it."

"What?"

"June did talk to me a little bit more that night, before she disappeared. I think she was looking for you, but she found me instead, and…well, remember how she wanted to talk to us about him?"

"Yeah?"

"Well…she said she was going to break up with him."

"Seriously? When she talked to us it seemed like they were having problems, but I thought June loved him. Like, *loved* him, loved him."

"I know. But that's what she said."

"Did she say why?"

"I didn't ask."

"Did you tell the police?"

"No, I…they didn't ask, and I didn't want to make him look any guiltier, you know? I mean, he's already her boyfriend, right? So the police have to be looking at him. And he was all over the place that night, so he looks even worse. I really don't think he did it, Emmy, I really don't. But if the police keep asking questions like that, I'm gonna have to say something."

I can't believe he would do it either, but this business about them breaking up is weird. If you had asked me a week ago, I would have told you they'd be married by next summer.

And then there's the gun in my room. Nicolas and I used to date. He's been in my house before. Could he have done it? But why? And why try to blame me even if he did?

"No, you're right. There's no way he did it. Let's just keep it to ourselves for a while, okay?"

CHAPTER TWENTY-FOUR

THE NEXT MORNING, I show up at Nicolas's house without calling. When he comes to the door, his eyes are red-rimmed, his hair sweat-smashed on one side of his head. He looks like he hasn't slept in days.

"I need to talk to you," I say.

He sinks into the couch. "Okay. Talk." He seems angry, irritated I'm here. We didn't work out as a couple, but I thought we were at least friends. I sit on the opposite end of the couch.

"Why don't the police know you guys broke up?" I ask.

His head snaps up, surprised. "What? We didn't—"

"She said she was going to."

"It was just...it wasn't for real. She got in these moods sometimes, but it never lasted. We would have been back together by morning."

"What kind of moods?"

"Like, I don't know, dark, opposite of what she usually was. She'd get to thinking that she was dragging me down, that I should be with someone better. It was always after things were really good for a while. Like she didn't know what to do when things were good."

"And then she'd break up with you?"

"Sometimes. For a little while. But I could always cheer her up, you know? Convince her that we were supposed to be together, and then everything would be okay again."

"And that's what happened the night of the lock-in?"

"Basically. She got this idea in her head that she shouldn't be dating anyone, that she needed to purify herself. That she was spoiled, because of, you know, her past. She wanted to get baptized. I told her, sure, that's great. I mean, they do it, like, every three months. But she didn't want to wait that long. She was trying to convince someone to do it sooner."

"Who?" I've never seen anyone baptize people but my dad. It's one of his favorite things about being a pastor.

"I don't know. I didn't ask. All she said is that she didn't think we could be together until it was done."

Something the police said catches in my mind. The swimsuit. You get baptized in your clothes, but women always wear a bathing suit underneath for decency. What if June wanted to get baptized the night of the lock-in? It would explain why she was up in the sanctuary.

You wouldn't notice it by looking, but behind the choir loft, under a platform, there's a baptistery big enough for my dad to stand in waist deep. The mechanized front panel slides back to expose a reinforced glass wall, so the whole audience can watch people get dunked, like it's a whale exhibit at Sea World or something. When the cover is over it, it just looks like part of the stage. Would the police know to look for it?

But if the murderer was trying to baptize June, why not just drown her? Why the gun? And why at the church? It seems like one of the worst places you could choose to do something like that. Unless, of course, you're trying to frame someone who was there at the same time.

Or maybe it wasn't the murderer trying to baptize her at all. Maybe someone else is the reason she was up there that night, and they're not saying so for fear of becoming a suspect.

Nicolas's words pull me out of my thoughts. "She didn't think she was good enough for me."

"She said that?"

"Yeah, I know, that's what I mean. It was crazy. I told her that it didn't matter what had happened to her before, that I didn't care, but she wouldn't listen." His voice gets all chokey. "It was kind of frustrating actually. It got to feeling like, I don't know, a test. A test I kept having to pass over and over and over again. I thought maybe she'd...I thought she could use some time to calm down. So I told her to think about it. I told her I'd leave her alone to think about it for a little bit, then we'd talk about it again. But then I couldn't find her."

His anger isn't toward me at all. The number one villain to Nicolas is Nicolas.

"I had one thing to do as her boyfriend, and I failed. I didn't protect her. Why'd I leave her? Why'd I have to do that?"

"Oh, Nicky." I grab his hand. "What would you have done against a gun?"

"I don't know. Something. Not let her die like that. All alone."

We sit in silence for a moment, then I ask, "Do you have any ideas about who could have done it?"

"Yeah, but the police won't listen."

"Tell me."

"You want to know the first thing I thought, when I found out she didn't do it to herself? I thought it was her dad."

"Her dad?" I know nothing about June's dad.

"She didn't tell you?"

"Tell me what?"

"He's, like, not a good guy. In and out of prison her whole life. Armed assault, bank robbery, drug possession. The sick bastard has killed people before. Sorry." He's apologizing because of the language. It's automatic. "And when he *was* around? Let's just say it was better for her when he wasn't. I know what the Bible says, but there's got to be an exception for men like that. He should be the one dead, not her."

"What do you mean it was better for her when he wasn't around?"

He looks away, says quietly, "He did things to her. Things that shouldn't happen between a father and a daughter."

"I had no idea." I really didn't. She alluded to things sometimes, gave testimony about a dark past, but everyone talks like that. The worse your past, the better your testimony. I never imagined anything like this. What did I really know about her? It feels like nothing at all.

"She even went to see him a couple weeks ago. She's been working through some of this stuff, trying to move on. She wanted to confront him, forgive him. I don't think it went well. She barely talked to me afterward."

"Have you told the police?"

"Oh yeah. But they think someone in our church did it."

Me.

"I thought maybe it was because they had some evidence that they weren't telling me about. But I haven't heard anything. Do you know anything? Like, from your dad?"

"No," I say.

"I mean a guy like that? You think he couldn't break in?"

"Of course he could."

June's dad is a criminal. It's a good feeling, like seeing a clean spot on a dirty window. I shouldn't be glad of anything having to do with such a terrible person. But I am; I'm relieved. There's at least one person who might have had a reason to murder June.

I go home right away to tell Mom. She's sitting on the back deck, wrapped in a blanket even though it's nearly eighty degrees out, a warm Colorado spring day soon to be chased away by a cold Colorado spring night. I think I can smell cigarette smoke, but I'm not positive. Something about her has been different since June's murder. She seems quieter, more introspective.

After I tell her, she gets on the phone to the police, and they ask us to come in. We're so excited we forget to call Mr. Graham, the lawyer.

I tell the police everything Nicolas told me.

"Okay. Anything else?" Boyer asks. She seems annoyed. I'm confused.

"No. That's everything." I say.

"Thanks for your time," she says and gets up to leave.

"So what are you going to do about this?" Mom asks. I feel the way her voice sounds, shrill, panicked. They should be apologizing by now, or at the very least interested. Something's not right.

"Unfortunately, ma'am, unless you can tell us something we don't already know, nothing has changed here."

"But her father was a professional criminal! He's killed people before! Couldn't he have done this too?" Mom says.

"We've already eliminated Mr. Stuckey as a suspect."

"That's ridiculous. Why?"

"Trust me, Mrs. Grant, he didn't do it. He has several witnesses who can attest to his whereabouts."

"So you think a known, violent criminal, someone who likely

surrounds himself with liars, is more trustworthy than my daughter?"

"There was no forced entry involved in the attack, so it had to be someone inside the building."

"But anyone who was there could have let anyone else in." I say. It gets her attention.

"Why do you say that? Did you let someone in?"

Shit. Watch yourself, Emma.

"No, of course not. I'm just saying it's possible."

CHAPTER TWENTY-FIVE

I DECIDE TO GO to June's house and talk to her dad myself. Maybe it's stupid, but I don't care.

It takes a while to figure out where she lives. I've never been there. I don't even know her parents' names. I find an article where they're quoted on the *Denver Post*'s website.

> *Police are searching for an unknown gunman who brutally murdered a teen girl, June Vogel, while she was attending a slumber party at Denver's Summit Christian Fellowship. Her mother, Trisha Vogel, was devastated by the attack. "I just don't know who could have done this to my baby. She was such a bright, cheerful little thing. Everyone loved her. Whoever she met, people'd always say how sunny she was. I miss her so much."*

It's weird how sentimental people can get. June wasn't close to her mother, not at all. She said they fought a lot. She said her mother hated her. I don't know why. I didn't really want to encourage her to think we were close, so I never asked. It feels so selfish now.

I Google *Trisha Vogel* and scroll past the news sites. I finally find one of those person look-up sites, enter my credit card, and have her address. It's farther than I thought, in a dinky suburb north of Colorado Springs, about an hour away. Which means it's unlikely that June was living with her family.

She didn't have a car, and a bus would have taken forever. With Focus on the Family centered in Colorado Springs, there are about a thousand closer churches she could have gone to. It doesn't make sense for her to attend Summit Christian unless she was living nearby. But where?

I jot down Trisha Vogel's address and drive. It's late now, nearly 7:30, but I can't wait until tomorrow. I need to know now.

It takes more than an hour to get there because I get lost. It's only about fifteen miles east from I-25, but the path is down one-lane prairie roads that go for miles without meeting another road. Google Maps doesn't seem to know that some of them just end. I have to double back a few times before I find it.

The place is called The Palace Arms, and it's a trailer park. June's house is near the back, by a depression that was probably a creek before the water got diverted to a reservoir or farmlands farther up. Trees spindle out from the ground beside it, leafless and wind-smooth.

I knock on the door and steel myself for June's dad. I imagine him big, hairy, menacing. I finger the phone in my pocket, ready to call 911 if I need to.

A woman answers. It's the woman who was holding Trisha's hand at the service. She's young. Maybe twenty? She has June's big blue eyes, framed behind dark-green Buddy Holly glasses. Her hair is black with an ombré to bleach-blonde tips, but her roots are June's same cornstalk blonde. She's got hipster written all over her. Great.

"Yeah?" she says. She's probably ticking off the reasons why she doesn't like me, why I'm the embodiment of all that's wrong in the world because my jeans are the new version of her retro-ironic ones. My dad's voice bubbles up in my head, *get a job.* And I realize, at the same moment, that she probably does have a job. I don't. I never have. I'm a jerk. Would we really look all that different, if you took away all the things we decorate ourselves with? No.

"Can I help you?" she says.

"Are you—I'm looking for— I was a friend of June's." Something clangs behind her. A pan? Trisha barrels toward me. She's sweat-pantsed and mush-bellied, a disheveled mess from the grieving mother at the funeral service. Red blotches streak her un-made-up face.

110

"Who the hell are you, coming here?" She says.

"Mom—"

"Don't you 'Mom' me. You think a little bit of college makes you in charge around here?" She turns to me. "And you, from that bullshit factory. I told the others not to come back here." Probably a visit from the Bereavement Ministry.

She takes a closer look at me, "I remember you. They had you on the news with your pretty little tears."

I don't know what to say. June's sister gives me a "sorry" face.

"If your Jesus was so great, why's my baby girl dead? Why'd somebody at that place kill my baby? You're not Christians. You're bullshitters." I can smell the alcohol on her breath.

"Mom—"

Trisha turns and smacks the girl across the face.

"I told you not to 'Mom' me." She turns back to me. "A bunch a shit-talkers killed my little girl. So don't come here thinkin' you can save our souls. That little girl *was* my soul."

She sobs then. June's sister puts an arm around her. "Why don't you lie down, Mom, okay?" Her words are strained. She's irritated, trying to do the right thing.

"Those people killed my baby."

"I know. I know." June's sister leads her mother away, motions to me to give her a minute.

"I'm sorry," I say, too soft for them to hear me. I turn to leave. This was stupid. Of course they wouldn't want to talk to me.

I hear her footsteps behind me then. June's sister is standing on the porch in the warm light of the doorway, clutching her arms around her. They wrap almost all the way around her small body, just like June's. Like she's trying to shield herself, but doesn't have enough shield.

Her face softens to me. "I'm May," the woman says, "June's sister." And all of a sudden it's hard to think of her as a woman, even though she's older than me, because her voice becomes soft, a child's voice, and the harsh edge in her eyes is gone. "Mom's in bed. Wanna come in?"

The trailer is big and looks newer. Most of them are around here. Bigger than the ones you see on TV shows about lowlifes. It's clean too. Pale-grey carpet, hunter-green sofa, knotty pine cabinets in the kitchen. The place is nice, I guess, for a mobile home.

"You said you were a friend of June's?" she asks. We sit on the sofa. There's a book lying there, *Jitterbug Perfume* by Tom Robbins. In my house the TV would be on.

"Yeah. I'm Emma," I say "I'm really sorry."

"Thanks." She looks like she's sick of hearing that. I am too. I wish I could think of something better to say.

"She told me once that you were the only person in her family who really loved her."

May bites down on her lip, kicking back the tears with her teeth. She nods. "She was the same to me." She sucks it down. "I don't get it. I'm sorry, but I really don't. She shouldn't have even been there that night. How did she get mixed up with you guys?"

I have to stop myself from smiling. *Mixed up.* I've never heard anyone say it like that. Like we're a gang or a cult. Maybe we are.

"Honestly, I don't know. She just showed up one night last summer. And then she was there after that. All the time."

"But why? Did she believe all that stuff?"

"I think so. Yes. She did. She really did."

May shakes her head. "I knew I should've taken her to school with me."

"What do you mean?"

"I'm a freshman at CU." So eighteen or nineteen then, only two or three years older than June. "I wanted her to move up there with me, but they have this rule about freshmen staying in the dorms, so...we couldn't figure it out. I was gonna get an apartment this summer, though."

"Wouldn't your parents be mad?"

"Our parents?" She laughs. "No. I don't think so."

"June said she didn't get along with your mom. What about your dad?"

"No. They don't get along. It's better for everyone that he's in prison."

"Prison?" My heart sinks. No wonder the police say he's innocent. "Since when?"

"Since forever or since the most recent time?" she asks. "First time was when I was five, for grand theft auto. That lasted two and a half years." She goes to the kitchen while she talks, pulls out a couple beers, hands one to me.

"Second time was when I was eight, this time for armed robbery. Some people got killed. He's not getting out anytime soon." She takes a big swig. I'm not sure what to do with mine. I've never had alcohol before in my life.

"I'm sorry," I say. I decide to take a sip, afraid she'll think I'm weird if I don't. It's bitter and loud in my mouth. I have to stop myself from making a face.

"After that me and June got stuck with good old mommy dearest over here and her parade of hands-y suitors."

"Wow. That's really shitty." She looks at me, smirks. I can't tell if she's impressed by my use of foul language or laughing at how awkward I still sound when I do it.

"Yeah. Super fuckin' shitty. Like, crazy, mega-awful, go-shoot-yourself shitty."

I'm way out of her league, swearing-wise. She probably thinks I'm bending my morale code to get on good terms with her. Sometimes it feels like I don't belong anywhere. I'm too hard for the church kids, too soft for everyone else.

She sits, leans her elbows on her knees. "Do you know who she was staying with up there? Where she was living?"

"I was going to ask you."

"No idea. My mom hadn't seen her for months. Since summer. We were e-mailing, but she said everything was fine. Never said a thing about Denver."

So she was staying with someone. But who?

CHAPTER TWENTY-SIX

I CALL NICOLAS FROM the car. He agrees to meet me at a park near his house. It's past eleven when I get there. We sit on the hood of my car, bathed in moonlight.

"Why wouldn't she tell me her dad was in prison?" he says, disbelieving.

"Maybe she thought we'd think less of her."

"Still. That's big. I thought I knew everything."

"Did you know where June was staying?" I ask.

"You didn't know?" He reads the confusion in my face. "Technically, June was homeless."

It hangs in the air between us, a puff of smoke. It can't be true.

"I always wondered why you didn't try to help her," he says.

"She never said anything." I would have helped her, wouldn't I?

"She was terrified of her mom. That's why she ran away in the first place. And obviously, living with her dad was out of the question. She had nowhere else to go. That's why she was living in the church."

"Living in the church?"

He looks at me like I'm the slowest person he's ever met. "She didn't tell me either, but I thought you would've figured it out. Ever notice how she's involved in everything? Around all the time?"

I did, but I thought she was just clingy. And besides, I'm around all the time too, so is Paige and Mike and half a dozen other kids whose parents work there. It doesn't seem that weird to me.

"How long?"

"Since the first night she came."

I remember that night. She arrived late, her hair soaked from the rain, and sat next to me. I talked to her about Jesus. "So she's been hiding in the church for nine months?"

"I know. I tried to get her some help but she wouldn't let me tell anyone. Runaways have no rights. Just the parents. She was too afraid they'd make her go back home."

"So, I just…I can't even believe this, where did she sleep? How did she eat?"

"She took a few of the nursery mats, set up a bed under the auditorium stage. No one ever goes under there."

I'm dumbfounded.

"I think she was eating stuff from Connections at first, the food bank too. Then she got a job. She even saved up some money for a place, but it was hard to find anyone to rent to a minor. After I found out I helped too, of course. I even tried to convince her to move in with my parents, but she didn't think it was a good idea. She thought she'd get them in trouble."

"I don't even know what to say. I just…wow."

"I was gonna find us a place, as soon as I turned eighteen. Just a couple weeks." His head is in his hands. "I really loved her, Em."

He pulls something out of his pocket then. It circles between his fingertips, no pretty box to present it in. He's been keeping it close. An engagement ring. It looks foreign in his hands, too old, an object the kid I dated, the sixteen-year-old with a beater truck and a baseball card collection, shouldn't have.

It makes me wonder about her, about all the things I didn't know that made her who she was. Nicolas is a popular guy—smart and good looking and a total gentleman. For him to want this, there had to be something special about June, something more than her making him feel strong. I wish I had taken the time to see it.

"Did she know?"

"Yeah. I proposed about a month ago, but she wouldn't take it. Not until she got baptized."

We sit there for a moment, the stars twinkling over our heads like little whispers in the night. Eventually, Nicolas tucks the ring back in his pocket. "If I tell you something, will you promise to keep it to yourself?"

"Of course."

"I just—I have to get it off my chest." He's tearing up, choking on his words.

"What is it?"

"I—it wasn't just her past she was worried about. It was us too."

"What do you mean?"

"We didn't, I mean—we didn't stay pure." He looks me in the eye, and it all tumbles out. "I couldn't control myself. She was so beautiful, and I loved her so much, and you know I how I used to struggle with that when we were together."

I nod. I do remember. Searching hands that I always had to guide back to where they were supposed to be, even though everything in me was telling me not to. I wanted his hands to stay where they were. I wanted even more than that. But I was convinced at the time that he needed me to be the one to set the limits. I remember the guilt in his eyes, the hushed thank yous for keeping him honest, feeling like I had won a battle against the devil, that both of us had, every night he would drop me off after a date.

"But the thing is, Em, I don't regret it." He looks me straight in the eye. "I'm sorry, but I don't. Especially now."

He looks up to the stars, like he's looking right at her. My eyes get moist, threaten to spill over.

"I'm thankful. We didn't have long enough together, but at least we got that." He turns back to me, "Do think that's wrong, Em? Do you think there's something wrong with me?"

"No, Nicky, I don't. Not at all." I take a deep breath, try to find the right words. "I think that things aren't always as black and white as we might have been taught."

"Thank you for saying that, Em," he says. "It means a lot, coming from you." He looks back up to the stars. "June and I may not have been married, but in my heart, she's my wife. I think God can see that. Don't you?"

He looks at me, his eyes wet and searching for my approval, my agreement.

I nod.

I get home just before midnight. My parents think I was out with Mike, so they don't ask questions. It's late, but I can't sleep. My mind buzzes with it all. June lived in the church. I can't believe I never noticed.

It feels important to understanding what happened to her, but I can't yet reason why. Is it because she could have seen something she wasn't supposed to? But what? What would be worth killing her for?

Maybe it's just because this seems like something I should have known, and not knowing it makes me uneasy about what else could be out there that I don't know.

I didn't know, for instance, that her dad was in prison. My heart was set on it being him, and now I'm back to nothing. At least I think it's nothing. He must have had friends. Could June have known something that could hurt her dad? I think about all the hit men I've seen in movies, scenes of drilling holes through floors to poison someone sleeping below or camping out in the building across from a target.

If June could have hidden in the church, then who else could have been hiding? The person that did this to her wouldn't have had to be attending the lock-in at all. They could have been waiting there all day, all week even.

It's 3 a.m., but I call Detective Boyer and leave her a voicemail. Then I call Mr. Graham and leave him a voicemail. It'll be at least five hours before I hear back. I should sleep, but I don't think I can.

I decide to research her dad. Maybe I can find some of his accomplices and hunt them down. I take a moment to let that sink in. My life now includes research into bank robberies and accomplices. It's unreal.

I enter his name into Google: *Lee Stuckey*. A lot comes up. There's a slew of articles from 2004 that list him as a suspect in a string of bank robberies, and finally convicted of armed robbery in one. I don't remember them, but I would have only been eight. I click on the one dated the latest, November 12, 2005. It says just what May told me.

Lee Stuckey, the last of the notorious Milk Gang, has been sentenced to life in prison for the deaths of Cassidy Surleaf and her baby boy, Cody Surleaf. The Surleafs were caught in the crossfire between a bank employee and the gang during the robbery of the Lafayette Credit Union last May 28. Forensic evidence later showed that the fatal bullets were shot from Stuckey's gun.

While the $200,000 they stole has yet to be recovered, all the members of the Milk Gang—Sara Jo Ford, Buddy Trent, Jay Peterson, Christina Bromegat, and Stuckey— were apprehended just four days later, on the morning of June 1. All have been formally charged and have begun serving out their sentences.

While the rest of the Milk Gang each accepted plea bargains for shorter sentences, Stuckey demanded a jury trial. It proved to be a mistake for Stuckey, who was convicted on two counts of murder, as well as armed robbery and possession of an unregistered weapon. Stuckey now has no option for parole.

The husband of Mrs. Surleaf and father of young Cody, Jason Surleaf, said nothing can ever replace the loss of a wife and child, but added, "I'm glad today that justice was finally served. I pray that Mr. Stuckey comes to find the error of his ways."

I research the prison he's in, the Limon Correctional Facility, thinking I might visit. How else can I make sure he's not involved? But the website says that I have to submit an application, which could take up to a month. I don't have that kind of time.

Then I get an idea. I call May. She gave me her number in case I needed to ask her any more questions. I mean to leave a message, but she picks up right away.

"Hello?"

"It's Emma. Sorry to call so late."

"S'okay. I'm up." Her voice is so groggy it must be a lie.

"Can I ask you a favor?"

CHAPTER TWENTY-SEVEN

I FAKE SICK ON Sunday morning to get out of church. It has to be Sunday because my parents will be gone all day. Ditching church isn't something I've ever done before, so seventeen years of consistent church attendance goes a long way in getting them to believe me.

After they leave, I find my oldest pair of jeans, the tennis shoes I used to help paint the homeless shelter, and a baggy flannel shirt I got for a ski trip a couple years ago and haven't worn since. The guidelines on the website are very strict about clothes.

When I meet May at a gas station later, she agrees that I should be good enough to pass and loans me her driver's license. I'm not on Lee's approved visitor list, but she is. If the police won't look into it, I will. It's time to go meet the devil in person.

I head east on I-70. Google told me last night that it would take two hours to get to the Limon Correctional Facility. I don't mind. It gives me time to think about what to ask.

Just a half hour outside the city, the landscape turns to vast plains that disappear to infinity at the horizon. It's endless, like looking out on the ocean, but instead of shimmering waters it's mostly brown prairie grasses and dust. Trees only grow near water, and that's hard to come by out here. The land is totally exposed. There's nowhere to hide. The sun glares down on it, and only the most resilient can survive its gaze.

I was born in the wrong state. My mind craves green moss and the sound water makes against rocks and the shade of trees and the smell of grass. I want to live in a place of secret nooks, not vast expanses. I want privacy and independence. I couldn't give a shit about transparency.

That's why New York will be so perfect. My Grandma Wellington took me there once, and I fell in love right away. There was an anonymity to the city, a way to disappear inside the crowds, inside the oom-pah-pah of the umbrellas on the sidewalks, dodging other umbrellas as they passed one another. It felt exotic and familiar all at once.

But New York, and my whole life, depend on staying focused now. I need information, but I don't know what information. All I need is a small connection between him and the murderer. But I can't imagine he's going to come right out and tell me if he's involved. I have to be careful.

I arrive at the prison and park. It's out in the middle of nowhere, far outside the main town center that makes up the city of Limon. It's a huge process to get inside. There's a pat-down and forms to fill out. There's a metal detector and stern warnings from the guard about the rules and what will happen if I break them. It makes me feel like I'm the criminal. My shoulders automatically slump from it, and I divert my eyes from the guards as though I'm the prisoner.

At the very last checkpoint in the line, a female guard asks for my ID. I hand it to her with a shaking hand. She stares down at it, then back at me.

"You clean up your look, Miss Vogel?"

"I don't know," I say, eyes downcast. "I guess so."

Please don't notice. Please don't notice. Please don't notice.

"Date of birth?" she asks.

I almost, almost, say my own birthdate, but catch myself just in time. "May twelfth, 1995."

"Middle name?"

"Crystal-Anne."

"Address?"

"Forty-three Girard Place, unit B."

"Relationship to inmate?"

"Daughter," I say.

The woman behind me in line, a chubby brunette with food stains on her T-shirt and a wiggling toddler in her arms to match them, says, "How long's this gonna take? I ain't got all day."

The guard turns to her, passing the license back to me, and waving me through. "It takes as long as it takes, Delia. Seems like you should be acquainted with the process by now."

Their voices disappear behind me as I walk forward. And just like that, I'm through.

I enter the visiting room, which is a concrete box peppered by tables and stools bolted to the ground. It occurs to me that I have no idea what he looks like. I find a seat and wait.

The inmates enter, and most of them pair up with their visitors immediately. The one left must be June's dad. I had been picturing a pockmarked face and a tattooed body, hardened by years of crime. But his skin is tan and, as far as I can tell, free of ink. He's in good shape, tall and fit, with dirty-blond hair, a touch darker than June's. Some might call him handsome. If he was in the outside world and not wearing an orange jumpsuit, I'd think he was a corporate executive.

I'm the only one left sitting alone. He spots me, and I give a small wave. He sits down across from me, his face wary.

"You ain't May."

"No, I'm not."

"So who are you?" The moment he speaks the image of the executive is erased forever. He has a twang, a slick-wet voice from the Deep South that's too sweet and too rich to be real. There's mud in it, and brine, and berries rotting on the vine.

"My name is Emma. I was a friend of June's."

"You knew my daughter?"

"Yes," I say. "From church."

"That church where..." his voice breaks, "...where she was?"

"Yes, sir." I wish I hadn't said that. The 'sir' is automatic, years of being trained to address my elders with respect, no matter if they deserve it.

"I saw the service. They let me watch it on the TV." He looks up at me. "Did she have...? Did she leave me something? A letter or something? That why you're here?"

"No. Sorry. I just..." I draw all my strength together. "I wanted to ask you some questions about June."

"She was a beautiful girl. Most beautiful girl I ever saw in my life. And I made her." The man in front of me, the one I once thought menacing, is crying. It gives me courage.

"She was." I agree, to the beautiful part, not the made part. It's one thing everyone who knew her could agree on. June was extraordinarily beautiful. "When was the last time you saw her?"

"She came to visit me about a month ago."

"What did you talk about?"

He leans back in his chair, crosses his arms, and huffs. "She had some ideas about some stuff, and I set her straight."

"Like what?"

"Said her mentor told her she should say sorry about our past, but there weren't nothin' wrong with anything back then as far as I was concerned."

What does that mean?

"She asked about wantin' to get married too, which was one of the stupidest things I ever heard her say."

"She asked you for your blessing?"

"Yeah. Said somebody told her she should. But I told her no. No way. No how. I told her if she even so much as thought about marrying that boy I'd call in some favors and make sure there wasn't a boy to marry at all."

"You threatened her?"

"What'd you say to me?" For the first time I can see what it must be like to be an enemy of this man. The tears are gone now, absorbed into his skin. For a moment I wonder if they were ever there at all. But his eyes gleam, still wet with them. They're hard pennies hurled from the top of the Empire State Building. He wants to kill me, I think. But he can't, I remind myself, not here.

"You hired someone to kill her, didn't you? One of your old gang. Someone who owes you a favor."

"Watch yourself, little missy," he says. "It's a federal crime to lie your way into a correctional facility. You want to end up in here with me?"

"Just tell the truth. You're already here for life. What's it matter to you?"

"Sweetie, everybody I got left to call in favors from ain't in no position to give them. They're all dead or in some place like this."

"That's not what you told June."

He crosses his arms and fixes his gaze over my head, silent. I can't tell if he's lying. Maybe he's as lost as I am. Maybe he just wants me to think he is. I decide to switch tactics.

"What about somebody who had a grudge against you? Could they have gotten to her?"

"Not unless the police are in the revenge business these days. I don't make enemies."

"You can't think of anyone? No one at all?"

He pauses for a moment. There's something he's thinking of, someone.

"Who is it?" I ask.

"No one," he says.

"You said you loved her, Lee. You said so."

"I did."

"Then help me figure out who killed her. That's all I want to do."

"You're trying to find the killer?" he asks.

"The police are useless," I say. "They're following all these crazy leads."

He scoffs, shakes his head. "Of course they are. Idiots." He leans forward, glances around to make sure no one's listening. "It's probably nothin'," he says. "I don't know."

"Okay. Just tell me."

"I wasn't even the one in charge of the job that got me put in here. Jay was. Why you think I'm sittin' in here, stuck for life, and nobody else on the crew took that kinda heat?"

"I thought everybody went to prison?"

"Yeah, they did. But not everybody for as long as me."

"What are you saying?"

"I'm saying I think there was a snitch. Maybe more than one. You look at who gets out first, my money's on them. Bet they got a nice little deal from the feds."

"I don't get it. Why would that make them want to kill June?"

"To get back at me."

"For what?"

"I dunno'. Same reason they all ganged up on me in the first place I guess."

"And that would be?"

"Well, you'd have to ask them about that. Never made any

sense to me."

I'm getting frustrated. What he's saying makes no sense. "But didn't they already get what they wanted if they made you take the fall for the murders?"

"I told you it was a long shot."

Something hits me then, something from the article.

"You've still got the money somewhere, don't you?"

"Don't be a goddamned fool."

"Is it still around?"

"You think it was, I'd tell you?"

"What if one of the people in the Milk Gang thought June had it?"

"The Milk Gang. Jesus Christ. You been reading the papers, haven't you?

"Did they know about June? Would anyone think she had it?"

"No."

"How do you know?"

"That's about the end of that conversation," he says. Which means yes, the money is still around somewhere. And no, he's not telling me where. I'm not getting anywhere with this guy.

"You don't seem like you really care about June at all," I say.

"You don't know nothin' about me," he says.

I can be hard too. "Yes, I do. I know all about you. June told me everything." It's not true, but I have to say it. "I think it was you."

He leans back in his chair, crosses his arms over his chest, bounces his leg up and down. I can't tell if it's a yes or a nervous tick. The tears come back.

"I would never, ever hurt her. I loved her. She was my baby, my girl."

He swipes at his eyes. The image makes me think of a schoolboy with a scraped knee—the sweetest boy in class, who everyone wants to comfort or cheer for or love. Maybe it's this, and not burly strength or animalistic rage, that's his superpower.

"You don't know what it's like to love someone that much," he says, reaching out and taking hold of my hand, trying to kill me with sincerity.

"It hurts you deep, especially when you're not together. You just ache for that person." He grips my hand tighter and rubs his thumb across the skin between my thumb and forefinger. It sends a shiver up my spine. "You look a little bit like her, you know, around the lips."

I yank my hand away and try to calm my breath. Stay focused, Emma. Keep him focused.

"So you didn't call in a favor? From anyone?"

"If June got herself killed, it's probably because she got into somethin' over her head. You gotta be careful who you trust."

"Is that what got you locked up? Trusting the wrong people?"

He shakes his head and clams up again.

I've had enough. I get up to leave.

"Wait. Can I ask you somethin'?" he says. "Last time I saw her, she was tryin' to give me some Jesus, and I said no." He bites the side of his cheek. "You think you could give me some Jesus?"

"I…" I shake my head no. "No. I'm sorry."

CHAPTER TWENTY-EIGHT

"HOW'D IT GO?" MAY asks when I meet her later to return her license. We're at a truck stop off I-70, splitting a basket of fries.

"Sort of useless," I say. "I don't know what I expected, but I didn't really get much from him."

"Hate to say I told you so, but yeah. He's a dick."

"Can I ask you something?"

"Yup."

"Did he have any money hidden away somewhere?"

"Like from the robbery?"

"Yeah. Or anywhere, I guess."

"Not that we ever saw. Money wasn't exactly plentiful growing up. Why? You think it could have something to do with June?"

"I was just thinking that if he had something stashed away, maybe he told her, and maybe—"

"Maybe she got killed because somebody knew?"

"Yeah."

"I doubt he would do that. He's a selfish prick. Stole my piggy bank for a liquor run once; didn't even apologize," she swirls a fry through a plop of ketchup. "Did June seem like she had extra money?"

"No. Just the opposite. She was always pretending to forget her purse and getting someone else to pay for her."

"That sounds about right. If she had it, she'd spend it. I remember this one time she blew all her birthday money on this discount prom dress. She was, like, eight years old maybe. The thing was ripped and didn't even fit her. But once she saw it she had to have it. She's always been like that. If she'd had money, you would have known."

"But what about if someone else thought she did?"

"Like who?"

"I don't know."

"I don't want to shit on your ideas here, but I didn't know where she was. I thought she was still living with my mom, and I'm her sister. How could somebody else find her? And why now? Why not a year ago? Two years ago?"

It's a good point. I sit for a minute, thinking.

"So what about him? Is there some reason why he would want her dead?"

"Honestly, and it pains me to say this 'cause I hate that asshole, but I don't see it. I don't see him being involved at all. It's not his style. The only way he'd be behind it is if he had something to get out of it."

"But he's killed people before."

"For money. June, though? The disgusting bastard is obsessed with her. He wouldn't have wanted her dead."

"What if he was jealous? She did ask him for his blessing, so he knew—"

"On the advice of somebody at your church. Who tells a kid she needs to ask a murderer for permission to get married? That's seriously fucked up."

"I know," I say.

And I didn't even tell her that June asked for his forgiveness about their past. What, exactly, did she think she had done wrong? A little part of me cringes. There are some people at church, not a lot, who might believe that any sexual contact between Lee and June would have been at least partially her fault, even as a child. It has to do with a verse in 1 Corinthians about not doing anything to cause your brother to stumble. So, since lust itself is a sin, causing someone to lust is a sin too. It's the whole reason why women are expected to dress modestly. But applying that concept to what happened to June? That's an older way of thinking, very dated and very legalistic. It still lurks around, though, the same way most people's grandparents seem to be just a little bit racist.

June was so concerned about being good enough for Nicolas. Could someone have told June that to purify herself she needed to ask for forgiveness from Lee? The only people I can think of who think that way are a million years old, and I don't know any reason why any of them would have had contact with June at all. So who would have put that idea in her head? Was it the mentor Lee mentioned? I didn't even know anyone was mentoring her at all, although it wouldn't be unusual for someone to offer to mentor a new Christian. I make a mental note to ask around about it.

"If Lee was jealous," May says, "he would have gone after the guy, that Nicolas kid, not her." She looks me straight in the eye. "I know you don't want to hear this, but I think it was someone she knew. Someone who went to that church. The news is full of sick fucks who hang out at places like that."

CHAPTER TWENTY-NINE

THE ALARM GOES OFF at 6:15 the next morning. Apparently, you still have to go to school when you're a murder suspect. Especially one who wishes to appear innocent.

Before getting ready, I open an e-mail Jackson sent last night. A picture of the Empire State Building pops onto the screen, lit up golden against a dark-blue night. Then his message beneath it:

>*I'm going to kiss you here too.*
>*My arms feel empty without you in them. When can I see you?*
>*Love,*
>*Jackson*

I type a message back:

>*Soon. I promise.*
>*Miss you so much it hurts.*
>*Love,*
>*Emma*

After I send it, I shower and do my hair, wishing the school had just decided to stay closed for the rest of the year. They're calling a special Chapel Day today for June. Usually, Wednesday is Chapel Day at SCHS, but they're adding one today too. This means I have to wear a dress to school. And not just any dress will do. Like everything else at SCHS, there are specific rules. The depth of the neckline, the length of the sleeves, the tightness around the hips and chest, and especially the length of the hemline.

Every Wednesday all the girls have to kneel next to their desks first thing in the morning. If your dress doesn't touch the floor you have two choices. You can either wait in the principal's office for a parent to bring a replacement and miss your classes, or you can wear one of their skirts, which are pretty awful. They look like something from *Little House on the Prairie*. It's super embarrassing, which is probably why they have them.

But do you know how hard it is to find a dress or skirt that goes all the way below your knee? Hard. You can't shop at Forever 21, that's for sure. It's mostly stuff you'd find in the petite section at Macy's, dresses that make all of us girls look like mini-executives, like we should be holding briefcases and carpooling and power-walking at lunch. I pick out a dress that won't get me skirted and head out.

Mike picks me up. It's part of the deal. He will drive me to school and home, and in between we will spend most of our time together. I am his disobedient child, and he must watch me to make sure I behave.

I wish Paige had ridden with him, but she didn't. She probably wanted to give us some time to ourselves.

"Morning," he says, his face bright and sunshiny as though everything between us is fine. I've always envied the ability some people have to lie to themselves.

"Hey."

"I brought you some breakfast. Oatmeal and an iced coffee." Mike is a utilitarian eater, and expects everyone else to be the same. He doesn't understand likes and dislikes. He understands best and worst. At some point, someone told him that oatmeal is the best way to start a day, and so this is what he chooses for me. I've already had breakfast, and I hate oatmeal, but I sip the bitter iced coffee and thank him. Rejection of his gifts will only make it worse.

"Can I ask you something?"

"Okay," he says, his eyes on the road, barely paying attention to me.

"Do you know if June had a spiritual mentor?"

"Why would I know that?" he says. "You led her to Christ, right?"

"Yeah, but I wasn't really mentoring her, at least I hadn't been for a long time. Did she ever come to you and ask for advice about anything?"

"No. Why would she?"

"I don't know, I just thought—"

"She did flash me once, though. She tried to make it seem like an accident, but it wasn't."

"Excuse me?"

He huffs, "Not so fun when the shoe's on the other foot, is it?"

"What happened?"

"We were on shift at the food bank together, stocking shelves in the back. Her shirt came unbuttoned, and she wasn't wearing a bra. You should have seen the way she looked at me. She didn't cover herself at all. It was like she just expected me to go after her or something."

"What did you do?"

"What do you think I did, Emma? You and I were together. I turned away and told her to cover herself up and have some freaking self-respect. Which, in case you're wondering, is what a real gentleman does."

"What did she do?"

"Ran out of the room crying, like a little girl. It wasn't long after that she and Nicolas got together. I guess if she couldn't have me she decided to settle for your leftovers."

"Okay," I say, not sure how to process any of this. Could Mike be even more old school than I thought? Could this incident with June be enough to set him off?

"Honestly? I'm not all that sorry she's gone. I mean, I didn't want her to die or anything, but I didn't like her. She was a bad influence on you. And she was definitely a bad influence on Nicolas. That's why I told him to break up with her."

"You did?"

"Yeah, but he wouldn't listen. She had him so blinded. Did you know he was planning to propose?"

"Really?"

So Mike knew.

"Yeah. He can be kind of an idiot sometimes. I can see why things didn't last between you two."

At school, Mike drops me off at my first class.

"Okay. See you at lunch." I take a step away and release his hand, but he doesn't release mine. Instead, he pulls me back and kisses me. It's our first kiss in a long time, and it's not a mistake that it's in view of everyone.

"Mr. Kent and Ms. Grant, that's enough." It's Miss Hope, frowning in disapproval. Miss Hope isn't just involved with the Dance Team and other Youth Ministries with Pastor Pete. She's also the history teacher at our school. Psychology too. And this semester, for me, homeroom.

It's a good thing this isn't Principal Hendricks. If it was, we'd probably both have detention, and an uncomfortable chat with him and our parents about purity with a capitol P.

"Get to class. Both of you," she says.

Mike squeezes my hand then trots down the hall. I pass Miss Hope to go into homeroom, then think of something and come back out to find her.

"Um, Miss Hope?"

"Yes?" she asks.

"You don't happen to know if anyone was mentoring June do you? Spiritually?"

"Not to my knowledge, no," she says, puzzled.

"Pastor Pete wasn't giving her any extra counseling or anything?"

"I'm sure he wasn't. He tries not to do too much one-on-one time with the girls because of how it looks. I'm sure you understand how a pastor has to protect his reputation."

"I do. Dad worries about that kind of thing too. Usually he asks my mom to be there if a woman needs some help, which is why I thought to ask you."

She smiles, "Sounds like my wonderful fiancé has picked up a trick or two from your dad. He's been asking me to do the same thing. It brings me a lot of joy to be able to help him out. Plus it gives me a chance to talk more with you guys, which I love."

"But not with June? She didn't, um, ask about getting baptized or anything?"

"No, I'm sorry. Why do you ask?"

"Just curious about some things she said before she died. I was hoping she had someone to confide in, but it sounds like maybe not."

"Well, I really wish she had come to me about her troubles. It would have been nice to spend some extra time with her before…" Her voice trails off. "It just would have been nice to spend more time with her."

I take a step closer, lowering my voice. "Did you know that Nicolas proposed to her?"

"Did he really?"

"Yes," I say.

"Poor thing. He must be devastated," she says. "It's really too bad he didn't come talk to us about that. June was so young, after all. I'm sure Pastor Pete would have advised against it, and maybe saved him a little bit of heartache."

I doubt that, but I don't say so.

"Emma, while we're on the topic of relationships, would you mind doing me a favor?"

"Sure," I say.

"Can you cool it with the kissing in the halls? It really is against school policy. I know your parents have their own rules for you, and I'm sure you're respecting them, but here it should be different. We just have a higher standard in these halls. It would be nice if you could be an example for everyone."

She saw the whole thing. Mike was clearly the one who initiated the kiss. Why is she ragging on me?

"I'm sorry, it was kind of a surprise for me too," I say, trying to argue without arguing.

"Well, sometimes we women need to be the standard-bearers. Temptation is harder on the guys than us."

"Of course," I say, swallowing my anger. "I'll talk to him about it."

"Thank you, sweetie, that will really help a lot."

I nod and follow her inside the classroom.

"Hem check, ladies," Miss Hope says when the final bell rings for first period.

All us girls kneel next to our desks. The boys stare at us, trying to see if anyone will fail. And maybe trying to see other things too. Who knows what's going through their dirty little minds. We all know what girls do for boys when they're on their knees. The whole thing is just embarrassing.

In front of me, Hannah Mansone is clearly trying to sit closer to her heels so that Miss Hope won't notice that her skirt is too short. Like, way too short.

"Sit up straight, Hannah," Miss Hope says, then stops right next to her. "Hannah." Her tone is clearly disappointed.

"I thought it was okay if you wear pants underneath," Hannah says. It's such a lie I almost laugh. She's been going to SCS since kindergarten, just like me. Around here, leggings aren't considered pants.

"You know the rules perfectly well, Miss Mansone. Gather your things." Miss Hope turns to the rest of us, who are still kneeling. "I know you girls think this is a burden, but you should really be thankful. In other schools, it's the opposite. You'd feel the pressure to show more and more, and lose yourselves little by little. Here, the boys know to respect you."

Yeah, my aching knees feel super respected right now.

"All right, everybody up. Homework out."

CHAPTER THIRTY

AFTER HOMEROOM I WALK toward my next class: British literature. Today we're supposed to be discussing the concept of filial ingratitude in *King Lear*, which I haven't finished yet.

People always think that because you go to a Christian school it means you spend all your time learning about the Bible and are clueless about everything else, which is sort of true, but not completely. We do have a required Bible elective every semester, and chapel once a week, and it's definitely intelligent design over evolution in science.

Otherwise our school is very competitive. With about a hundred students in each grade, we test in the eightieth percentile on all the national tests, and 91 percent of our graduates go to college, including some Ivy League schools, every year. We're also considered one of the top ten athletic schools in Colorado, with twenty-four state championships since the school opened fifteen years ago. Paige will be the hundredth student of ours to get some type of Division I A scholarship. Lots of kids attend who aren't even religious, because of its reputation and the .

On my way to class I see the first promposal of the year. Yes, we have a prom. At least it's called a prom. It's not much like a prom you'd see at a public school; it's really more of a banquet. There's a catered dinner with games and photo booths and performances. There's a band, but not all night, and there's dancing, but not with your date. It's mostly in a circle of your friends and is closely monitored by the chaperones for lewd or suggestive movements.

This year's prom theme is "A Night with the King." It's going to be a masquerade ball. Last year's medieval castle theme was "The Kingdom." Do you see a trend?

Vicki Martinez's locker is a few down from mine, and I see it all happen. She opens it after first period, and a bunch of red helium balloons come out with "PROM?" written on them in black sharpie. They're from Gus Stead, who's hiding down the hall with a video camera and a dozen roses.

Half the drama of prom is the promposal. I've heard other schools call it the "prom ask." The measure of the guy you go with is how he does the promposal. You want to be the girl who gets flash-mob serenaded in the cafeteria. You do not want to be the girl who gets handed a limp carnation in the hallway with a smirking, "Wanna go?"

It's mostly about bragging rights, for both the girls and the guys. Treasure hunts are popular. Animal costumes are common. Semi-homoerotic dance routines where your football buddies wear matching sweats and shake their booties, bare chested, to Roy Orbison's "Pretty Woman" are normal. Last year, Mike rented a hot air balloon for us to ride in while we flew over the football field where he had people lying on the ground spelling out "PROM?" As far as the girls were concerned, he won. It's hard to beat that. You can't say he doesn't try. I'm dreading whatever he has cooked up for this year.

Gus's promposal to Vicki gets points for originality, I guess, but loses points for timing. It's tacky to do it today, even if it's sort of that time of year. He should have waited. It's weird to see all this normal happening when everything is so upside-down right now. June didn't go here, but most of us knew her. It's too soon. And now that I know she was living in the church, I'm guessing she wasn't going to school at all.

It starts in British lit. On my desk, for everyone to see, is a giant red puzzle piece, hand-cut out of cardboard, as big as the desk. I have a moment of hope where I think it's there by mistake, but then I see an envelope with my name on it. I cringe as I open it.

CHAPTER THIRTY-ONE

THIS IS WHAT THE handmade card says:

Emma, Emma, fair and bright,
A beacon against the dark night.
Your vision steady, your heart true,
And now a little puzzle for you.

Eight pieces to my heart
This one is just the start.
They'll be waiting throughout the day
Put them together to see what they say.

Oh god. He just had to pick today, didn't he?

"Nice," Katie Reed says, her voice dripping with sarcasm. "Do you really think today is a good day for that?"

Like this is my fault.

Katie and I are sort of surface level-only friends. We've never really gotten along. She's the kind of person who's always competing, no matter what's going on. Cheerleading, boys, grades, drama team, everything. I hate that kind of stuff. It makes you feel awful whether or you win or lose.

"Well, maybe you should have told him," she says. "Guys are clueless about this stuff."

She would have told him, I'm sure she's thinking, if Mike was *her* boyfriend. I wish I could tell her to take him if she wants him so bad. That might solve all kinds of problems. But unfortunately for both of us, Mike has never been interested.

Girls titter nearby. Most of them would be ecstatic to get asked to prom like this. But I just wish it would go away. I tuck the puzzle piece under my seat and look to the front, hoping the girls will stop with the giggling. They don't.

"Aww. She's embarrassed. That's so cute!" It's Erica.

"Some-body la-oves Em-ma!" says Angela.

I laugh and roll my eyes at them. "Shut up."

"Couldn't you have waited a couple days?" I ask Mike when he picks me up from class.

"What are you talking about? Waited for what?"

I lift the puzzle piece. "To ask me to prom."

He grabs my elbow and steers me into a corner.

"Somebody's asking you to prom? What the heck, Emma? Didn't you believe what I said?"

"I thought it was from you."

He snorts, "I'm not going through that nonsense again. Not this year. I know you're coming with me. You have no choice."

I'd really, really like to punch him in the face right now. Maybe it was a mistake to stop Jackson.

"This is that boy, isn't it?" he says.

"I…," I say, unsure. I allow myself the momentary fantasy that it is Jackson, that he's doing exactly what I've asked him not to do and is about to put Mike in his place. But this whole cutsie, public-display thing isn't really his style. Besides, he promised.

"No," I say. "It's not him. I was very clear that it was over."

But as to who it actually could be? I honestly don't know.

"Then who have you been flirting with? Who thinks they have a chance? Guys only go after girls like you if they know you want them to."

"Seriously, Mike? You know that's a messed-up thing to say, right?"

"Yeah, 'cause you're the expert on what's messed up." He snatches the puzzle piece out of my hand. "Give me that."

CHAPTER THIRTY-TWO

THERE ARE PUZZLE PIECES waiting in every class, on a wall or a door or computer, all with my name on them. Mike's there to meet me at all four classes before lunch. I never knew he had my schedule memorized like that. Another sort of girl might find that charming. I might even find it charming for a little while. But under the circumstances, it's not. Every time he sees me with a new piece, he gets angrier and angrier.

In the cafeteria at lunch, I have to listen to him pontificate with Ben about whether or not we should be strictly following Old Testament laws. Bible class is the one class where Mike aces everything, which makes this conversation even more annoying.

He's practically panting in excitement as he rattles off verses. "John 7:19. Luke 16:17. Timothy 3:16. The New Testament specifically states that we should be adhering to all of God's laws, not just the ones in the New Testament."

"So you really think we should go back to the days of having to wear giant beards or not eating fat or cheeseburgers or shellfish?" Ben says.

"It's not up to me, man. I'm only telling you what the Bible says."

"What about slavery? The Old Testament is pretty clear about that being okay too," Ben says.

"This is all theoretical. I'm not saying I agree with it. I'm just saying that, '"All scripture is inspired by God,'" Mike says, quoting the verse in Timothy, chapter 3. "So there has to be something that we're supposed to learn from everything, not just the parts we pick and choose."

They go on and on and on and on, but all I can think about is who those puzzle pieces are from. There are forty or so guys in my class, but most of them are either already paired off or not in my social circle.

Chuck is a strong possibility. He's always had a thing for me, even though I've been putting water on that fire since day one. But is he really bold enough to go up against Mike? I doubt it.

Maybe Ben? It's unlikely as he's barely spoken to me beyond small talk since middle school, when I noticed he had a boner in his pants and laughed at him. I know it was mean, but give me a break, okay? I didn't mean to. It was the first boner I'd ever seen. But yeah, he hasn't talked to me much since then. He did break up with Chrissy Hillis a couple weeks ago, though. So it's not totally impossible.

It could be Anthony Severn, the hot ginger guy in the Media Club, but this doesn't seem like his style. He'd do something more unique, not some lame puzzle that's been done a thousand times.

I can't think of anyone else.

Mike's voice pipes back into my head. "But if you start ranking them by their occurrence in the Bible, then what happens to, say, homosexuality?" Mike guffaws. "You just gonna go out and get a boyfriend?"

"Oh. My. Lord. You *guys*. Shut up already," Paige says, pulling me out of my thoughts.

The boys just stare at her, a little surprised that anyone exists besides them. She stands up.

"Maybe, instead of trying to find the secret code to the little stuff, you should look at the big parts you know are true and take action to follow them. Like, *I don't know*," she says like it's the most obvious thing, "loving people. And figuring out how to help them."

Where did that come from? Maybe it's that her parents always fawning over Mike's spirituality, but Paige isn't exactly the most vocal when it comes to theology. All of us are looking at her like she just landed from Mars.

"Come on, Emma," she says. "These lunch trays aren't going to clear themselves." She tugs me toward the trash with our two trays stacked in her hands.

"What was that about?" I say.

"Doesn't it ever get under your skin? How they think they know everything all the time?" She shoves our trays under the trash flap so hard she almost loses them in there.

"Yeah. But they're always like that. Why is it suddenly bothering you today?"

"I guess I'm just in a mood," she says, hooking her elbow into mine as we walk out of the cafeteria. "So who do you think is behind this promposal business?"

"I wish I knew. Mike's getting so upset."

"I know. Everybody's talking about it. They aren't saying so, but they totally want to see him unload on the guy."

"I hope not."

"Why? He is your boyfriend, Emma. Everybody knows that. It is sort of insulting."

"I know, I just…it seems like a stupid reason to fight. I'm obviously going to say no."

"Obviously."

"Can we talk about something else, please?" I ask.

"Okay…have you thought about what you're going to wear to prom yet?" she asks.

"Not really," I say. Nothing because I'm not going at all if I can help it? "Have you thought about who you want to go with?" I ask, changing the subject.

"Nobody's asked me."

"Who do you want to ask you?"

She hesitates for a moment, then says, "I don't know. No one special. I don't even know if I want to go yet." Which means, of course, that there is someone special, someone very special, and she's afraid to jinx it by saying his name out loud. I grin.

"I'm sure he'll ask you soon."

"There's really nobody."

"Uh huh," I say. "Sure."

"Drop it, okay? I'm serious. There's no one. If I go at all I'm going solo."

"Okay. Whatever." It's not worth it to press her about it. She won't tell. Paige is a vault. She can keep a secret like no one I've ever met.

There are more puzzle pieces after lunch too. I try to decipher the message as I get them, but I can't make out the P-R-O-M-? that I know is coming. There's an F-O on one. An M on another, but no question mark after it. An E-L-D. And the number six.

The only thing I've figured out is that it's in the shape of a heart. The last piece will be the middle piece. It's on my locker after eighth period. There's a crowd when I get there. Of course there is. Everyone has heard about this by now. Everyone is trying to guess, just like me, who in the world would be stupid enough to piss off Mike.

Paige, Naomi, and Beth make up the center. Katie, Angela, and Erica smirk on the sidelines. Anthony and Chuck are there, but they both look like it's by accident, like they just happened on the scene. Maybe it's an act, but I don't think so. Chuck looks downright disappointed, and Anthony is texting. A ton of freshman and sophomore girls round out the crowd, fueling their dreams for their upperclassman years and thirsty for a fight. I give them all a halfhearted smile.

Mike comes up and yanks the piece off my locker, fire in his eyes. But with everyone watching, he seems to sense that now is not a good time to lose his temper.

"Somebody here's a real comedian," he says. "Anybody want to fess up?"

There are giggles and whispers, but no one answers.

"Come on, who is it? Anybody?"

Still, there's no one.

"What does the puzzle say?" someone yells.

"Put it together!" someone else says. The crowd claps.

So he does. Right there on the floor, in the middle of everybody. When it's finished, he steps back. The message isn't what I thought it would be. All it says is:

Football Field
6:30 p.m.

My heart sinks. This isn't over.

Mike puts an arm around my waist and squeezes me close to him. "This is all very sweet," he says. "I mean, I know she's beautiful, guys, but she's sort of spoken for." He pecks me on the cheek, and the crowd seems to erupt in sighs and "awws," like the air getting let out of a balloon.

He takes my hand, and we walk away, leaving the heart on the floor behind us.

"We're coming back at six thirty," he says to me. "And I'm going to watch while you tell whoever this is that you're not interested."

CHAPTER THIRTY-THREE

MIKE HAS LACROSSE PRACTICE until four thirty, so at least I get a little break from him. Which gives me plenty of time to dread what's coming up tonight. I mentally brace myself for discovering my would-be suitor. I have no idea what I'm going to say, or rather, how I'm going to say it. Guys never understand this, but I think it's harder to say no to someone than it is to ask. I've never wanted to be in the heart-smashing business. Today I'm certain I will be.

I decide that instead of thinking about it anymore, I'll go look for something I've been thinking about ever since I talked to Nicolas. I walk across the overpass into the church building. A lot of kids are hanging out at the Connections Café, doing homework and chatting. But what I'm looking for is a little farther down.

I open the door to the auditorium, which is dark, totally empty right now, and make my way toward the stage. There's a fabric curtain on the front of the apron, which is about four feet tall. The curtain hides the structure that holds up the stage. Before I would have thought that the only thing under here was storage for extra chairs, but now I know better.

I duck behind the curtain, and all the light disappears. There's a flashlight app on my phone, so I turn it on and crawl through the space. I go past a row of chairs that's on a rolling cart, past a Nativity cradle and some stage flats, but I don't see anything until I'm almost to the back wall.

It's right there, just like Nicolas said it would be: a couple of nursery mats and a sleeping bag. This is where June lived. If she

144

had anything else here though, it's gone, probably taken away by the police as evidence.

I crawl onto the mats and lie down, thinking about what it would be like to have this as my home. It's hard to imagine anyone being comfortable here. But it makes me a little proud of June for thinking of it. Hiding inside the church is very resourceful. There's always stuff going on. It would be almost impossible to notice her. She had access to food and water and showers off the gym. The church is heated in the winter and cool in the summer. And setting up under here where no one would ever look, even by accident? It was really smart.

I shine my phone around the walls and see, overhead, a heart scratched under the stage. Inside the heart is written:

N & J

4ever

Oh, June. This part of you I think I can understand. The part that knows what it's like to be in love. I miss Jackson so much right now. I wish I could hide him away down here, just so I could sneak off to see him whenever I want.

When 4:30 rolls around, Mike is done with practice. I promised to meet him in the Connections Café, and I make sure I'm there before he is. We sit with Paige and some other kids, all of us buried in books and the pile of catch-up homework the teachers have assigned. The downside of going to a good school is all the homework, sometimes five or six hours a night, and this week it's double the usual.

I spend the next couple hours working through the homework and checking e-mail. There's one from May; she says she's going back up to CU in Boulder this week. Her spring break is long over, and she doesn't want to fall any further behind. Things with her and Trisha have gone sour. She gives me her address in case I need to visit. I wish her well and thank her again for loaning me her ID.

It's 6:15 before I know it.

"Ready?" Mike asks.

"I guess so," I say.

We pack up and head across. It's starting to get dark. The windowed overpass is neon orange with the setting sun, like being inside molten glass before it takes its final shape. I am the dark spot against its glow, within its fiery center.

There's a crowd down there, but I can't make out faces. At least twenty-five people, and more driving up, their headlights cutting through the warm haze of the evening, gossipy girls popping inside like corn kernels.

I make an effort to smile when I walk out on the quad. For a second I get caught up in their attention, and the smile comes easier. I can't lie. There's a little bit of magic being me in this moment. Me the prize in a fight between two boys, one of them a mystery, and all these people gathered to see it. Our curiosity is amped-up the way the sky feels electric before a thunderstorm.

Mike takes my hand in his, reminding me he's there at all, reminding me that doing this is really more for him than for me. The whole point is to hurt someone's feelings so Mike can look like the top dog. I guess I'd be hurting someone's feelings either way. If it wasn't for Mike, I wouldn't go to prom this year. My parents would never agree to let Jackson take me, and why would I go with anyone else?

The crowd parts like the Red Sea as we walk through them. And beyond, I see it. Not him, but it. Instead of a person waiting, there's something set up in the middle of the field.

We walk toward it, Mike and I. The other kids follow in a hush of excited whispers and sneakers swishing through grass. As we get closer, the object on the green grows clearer. It looks like a big rectangular picture frame, maybe five feet wide and half that tall, set up on an easel. But instead of holding a painting, it's covered in black paper, with my name scrawled in big silver letters across it. Am I supposed to unwrap it?

No. When we get closer I see a small envelope taped to a white string dangling below the left corner. I pick up the envelope, and inside is a cigarette lighter wrapped in a note:

Light me.

Well that's a little more original. That's when I notice the smell. It's sharp and strong, like gasoline or lighter fluid or propane. There better be someone with a fire extinguisher nearby.

I look over at Mike, and he shrugs, rolling his eyes. From the hot air balloon guy, this probably seems pretty lame.

What else can I do with everyone watching? I flick the lighter

146

to life. With a shrug to the crowd, I place the flame on the edge of the string, and it feels like I'm lighting one of those cartoon bombs, black and round and ready to leave everyone with crazy hair and smoky faces.

It takes. The flame dances up the string, onto the paper.

The paper catches with a whoosh, and I stumble back from the blaze. In an instant, it's ashes on the air. And there's something else burning, orange-hot flames licking rope, nailed to a metal backing in a pattern.

There are gasps from the onlookers.

It takes me a moment to register it, for the mess I'm seeing to switch from a jumble of letters to something that has a meaning, for my mind to adjust from what I was expecting to what this really is.

On the board, spelled out in flaming rope, is a single word: *KILLER*

CHAPTER THIRTY-FOUR

THERE'S CHAOS ALL AROUND me, but my hearing goes fuzzy, blending everything together into mush. It's like I'm wearing earmuffs, like when I was a little kid going out to play in the snow.

Mike yanks me away from the blaze. I stumble, but he holds me up.

The fire spreads to the easel. Some boys race back to the school building to get a fire extinguisher, Mike among them.

I feel woozy and sit down on the ground.

Then Paige is in front of me, holding my shoulders, saying something, but I can't make out what.

Focus, Emma. Focus.

"Emma!" Paige says. She looks worried, terrified.

All my senses return at once. The sharp smell of the smoke, the feel of the air—hot and scratchy in my throat, the sound of the other kids—some spooked and tugging their friends away, others standing shocked, waiting for me to explain.

"Are you okay?" Paige asks.

"I'm fine," I say. "I'm fine."

The boys come back, spray down the flames, but not soon enough to avoid leaving a blackened spot on the field. With how dry Colorado is, we're lucky it didn't spread farther.

I struggle up to my feet, staring at what's left of the crowd. It's mostly just the kids in my circle now, maybe ten of them.

"Did anyone see who set this up?"

A couple people shake their heads no, wide eyed and confused.

148

"It's really important, you guys," I say. "Someone is playing a very sick joke, and I need to know who it was."

"I was the first one here," Chuck says. "Me and Ben. That thing was here when we got here."

Ben shakes his head, "Yeah. We didn't see anything. Sorry, Emma."

I look out to the rest of the kids. "How about at school today? Did anyone notice who put those puzzle pieces up?"

More nos.

"Katie, you have Bible in Mr. Stearn's class right before I do. You didn't notice anyone putting that piece up on his bulletin board?"

"It was already there," Katie says.

Ruth pipes up, "I have homeroom in there. It was there before the first bell rang."

"Same in the science lab," Chuck says. "There was a puzzle piece right at your spot in first period. Casey French sits there and asked what to do with it, so Mrs. Boris took it and put it on the chalkboard."

"Math too," Ruth says. "I saw it on the computer station in fourth period. Isn't math your last class?"

I nod. Whoever did this taped up those pieces before school even started, then snuck back to the school after all the sports practices and clubs were done for the day.

Mike's voice booms out, "I think we should get out of here, guys. It's not safe."

For once, Mike is right.

We clear out of the field and head back to the Connections Café, where somebody calls the police. They come and take a look at things, but seem to write it off as a prank in poor taste. Detectives Boyer and Simms don't even show up. And after the police go, everyone else seems to take the same attitude. Just a prank. Just a really, really tasteless prank.

I'm the only one who knows it was something more.

With everything that's happened and all the thoughts rushing through my mind, I almost forget that I still have to go to dance practice tonight. I consider skipping it, but the idea of going home alone and sitting in an empty house sounds so much worse than dancing right now.

I race into the room and drop my backpack on the floor. The other girls are just starting to get into formation: symmetrical like always. I wouldn't exactly call Miss Hope a gifted choreographer. All our moves are always completely symmetrical: if one half of the girls do something, then it's a pretty safe bet that the other half of the girls will do it too. It's all so neat and tidy it makes me want to break something sometimes, just for balance.

To make it even worse, the choreography for all the choruses is always identical too. We repeat the same set of movements every time the chorus rolls around until it's so predictable the audience could probably get up on stage and do it with us by the end. Apparently, Miss Hope only has a limited number of ideas and has to spread them out evenly across the song.

"Hurry up, Miss Grant, you're late."

"I know, sorry," I say as I run over to them.

"Okay. Gather up, ladies. We almost forgot to pray," Miss Hope says.

We group into a circle around her and bow our heads.

"Dear Jesus," she says. "We know You have a brand-new angel tonight."

June. I nearly forgot that she should have been here. This is our first practice since she died. I don't dare open my eyes, but I can hear the girls around me sniffling.

"We know You're holding her safe in Your arms now and that one day we'll be able to rejoice in Your presence with our beloved sister. We ask for Your peace and guidance tonight as we rehearse without her. May our movements, and all of our actions, be for the glory of You and not ourselves. Amen."

We do a big group hug, then line up in our starting positions, only no one seems to know where to go. June was the featured dancer in this one. She never had a dance lesson in her life, or so she said, but she was so naturally good that Miss Hope couldn't throw enough parts at her. There was just something about June that made you want to watch.

Without her, everything is off in the lineup. June should be front and center, and we should be lining up in a triangle around her. We all look toward Miss Hope. No one wants to say it.

"Right," Miss Hope says. "Emma? Do you think you could

take over the lead?"

I nod and take my place in the center. The other girls form the triangle around me. Paige is in the back, directly behind me at the point, where she always is because she's really kind of awful and Miss Hope always tries to hide her. Ruth and I used to be on either side of June, but now it's only Ruth. June's absence is a literal empty space.

"Paige, please take Emma's place." Paige nods solemnly and steps forward. Then the music starts. "How Beautiful" by Twila Paris. It's for Pastor Pete and Miss Hope's wedding, which is coming up in a couple weeks. It's a good thing we've done this number before, or we wouldn't have enough time to put it together. They play the song at basically every single wedding at the church. Even if I hadn't danced to it a million times, I'd still have it memorized.

I try to concentrate on the movements, but I can't get it out of my mind. June isn't here. Someone killed her. And that same someone is trying to blame me for it.

As the chorus starts, I lift my leg and point my toe for the extension.

"Too high, Emma," Miss Hope shouts, but I don't care. I need to feel my leg stretched all the way out. I need to push it as far as I can go. I do it again when the chorus repeats.

"Stop. Stop. Stop." Miss Hope grabs her iPod off the floor, where it's piped into the sound system through a cable, and stops the music. "You have to think about what that will look like in the dresses, Emma. What will people in the audience see?" One of us is dead, and all she cares about is whether or not some perv watching teenage girls dance in a church will catch a fleeting peek of my completely covered crotch.

"But aren't we wearing leggings underneath the skirts?" I ask, using the same lame argument Hannah tried this morning.

"It doesn't matter. It's not decent above your waist. Try it again." She starts the music back up, and I can feel my blood boiling as I go through the movements. What's the point of any of this?

When the chorus starts, I kick so high that my legs strike a straight line from the floor to the toes above my head.

"Emma! What did I just say?" Miss Hope shuts off the music again.

"Why does it fucking matter?!" I shout.

The whole room goes silent. There is no shuffle of feet on concrete, no swish of ponytails. All their eyes are on me. Miss Hope is speechless, trying to decide if she heard me correctly. Certainly, perfect Emma Grant didn't just say the word fuck?

I glance at Paige; she's staring at me with her mouth wide open. It's the first time she's ever heard me say it.

My chest is heaving. I'm hyped up and out of breath from the dancing.

"What did you say?" Miss Hope says.

"I said," I say, trying to calm down, trying to speak evenly, "why does it matter?"

"It matters," Miss Hope says. "Because we are charged with being an example to others. And what you just said proves to me that you're not ready to do that."

"Oh please," I say. What a joke. It's all such a complete joke.

"Get your things. You can come back when you get your attitude straightened out."

"Fuck this," I say under my breath, the word new and dangerous on my tongue. Then louder, "I quit."

CHAPTER THIRTY-FIVE

I STORM DOWN THE halls, out the door, to my car, slamming the door shut as I get in. It doesn't matter. None of it matters.

I shouldn't be spending time dancing to some stupid church song I don't even believe in anymore. I should be figuring out who made that sign tonight and who put that gun in my bedroom so they don't have a chance to do it again.

I drive until I can finally see straight, then see the line of people outside Voodoo Doughnut and realize where I am: a little neighborhood just outside of downtown Denver called Capitol Hill. It has a bunch of hipster bars and a couple aging concert venues that were once movie theaters with big, bulbed signs. Jackson took me to a coffee shop here once. I drive a little more until I find it, then drive a few more blocks until I spot a place to park.

Inside there are lines of long wooden community tables. I take my tea to an open spot and sit down. I need to think things through, figure this out.

The first thing, the glaring thing I have to face is that May was right. Whoever killed June most likely knew both of us, which means they probably go to the church. The killer knows where I live, knows where I go to school, and enough about my schedule to time things just right. That message today wouldn't have worked an hour earlier or an hour later. There was too much going on at school before, and too much going on at church after.

I have to face the facts. The best place to start might just be with the list the police are working off of. I pull out my notebook and write down the names:

There's me and Jackson, though I can eliminate us. Jackson only left my side for a few minutes to use the restroom, which would barely have been enough time to get down to the sanctuary and back. And even if he was physically able to pull it off, he never even met June.

Paige. I scratch her name out right away. Yes, she was alone for a while when Mike was snooping on me, and yes, she even knew I would be out of the main Youth Center room at the time the murder was committed. But if my best friend, the person I know better than anyone, the person I trust more than anyone on the planet, is somehow guilty, then I don't care what happens to me. It would mean the world was the kind of place that I didn't want to live in anymore. I refuse to believe she's capable of it.

Chuck, Pastor Pete, and Miss Hope. They're also easy to eliminate because they were together, though it might be worth asking if any of them left at any point, just to make sure. What would be harder to believe out of this group is why anyone would want June dead, or hate me enough to try to frame me, much less do both.

I've always gotten along with Pastor Pete, and I can tell that he really cared about June. And I hadn't even thought about this before, but he's one of the few people in church who's anti-gun. There was an incident a couple years ago when he tried to convince some kid not to join Brothers in Christ because it's so weapons-focused. The family left the church over it. A lot of people around here don't like him because he's too liberal, but my dad sticks up for him because he says he thinks it's healthy to have multiple viewpoints represented within the Body of Christ. It would be a stretch to imagine Pastor Pete shooting anyone.

Miss Hope can be a little strict sometimes, and I get the sense that she'd definitely like my family to be stricter too. But it's a far cry from disagreeing with the way my family interprets the Bible to trying to frame me, and I can't imagine any reason she'd have to kill June.

I guess if I'm honest with myself, there's Chuck. Could me not being interested in him have hurt his feelings more than I realized? It's hard to say. He's never done much more than elementary-school teasing. Would he even have the guts to go through with all this? And even if he did, why kill June? I can see why he might secretly hate me, but June?

None of them seem likely. I move on.

Mike. I can't take him off the list. He was wandering around in the church alone twice around the time June was shot: once looking for a hand truck, the other time returning it. Or so he says. Of all the kids in the youth group, he's by far the most conservative. He's the only one I can even imagine telling June it was her fault that her father did what he did to her. Though that might be a stretch, even for him.

And what about that story he told me about seeing June with her shirt unbuttoned? That was weird. Why would June act like that? Is there more to the story than Mike said? Could he have done something with her that he regrets? Could she have been threatening to tell me? He's in Brothers In Christ so he obviously knows how to shoot a gun. And he's very upset with me right now. There are too many pieces that make him a possibility. I resign myself to be more careful, more watchful around him from now on.

Then there's Nicolas. I don't want to think that he's capable of it, but there are a lot of factors working against him. He might be underplaying how upset he was that June refused his proposal. In the video Paige took, he looked pretty agitated. According to the police, not a single person can verify where he was when June was killed. And he's in Brothers In Christ too, right along with Mike.

Lastly, though it's not on the police's list, is everyone else who goes to the church, over eight thousand people every week. The truth, the daunting, I-wish-I-could-ignore-it truth, is that I, and my whole family, aren't exactly afforded a lot of privacy. Anyone could follow us home at night. Anyone could tell where I went to school, and maybe even figure out which classes I was taking if they asked the right people or snooped in my backpack when I left it unattended. Anyone could have hidden in the church, just like June did every single night, and waited for some stray person to wander by. What if it wasn't about June at all? What if she was just the first person to cross his path? If someone has a grudge against the church itself, or one of my parents, I might be the perfect target.

I close my notebook and go up to the counter for a refill on my tea. Maybe I need to think in a different direction for a while, change it up to see if it jogs anything loose in my brain.

But what other directions are there? Talking to Lee Stuckey was a joke. It didn't feel like he was talking straight about anything. And there's no way he could have done it himself. But still, he's a convicted murderer, and his daughter was killed. Maybe it's worth researching what he told me, even if it's just so I can rule it out.

Back at my seat, I power up my laptop and pull up the article about the bank robbery to see if there's anything I missed. Maybe I should try to talk to the other people involved, see what they have to say. I jot down a list of their names:

Lee Stuckey
Sara Jo Ford
Buddy Trent
Jay Peterson
Christina Bromegat

Five people, all convicted of the crime, but Lee was the only shooter. Does that mean they're all in prison too? I have no idea how it all works.

I do a quick search on the Colorado Department of Corrections website, and find records for most of them. The records don't say much, but they do show their current photo, list their arrest dates, their future release dates, and how long their sentence was originally for.

The only one I can't find is for Jay Peterson. Was he released? Could he have been transferred to another facility outside of Colorado? I don't know how to begin searching for him, or what not finding him even means.

I call Mr. Graham on his cell. Maybe lawyers have access to records I don't. He never returned my message last night; neither did Boyer, so I'm not leaving another message.

"Yes, Emma. What is it?"

"Did you get my message the other night?"

"I did, and I passed along your ideas to the police, but Emma —"

"I was wondering if you could look into someone for me?"

"Like a background check? I'm not an investigator, Emma,

I'm a lawyer. What is this about?"

"I think there's a small chance that June's dad was involved with some bad people who might have wanted to kill her."

"Oh? What makes you think that?"

"He's in prison. For killing a woman and her baby when he robbed a bank. So I went to talk to him and—?"

"You did what?"

Shit. I didn't mean to let that slip out.

"I went to the prison to talk to him. I had to."

"Emma. That's—you can't just do things like that."

"Why not? The police aren't doing anything."

"That could be very dangerous. You have no idea what sort of people—"

"Well somebody has to do something."

"I specifically advised you to stick to your normal routine. We can't afford for the police to think they spooked you."

"Can't afford? Why?"

"Look, Emma, this isn't something we should discuss over the phone. Why don't you have your parents bring you to my office?"

"Is something wrong? Did something happen?"

He pauses for a moment. At first I don't think he's going to tell me, but then he takes a deep breath and speaks.

"The police have narrowed down their suspect pool considerably. My contact wouldn't tell me who else they're looking at, but he did say that there were only three and that you're on the list."

I say goodbye, hang up the phone, and take a deep breath. This changes nothing. Nothing at all.

I wake up my computer and look at the list again. Jay Peterson. He's the only who I can't find in the system. If he's been released from jail already, maybe Lee was right. Maybe he would have a reason to hurt June. Maybe he thought she had Lee's share of the money or maybe he was trying to get back at Lee for something he didn't tell me about.

As for the rest, they're all still in jail for at least another five years before they're even eligible for parole. There's no easy way to talk to any of them. Even if I could convince them to see me, I'm not eighteen yet, and the Colorado Department of

Corrections won't allow me to visit without a parent or guardian unless the person I'm visiting *is* a parent or guardian. I can just imagine how that conversation would go down with my parents.

But the better question is May's—why kill June now? Why not wait until they're released? If Lee's theory is correct, if someone from the gang turned him in and then went after June, Jay Peterson is the only one that could be responsible. It's worth looking into.

I search for him again in the Colorado Department of Corrections database, just to be sure, but he's not there. A Google search yields different results. I turn up a whole list of men named Jay Peterson. After a little digging, I narrow down the pool to people who were at least eighteen when the crime was committed in 2004, which would make them at least twenty-eight now. I also eliminate anyone who was older than sixty-five at the time.

Then I start digging deeper, looking through Facebook profiles and LinkedIn profiles and webpages for dentists and lawyers and real estate agents. Anyone even remotely connected to anything legal is out, because they'd have to pass a background check to do the job, just like we require at church. Anyone who looks like they got married or had a baby or started a business in 2004-2006 seems unlikely. He would have had to serve at least two years for a crime like that, probably a lot more, which is why it's so strange that I can't find him.

I go through page after page, and no one seems right. I have nothing.

I decide to plug him into a background check service online. I type in Jay Peterson, and find one person who lives in Denver and lists having a criminal record. His age seems about right, thirty-three, so I pay the $24.95 for a background check with the credit card my parents opened in my name for emergencies.

Bingo. This Jay Peterson was arrested in 2004 for armed robbery in Lafayette, Colorado. Last known address, in 2005, was in Limon, Colorado. So shouldn't that mean he went to prison and is already out? Then I scroll down.

Jay Peterson is listed as deceased.

The death record lists him as dying at the Limon Correctional Facility, the same place where Lee Stuckey is incarcerated. It doesn't say how. There's not much more information.

There goes that theory.

CHAPTER THIRTY-SIX

I'M DRIVING BACK HOME, going slow through some post-Rockies traffic, when my phone rings. It's my mom. Shit. I pick up.

"Hey," I say.

"Where are you?" she asks. "Because I know you're not at church."

"On my way home."

"How far?"

"I don't know."

"Well, I expect you through these doors in the next ten minutes, young lady." This drive will take more than twice that.

"Okay," I say, knowing for sure there's no way it's gonna happen.

By the time I get through traffic, it's been nearly forty minutes, and my mom has called three more times. I didn't pick up. She starts in on me as soon as I'm through the front door.

"Where were you?"

"Just driving around."

She looks at me like she knows better. "Uh huh. Not going to visit anyone in prison this time?"

So she talked to Mr. Graham. Dammit.

"When, exactly, did you do it?"

"Sunday," I say, avoiding her eyes.

"So you lied to us?"

"Yes, ma'am."

"That's not very trustworthy behavior from someone who very much needs to be focused on showing the police she's trustworthy right now."

I stay silent.

"And how, may I ask, did you even get in?"

I tell her about borrowing May's ID, and her face goes white.

"You can't be doing things like that, Emma. You just can't."

"Somebody has to."

"That's right. The police."

I roll my eyes. "Yeah. 'Cause they're doing such a great job right now."

"I do not appreciate the attitude, young lady. Frankly, I'm surprised by it." She paces in front of me, agitated. "I had a very interesting talk with Miss Hope. You want to tell me about what happened at Worship Dance Team?"

"I quit the team."

"And?"

I decide to play dumb. "And what?"

"If you can't be honest with me, we're done talking. You're grounded."

I go to my room and hear my parents' door close down the hall. I'm grounded. Fabulous. As if they could make my life any worse than it is right now.

My phone buzzes in my pocket. A text from Jackson.

Check flower pot in back yard, by trees.

Is he here? I'd love to see him right now, but this is the worst possible night for him to just show up. I race to my window, but it's too dark to see. I text him.

Why?

He texts back right away.

Just check.

I tiptoe out of my room and down the stairs, sliding open the door to the back yard as quietly as I can. Of course, the motion-sensor light fires on, lighting up the whole patio and I'm sure notifying my parents I'm back here. But maybe not? Their window faces the front of the house, not the back.

I scan the backyard, half hoping to see his face and half hoping not to. There's no one back here. The yard is a stretch of empty green.

I race over to a small patch of aspens. At the foot of them is a huge ceramic pot. There's nothing growing in it yet, the weather is still too cold for planting. But there are some branches and twigs, knocked down from the weight of winter snow. Underneath them, I see a patch of red peeking out.

I reach in and retrieve a small box, squirreling it into the pocket of my hoodie. I turn back to the house, just in time to see the shadow of my mother walking through the kitchen and reaching the light of the back door. She's in her bathrobe now, and isn't exactly smiling.

"What are you doing out here?" she asks.

"So I'm not allowed to have fresh air either?" I ask. I'm panicky, and the words are too bratty, even for me. I can feel their wrongness as they tumble past my lips.

"Get to your room. Right now."

I walk past her, fisting my hands in my pocket to mask the bulk, and run up the stairs. As soon as the door is closed behind me, I pull it out. The box is oblong, papered in red foil, the kind of box jewelry sometimes comes in at Christmas. There are scuffs on the edges that make it look like it might have been used before. I imagine Jackson in his dark basement, digging through a bin of old holiday gift wrap and picking this.

The lid comes off easily. Inside, on a bed of cotton, lays a mini-figurine of the Statue of Liberty. It too looks weathered, cold and metal with a chipping mint paint that gives it an antique character. Where did he find this? A thrift store? An antique shop? A smile stretches across my face as I hold it in my palm. It's perfect. I love it.

Nestled under the figurine is a hand-written note. In Jackson's handwriting, it simply says:

I'll kiss you here too.

I grab my phone and text him.

I can't wait.

The terms of my grounding are this: surrender the keys to my car, drive back and forth from school with my parents every day for two weeks, and I'm only allowed to go to church or school activities, nothing else. At least it gives me an excuse not to go out with Mike for a while.

Paige seems to be hovering by my locker when I arrive at school the next day.

"You gonna start returning my calls someday?" she asks. She

seems a little pissed. I should have remembered to call her, but my mind was on other things.

"Sorry. It was kind of a crazy night. I'm totally grounded. I basically lost my car for two weeks, plus a whole bunch of other stuff. They're not letting me go anywhere."

"The dance thing?"

"The dance thing."

"I can't say I'm surprised. What was that, Emma? I've never seen you act that way before."

"I know. All this stuff with June has really been getting to me."

She looks at me like she knows it's an excuse as much as I do.

"Still," she says. "That was, like, weird. Especially for you. Are you sure there's not anything else going on?"

I wish I could tell her everything. I really do. It would be so nice, *so nice*, to be able to talk to her about all this. Mike, Jackson, Lee Stuckey the gun. Especially the gun. But telling her a little means telling her everything. And telling her everything means losing her forever. I can't.

"No." I change the subject. "How was practice last night?"

"Oh fine, you know. Miss Hope gave Ruth the lead part and called Katie to see if she could fill in since she danced with us last year. Let's just say Ruth had a little bit of a hard time learning it. As usual. I mean, I know I suck at doing all the moves, but at least I remember when to do them."

"You don't suck."

She raises her eyebrows at me, "Know thyself, woman. And know when thou sucketh. I sucketh. A lot-eth."

"Whatever," I laugh. Then I think of something I've been meaning to ask her. "Hey, do you know if June was being mentored by anyone?"

"I never saw her with anybody. I mean, she came to you a lot, but other than that, no. Why?"

"I don't know. Nicolas told me that she really wanted to get baptized and the police said she was wearing a swimsuit when she died. I thought maybe, I don't know…it's probably nothing, but I can't get it out of my mind."

"Well, don't take this the wrong way or anything, but your dad kind of has a thing about baptizing people. No one on staff would have agreed to do it but him."

"He likes it, yeah, but—"

"No, Emma, it's like a *thing*. My dad has *never* baptized anyone at this church, even though lots of other assistant pastors do it in other churches, and he did it in Bible College all the time. There was this one time when this guy he was mentoring, Gregory Foster, specifically requested my dad to do his baptism, and your dad said no *and* chewed out my dad about it."

"Really?"

"I mean, and you have to swear you're never gonna tell your dad this, but the rest of the staff sort of makes fun of him about it. They think," she smiles cautiously, "they think he's keeping score."

"Wait, what?"

"Of souls. The joke is that he's gonna show up in heaven with a spreadsheet."

"Wow," I laugh. "I had no idea."

"Yup," she says. "Like I said. It's a thing."

"So you don't think anyone else would agree to baptize June?"

"Not anyone on staff. Your dad would be all over them about it. You promise you're not gonna tell, though, right? 'Cause my dad would kill me if he found out I told you that."

"Of course not," I say. "Did June say anything to you about getting baptized, or, you know, anything else?"

"No," she says. "To be honest, she didn't really talk to me much unless you were around. I don't even think she really wanted to be my friend, not really. I think...I think she only wanted to be friends with me because of you."

"That's silly."

"Didn't you notice how she was always tagging along, paying so much attention to you? That's why she wanted to be friends with me. I think it's even why she started dating Nicolas. I'm sort of surprised she never went after Mike."

"She might have. I don't know. You didn't see them talking ever, did you?"

"A few times, but never for long. Why?"

I tell her the story Mike told me.

"See? That's what I mean. She didn't just want to be like you, she wanted to *be* you. It kind of, I don't know..." she turns away from me, bites her lip. "It bothered me sometimes."

CHAPTER THIRTY-SEVEN

EVERY DAY THAT WEEK, I have to go straight to my mom's office after school and sit there with her, doing homework until she's either ready to leave or another church activity starts up, which is pretty much every night. With them watching me so close, there's absolutely zero chance to look into any more leads about June's murder. It's infuriating.

The next Monday, I go to her office again after school to begin my second week of punishment. She's the Women's Ministry director, and has an office on the second floor of the North Wing. It's smaller than my dad's, and positioned almost directly below his. Both of their windows face west toward the mountains, but only my dad can actually see them from his higher vantage point. My mother's view is almost totally blocked by the school across the street. Only the very tips of the mountains peak out from above the roof.

While I do trig, she chatters to someone about table decorations for a banquet to raise money for some missionaries the Women's Ministry is sponsoring in the Middle East somewhere.

I'm working through the first problem when my phone buzzes in my pocket. I glance up to see if my mom is looking, but she's still talking, nearly oblivious to my presence. I sneak the phone out and look at the screen. There's a text from Jackson.

I slide it back into my pocket. "I'm going to use the restroom," I say.

She looks over and nods absentmindedly. Whatever she's

working on, she's absorbed in it as usual.

I go to the restroom where I lock the door and press my phone to life. His words jump out at me from the screen.

Going crazy. Need 2 see u.

I think we should come clean.

Can u meet me?

What the hell does that mean? I text back fast.

?????????

Lots to tell u, but grounded, can't meet.

Hang tight. Will call 2nite.

Love you.

I wish I could call him now, but it's not worth the risk. He texts back immediately.

Please. I need u.

The park? After bed?

Please.

Something is wrong. I have no idea how, but I need to figure out a way to see him.

Ok. midnight. See u there.

Love u. B strong.

It's only a little after four. This is already killing me. I walk back to my mother's office. How am I going to get through until midnight?

The following hours pass like a hot summer day: slow and relentless, where all you want is escape but the sun won't let you, refuses to go.

First, it's home for a too-silent dinner, then it's back to church where my parents have their weekly Parents of Teens Bible Study. I should be at dance, but since I quit I'm hoping the night will be free and I'll get a chance to call Jackson. Not so. When we get to church, my mom informs me that she's volunteered me for childcare duty in the preschool area of the Kid's Korner.

Ugh. I hate working in the Kid's Korner. I spend the next two hours avoiding snotty noses and sticky palms and generally hating life.

When parents start showing up, I want to go, but I can't yet. The kids and parents get matching bar code bracelets. We have to scan them all and make sure every parent gets the right kid.

Like somebody's gonna take one of these brats if they don't have to. It takes forever.

Eventually, when we're down to a handful of kids, I make an excuse and take off. I race over to the main floor of the North Wing, where the adult Sunday school rooms are. I peek through the window of my parents' classroom. Things were supposed to end at 9:00, and it's 9:15, but they're still in there.

They stand in the center of a circle. The other adults pray around them, their hands extended. I can't make out what's being said, but I can guess it probably has to do with me. Around here, everyone always knows all your business. Prayer requests spread gossip fast, and without all the guilt.

The prayer comes to a close, and people start to gather their things. Several husband-and-wife duos stop to say a kind word to my parents as they filter out. I've slept over at these people's houses, gone to their sons' and daughters' birthday parties for years. But none of them say a word to me as they exit, even though I know they notice me standing by the door. It's like they're banded together, wounded veterans in a war against teenagers.

My parents are the last to leave, and they're surprised to see me when they finally come through the door. I tell them I'm tired. I tell them I want to go home. But my dad has something to get from his office, and we're interrupted by someone who wants to talk to my mom. I say I will wait in the car.

It takes another thirty minutes for them to join me. There are always hands to shake, small talk to make, questions to answer of a congregant who wants one more piece of you before you go. It was stupid of me to hope to leave right after their class. But we finally do.

I go straight to bed. I wait for the sounds of the house to die down, wait for FOX News to silence, wait for the lights to go dark and listen for my parent's door to close all the way upstairs. Then I wait some more.

CHAPTER THIRTY-EIGHT

At eleven thirty, I creep through the house and enter the night. My car is in the garage, and it would wake my parents to take it, so I have to go on foot. It's probably better this way anyway. I'm certain there's an undercover police car parked at the mouth of my cul-de-sac. I've been trying to notice which cars seem to be around a lot, and there's no question that I've seen the one on the end of the block at both school and church too. So I can't drive my car anywhere I don't want the police to know about, or go through the front door.

I turn off the motion-sensor light out back and use the storage chest to scale the back edge of the fence. I hop into the neighbor's yard, then go through their side gate to the block behind ours.

It takes me several blocks to stop looking over my shoulder to see if I'm being followed. The air is crisp, but not cold enough to see your breath tonight. It's nice being out in it, alone, free. It's usually my favorite time of year, and would be even more if everything was the same as just a few weeks ago. But it's not.

I let my mind wander to the things I used to conjure up when I needed comfort: dorm rooms and Jackson's guitar and new, interesting friends and salty sea air and a world without limits. But instead of comforting me, they make me sad. They feel farther away than ever now, almost impossible.

The park isn't far, just a couple of miles. I'm on a main road now, Colfax, and nearly there. Cars whizz past even this late on a weeknight. My heart jerks. Was that last car the one parked in my cul-de-sac? I watch to see if it turns around, but it's hard to tell in the dark.

What if they are following me? It will lead them straight to Jackson, to our meeting secretly in the middle of the night. I can't let that happen. I just can't.

I text him right away, hope I'm not too late.

Not our spot!
Police might follow.
Safeway on Alameda.
Go in, wait by milk.
I'll find you.

This is all so much to keep track of. I feel like I'm losing my mind. Jackson texts right back.

See u @ Sfwy in 10

I release the stale breath in my gut, and take in the fresh air. That was too close. I feel like I'm getting sloppy, like my brain is too small to hold all the twists and pockets of possibilities.

What would life be like if I could always be honest? If I could always be who I really am? The thought of it feels as free as dropping down the highest hill on a roller coaster, hands up and screaming the fear away from me. But that's not really possible, at least not right now.

I see the sign up ahead and cross over to the next block. From the direction I'm coming, I'll be able to see the back first.

A low rumble comes up behind me, turning from Alameda onto my street. I look down at the sidewalk to hide my face, just in case. The headlights grow brighter as the car gets closer, then it goes past, and all I see is a blinking turn signal as it rounds the next corner.

I take a deep breath and turn on the opposite corner, almost there. Tall street lamps illuminate the loading dock behind the grocery store. All I can think about is seeing his face. It feels like I haven't seen him for years, even though it's only been a little over a week. I try to calm myself down, I'll need to wait a little longer. He may not even be here yet. It's only been a few minutes since I texted.

I start to cross the last street between me and the back lot. Then I hear it.

A low rumble, and a screech. It's a car, I think, but I don't see headlights.

The sound grows louder. Too loud and too urgent. I look toward the noise as I approach the middle of the road. A maroon mass flashes under a streetlight. It's hurtling straight toward me, only half a block away.

It takes a second for my brain to register it. And another to process that it doesn't matter which side I go to. I just need to move.

I dash across, toward the parking lot, toward where I hope Jackson is waiting.

I chance a glance at the car, but I can't make anything out but a blurry black shape behind the wheel. The glance costs me. My legs pump hard, but not fast enough.

SLAM.

The car catches my back foot in midair and twists my body into a grotesque pirouette. I spin into the air, then crash into the pavement, my left foot screaming.

Ahead, the car stops. Maybe they didn't see me. Maybe they're stopping to help, but nobody's getting out. I lift myself onto my elbows to get a better look. The first three digits of the license plate read, 8MK-.

White reverse lights blink on.

No.

The car revs to life. Another squeal.

This is no accident. I have to move.

I roll away, toward the curb. My cell flies out of my pocket, but I don't have time to grab it. The car is milliseconds away.

Fear drives the adrenaline I need into my muscles. I pull myself onto the sidewalk as the car whizzes past, crushing my phone to pieces underneath its wheels.

The car stops again. It's going to take another pass, run me down, sidewalk be damned.

I only have one chance to escape it. I have to get inside that store.

I force myself up to standing. The pain in my foot is excruciating, but I propel myself forward. There's another screech as the car lurches toward me again.

I race to the store. Only twenty feet separates me from the loading dock.

I hear a grumbling clunk as the car jumps the curb, but I can't look back.

Only five feet now.

The car is close. I feel the heat of the engine licking my heels.

I scream, force my body forward until it slams into concrete and I launch myself up onto the loading dock.

I am out of the car's reach, but not the reach of the person driving it. I have to get inside.

I pull myself up, yank on the back door. It won't open. It's locked.

I pound on the door.

"Help! Please! Help me."

I see a security camera mounted above the door and wave furiously at it.

"Help! Help!"

The car has stopped. It's idling in the spot reserved for delivery trucks. The driver is bent over, reaching for something.

I bang on the door. I imagine elevator music and a sleeping security guard at this late hour.

"Please! Please!"

I hear the click and push of the car door as it opens. And then I hear a buzz.

I try the door, and this time it opens. I tear inside and slam straight into the bloody chest of a butcher's apron. The door slams shut.

"Whoa, honey. What's the matter?" a heavy voice asks.

"8 M K, 8 M K, 8 M K" I keep saying it, over and over. I can't forget, no matter what.

"I can't understand you." The butcher puts his hand on my shoulder, leans down to look into my face.

There's a screech outside. I pull the door open. The car is gone.

CHAPTER THIRTY-NINE

I HAVE NO IDEA what time it is. Hospitals look no different in the middle of the night than they do during the day. The halls are always dark, the fluorescent lights always flickering. I'm in the intake room, sitting in a bed whose only privacy from the ten or so other beds is a thin curtain.

My parents are off somewhere speaking with the doctor. What they could possibly need to discuss with a total stranger that they can't discuss with me, I don't know. When my parents arrived at the hospital they didn't chastise me for sneaking out. They didn't say anything at all. They didn't have to. Their eyes said everything.

I shift, trying to get comfortable. It's impossible. Everything hurts. My body feels hard and weak at the same time, frozen taffy one strike away from shattering. There are scratches on my knees, on my palms, purple splotches on my arms and thighs. My foot's gone numb from the ice. I'm lucky, they say. It's not broken. But everything below my ankle is swelled up to double what it normally is.

But what really hurts isn't my body. My greatest pain is internal, my head flooded with questions. Jackson never showed. I kept looking for him, hoping to see his face break through the throng of police, illuminated by the flashing lights of the ambulance, but he never came. He's the one who texted me. He's the one who asked me to meet him. Okay, maybe he got spooked by the police, but didn't he even care enough to check and see if I was okay?

There are darker thoughts too. Could he have had anything

to do with what happened tonight? Could he have had anything to do with what happened to June? There has to be some explanation, doesn't there?

The pain killers are starting to kick in, and all I want to do is sleep, quiet my mind of these ideas for even a little while. I shut my eyes against the light and hear the curtain slide open on the metal rail.

But it's not my parents behind it. It's the detectives: Dumb and Dumber. Fabulous.

"Did you find him?" I ask. I've already told my story to the police who showed up at the store.

They look at each other, deciding who should talk first. It's Boyer who does.

"Why don't you tell us exactly what happened, Emma?" She seems almost sarcastic, like her showing up at all is just her humoring me.

"So no, then?" I ask, angry. Of course they haven't.

"We need a little more information," Detective Simms says.

"You want me to draw you a map?" I ask, tired of jumping through their hoops. "Maybe give you his name and address and favorite animal and childhood best friend?"

"If you've got it, sure." Boyer says without missing a beat. "Lucky break, by the way, getting hit by a car without breaking a single bone. If I were religious, I might call that a miracle."

"What do you guys actually do for a living? Because they can't possibly pay you for this."

Boyer scowls at me. "Listen, kid, I've had just about enough of your bullshit to last me two lifetimes, okay? We got questions, and you're gonna answer them."

"I thought you couldn't question me without my parents around?"

"Rules are different when you're the victim of a crime. And that's all you are, right?" Boyer says.

Simms steps in, probably stopping Boyer from punching me in the face. "All we want is to verify the information you gave our colleagues," he says. "Shouldn't take more than a couple minutes."

I glare at them both. "Somebody tried to run me over three times and crushed my cell phone in the process. I'm sure you can see the pieces if you look in the street. They were driving a maroon car, four doors, no idea of the make and model, but the first three digits of the license plate were 8MK. That's all I know."

"Why didn't the butcher, Fred Hughes, see this vehicle?" Boyer asks.

"How should I know? Why don't you ask him?"

"We did," Boyer says. "He said he didn't see any car, just you."

"What about the security camera? I saw one above the door," I say.

"The camera only shows the door, not much beyond it. It didn't see a vehicle," Simms says.

"Okay. But I did see it, and I'm telling you it was maroon, four doors, license plate 8MK-something. I mean, how many cars could possibly fit that description?"

"We've got people checking into it," Simms says. "How about you tell us what brought you to be in that area so late at night?"

Should I tell them or not? If I don't, and he's guilty, it will look exactly like what they're thinking. Like I made it up. But if I do, and he's innocent, then it could be even more damaging. To both of us.

"I just wanted a little fresh air," I say.

"You got plenty of trails in that fancy neighborhood of yours. Why didn't you walk down one of those?"

"I don't know. Maybe I got a little nervous because you guys have been following me everywhere lately and everything I do seems to make you think I'm a killer?"

Boyer leans back in her chair, satisfied with herself. She shrugs. "Say we are keeping an eye on you," she says. "Why should you be worried about what we see tonight?"

Simms shoots Boyer a "watch yourself" look, making me wonder exactly what the rules are right now, and if they're really following them.

"If there's anything you haven't told us before, Miss Grant, now would be the time," Boyer says.

There's plenty more I could say, but I don't. If Jackson was involved, I need to find out on my own first.

"You guys are useless. I'm done talking to you without my lawyer."

CHAPTER FORTY

IT'S AFTER 4 A.M. when we leave the hospital. My mother wakes me at 6:30.

"Wha…?" I ask, my speech slurred by exhaustion.

"I said wake up. It's time to get ready for school."

The glare I give her must be the glare-iest of my life. Or maybe not. I'm not sure I have any control over my face right now.

"On two hours sleep?" I ask.

"What you choose to do with your evenings has no effect on whether or not you go to school the next day."

"But—"

"Now."

She leaves. I guess I shouldn't be surprised. Before I went to bed last night they grounded me for another month, which puts me on lockdown past graduation and into the summer. Hopefully I won't be around that long. Is there still a chance for New York? I have to believe there is, or I won't make it through even today.

It's a fight to sit up, a fight to stand, a fight to haul myself to the shower. Every motion is slowed by my aching body, my swollen foot, and my heavy lids. The only thing that keeps me going is the thought of how much bigger a fight it would be to stay home.

I throw on a baggy sweatshirt and yoga pants and throw my hair into a bun. With the laces as loose as possible, my foot just barely fits into my tennis shoes, as swollen as it is. Luckily the ACE bandage the doctor wrapped my ankle in last night is hidden by my pants. I can't imagine having to explain all this to everyone at school, on top of everything else I'm dealing with.

Neither of my parents says anything to me as I slurp down my green tea. They don't even look at me. There are bags under their eyes, but they zoom around like toddlers who know they'll fall asleep if they stop moving. It's a fight for them to be awake too. They're making a point. The Grant family does not negotiate with terrorists, especially teenage ones. It's infuriating, but there's no way I'm going to be the first to back down.

They drive me to school early. The halls are nearly empty. Only the quiet movements of teachers in their classrooms.

It's hard to recognize my reflection in my locker mirror. My face is puffy, dark half-moons hang under my eyes. If anyone else looked like this I'd probably think they were on drugs. The thought suddenly seems hilarious. I laugh.

"What's so funny?" Mike stands two feet away.

"Everything," I say, then stuff the laughter away. "Nothing. I'm just tired."

"What's the matter with you? You look like crap."

I should keep a tally of how many times I want to smack him, so that I can accurately deliver after all this is over.

"Thanks for noticing," I say. "I barely got any sleep last night."

"You don't have to get all snappy with me. I came early today so I could see you."

"Okay," I say.

He grabs my hand. "I've missed you." He leans in, but I lean away.

"Mike." My voice is a warning, not an invitation.

He doesn't listen. Instead he kisses me, his mouth covering my lips entirely as he searches with his tongue. It's revolting. I pull away.

"Mike. Knock it off."

But he doesn't, he presses me against the locker, his chest to mine. "It's fine. There's nobody here." He kisses me again.

"I'm not doing this with you." I say, and turn my head away again.

He grips my wrist tight. "Yes, you are," he says. "You owe me."

"Excuse me?" I say, trying to free my wrist from his grasp,

but he's holding it so tight. "I don't owe you anything."

Then he has my other hand too, and he's pinning both of them above my head with just one of his, against the locker's vent, its flaps digging into my flesh.

He whispers in my ear. "I want it too. I want what you gave him."

His other hand darts down between my legs, that place he's never been. I shove him with my knee as hard as I can, and he stumbles backward.

He looks up at me, breathing hard, his eyes nearly as shocked as mine.

"What's wrong with you?" I say.

There's a look on his face then, a realization of what he's done. "I'm sorry. I crossed the line. I'm sorry." But the tone of his voice is noble, not apologetic. He's sorry for the wrong thing. He's sorry he went too far, yes, but not because I didn't want him too. He's sorry because it's further than he's supposed to go in general. Further than God wants him to go. I'm not a part of the equation at all.

"Leave me alone, Mike. Seriously." I walk away, limping on my bad foot.

"Emma, come on." His voice is pleading. "I messed up, I'm sorry. Let me… At least let me apologize?"

I keep walking, but he's right behind me.

"I got carried away, okay? But it's only because I love you. I'm only trying to do what's best for you," he says.

"Really?" I say, turning to face him. "You…are…so… ridiculous! Do you know what a joke you are?"

My voice sounds hysterical. The words are mean, I know they are, but his actions and my pain and lack of sleep have reduced my filter to nothing.

He sputters, and his face twists into an expression I've never seen before. He looks like an ape, befuddled by a banana.

"No, *you* are," he says with all the force of a child, unable to come up with anything better, pouting like he used to when Paige got a bigger slice of birthday cake.

A laugh explodes from my mouth. He's wanted me to be afraid of him, and I have been. I've let him intimidate me into this stupid arrangement. But now? He looks like an idiot.

"Shut up," he says.

But I can't stop. My stomach hurts from it. I double over, use the locker wall for support. Ben and Chuck walk up.

"What's up with her?" Chuck asks, a smile behind his voice.

"She's acting all crazy," Mike says.

"Okay," Chuck says.

They all seem to stop, take a closer look at me. I'm not sure if they've ever seen me like this before—messy, tired, no makeup. My usual polish has disappeared.

"What's going on with you, Emma?" Ben asks. "Like, for real?" The tone in his voice is curious. Not good curious, disappointed curious. If he sounds like that, then I must look even worse than I thought. The realization helps me out of my fit.

"Nothing…nothing," I say, gulping deep breaths and wiping my eyes.

"She needs to get right with God, that's what," Mike says.

"Oh my god. You seriously have to stop. That's what an insane person would say." Only I'm the one who sounds insane and I know it.

Ben turns to Chuck. "Is she like, on something?"

Chuck shrugs.

"Oh my god, you guys," I say. "You can't be serious."

Mike scoffs. "Listen to yourself, Emma. You're so lost right now."

I catch his eye and hold it. I can see his confidence waver. Not a lot, but enough. I grab his arm.

"I'm done pretending, okay? Leave me alone. Or you will regret it. I promise you."

He yanks his arm away from me. "Maybe you're the one with more to lose, Emma. Maybe you should think about that."

Shit. Shit. Shit. Shit. Shit. I shouldn't have said that. I shouldn't have said any of that.

"I'm sorry, okay?" I say. But the look on his face tells me it's too late.

"Let's get out of here," he says, and the guys go.

I fall asleep in homeroom. I fall asleep in British lit. When Mr. Stearns has to yell my name to ask me about a passage in Leviticus I startle awake and almost scream. Usually something like that would make us all crack up, but today the whole class just stares wide eyed at the mess I am.

Paige whispers to me during quite study time.

"What's wrong?"

"Nothing. Just tired."

"Clearly. But you're more than tired, Emma. You're limping. What's going on?"

I don't trust myself to just tell her about last night. If I open the bottle, it's all going to spill out.

"I took a walk last night and fell. Had to go to the hospital. Didn't get much sleep."

"What did you say to Ben this morning? Do you know what people are saying?"

"No talking, ladies," Mr. Stearns says.

Paige leans back in her desk but doesn't stop staring at me. I excuse myself to the restroom and sleep in the handicapped stall until the final bell rings. When I wake up, my head feels a little clearer.

I wait for the din in the halls to die down then venture out, sneaking through the back exit instead of going to my mom's office. When I'm sure there's no police following I walk a few blocks to catch a bus back home, and find the spare key to my car so I can drive to Jackson's house. There are some things we need to talk about.

CHAPTER FORTY-ONE

EVEN THOUGH IT'S LESS than ten miles away from my house, Jackson lives in the kind of neighborhood most people at church would call "seedy." Which is a totally stupid thing to say, especially after you spend any time here. I have, and I've never felt any sort of danger at all. I doubt the crime stats are any different than my neighborhood.

But the people I've grown up with find things like gnomes on the lawn and motor homes in the driveway distasteful. I used to too, before I knew not to. Jackson laughed at me outright the first time we came here and I asked if there was gang activity in the area. I was such an asshole back then.

His house is a ranch with blue siding and white trim and a miniature Dutch windmill in the flower bed up front. There are three bedrooms, a living room, a bathroom, and a kitchen on the main level, but you could fit most of that in just our family room. He lives here with his parents and two brothers. One of the brothers goes to community college and hogs most of the basement.

I see Jackson's lime green 1972 Gran Torino in the driveway. His grandfather gave it to him a couple years ago, and he's been working on restoring it ever since. It's his baby. There's no way he'd be anywhere without it.

I park on the sidewalk and walk up to the door. There's a television blaring inside, or maybe a video game. There are lots of explosions. I'm hoping his parents aren't home. I've never met them, and I'm not sure I want to, at least not now. I definitely don't want today to be the first time. Besides, Jackson says there won't be much to miss family-wise when we go. I've never asked him to explain.

I ring the doorbell, and the noise stops. Jackson opens the door. He's wearing jeans and an old orange T-shirt. It's the kind of clothes that make me wish I was a boy sometimes: anti-heel, anti-tights, anti-spanks.

When he sees it's me, he breaks into a grin. "Em! What are you doing here?" He snatches me into his arms and lifts me right off the doorstep. "Why didn't you let me know you were coming?"

I pull away from his grasp. He looks confused. It's so hard not to kiss him.

"Where were you last night?"

"Last night?" The look on his face says he has no idea what I'm talking about.

"You texted me. I snuck out to meet you."

"I didn't text you, Em, I couldn't have," he says. "My phone got stolen yesterday."

"You didn't text me? You swear?"

"I swear. I was working after school yesterday. You know how they don't want us having phones on, so I left it in my trunk with my backpack. Somebody broke into my car and took everything."

He shuffles off to find something. "Look. Here's a copy of the police report."

"Oh my god," I say.

I read it over, and it's written down exactly like he said. The realization of what really happened last night sinks in.

"Em, what the hell happened to you?" he looks irritated, not mad at *me* exactly, but mad. "I wasn't gonna say anything, but you look like you got the shit beat out of you."

"Can I have a glass of water, please?"

We go inside. I limp into his kitchen where I sit down and he hands me a cup. He toes at a loose corner of linoleum on his floor while he watches me drink it down. I had no idea how thirsty I was.

"Can you please tell me what's going on now?"

I do. I tell him the whole story. The texts I got from him, the midnight meeting, how I was attacked.

"Seriously?" he says.

"Seriously."

"I didn't text you, Em. And there's no way I would have been cool with you walking around in the middle of the night by yourself like that. You know that, right?"

"I know." I say, even though I wasn't so certain last night. I lean into his chest, pull him toward me. He crushes me against him, and I wince.

He pulls away immediately. "Oh god, sorry."

"Don't stop. It's okay. I'm fine." I can trust him. That's all I need right now. Everything else will heal.

And then I think of something else. "You know what? That text said to meet you at the park. Not our spot. The park. We never call it that."

He shakes his head. We both know what this means.

"Somebody texted me with your phone," I say. "Somebody's been following us enough to know we meet at City Park. Which means they know a lot about me. And a lot about you too," I say.

"It also means they went pretty far to try to hurt you last night. Stealing my phone, getting you alone? That's seriously fucked up."

"I know."

He grabs his keys from the counter, and then my hand. "Fuck it. I'm not doing this anymore. We're going to the police."

I call my parents before we leave. We take his car. I sleep on the way there. When I wake up we are in the parking lot of the police station, and the sun is shining through the window and Jackson is stroking my hair. I look into his eyes, and I imagine us in Central Park. I imagine us on the Brooklyn Bridge. I imagine us in a tiny, shitty apartment making pancakes on a Sunday morning. My dreams seemed so small once, so easy.

Now? I might be kissing every single one of them goodbye.

"Are you sure we should be doing this?" I ask.

He pulls his hand away from my hair, takes his keys out of the ignition. "I'm not cool with this anymore, Em," he says. "I'm not gonna just sit around all day wondering if someone's trying to hurt you. Come on. We're going inside."

CHAPTER FORTY-TWO

"I'M SORRY I LIED," I say. "I shouldn't have done that. But now you know everything."

My dad's face has turned to stone. My mom's propping her head up with her hand. They put Jackson in another room with some other detectives before we even started.

I've told Detective Boyer exactly what happened the night June was killed, and everything that's happened since. Well, everything except the gun. Even I'm not stupid enough to tell them about that.

"So you were cutting a demo tape of the two of you? In the recording studio at your church?"

The look on Boyer's face says it all. Why on earth would she believe me?

"Yes," I say. It's not the only thing we were doing, but it's why Jackson was there in the first place. I fish something out of my purse. Luckily Jackson was smart enough to think of bringing it.

"What's this?"

"It's a CD with the audio files that we recorded that night."

"You got any record it was that night, and not some other night?"

"No. Jackson wiped the files off the computer, so no one would know we used it."

Detective Boyer taps the CD against her hand, then pops it into a laptop that's sitting in the room.

"We don't need to listen to it," I say.

"What? Why? You've got such a pretty voice. I'm sure we'd

all like to hear you sing."

"It's private."

She double-taps her index finger on the laptop. "I thought you wanted to be famous, Emma?" She presses play. My voice comes out of the tiny speakers. My voice and Jackson's guitar. It's faint at first, then stronger as Detective Boyer turns up the volume. I lower my eyes, stare at the table, stare at anything but my parents.

Sunlight on your back, in my eyes.
Feeling the weight
Of your heart over mine.
The feel of your hands.
The feel of you.
My love. My love. My love.

I look up to see my mom trying to press the tears back with a Kleenex. My dad is staring at the wall across from him, his face hard. It's not exactly how I imagined someone hearing it for the first time. I imagined smoke-filled bars and heads nodding along in the darkness. Not this.

Finally, Boyer turns it off. "Now isn't that sweet?" Boyer says. "We've got ourselves a couple of lovebirds here, don't we?" She leans forward in her seat, "Did you write that yourself?"

"Yes."

"Wow. That's pretty impressive. A little sappy for my taste, but not bad, as far as those kinda songs go." She crosses her arms over her chest. "You know what I don't get, though? If you were really just recording a CD, well, that seems like a pretty stupid lie to tell, don't you think?"

"My parents didn't know about Jackson. They wouldn't have approved."

"No kidding we wouldn't have approved," my dad says.

"Frank. Calm down," my mom says.

"But still, keeping a secret like this when you know we're looking into you?" Boyer says. "Why would you do that?"

I pull out the final card in my hand. "Ask Mike. He knows. He saw us…kissing." He saw a lot more than that.

"Michael Kent? That's not what he told us."

"Ask him again. He'll tell you. I'm surprised he hasn't called you already."

"Here's the thing. I believe you." The tone in her voice makes me think there's a catch coming.

"You do?" I ask.

She pops out the CD from the laptop, puts it back in its case. "Well, this? I don't know about this. This you could have made any time. But I believe you were with Jackson that night. That much I believe. Kid has quite a record."

She takes a deep breath and blows it out slowly.

"Do you remember what I told you about lying, Emma? About how I don't like it?"

"I remember."

"Good, good. I'm gonna ask you a few questions now. And this time, I want the truth."

We go through the whole story again and again and again. I'm so tired. She must see it, but she doesn't let up. It's the same questions over and over, stated differently, but all the same. She's trying to catch me in a lie. But it's so much easier to avoid the trap when I stick to the truth, and that's all I'm telling anymore.

My head sinks down to the table. I'm drifting away again when she asks:

"Are you familiar with the name Trixie Burnette?"

This question is new. She threw it in hoping to catch me off guard. It works.

"Yes," I say.

"How do you know Mrs. Burnette?"

"She goes to our church. She's kind of like a grandma to everybody. We call her Aunt Trixie," I say. "Why do you ask? Is she okay?"

"She's fine. A little head cold at the moment, but she'll be okay. Have you visited Mrs. Burnette lately?"

"No. I've never visited her," I say.

"Yes, you have," my dad says. "We dropped off some soup for her."

"Frank," my mom says. Her tone is a warning. She's telling him to stop talking.

"No. We're telling the truth. Come what may, we're telling the truth."

"So you've been to her house, Emma?" Boyer asks.

"I guess so. I totally forgot about it, though. We weren't there long. I didn't even go inside. We just handed it to her at the door and left."

"When was this?"

My dad speaks up. "A year ago? Maybe more? She was going through chemo at the time. Why? What does Mrs. Burnette have to do with any of this?"

"Do you know what kind of car Mrs. Burnette drives?" Boyer asks.

"No," I say.

Detective Boyer opens a file. I realize it has been sitting there the entire time we've been in here. She's been building up to this moment for over an hour. I get nervous. Anything this important to her can't be good for me.

She pulls out a photograph. It's a maroon sedan. A Cadillac I think, with four doors.

"Does this car look familiar to you?" she asks.

"Yes," I say, surprised. I picture it in the dark. I picture it with the tail lights lit up. I picture it bearing down on me, its wheels squealing. "I think that was the car from last night."

"You think or you know?" Detective Boyer asks.

I take a second look. The license plate reads 8MK-42A.

"That was the car," I say. "But there's no way Aunt Trixie could have been driving it. She's tiny. I think the driver was taller. It's hard to tell when somebody's sitting down."

"You know what? I think you're right," she says. "Here's the funny thing about this car. Mrs. Burnette reported it stolen yesterday, right out of her garage. Turned up abandoned in a tow-away zone this morning."

"Do you know who was driving it?" I ask.

She doesn't answer, just leans back in her chair, satisfied. "You know the other funny thing about this car? That's not the right license plate. We were a little stumped last night. Turns out those three digits are pretty unique. Only car that had them was a Nissan Pathfinder. But that's an SUV, not a sedan."

"So the driver switched the plates?"

"That's right, Miss Grant. That's right. You wanna know the last funny thing about this whole thing? That Nissan Pathfinder? Turns out it belonged to your boyfriend's next-door neighbor."

"Somebody is trying to frame me," I say. "Do you think if we'd actually done it we would have used a plate from Jackson's neighbor?"

"You ever heard of Occam's Razor?" she asks. "Basically says that the simplest explanation is probably the right one. You think that sounds like the simplest explanation?"

"It does to me, because I know I didn't do it. So the simplest explanation is that someone wants you to think I did."

"Uh huh," she says. She pulls out another piece of paper from the folder. She slides it toward me. "What does 'come clean' mean?"

I look at the paper. It's a transcript of the texts yesterday afternoon.

Jackson's phone to me:
Going crazy. Need 2 see u.
I think we should come clean.
Can u meet me?
Me to Jackson's phone:
?????????
Lots to tell u, but grounded, can't meet.
Hang tight. Will call 2nite.
Love you.
Jackson's phone to me:
Please. I need u.
The park? After bed?
Please.
Me to Jackson's phone:
Ok. midnight. See u there.
Love u. B strong.

The fact that they have this, so soon after we came in, maybe even before, makes me wonder if they knew about Jackson all along.

"What does 'come clean' mean, Emma?" she asks again.

"Just look up the police report he filed. Jackson didn't write that." I lift up the paper. "So this? It means someone is being very deliberate about trying to frame me."

"You think no one's ever filed a false report before? We get them for insurance all the time."

I sink back into my chair.

"Why don't we go through your story again?" Boyer says.

It's nearly nine when I finally get out of the room, and it's only after I ask if I can go. It was going nowhere. They don't believe me. I'm the boy who cried wolf, and soon I may be eaten by one. I should have been honest with the police from the start.

I go through the hallway into the lobby alone. My parents sent me out so they could have a private talk with Boyer before we go.

I'm guessing Jackson's been waiting for me for a while, but he's not in the lobby. I scan the parking lot and see his car is there. He must still be talking to the police. I ask at the front desk.

"Has Jackson Thomas finished up yet?"

"I have no idea, Miss," the guy says. He has that eye-rolly tone in his voice that's supposed to make me think I'm wasting his time.

"They're still back there," a woman's voice answers. I hadn't noticed her before, but it only takes a glance for me to have a pretty good guess about who she is. She's sitting in a chair in the corner and looks as exhausted as I feel. She's thin and tall with split-end prickled hair that looks on the verge of giving up. She clutches a raincoat to her chest. Her long, boney fingers look like they belong on a woman much older than her forty-ish years. The thing that makes me know, though, is her eyes: dark fields that shift like wheat on a moonlit night. They're exactly like Jackson's.

"He was doing really well, getting his life back together," she says.

I don't say anything. I don't know what to say. We've never met, his mother and I. It's not exactly a good first impression.

"It was a girl last time too, you know. He did all that stuff for a girl." Her words bite. Whatever trouble she believes her son is in, it's my fault. I'm mute because she's right. Jackson wouldn't be here right now if it wasn't for me.

"What is it about boys that makes them do damn near anything for a little pussy?" She looks me up and down. "At least the last girl was pretty."

Tears prick my eyes. "I'm sorry," I say. "I didn't mean to get him into trouble."

"Sure you didn't. You do that little-miss-innocent act for him too? I'm a girl too, sweetheart. I know all the tricks."

I swipe at my eyes. "You can think whatever you want about

me, but your son didn't do anything wrong. He was just in the wrong place at the wrong time."

"You think it matters if he's actually guilty?" She scoffs. "That's the thing about the police. They don't need real guilt. All they need is enough to make a jury believe he is. And a kid with his background? He wasn't guilty last time either, but it didn't make a bit of difference. Not after what that girl said."

"I don't understand." Jackson never said anything about a girl.

"It was the girl that wanted to shoot that kid, not Jackie." Shoot? Jackson didn't say anything about a gun. "She made up a story about that kid attacking her so of course Jackie lost it. He didn't even put bullets in the gun, just wanted to scare him. But all the police found afterward was the gun in his room. The rest didn't matter."

She stands, and she's even taller than I thought she was, nearly six feet, I'd bet. Jackson said she used to be a model when she was a teenager, and I can almost see it. Under the cry-puffy eyes and wind-ravaged hair there's a bone structure and symmetry to her face that's piercing.

"I won't let that happen to him again, understand?" she says. "I won't."

"Mom? What's going on?" The voice is Jackson's. He's standing behind me with someone who must be his dad. He's tall, six-five probably, and lumberjack strong.

"I should go," I say. "I'm really sorry."

"Emma, wait," Jackson says. But I don't.

I hurry outside. It's raining now. It's the kind of hard spring rain that can't decide if it wants to be liquid or ice. It feels like shards of glass hitting my face, but I like it. Out here, no one can see the tears. I fumble for my keys and remember. Jackson gave me a ride. I have to go home with my parents.

Jackson bursts out the door. "You can't listen to her," Jackson says. I don't say anything. Slowly, the rain dots on his shirt blend together until there are no more dots, just wet. "She's just trying to protect me, okay? She'd say anything."

"Like that you pulled a gun on somebody?" I ask.

His forehead wrinkles in pain, and I know it's true. He shoves his hands in his pockets and looks down at the ground.

"Why didn't you tell me? Especially after all this?"

"Would you really be with a guy like me if you knew that?"

Maybe he's right. I don't know if I would have, especially not back when we first met. Now, everything twists up in my mind, throwing all my fears into the spotlight and mixing them up with all that we've shared since.

I start to speak, not sure what words will come out. Not sure whether this is something I can forgive or whether it means so much more. But just as I get the breath into my lungs, my parents walk out.

My dad glares at Jackson. I've never seen so much hate in his eyes. I've never seen Jackson look so small.

"Come on, Emma. We're leaving," my dad says.

He grabs my elbow, actually grabs it, and yanks me toward the car.

I don't say goodbye, just look back at him and see his rain-wet face, and his shoulders, shivering in the cold. At least that's what I try to tell myself, that the shaking is because of the cold.

CHAPTER FORTY-THREE

"I'M AT THE END of my rope, Emma. I really am," my mom says. She's pacing, walking a path in front of me on the couch.

I don't say anything. There's nothing to say.

I look over to my dad. We're in the family room, and he's sitting on a stiff wingback chair that's really a recliner. He's staring at his folded hands. He has the same look he used to get before he spanked me as a child. If I was younger, he probably would.

Finally, he speaks. They're the first words I've heard from him in two hours.

"What would you do, Emma, if you were in our position?" he asks. He's not really looking for my opinion. He's illustrating his own frustration.

"I don't know," I say. Believe me? Help me? Defend me?

"We're worried about you," my mom says.

"I know you are. I'm sorry. I should have been honest about Jackson."

"It's not just that," my mom says. "It's the lying and the secrets and the way you've been acting lately. Principal Hendricks came to see me today. He said that your grades are slipping, that you failed two tests."

"I've just been under a lot of pressure."

"He also said some of the teachers and students had concerns about whether you were on drugs today. They even went so far as to search your locker." Her voice is shaky, unsure. It comes out as almost a question, but not quite. She wants me to tell her she's wrong. "Are you on something, Emma?"

"Of course not," I say. "I got hit by a car last night. I got no sleep. I could barely stay awake at school today. I shouldn't have been there at all."

She just shakes her head.

"Stop it with the excuses. We heard the song, Emma. We saw the texts. We know you're far more involved with that boy than you've told us," Dad says. His face has gone apple red. This is the last thing he wants to be talking about with his daughter. There's no manual for Your-Daughter-Is-Possibly-A-Slut-And-A-Murderer. I almost feel sorry for him.

My mom gives him a look to back down then crosses the room and sits next to me on the couch, her knees angled toward me, ankles crossed, back straight. She's always careful of every nuance in her body and demeanor, a side effect of her upper-class upbringing. Right now she could just as easily be talking to the Ladies Aid Society circa 1950 as sitting in her own living room with her disgraced teenage daughter.

When I was a child, I used to imitate her, sitting prim and proper, but I got the sense eventually that she didn't like it. She'd see me at the dinner table folding my napkin across my lap, trying to impress her. But she'd look away, intentionally not giving me attention for the behavior. The generous part of me likes to think she didn't want to subject me to the same standards she grew up with, didn't want to Stepford-ize me the way she felt she had been. The less generous part wonders if she married my father because in his world she was rare and precious, and didn't want anyone, including her own daughter, to have a piece of what made her special.

Seeing her now, just as untouchable, just as perfect as always, makes me recoil. I fold myself into the corner, hugging my knees to my chest.

"What's going on between you and that boy?" she asks.

"Nothing. Really," I say. "It's not a big deal."

"Don't lie to me. I can see it on your face. And frankly, I've been seeing it for months," she says.

"I don't know what to tell you," I say. It sounds like a challenge coming out of my mouth. Maybe it is.

She sighs, and then scoots back into the couch. She tucks her knees under herself, still like a proper lady at a picnic, but at least more relaxed. She stares out the window into the slowly darkening backyard. We're both quiet for a long time.

"Can I tell you something?" she asks, though it's not really a question. "I wasn't a virgin when I married your father."

"Gloria—" my dad says.

What did she just say? My eyes lift cautiously from my knees to her face.

"No. It's time she knows." She turns back to me. "You know my parents aren't believers. I didn't come to Jesus until my senior year of high school, and by then it was already too late."

I can't believe this. My perfect mother wasn't a virgin when she got married?

"And once you've crossed that line, well, it's very difficult to stay on the other side of it. I struggled with it quite a bit, even after I called myself a Christian, until I met your father."

I'm equally shocked and fascinated. This little dent in her makes her more human to me than she's ever been before. I want to ask her questions, figure out who she was back then. I want to know everything, except maybe the bits about my dad.

"He was the first man who respected me enough not to pressure me."

I sneak a glance at him. He's looking away, probably wishing he wasn't here, clearly angry that she's telling me this story. He probably thinks it's giving me permission.

Mom scoots closer, reaches out her hand to mine. It feels good. "So whatever you have to tell me, it can't be as bad as what I've done in my life, okay? All I'm asking is for you to be honest."

She's looking me right in the eyes now. I want to tell her everything, but I'm scared.

"There's nothing we can't figure out together, but not unless we're honest with each other, okay?"

I nod. It would feel so good to let it go, put it behind me. But the words won't come out of my mouth.

"Have you and Jackson had sex?"

I nod yes.

Tears dot the corners of her eyes, but she fights them back. I think she doesn't want me to know how much this hurts her to hear, but I do know. I've always known it would. She blames herself.

"Thank you for being honest with me," she says, but her tone has gone icy. I know right away I've made a mistake.

My dad speaks, his tone direct and even. "You've demonstrated an extreme lack of discretion and self-control in your personal relationships and at school and in your behavior toward your mother and me." Discretion. Of course. It all leads back to them. "It's as though a thief has come in the night and stolen the daughter we loved. You're not the person we thought you were."

"No, I'm not," I say. "I can't be." My voice is choked. I didn't plan to tell them yet, but I've come this far, haven't I?

"What do you mean?" It's my mom. Her voice is almost broken. It's the most unsure of herself I've ever heard her, and exactly why I wanted to avoid having this conversation until I was long gone.

I am their only child. They look at me as an accomplishment. Who I really am will not just disappoint them, it will rock their own beliefs about themselves. It feels selfish of me, wrong, like something I would say for the sole purpose of hurting them. But it's not to hurt them, not at all. It's just the truth. And the truth is the only way forward.

"I don't know if I believe in God anymore," I say. "At least not the way you want me to."

My mother drops her face to her hands. My father leaves the room.

CHAPTER FORTY-FOUR

IT HAPPENED AT CAMP IdRaHaJe last summer. Well, it started a long time before that, but it ended there.

IdRaHaJe is the summer camp everyone in our Rocky Mountain Church District goes to. And it's not some name for a Native American tribe that you've never heard of. It stands for I'd Rather Have Jesus. I mean, seriously? No one ever asks, "Rather than what?"

It was the last night of camp. We'd been there all week, and I remember thinking that this was it. My last chance, His last chance.

It was sweat sticky and July hot. The crowd inside the barn-turned-church was teeming with an invisible energy that tore through them like a tornado through brush, only I couldn't feel any of it. There were kids dancing and crying and raising their hands to the sky. There were kids speaking in tongues, kids slain in the Spirit, lying on the floor in spiritual comas as others huddled around them, their hands outstretched to pray over them.

I wanted it too.

I'd been wanting it forever. Receiving your spiritual gifts for the first time is sort of like getting a letter from Hogwarts. You either get one or you don't, and it's kind of a big deal if you don't. I'd been jealous ever since Chloe Aster started speaking in tongues at our sixth grade outdoor ed trip. It was like a domino effect after that, everyone finding their gifts of the Spirit. When Ruth started singing in tongues a year later, clear and full and heartbreaking, it was the most beautiful sound I'd ever heard. And when Mike gave his first prophecy a year after that, we all felt blessed and awed.

But that night at camp was five years after sixth grade, and I still hadn't had that moment all my friends had had, the moment when I felt the Holy Spirit move through me like wildfire. When I turned fifteen, out of embarrassment and jealousy, and also a little hope that the idea itself *was* God speaking to me, I started faking it, speaking in tongues so that others would think I hadn't been left behind.

It was surprisingly easy to mimic the sounds, to make up nonsense words that sounded nearly identical to what others were speaking. I figured it would happen for me eventually, and making others believe that I was the same as them would take the pressure off. But it only made me feel the pressure more, especially after nothing happened.

There were only two possibilities. Either I was unworthy, or everyone was lying, faking it just like me. Neither seemed possible, but one of them had to be the truth. I decided it was me.

So I studied more. I prayed more.

But after a year or so of being perfect, of doing everything I could think to do, even breaking up with Nicolas, who was a sexual temptation, and dating Mike, who was a spiritual leader, the growing doubts dug deeper into the cracked crevices of my heart. At youth camp, after a week of devotionals and study and prayer, I was out of ideas and spiritually exhausted.

Kids younger than me, kids who had done terrible things and average kids who seemed like lukewarm Christians at best were getting the gifts of the Spirit left and right—callings into ministry, even. Missionaries, pastors, pastors' wives, doctors, lawyers, actors, musicians—everything.

Every time I saw it happen, the same question glared in my mind like a neon sign at midnight: is it fake?

Could they all be lying, just like me?

I stopped faking it the second day of camp. It felt too false. And I thought it would help me listen. Listen and hear nothing.

Which brings me to this night, this one particular night. The last night.

The touring pastor/comedian was calling for people to come forward and receive the blessing of Jesus. His name was Pastor

Max. He was done speaking, done telling his age-appropriate jokes for a Christian crowd that eventually led back to a message. The rest of the night was supposed to be for prayer and worship, which meant we'd probably be there until 3 a.m., caught up in a Godly teen hysteria that looks something like those videos of girls at a Beatles concert, except with all the panties firmly in place.

"Who will come forward and accept the blessing of the Lord in your life? He wants to bless you. All you have to do is humble your heart and ask."

I watched someone step up toward the stage, another girl who seemed a lot like me. Not pretty, not ugly, not fat, not skinny. Just average. Long brown hair, modest jean shorts and T-shirt.

"Praise Jesus," Pastor Max said. He turned to the side and positioned the girl in front of him. He hovered a hand over her head while holding the microphone in the other. "The Lord blesses and *keeps* His children!" he shouted, and his hand came down on her head. She crumpled to the ground. I swear to god. It was like a slow-mo video of a water balloon getting popped, all the water spilling out without a form to hold it in anymore. She just wilted.

And it wasn't just that girl. The stage was littered with other kids just like her. Two waiting assistants dragged her to the side to make space in front. I watched as her head hung back, her jaw slack, watched the tears streaming down her cheeks. This was what I wanted, to be knocked out cold by the power of Christ.

I stepped forward, a little prayer humming in my heart: Show me you're real, God. Please be real, please be real, please be real.

Pastor Max stood across from me. He raised his hand above my head. "I bless you in the name of Jesus!"

His hand smacked against my skull, so hard I stumbled from the force of it, tripped, and fell backward. But I was fully awake, fully aware. It wasn't the power of Jesus. It was the power of Max.

So I stood back up. I stared at Pastor Max. Last chance, I prayed. Show me, I prayed.

The pastor turned back to me. A wrinkle crossed his brow,

and a frown threatened the corners of his mouth. He was looking at me like I was intentionally making trouble. I wasn't.

He set the microphone down on the pulpit and placed both hands on my shoulders.

"In the name of Jesus!" he said, and shoved me so hard I fell straight to the ground.

Even though my eyes were open, everyone took it to mean that I passed out. Pastor Max turned away to speak to the next kid who had come forward. I lay there for a moment, fully present, not basking in the glow of Christ, and not wanting to accept the clarity of this answer.

No one seemed to notice when I stood up and left.

CHAPTER FORTY-FIVE

"I KNOW WHAT YOU'RE going to say," I say. "So don't bother."

"How could you possibly know what I'm going to say?" Miss Hope asks.

We're sitting in the lounge side of Pastor Pete's office. My parents have scheduled this meeting with Miss Hope before school today, hoping she can talk some sense into me.

"Let me guess," I say. "I may not know it, but God is real. He's in this room with us right now. I have to trust, have faith, and then I'll be able to feel His presence."

"God isn't a genie, Emma. We can't rub a bottle and expect Him to appear. There's no formula that can make His presence felt. It's up to Him when he chooses to reveal Himself to you. So sometimes you feel it, and sometimes you don't."

"Well I don't."

"Does that mean that He doesn't exist? That if He doesn't choose to show Himself to you—Emma Grant, in Denver, Colorado—then it means there's no God at all?"

My heat rises. I feel all the arguments churning inside me, even though I know the best thing to do would be to stay silent, not engage her at all. "If He does exist, then why is it just me that He's not showing himself to, and nobody else?"

"Ah. I see what this is about. Jealousy."

"That's what I'm talking about. That right there. The minute someone starts asking questions, real questions, then it's always their fault. There's always another reason to blame them. I've tried everything I can think of, but still, nothing."

Miss Hope leans back in her seat for effect, which proves

hard to do as we're both in beanbag chairs. She fastens her gaze on me. "Really, Emma? You *really* think you've tried everything?"

"You're right. Maybe I haven't. But neither has anyone else. And the whole idea behind Christianity is that God loves us despite our faults. If that's true, then why am I expected to be perfect in order to feel His presence?"

Miss Hope sighs. She shifts forward again, rests her elbows on her knees. "Let me let you in on a little a secret," she says, her voice soft, a smile curving her thin lips. "I don't care what you believe. I really don't."

I stare at her for a moment, dumbfounded.

"It has absolutely zero effect on me whether you think there's a God or not. Absolutely zero. I'm not the one who's going to have to answer to Jesus for your sins. I'm not the one who's going to have to stand in front of our Savior and tell Him that I doubted Him, that I gave in to sexual temptation, and who knows what else you've been up to lately." There's a self-satisfied smile on her face and fire in her eyes. "James 4:4 says that whoever wishes to be a friend of the world makes himself an enemy of God. And it sounds like you've been making pretty good friends with the ways of the world lately. That, Emma, is on you."

Her words sting, and I bite my cheek to keep myself from crying. I will not cry in front of her. I look away, over her shoulder toward the door. If there was any way for me to bolt right now, I'd do it.

"I don't care what you believe, Emma, because I know what *I* believe. I know that Jesus is real. I know He died for my sins and I know that one day I will see Him in heaven and He will welcome me with open arms. And don't think that my path has been easy."

I can't look at her. My eyes drift back to Pastor Pete's perfect collection of toys and games, and they settle on the pig, the one that Pastor Pete loved so much as a kid, sitting right next to me on a low shelf. But as I'm looking at it again, something feels off about that story. All my childhood toys, especially the dolls and the teddy bears, barely survived. They're ripped and sewn back together, soiled and scrubbed a thousand times. Some of them barely have any hair left at all. I pick it up, examine it for any stains or tears. There are none. This doesn't look like a favorite toy. It looks like a new toy. Even the manufacturer's tag is still attached, printed with a clearly legible: Joya ToyCo.

"Emma, put that down. I'm speaking to you."

My eyes flash back to Miss Hope's, who is all but outright glaring at me. Sorry for not being riveted by your boring story, I want to say. I put the pig back on the shelf.

"As I was saying, God has tested me and tested me and tested me. I didn't grow up like any of you kids here. I learned to trust God the hard way. I had four brothers and six sisters, and we were very poor. My mother died giving birth to my little sister, Mercy. My whole family had to work hard on that ranch every single day just to survive."

Here we go again. Another inflated story of a sad-sack upbringing. I nestle into my beanbag chair and cross my arms. I've heard so many of these things before that I can predict where this one is headed. Soon she will find God, and everything will be magically better. It might be unfriendly of me to discount stories like this, but it's because so few of them are actually true when you start asking questions.

"But luckily, God also granted me a God-fearing father, who raised us kids right. He raised us to trust in His plan, not our own. God's plan for me is to be a pastor's wife. He called me to it at a very young age, but it was no easy thing to believe in. How old do you think I am, Emma?"

"I don't know."

"I'm thirty-two. Most women my age here have already given birth to all their children by now."

"So?"

"Don't you think it's kind of miracle that, at my age, I was able to find not only a strong Christian man, but a pastor?"

I just shrug.

"My daddy named me Hope for a reason, Emma. God had a plan for me, and I had to hope, and to pray, and to trust in that plan to see it come true. But you're failing to do that right now. Ezekiel 36:26 says, 'I will give you a new heart and put a new spirit within you; I will take the heart of stone out of your flesh and give you a heart of flesh.' So you have a choice. Right now. You can either let your doubts rule you and be content with a heart of stone, or you can accept that God's plan for you is on

His schedule, not yours, and open up your heart to receive His Spirit."

She stands up and walks to the door. "Up to you."

"Look, I appreciate what you're trying to do here, but I just don't buy it anymore."

"Very well," she says.

She goes out into the hall, and I can hear heated whispers between her and my parents but I can't understand anything they're saying. Miss Hope was obviously hoping that her little story would get through to me. But it only seems to prove exactly what I've been feeling all along. Even if her story is true, it just feels like another broken person who makes up Jesus to feel like there's some noble purpose to their pain. But what about me? What if I'm not broken?

CHAPTER FORTY-SIX

I MAKE MY WAY over the overpass and toward the upperclassman hallway, still moving slower than usual with my ankle. The swelling has gone down a lot, but there's still a pinch with every step. As I walk I try to put the whole conversation with Miss Hope behind me. It feels played on repeat in my mind. I shouldn't let it get to me. It doesn't matter what she thinks. It doesn't.

I wish I could call Jackson. He was the only one I could talk to about this kind of stuff, the only one I knew would listen and tell me I'm not crazy. But I'm just too confused right now. I need to process everything first.

I hate that he wasn't honest with me. I hate thinking of him with a gun, threatening someone. But a little part of me, the darkest part, wonders what I'm really more upset about—that Jackson lied about his past or that he cared about someone else so intensely (loved her?), enough to do what he did.

There's still a little time before class starts. Instead of going to my locker, I slip outside and find a quiet spot between the high school and elementary school buildings where no one hangs out. I just want a little time alone to think. I sit under the biggest tree and lean against the trunk, closing my eyes and soaking in the morning sun.

"Em?"

His voice is like a mirage, like I conjured him up from my desire to see him, but when I open my eyes, he's really there.

"Jackson? What are you doing here?"

"I needed to see you. I went to your house last night, but

your dad wouldn't let me in."

"You did?" I was so exhausted. I fell asleep as soon as my head hit the pillow.

He sits down next to me, resting his elbows on his knees. "Look, I owe you an apology. You should have heard the real story from me. I'm sorry."

"So it was like your mom said? You threatened someone with a gun?"

"Stupidest thing I've ever done. But it wasn't loaded, Em. I swear. I didn't trust myself with bullets."

It's hard to hear him say that, hear him acknowledge his own capacity for darkness. I honestly don't know what to say.

"I get why it has you freaked out. You have every right to be upset. But I swear I had nothing to do with what happened to your friend. Back then things were different. I thought I loved Christy. I thought she loved me."

"But you were wrong?"

"Yeah."

It's a moment before I speak, a moment before I can say the words out loud. "What if you're wrong about us too?"

He turns to look at me, his dark eyes flashing. "No. That's the one thing I'm absolutely sure of. Even more after what I've been through."

He takes my hand, and I let him.

"When I got out of juvie, I promised myself I'd turn my shit around, and that's what I've been trying to do ever since. Football helped. Getting back into school helped. Ditching my old friends too. I've done absolutely everything I could think of to make sure I don't mess up again. That includes dating a girl like you."

"Like me?"

"You're good, Emma. You're really and truly good. I wanted to be around someone who would make me a better person every day. You do that. You've changed me."

My heart spills over. I want to tell him that he's changed me too. That I was so sad before I met him, so heartbroken by the church and my life and that he showed me it wasn't the end of the world, just the end of this one. I want to tell him that he makes a universe without God in it even more beautiful and exciting and wonderful than when I believed.

But before I can, a shadow blocks the sun. "Well isn't this sweet?" Mike stands over us, stone faced and surly. "The harlot and her lover boy."

Before I know what's happening, Jackson is on his feet and throwing a punch. His fist hits Mike's face with a hard thwack, and Mike goes down. Jackson rushes forward to hit him again.

"Jackson!" I yank his elbow and he pulls back. "That's enough."

He paces, shakes it off. "Piece of shit," Jackson says. "You don't fucking talk to her like that. You don't fucking talk to her, period. Ever again, understand?"

Mike clutches his face but says nothing. He just glares. For all his talk, I doubt he's ever been in a real fight. I've never seen him so outmanned, so totally scared shitless and unsure of himself. I'd be lying if I said it wasn't a little bit satisfying.

"Did you hear what I said, motherfucker?"

Red faced and fuming, Mike scrambles backward like a crab, and runs away.

"You have to get out of here," I say to Jackson. "He's going to tell."

"So let him," Jackson says, still amped on his own testosterone.

I grab his arms and force him to look me in the eye. "You don't need the police involved in this. Go. Now."

He nods, takes a deep breath, and turns to go. But at the last second he pulls me against him and kisses me so deeply it sends a wave of electricity down to my toes. I have to fight the urge to tell him to stay, police be damned. Thankfully, he pulls away before I can say anything at all and, with a cocky grin, runs toward the parking lot.

I don't see Mike all day. I overhear someone saying he's out sick, which means he must be at home licking his wounds. Surprisingly, he didn't go to the teachers as I expected. He didn't even call the police. Jackson must have really scared him.

By the next morning it's starting to feel almost normal at school. Being grounded has given me a chance to catch up on some of my homework, and it feels good to do something so ordinary. I walk into the building with a backpack full of assignments to hand in.

The first bell rings, telling us to head to class. I pick up the pace as I head to my locker. On the way, I smile at Naomi, but she doesn't smile back. She looks away and shuffles off. That's odd. Maybe Katie finally made her a convert of the we-secretly-hate-Emma-club.

But it's not just her. Erica, Hannah, Ben, and Angela do the same exact thing. Even Chuck won't make eye contact with me. Now I'm worried. What's going on?

I see it once I turn the corner. There, in bright orange letters sprayed on my locker:

SLUT

The word sears into me. It must be Mike.

Katie walks up with a cotton-candy simper on her face. She hands me a folded paper.

"I just wanted to give you these. They're verses about seeking forgiveness."

"Did you do this?" I ask. I can barely contain my rage.

"No, sweetie," she says, her face in a best-actress mode of surprise. She puts her hand on my shoulder in a gesture of sympathy. "I'd never do anything like that to you."

Sure she wouldn't.

"It really could have been anyone, though. Everybody heard," she says.

"Heard what?" I ask.

"Mike told everyone," she says.

Shit. Shit. Shit. Shit. Shit.

It's his one last weapon against me. I thought I was ready for this, ready to tell everyone the truth, but I'm not. My face blanches so white that Katie's confidence falters. She's just staring at me now.

"What did Mike say?" I ask.

"Look, maybe you should talk to him about it." Her face is suddenly unsure. She may be happy for me to fall, but it's a very different thing to want power and to actually have it.

She tries to walk away, but I grab her arm. "Katie, please, what did he say?"

Her eyes go downcast. It's so awful she can't say it to my face.

"He didn't say it. He posted it," she says. "I gotta get to class." I release my grip, and she walks away. "I'm praying for you," she says over her shoulder, and this time I think she really means it.

I twist the lock with my combo and dump my stuff inside. Then I reach into my purse for my phone before remembering that it's sitting on the street outside Safeway, crushed into a million tiny pieces.

The halls are almost empty; I'm running out of time. I race toward homeroom. The last thing I need right now is more attention for being late.

The final bell rings right as I have my hand on the door. Miss Hope scowls at me as I enter, but doesn't single me out. Today is free study period in homeroom, and I intend to use it to see what Mike posted about me online. I have my iPad with me, but we're not allowed to use them in class, so I go to a computer and fire it up. I'm almost logged in when there's a knock on the door. It's Vicki, she's the main office student assistant this hour. She hands a note to Miss Hope.

"Emma?" Miss Hope says. Of course it's me.

"Yes?" I say.

"Principal Hendricks would like to see you in his office. Go ahead and take your things with you."

Everyone stares, whispers.

I expected this, I guess. It was only a matter of time until word reached the principal. But still, that Miss Hope told me to take my things is serious. It means I'll either be in there for a while or won't be back at all. I want to snatch the note from her hand to see what it says, but I don't. I collect my backpack and head toward the main office.

Principal Hendricks is waiting at his door for me. "Come on in, Emma," he says. His face is stern, angry, but also a little amped up. He lives for moments like this, I think. He always looks a little too excited to punish us.

I enter and settle into one of his chairs. He sits behind his desk.

"It has come to my attention that you may have broken the student conduct code," he says. "As you know, we expect our students to be ambassadors for Christ at all times. Therefore, it is against our policies for students to engage in intimate behavior with one another or non-students, either on or off school grounds. Violation of this policy can lead to immediate expulsion, at my sole discretion."

"Okay," I say. I'm aware of the policy. We all are. If your parents are forcing you to go here, the easiest way to get expelled is post something racy online. It has happened before.

I, however, do not want to get expelled. I can't even imagine the hoops I'd have to jump through to graduate at any other school at this point. The science classes alone would have me stuck in summer school. It's one of the reasons I've tried to be so careful about Jackson. Not that it worked. The police know. My parents know. And, more importantly, Mike knows.

I know what Principal Hendricks wants here, and I should do it. He wants me to grovel, confess my sins, and ask for his forgiveness so that I can walk around with a virtual scarlet letter on my chest for the rest of the year. But I don't think I can. I feel torn between what I feel is right and what will help me graduate.

The problem is that I don't feel guilty about what I did with Jackson. Not one bit. Even after everything that's happened, I don't regret making the choice that I did.

I sense a shift in myself lately. Maybe all my hiding and all my secrets were mistakes. Maybe what would have been best all along was a fight.

"I've already spoken with Michael Kent. He came to me this morning of his own free will," he says.

Something about that statement isn't right.

CHAPTER FORTY-SEVEN

I DON'T GET IT. *'Of his own free will'* implies Mike, too, is guilty. Did he say we did something together? But why?

Principal Hendricks stares at me, waiting for a response. I wish I'd had time to read what Mike posted. What I say now could affect my entire future. Does Principal Hendricks think I slept with Jackson…or Mike? It's a gamble. A huge one.

But the pieces are falling into place. Mike knows the routine as well as I do. Sin big, confess big, gain even greater respect. People would think Jackson took advantage and I was weak. But eventually, I would be forgiven for Jackson, as long as I felt bad enough about it.

So what's worse than being seduced by a non-believer? Seducing a golden boy.

That wouldn't be forgiven so easily. I would be marked as the temptation, marked as easy. Mothers would warn their sons against me. The other girls would band around their boys, righteous, holy protection from me. He doesn't just want to ruin my reputation. He wants to make me a pariah.

"I have no idea what Mike told you, but I know for certain we've done nothing together that has in any way violated the student conduct code," I say, going all-in on Mike lying about me. I hope it works.

Principal Hendricks stares at me. I can't tell if he's scrutinizing my honesty or galled that I would try to hide my relationship with Jackson under such a flimsy cover.

I hope, more now than ever, that my flawless history will count for something. But Mike has the same history I do.

Whatever he's said, it's his word against mine. I decide to continue.

"I only learned this morning that Mike posted something online that challenged my character. I haven't had a chance to look at it yet and have no idea what he said against me. But I think you should know that we broke up recently, and Mike was not happy about it."

"And you believe he's retaliating?" Principal Hendricks asks. I still don't know what he knows. I still don't know if Mike has told him about Jackson. But it's too late now.

"I don't know what he's doing," I say, too angry, and I'm tearing up, and my voice is getting shaky because all of this is so unfair. Mike and I have done nothing, and even if we had, why is my sex life any of the school's business? In any other school this would be a vicious rumor. Embarrassing, maybe, but nothing more. Here, it's linked to my whole life. I can't stand it anymore.

"Please calm down, Miss Grant," he says. "There's no need to get emotional." He slides a box of tissues toward me, then leans back in his chair, scrutinizing me again.

I dry my eyes and try to get my breathing under control. I have to be the rational one. Principal Hendricks is not the type of man who responds to tears.

"It saddens me very much to think that one of the two of you is lying to me," he says, "and one of you most certainly is. Whoever it is, they will be severely punished."

"It's not me," I say in the most controlled way I can manage, and look him straight in the eye.

"I'll give you one last chance, Ms. Grant, to tell me your side of the story, to save yourself from possible expulsion. If you have anything else to say, you'd better say it now."

"I have nothing else to add," I say.

"Very well. I will take this matter under consideration and notify you as soon as I've made my decision. In the meantime you will be allowed to attend classes as usual."

"Thank you, sir," I say, and get up to leave.

"Oh, and Ms. Grant?"

"Yes, sir?"

"Please speak to the custodial department about obtaining the necessary materials to clean off your locker. I expect it to be spotless by the end of the day." A punishment. In his eyes, no matter what I've done, I am guilty by association.

"Yes, sir," I say, and it takes everything in me not to spit the words back in his face.

Out of his office, I race to the bathroom. Tears are blurring my vision again, and I have no idea how much time is left in first period. I really don't want anyone to see me like this, and I have to know what Mike said. I make it into the farthest stall and fumble inside my backpack for my iPad. I turn it on and go directly to Mike's Facebook page. I read through the post, and I feel both victory and alarm as I process what he wrote last night.

> *I need to ask all of you for your forgiveness, and I picked Facebook because I just can't stand hiding this from anyone anymore. I'm not as strong as you thought I was. I've fallen in the worst possible way. I'm not a virgin anymore.*
>
> *I know this will shock a lot of you. It sorta shocks me too. I believe exactly what I've always believed, that sex is a sacred rite reserved for marriage. But I messed up. I thought I was following my heart. I love her so much, and I just wanted to make her happy. She said she'd done it before, and I didn't want to lose her. I should have been her spiritual leader, but I wasn't strong enough to say no. I broke a promise to my Heavenly Father. I'm so sorry. I'll understand if none of you wants to be friends with me anymore.*
>
> *I'm praying a lot, and I'm not seeing her anymore. It wouldn't be right. And frankly, it's too much of a temptation still. Please pray for me.*
>
> *Your Brother in Christ,*
>
> *Mike*

I feel a small sense of victory, because I was right. Mike said we slept together. Not outright, but the meaning is there. He doesn't have to mention my name. Everyone will assume he's taking the high road, and everyone will know it's me anyway. They haven't seen Mike with anyone else for nearly a year. At least my defense to Principal Hendricks was the right move, the only move. If I had said anything else, I would have buried myself so much deeper.

Mike's post is crafted so well, though, that I can't imagine anyone believing my side of the story, ever. If he had been boastful or angry, I would have had a chance. But he's not. He's humble and regretful. I actually marvel at the genius of it. I didn't know Mike had it in him.

My anger's been replaced by a sense of defeat so strong I can't force myself to leave the stall. Everything is falling apart. The police think I'm guilty of murder, my parents hate me, my friends won't trust me anymore, and I might get expelled.

The bell rings, and I stay inside as the room fills up with chatter, trying to be silent so no one hears me. I can't stand them looking or not looking or their whispers or wide-eyed surprise. It's just too much.

I hear Paige's voice.

"No, I didn't, but it's really none of our business," she says.

"Do you think it's true?" It's Katie. "It's just, when I talked to Emma this morning she seemed, like, genuinely shocked by the whole thing." It's weird to hear Katie defend me, even a little bit. I thought she'd be dancing in the streets when she heard we broke up.

"Only they know the answer to that," Paige says, "but I don't see any reason for Mike to lie about it."

"I guess she could have been surprised he told everyone," Katie says, and I realize from her tone that she wasn't defending me at all. "She probably thought she had him wrapped around her little finger," her voice is so haughty, so gleeful that my anger is coming back. I want to slap her.

I put my hand on the stall door, ready to slam it open.

"Shut up, Katie!" Paige yells, really yells, at her. "It's none of your business either way, okay? You shouldn't be talking about it."

I hear Katie snort, and I can imagine the look on her face,

eyes wide, pretending Paige is the one whose behavior is inappropriate. It's the last straw.

I storm out. "Yeah, Katie, shut the fuck up," I say. "You have no idea what you're talking about."

"Wow. *Language*," Katie says. "You really think you need to get in any more trouble than you already are?"

I could tell her everything, but I refuse to defend myself to her. She's not worth it. I will forget her the minute I have my diploma in my hand.

"Don't lecture me, Katie. You're only a technical virgin yourself. Isn't that right?"

"Shut up," she says, and blanches because she knows exactly what I know about her. She told me herself. I continue, heedless of the fear in her eyes.

"Paige, did you know Katie let Derek Halls have anal with her after the Harvest Festival junior year?"

"Emma. Stop it." Paige says.

"So, by all means, please go around telling everyone else that I'm the slut. See how that works out for you."

"I told you that in confidence," she says. Her eyes are welling up, and I can tell my words have hit her hard.

All of a sudden I realize that none of this matters. I'm holding her to a standard that I don't even believe in anymore. I'm so messed up. I don't know how to navigate living both inside and outside this world at the same time. I don't belong anywhere.

Katie turns to Paige. "Please don't tell anyone. It only happened once."

"I don't care what you do," Paige says.

Some freshman girl bangs the door open, but when she sees our faces, she leaves.

"I'm sorry, Katie," I say. "You're right. That was private. I shouldn't have said it."

"Whatever," Katie says, and I know it's as close as I'll get to an apology from her. It doesn't matter.

The second bell rings, and Katie wipes at her eyes quickly in the mirror.

"Come on, Paige, we have to get to class," Katie says.

She starts to go, but Paige doesn't move.

"Are you coming?" Katie asks.

"In a minute," Paige says.

Katie huffs out, biting her lip so she doesn't cry again. It makes me think of her when I met her in first grade, blonde pigtails and an awkward, too-toothy smile. It was hard for her coming in even a year after the rest of us had started. She used to give away parts of her lunch, and go home hungry, just so people would like her. It's the same with her today, some part of her believing that she's not worth friendship, only now her fruit snacks are tiny bits of gossip.

I turn and realize Paige is still standing there, staring at me. I meet her eyes.

"What's wrong with you, Emma? That was really mean."

"I know. I'm sorry. It was stupid."

Paige purses her lips and looks away from me. "Is it true, what he said?" she asks.

"No," I say. "I'm sorry, Paige, but no."

She nods. I can't tell if she believes me or not. I get the sense that she's tucking away these details for later when she'll have time to figure it all out, just like me. I wish I could tell her everything. I wish I could be honest without losing her. But a part of me knows I already have lost her.

CHAPTER FORTY-EIGHT

IT TAKES ME MOST of the day to clean off my locker. All the janitor, Mr. Rassmussen, gives me is a scrub brush and a bucket of bleach water. No hard candy today. The bleach water doesn't do anything at all, but it takes two hours of scrubbing, my fingernails spongy and splitting, my skin raw from the chemicals, before he believes that elbow grease will not do the job.

I wait for another hour while he goes to the hardware store and comes back with an assortment of cleaners to try. My cuticles crack from the harshness of the chemicals, but eventually they work.

After school I force myself to go to cheerleading practice, just to have something to do. There's not much in the way of sports left to cheer for. All we have left are a couple of routines we're planning to do for the end-of-year assemblies. We've done them a thousand times by now, and it feels good to get lost in the movements.

Once practice is over, I barely have enough time to shower, change, check in with my mom, and grab a quick bagel from the Connections Café before youth group starts.

I find Pastor Pete before things get going. My parents have told him everything. He's the one who suggested I speak with Miss Hope.

"I really don't think I should be leading worship services anymore," I say, and it feels like such a relief.

He frowns, "Come on. I know everyone would love to see you up there. Maybe singing will help you feel better."

216

Singing would make me feel better. But not these songs. Jackson flashes in my mind, playing his guitar, us sitting on his bed a couple months ago, me singing along. I wish I could go back to that night. I wish it so badly.

"I'm sorry. I can't anymore."

He hesitates, not sure what to say, then falls back on, "Okay. It's up to you."

Then I remember something else.

"Oh, and…" I start, not knowing how to ask the question. "I was in your office yesterday with Miss Hope, and I saw that pig again, and…"

"Yes?"

"It's just, you said it was your favorite as a kid, but…um…it looks brand new. All my old toys are pretty beat up."

His brow furrows. Then he smiles and leans in conspiratorially, "Don't tell anyone, but I was a little bit of a neat freak as a kid."

"Oh, okay," I say, even though it's hard to believe. What sort of toddler is a neat freak?

"Can I ask you something else?"

"Sure, what's up?"

"I was just wondering. Did Nicolas or June ever come to you for any counseling?"

"I'm afraid that's private, Emma. Just like I wouldn't talk to someone else about the things we've discussed, I can't talk to you about them."

"Did you know Nicolas proposed to her?"

He looks at me, confused. "But she was so young."

Unless he's a good actor, the answer is no.

"She didn't accept, but…" I say. "I don't know, I think she was trying to. She wanted to get baptized first."

"I'm sorry she didn't have that chance."

"Were you planning to baptize her?" I ask.

"No," he smiles softly. "I usually leave that kind of thing to your dad. Why do you ask?"

"No reason, just some things she said before she died made me wonder."

He tilts his head, curious. He seems to sense that there's more to the story than that, but doesn't press me. Instead, he puts a hand on my shoulder, looks into my eyes. "Remember our conversation?"

"Um, yeah."

"You don't have to make any decisions about God right now. Just remember to keep listening, okay?"

I nod. I'm not about to get into that discussion again.

"I'm praying for you, Emma."

Everyone is praying for me.

What Pastor Pete said about the toy doesn't make sense, and it's weird enough to make me uneasy. Then I remember that there was a manufacturer's tag on the pig. Maybe I can look it up and find more information.

There's still a few minutes before youth service starts so I go across the hall for a little privacy, into the empty gym. I pull out my iPad and look up the toy's manufacturer: Joya Toyco. They have a website, and I click over to their Products page, but it's just a paragraph explaining that they specialize in plush toys, not a list of any of their specific products.

I move on to their About page. Sure enough, it says the company wasn't even formed until 2002, way too late to be Pastor Pete's toy in the '80's.

It's definitely a lie. Why would Pastor Pete lie?

And how much do I really know about Pastor Pete?

I know he's been at the church for five years. I know he graduated from Bethany Bible College and that this is his first job out of school. Which, honestly, is sort of incredible. Most pastors have to put in a lot of time in smaller churches before getting hired at a place like this. He either impressed the heck out of my dad, or he had some very powerful connections.

I doubt it was connections. I've never met his parents, or seen any brothers and sisters, or any other relatives for that matter. Paige's grandparents and aunts and uncles visit all the time. Why wouldn't Pastor Pete's do the same? He's always said that his parents raised him as a Christian. But they haven't visited even once to see him preach?

Maybe it's just my head being soaked in all of this June stuff right now, but all I can think of, the only thing I can think of, is that the pig in his office *is* the toy from June's testimony. Did she give it to him? Did he take it from her? Or am I making too much out of this? Plush pigs aren't exactly rare. Is there some other story behind that toy that he doesn't want to tell for a totally innocent and unrelated reason?

I feel jittery. What if there's more to Pastor Pete's story than I know? Or what if, more likely, I'm seeing something that's not there? What if I want to find a scapegoat so badly I'm making connections where there are none at all? I have to be careful. All I know for sure is that I need to find out more.

I hear the music starting across the hall, the slow strum of his guitar, and know I have to get myself under control. Youth group is starting. I need to get back over there.

Instead of my usual place in the second row, where I sit with everyone after the worship part of service is over, I pick a spot in back. Paige stares at me from her place at the piano, not so much confused as she is disappointed. There's a long, hard conversation ahead of me with her. But it's going to have to wait until I have this all figured out.

Soon Ruth takes my place at the mic, and it's as if I never existed. Several people glance back at me, curious, but no one seems brave enough to ask. They're probably thinking it has something to do with Mike's Facebook post. They're probably thinking that not being on stage isn't my choice at all.

It's been a long time since I've seen things from this angle, down in the seats instead of up on stage. What felt earnest and smooth, even at my worst, now looks amateurish and hacky. Pastor Pete's strumming on the electric guitar feels simple. Greyson's drums are off beat. Paige is competent on the keyboard, technically proficient but not passionate. And it may be my own pride speaking, but Ruth's voice sounds sharp— shrill and trying too hard to impress.

There's this trend in Christian music right now, maybe for a long time, to make it sound like secular music. But when they do that, it always sounds so wrong. Whether they're mimicking sexy ballads (for Jesus) or emo crooning (for Jesus), or rocking hard (for Jesus) it just makes you feel a little icky. Especially the sexy stuff. I mean, all that breathy groaning is about sex, right? So it kind of feels like all these Christian kids are totally horny for Christ.

Just as I'm thinking this, Ruth hits one of those breathy groans and closes her eyes. She's trying to show how totally into

God she is right now, how totally drowned she is in the Spirit, but it makes me certain, absolutely certain, that this is the exact face she makes when she has an orgasm, if she's ever had one at all.

I let out a little giggle. Okay, maybe not a giggle. The laugh explodes from my nose in a snort. If I was drinking milk it would bubble out of my nostrils. The guy sitting a couple chairs down turns to look, and I see that it's Chuck. Making eye contact with him only makes me laugh harder, and soon he's laughing too.

An adult at the back of the room, Roger Smith, standing watch for troublemakers, gives us a harsh look. Chuck scoots closer as I try to stifle the urge to break out in full-blown howls of laughter.

"What's so funny?" he asks in a whisper.

"Ruth…Ruth's face. She looks like…she looks like she's about to…"

Then we both look up and, I swear to god, Ruth does this little grinding sway with her hips and makes that face again, and I lose it. I absolutely lose it. Chuck does too. He knows exactly what I mean.

I feel a hand on my shoulder and hear a harsh whisper. "Okay, you two, out of here." Roger Smith is hovering over us with a scowl. I turn to look at him and he seems surprised that it's me. It makes me laugh harder.

"You're both excused until you can get yourselves together. Some people here are trying to worship the Lord."

He gives us a little shove, and Chuck and I shuffle out the back row and out the room. Everyone's giving us a look. We are definitely misbehaving. Hooligans! Troublemakers! I've never been a troublemaker before. The feeling makes me giddy.

Chuck and I wait until we're outside, and then we explode. I'm laughing so hard tears run down my cheeks. My stomach cramps from it. I take deep, full breaths trying to calm down.

"I thought she was gonna make out with the microphone." Chuck says.

And I start up again. It feels good to laugh, really good, like a friend you haven't seen in years showing up as a surprise on your doorstep.

"I know. I know," I say, finally getting myself together. "I thought she was full-on gonna, you know…finish."

"Emma Grant." Chuck raises his eyebrows in shocked respect. "We should ask Ben about that. He'd know."

"What?! Are you saying—?"

"Yeah. They definitely did it."

"When? She always acts so perfect."

"Camp last summer. They snuck away during chapel. I saw them when I got turned around coming back from the outhouse. His shorts were down. Her skirt was up."

"No way."

"Yup. Swear to God!"

"Ruth Stanger and Ben Devine?" I've known these two since they were babies. It's not like no one in youth group *ever* has sex, but it is pretty rare. And usually when they do it's followed by a tearful confession and lots of very public prayer requests. The fact that they've kept it a secret this long, even after breaking up, is pretty remarkable. It makes me wish the rules were as simple where pastors' daughters are concerned.

"I know," Chuck says. "And I'm supposed to be the black sheep. I've never done it with a girl. Not that I wouldn't." He looks me up and down, an invitation.

I give him a look that makes it clear he won't be losing his virginity to me tonight.

"Anyway. I'm just saying, everybody thinks I'm so bad, but I believe in Jesus and I haven't done half the stuff that some kids here have done."

I look at him and shake my head. I used to be one of the people that thought of him as a bad boy. He was a problem. Someone who needed to be fixed.

"I'm sorry if I ever…thought of you like that."

"No big deal," he says, looking away. But it is a big deal. I can tell. He looks so vulnerable, like a little kid clinging to his teddy bear.

Then I think of something.

"That night, did you…did you see anything weird when Pastor Pete and Miss Hope took you upstairs?"

"Naw. We were up in Pastor Pete's office. He was going at me like he usually does, like making people laugh is the worst thing a person could possibly do."

I put a falsely stern look on my face and say, "Lighting your farts on fire is a very serious matter, Chuck. You need to get right with God."

He laughs. "Yeah. That was pretty much it. He even asked Miss Hope to wait outside so he could ask if I nearly set my ass on fire to try and impress a girl. Which I was, but I wasn't going to tell him that."

"Oh really?" I say, grinning. "You dirty dog. Who was the girl?"

"Doesn't matter. She's not interested." I suddenly get the distinct feeling he's talking about me. "Anyway, then we prayed and went downstairs again. I didn't see the guy who did it."

"So Pastor Pete was there the whole time? You're certain?"

"Oh yeah."

Well, there goes that idea. At least part of it. If he was with Chuck the whole time then he couldn't have been the one who killed June. But I do have another theory. What if he agreed to baptize her in secret, because of my dad? They might have set up a meeting that got delayed when he had to deal with Chuck. But why not tell the police? Is there something else he knows that he's not saying?

Just as I'm thinking up another question to ask, I spot the flashing lights of a police car cresting the hill.

No, not one.

Five.

And they're speeding right into our parking lot.

CHAPTER FORTY-NINE

I STAND BY THE door, ready to face them. Ready for them to take me in. But as they shuffle out of their vehicles, they walk right by. Then I spot Boyer and Simms rounding up the end of the herd.

"Looks like it's your lucky day, kid," Boyer says, and goes inside.

I don't get it. I look over at Chuck.

"What was that about?" he says.

"I have no idea."

A few minutes later the police come out again. This time, they're carrying someone with them: Rick Rasmussen, the church janitor.

The story comes out in drips and spurts over the next few hours. Apparently, Mr. Rassmussen, giver of hard candy, the person everybody loves, the person no one would think twice about leaving their child with, has a computer stocked full of kiddie porn.

He made it onto the suspect list because he didn't have an alibi for that night and, as the only paid janitor on staff, also had an all-access key to the building. He told police that he was home alone that night, but he could have gotten in and out with no trouble at all. The police got a search warrant and entered his apartment by force the minute he left for Wednesday night service.

The papers are calling him Mr. Clean.

Now everyone has a theory. Some are saying he tried

something with June, and she resisted. Some are saying he was already doing things to June, and she was threatening to tell. Some are saying June saw him doing things to some other kid and was threatening to tell. The parents are in a panic, and the church elders are sweating.

The church office is supposed to run a background check on every employee before they're hired, but somehow Mr. Rassmussen was hired without one. If anyone had looked at it, they would have seen that he had been convicted of sexual assault of a minor when he was twenty-two. Which was more than thirty years ago, but still. It's a huge oversight. By morning, the human resources director, Janet Evans, puts in her resignation. They let her make it look voluntary, but I overheard my dad talking on the phone with some members of the board. It definitely wasn't voluntary.

To calm people down, my dad announced a full review of all the employment records, just to be safe. He is personally looking over the files of every single church employee and all volunteers who work with kids or teens. There are over two hundred manilla folders stacked in his office at home.

But people are still scared. Some of them are demanding that the prison outreach program and the sex offender buddy system be suspended, which is sort of a mixed-up way to look at things. The buddy system was something the Security Ministry came up with to solve the whole sex-offender-in-church problem.

See, everyone who comes to our church for the first time is invited to a welcome breakfast after service where they all fill out cards with their contact info. The cards are mostly to get people hooked up with the different services the church offers —if they have teenagers, Pastor Pete calls later in the week to invite them to Elevate Youth Ministry, if they're college students, Pastor Ken calls to invite them to The Peak College Ministry, that sort of thing.

But the Security Ministry looks at the cards too. They do a simple check in the sex offender registry on every new visitor. If they find anything, they assign an escort to them who doesn't leave their side while they're on the property. At the time they came up with it a few years ago, it seemed like a good way to both protect the congregation and make sure that everyone who wanted to come to church could. So the problem isn't that we have the program. The problem is that the Security Ministry never got around to checking out current members, only new ones. People who have been coming for a long time, like Rick Rassmussen, never got checked. It's all a total mess.

But honestly, it's a mess that makes me want to dance and sing! I'm lighter now. A thousand times lighter. A million! The pressure has been released. I wish Jackson and I had waited a couple days, sure, but I can't change that now. And maybe it was for the best. My parents had to find out sometime.

I'm still grounded, but I send off a quick e-mail to Jackson to let him know the good news. For the first time in a long time my future feels bright again. It's only three and a half weeks until I graduate and we can get out of here. However rough the next month will be, my future is crystallizing in front of me once again. I have a destination. I have hope.

The next morning I wake up to a world that doesn't include the threat of going to prison for something I didn't do. Everything about me feels lighter. Even my ankle seems to have finally healed.

I bounce out of bed early and go for a run, which is something I haven't done in ages. The cool May breeze flushes my cheeks to pink dots and makes my mind feel suddenly clear.

What I need to do, I decide, is to show my parents that I haven't changed, not really. I may not be a Christian anymore, but that doesn't mean I'm a bad person. My values haven't changed, just the reason behind them.

When I get home I go straight to the kitchen and make everyone breakfast. When my parents come downstairs I have eggs, toast, bacon, and orange juice laid out for them.

"I just wanted to say that I'm sorry for the way I've been acting. I shouldn't have ditched school, and I should have been more honest with you about a lot of things. I've been going a little crazy lately. I'm sorry."

"Thank you for saying that," my mom says, though she still seems a little wary of me. "And thank you for making breakfast."

"I appreciate the attitude adjustment, but this doesn't change anything," my dad says. "You're still grounded. There are still some serious things we need to discuss."

"I know. I know. I'm not asking for anything. I just wanted to say sorry."

He gives me a cautious smile, the first one in weeks. I can do this. I can make them understand.

CHAPTER FIFTY

WHEN I ARRIVE AT school that morning, someone tugs at my elbow. It's Paige. My face explodes in a smile. It makes me feel warm just to see her. It might not be simple, explaining what happened between me and Mike. But now that they have the killer, all my old problems seem manageable, possible.

"Hi!" I say.

"What are you doing here?" Then I register the look on her face. She's upset about something. Really upset.

"What's going on?" I ask.

She looks into my eyes, trying to read me, trying to figure me out. "You haven't seen it," she says. "Have you even looked at your phone this morning? Or your e-mail?" she asks.

I still don't have a phone. My parents aren't replacing it until I'm done being grounded. "No. Not yet. What is it?"

She just shakes her head. "Check it. It might be a good day to call in sick." She walks away.

What does that mean? I race over to the computer lab. I might be late to class, but I have to know. As I rush through the halls no one even makes eye contact with me. No one says a word, they just steal glances then avert their eyes. I feel both exposed and invisible. What could have happened?

I log into my account. There are hundreds of unread messages, but one stands out. The address is listed as being from TruthSeeker82@hotmail.com. It was sent late last night. The subject heading is in all caps. *EMMA GRANT: HYPOCRITE, WHORE, MURDERER?*

I click it open and see that it has been sent to hundreds of people. There are e-mail addresses for the entire school. It's only a matter of time until someone forwards it to my parents.

The message reads like a call to war:

> *Who is the real Emma Grant? She'd like you to believe she's an innocent pastor's daughter who makes videos like this:*

I recognize the video below the words immediately. It shows my face frozen in a smile. It's from a vlog I was posting on regularly up until last fall. All of the youth leaders contributed to it. This one is almost two years old. In the video, I talk about the virtues of abstinence and some of the ways teens can combat sexual pressures. It feels like a thousand years ago. I scroll past it.

> *But what would you say if you knew that sweet Emma Grant was STILL a suspect in the murder of June Vogel, even after Rick Rassmussen was arrested?*

Could this be true? How?

> *Police have been stationed outside her house for the last few weeks, watching her every move. Last week she gave them the slip and DISAPPEARED. Why? Where did she go?*

> *And there's more. Take a look at what good little Emma's been up to lately.*

There's another video embedded beneath the words. The thumbnail is blurry and dark. I press play. As soon as it begins, I know exactly what I'll see.

The camera, the one in his phone, lifts up. I'm sitting on the edge of Jackson's bed. The bedroom is dark. I'm wearing my cheerleading uniform with the SCHS emblazoned across my chest. There's no question it's me. The smile on my face is playful, smirking as I stare at a spot above the camera lens. Then I hear Jackson's voice.

"Please?" he teases, "Come on."

"No way," I say faux annoyed. "Turn it off."

"But you're gonna be gone so long."

"You'll survive," I say, and roll my eyes. "It's, like, a week."

"It's ten days, and I won't." He sets the camera on top of something and steadies it. He crosses over to me, kisses me.

"So watch, I don't know, *something else*."

"I don't want to watch something else. I want to watch you." His lips move to my neck.

I don't see the video anymore. I see his eyes staring into mine. I feel his hands in my hair. I feel his breath on my neck, his lips on mine, the pressure of our bodies pressed close.

"I need you," he says.

"You promise it's just for you?" I hear myself say breathlessly.

"I promise," he says.

I shut the video off. I know what comes next. I know what everyone's seen. They've seen me. All of me. And him too. It wasn't sex, not then, but it was practically everything but.

My face is white hot, drained of blood and on fire. He said he would delete it as soon as I got back. He promised.

There's more to the e-mail. I don't want to look but I have to know. I brace myself and scroll down.

> *Is this the kind of person you want in your school? In your church? Babysitting your kids? Dating your sons? I didn't think so.*
>
> *TAKE ACTION!*
>
> *Tell the police what you know about Emma on the night June was killed. Do you know where she was? Neither do I!*
>
> *Tell SCHS to kick her out so she doesn't endanger the good students there.*
>
> *Tell the board at Summit Christian Fellowship to fire her parents and ban them from attending.*
>
> *Tell her she doesn't belong with the rest of us. She belongs in JAIL!*

My throat closes so tight I can't breathe. I hear the sound of my breath like it's coming from far away. It's wheezing and shallow and fast. I try to suck in oxygen, but there isn't enough.

My heart's beating too fast, too hard, thumping against my ribs like it's trying to break free.

And suddenly I have to break free too. I have to.

Before anyone can stop me. Before anyone can tell me no.

I run.

CHAPTER FIFTY-ONE

I RUN AND I run. Down the hall, out the doors, down the street to the gas station, my arms pumping and my chest heaving and my backpack tossing back and forth across my back.

As soon as I spot the newsstand, I stop. The headline on the front of the *Denver Post* reads:

MR. CLEAN NOT MURDERER

I fish out quarters and pull the paper out, scanning until I read:

> *While still in custody for the content on his computer,*
> *Rick Rassmussen, known as Mr. Clean, is not being*
> *charged for the murder of June Vogel that took place on*
> *April 19 at Summit Christian Fellowship. Further*
> *examination of Rassmussen's computer revealed that he was*
> *in an online chat room, posing as a teen boy and chatting*
> *with an unknowing teen girl at the time of the murder.*

I throw the paper in the trash. I don't care what else it says. My life is right back where it was two days ago.

Then I see the pay phone, like a unicorn, a rare relic. I find more quarters. Dial.

"Meet me," I say into the phone, barely able to keep the tears from escaping. My voice sounds odd, my throat tight from holding them back. "The Starbucks on the corner of Westlake Road and Sixth Avenue."

"I'll be there. What time? I'm out of school at 3:35."

"Now. It's important." A sob escapes. I'm too weak to keep it in any longer.

"On my way."

I walk to the coffee shop and wait for him in a booth near the back. The place is as crowded as I expected. There are people at almost every table—moms with small children, men on laptops, some women in suits passing around papers with colored pie charts. The din of steaming espresso and clattering spoons and people's voices as they chatter comforts me.

It takes him less than twenty minutes. He wades through the line at the door, finds me, and sits. I got my crying done before I arrived, but my eyes are puffy and telling all my secrets.

"What happened? Are you okay?"

"Someone found the video," I say. "Someone e-mailed it to everyone I know."

His face darkens. "Oh, Jesus." He leans his head into his hands.

"You said you deleted it."

"I was going to."

I can feel the breath rising in my lungs, getting hot and fast. "You were going to? When, exactly? Before my parents saw it or after?"

"I don't know."

"You don't know. Okay. That makes me feel so much better."

The din around us has grown quieter. People turn to stare. I take a moment to get my voice under control, make an effort to speak quietly. By the time I'm ready, people's attention has shifted back to what they were doing before.

"Do you know what this has done to me? To my family? I'm going to get expelled. No question. My parents might even get fired."

"I'm sorry," he says, his throat bobbing as he chokes the words out. "I'm so sorry."

"Did you show it to anybody else, Jackson? E-mail it to anyone?"

He leans in, his eyes fierce. "Jesus Christ. No, Emma. Do you think I'm the kind of person who would do something like that?"

"I didn't think you were the kind of person to break a promise to me either."

"How was I supposed to know something like this would

happen?"

"I told you to delete it specifically because something like this could happen. I would have never done anything like that if I thought for a second you would hold on to it."

"I didn't twist your arm. You're not exactly a pushover, Emma. You wouldn't have done it if you didn't want to."

"Excuse me?"

He looks away, shakes his head. "Nothing. I didn't mean that."

"It's not about what we did," I say, even though it's not *not* about what we did either. It was so stupid of me. "It's about what you promised."

He doesn't say anything. He knows how bad he messed up. But I say it anyway. Not for him. For me. If I keep these words inside they'll kill me.

"You lied to me. Twice. You broke a promise."

"I'm sorry, Emma. Fuck. I'm so sorry."

I stand up, not trusting myself around him right now. I want to forget this ever happened. I want to go back to the way things were a month ago, me in his arms. But can I after this? It's a lot to forgive.

"I have to go."

He grabs my hand. "I love you, Emma. I love you so much. Just tell me what to do. I'll do anything."

"I don't know if you can fix this," I say, and pull my hand from him as I walk away.

"Fuck," I hear him say behind my back, the sound of his fist hitting the table sending a shockwave of silence through the restaurant. "Fuck, fuck. fuck."

I won't say that I cried all the way home, because what's the point? Of course I did.

CHAPTER FIFTY-TWO

"WHAT IS GOING ON with you?" my mother asks, in almost a shout. "I don't understand anything you do anymore."

After I left Jackson, I spent a couple hours walking around to calm myself down. I knew my parents would be upset, really upset. I knew they would have heard all about the video, if they hadn't already seen it with their own eyes. I knew what I'd be coming home to.

We're in the family room. My dad is in his wingback chair. He hasn't said a word to me in an hour. I have a feeling he'd like to go back to when I was five, and my disobediences could be solved by a good, hard spanking.

My mom starts up again. "I don't get it, Emma. I really don't. You go from a straight-A student to acting out at church. Lying to us about everything. Ditching school. Promiscuity with juvenile delinquents. And now this video too?" Her voice crumbles. "I don't even know who my own daughter is anymore."

"It was a mistake. A big one. But I'm exactly the same person I was a week ago," I say.

"No. You're not," she says. She sits down on the couch, looking exhausted and empty. "I'm at my wit's end. There's nothing else I can do to punish you that we haven't done already. Do I have to go to every class with you? Stand by your side every moment? Is that what I have to do?"

"No," I say.

My dad stands up, his face red and angry. "I think you've got a very big shock ahead of you if you think your mother and I

234

are just going to tolerate this kind of behavior."

"What do you have to say for yourself?" my mom asks, but I stay quite. What can I say? "Say something, Emma."

"I don't know."

"Emma, please," my mother says. "Just tell me why. Was it something we did? Something you read? Something you saw? What was it?"

The truth? None of that. What kind of reason can I give them that they'll understand? Jackson was right. I wanted to do it. I didn't think anything bad would happen, and I wanted to do it. I liked the idea of him having this little piece of me, something private to look at when I was gone.

"Oh, please, Gloria," my dad says. "She's had every possible opportunity. Every possible privilege. At some point she has to take responsibility for her own choices."

My mom turns away from me, stares out the window into the dark backyard.

"Your mother and I have some serious thinking to do."

They go upstairs. I go to my room.

I've already cried so much today that I have no tears left. I try to sleep instead, but my mind is spinning. The thing I haven't even had the time to really think about today is…who? Who e-mailed that video?

It came from Jackson's phone. But whoever sent it was clearly from the church. They knew exactly who to send it to. Which means the killer either hacked into my e-mail account, or knew the same people I did.

That's if it was the killer at all. People at church have been up in arms about all the stuff that's been going on lately with Mr. Rassmussen. Could someone else have gotten that video? Could Jackson have shown someone and lied to me?

Which brings me to Jackson. My heart screams that it wasn't him, but I can't logically ignore the possibility that he was involved anymore. He had the opportunity to do it when he went to the bathroom. It would have been hard to pull off, but not impossible. It was getting a text from his phone that lured me out that night the car tried to run me down, and his phone that had the video on it. Could Detective Boyer have been right? Could Jackson have been lying about someone breaking into his car?

There's also his record. He pulled a gun on someone before, actually pulled a gun on someone. And lied to me about it. But why kill June? And why frame me? Do I really believe that what we shared together was all an act? No. I don't. But I can't tell anymore if I can trust my own judgment where Jackson is concerned.

Maybe I should start from the beginning, review what I know.

I pull up the article on June's dad again. Lee, with his conspiracies that his gang betrayed him in exchange for a deal from the police, only all of the possible conspirators locked up just like him. Locked up or dead. It's probably not even worth it to think about him anymore. But there's nothing else I can do from my bedroom tonight, so it's worth a try. There has to be something somewhere, something I'm missing.

> *Lee Stuckey, the last of the notorious Milk Gang, has been sentenced to life in prison for the deaths of Cassidy Surleaf and her baby boy, Cody Surleaf. The Surleafs were caught in the crossfire between a bank employee and the gang during the robbery of the Lafayette Credit Union last May 28. Forensic evidence later showed that the fatal bullets were shot from Stuckey's gun.*

> *While the $200,000 they stole has yet to be recovered, all the members of the Milk Gang—Sara Jo Ford, Buddy Trent, Jay Peterson, Christina Bromegat, and Stuckey— were apprehended just four days later, on the morning of June 1. All have been formally charged and have begun serving out their sentences.*

> *While the rest of the Milk Gang each accepted plea bargains for shorter sentences, Stuckey demanded a jury trial. It proved to be a mistake for Stuckey, who was convicted on two counts of murder, as well as armed robbery and possession of an unregistered weapon. Stuckey now has*

no option for parole.

The husband of Mrs. Surleaf and father of young Cody, Jason Surleaf, said nothing can ever replace the loss of a wife and child, but added, "I'm glad today that justice was finally served. I pray that Mr. Stuckey comes to find the error of his ways."

I wonder what it was like for June to grow up with her dad in prison. I do the math. The article was written ten years ago. June would have been only six years old, which makes me even sicker on her behalf to know what her father did to her before he went away. Something jogs my memory, and I pull it up just to be sure. June's testimony is still up on our youth group website. I press play, and there she is again, so alive, blinking against the bright stage lights.

"My sixth birthday party was at Six Flags. My birthday is on June first in case you want to buy me a present. It's easy to remember because it's my name too."

I scroll forward to something else.

Her voice rings out over the crowd, "Once I sat down the best thing happened! My dad sat down right next to me!"

If her dad was arrested on the morning of her sixth birthday, then how could he have been with her at Six Flags? Did they celebrate her birthday on a different day? Or did June just make that whole story up? I wouldn't doubt it. She had her head in the clouds about everything, like she was stuck being a little kid in her mind.

But why? The answer comes to me fast and simple. Because everyone else does. She wouldn't have been the first to feel pressure to have a good testimony, true or not. But wasn't June broken enough without it?

I sigh and push away from the computer. This is getting me nowhere.

Thinking of June's testimony brings my thoughts around to Pastor Pete. Chuck said he was there the whole time, but the whole thing about that pink piggy still isn't sitting right with me.

Then I remember the files on my dad's desk, the ones he's been reviewing ever since they discovered the background check problem. I wonder if they're still there. Maybe Pastor Pete's file is with the others.

I sneak downstairs, past the door to my parents' bedroom, which is already dark and silent, and into my dad's study. Sure enough, the files are still there. I shuffle through the boxes until I find Pastor Pete's.

The first thing I see is his resume. It shows he graduated from Bethany in 2009, just five years ago like I thought. There are mission trips and volunteer organizations listed, but they all appear to be while he was in school.

There's some tax filing paperwork and a copy of a letter, signed by my dad, offering him the position as youth pastor. There's a copy of his driver's license and Social Security card. He was born in January of 1981, which makes him thirty-three, the same age Jesus was supposed to be when he died.

I do the math. It's never occurred to me before, but he didn't go to college until 2005? When he was twenty-four? I guess it's not unheard of to begin school so late, but most people start when they're eighteen, right after high school. Pastor Pete has never talked about it. Once again, not a big cause for suspicion, but why *not* talk about it?

I flip over to the last page in the file—the background check. He has a few credit cards, all of which he got while in college, and all of which are paid on time. No student loans, though, which means he either had a scholarship or parents who could pay. Bethany is expensive. Twenty-five thousand a year just for tuition, not to mention dorms and books. But there's no mention of his family or relatives. And there's no criminal activity listed, not even a single parking ticket.

I'm chasing wild geese here.

I go back up to bed. It's late, and I'm tired.

CHAPTER FIFTY-THREE

AGAIN THIS WEEKEND, I'M on lockdown. No driving, no leaving the house, no calling anyone. The last part is the easiest to live with. Who do I have to call?

On Sunday morning, my parents drag me to church like always. The moment I walk through the door I know it's going to be a tough day.

Word about the video has spread through Summit like chicken pox in kindergarten. Mothers tug their children away from me. Men chastise me with their glares—*You should be ashamed of yourself, showing your face!* Others look away, whisper to their neighbors: "*I heard the girl stole her boyfriend. That nice Nicolas boy. That's why she did it.*" A handful stare at me with compassion, shake my dad's hand, put an arm around my mom—*God will help you through this.* No one says a single word to me. Yesterday I was their princess; today I'm their worst nightmare.

I don't sit with the youth group today. Mom leads us both to her regular seat, front and center, the last place I want to be. It's a challenge to everyone, a proclamation of my innocence. I'm actually thankful for her faith in me, maybe it's stronger than I thought. Maybe she's stronger than I thought.

Dad's service is about seeking the forgiveness of God. I wish I could preach a sermon about subtlety.

He booms from the stage. "Isaiah 1:18 says, 'Though your sins are like scarlet, they shall be white as snow; though they are red as crimson, they shall be like wool.' It's a powerful thing, isn't it, the love of Christ?" Amens everywhere. "That means that no matter our sins, no matter the terrible things we have done, no matter the darkness in our hearts, Jesus is ready to put His arms around you. To envelop you in His love and make you white as snow." He strolls the stage, letting us ponder the words.

"We've recently had a terrible reminder about the impermanence of this life, about the sins that can overtake our hearts, haven't we?" Hmms and nods from the crowd. "My heart is broken for our church today. At times like these it's difficult to understand the plans Our Heavenly Father has for us. But there's a lesson here, I think, a tiny ray of hope in our darkness. Because while life on Earth is limited, the Kingdom of Heaven is eternal. I know, beyond a shadow of a doubt, that Jesus is cradling that little girl in His arms right now." Soft hallelujahs echo from the ceiling.

"I know that He's drying her tears, and dressing her in His finest linens. Revelation 19:8 says, 'And to her was granted that she should be arrayed in fine linen, clean and white: for the fine linen is the righteousness of saints.'"

He says it again for emphasis. "'The righteousness of saints!'" He's holding her hand and saying, 'My dearest child,'" he smiles now, "'My dearest child, welcome to the Kingdom of Heaven.'"

I'm seething. How dare he claim to know her soul? He didn't even know her name until she died. And using her like this, as an object lesson, as though her whole life was only for the purpose of illustrating some stupid idea to others? June's life was wasted, and saying it wasn't, saying that she was used by God, that her life was snuffed out just so others can believe? It makes me burn.

The deacons are lining up at the front, and I know what's next. "This morning, I'd like to invite you to follow that child's example. Jesus is waiting for you. He's waiting to wash your sins white as snow, to turn your private sorrows into joy. Won't you come forward right now and confess your sins to Him?"

A thousand eyes buckshot toward me. Mom grabs my hand.

"Come on, sweetheart." Her eyes are brimming, and I realize why she chose her regular place so near the front. It wasn't her having faith in me, it wasn't her standing by my side. She wanted to be close so I can seek forgiveness for my sins. The thing to worry about now is my soul, my ticket to heaven, the only thing that can save me. Because my guilt isn't a question in her mind anymore. It's absolute.

"Mom."

"Come on, baby. Let's go pray, okay?"

The singers take their places. The band starts up, slow and reverent.

"What can wash away my sins?
Nothing but the blood of Jesus.
What can make me whole again?
Nothing but the blood of Jesus."

"We're waiting to pray with you, so come forward," Dad says, in that dripping cadence that's supposed to make me believe he cares.

Mom takes my other hand in hers. "I'll be right there with you."

I see then that it doesn't matter what I do. If I step forward, I'm guilty. If I stay, I'm rebellious. The band gets to the chorus.

"Oh! Precious is the flow
That makes me white as snow-oh!
No other fount I know,
Nothing but the blood of Jesus."

Others are flooding toward the front. Deacons step forward to pray with them.

"It doesn't matter what you've done," Dad says, "Jesus sees your sinner's heart. He knows! Come now, come today, and let Him forgive you. Let the blood of Jesus wash away your sins."

But asking for forgiveness would be a lie. It would be more than one lie. I didn't do anything that needs forgiveness, and even if I did, I don't believe it's possible to be saved anymore. I turn to Mom, "No."

"Oh, Emma." She's crying now, "please."

Dad sees us from his place on the stage and looks right at me, "Please don't shut your heart to God. Repent. Make your wrongs right." Then he sets the microphone down on a chair and walks straight toward us as the band continues to play.

"This is all my hope and peace.
Nothing but the blood of Jesus.
This is all my righteousness.
Nothing but the blood of Jesus."

"Please, Emma," he whispers to me when he reaches us.

"Please don't shut your heart to God. He wants to heal your heart. He does." He leans in close. I wiggle away.

"No." My voice is louder than I mean it to be. People turn to gape.

Pastor Pete sees us. He steps down off the stage and makes his way through the crowd already praying at the front, a throng of people seeking forgiveness for petty sins, more guilt ridden than guilty.

"Can I pray with you, Emma?" he asks. People are staring now, without shame. The whole row behind us has stopped singing.

"I won't ask for forgiveness for something I didn't do." His heart breaks a little for me. I can see it. There's sympathy in his eyes, but whether it's because he believes me or because he thinks I can't own up to my mistakes is impossible to tell.

"Then let's just pray, okay?" It isn't a request. He starts before I agree.

He lays his hands on me, right there in the front row. Before I know it, others do too. They crowd around me, all of them grappling for a piece of my salvation.

I can't breathe. They're pushing each other farther and farther in. Hands reach and hold. Layers of hands around me, three people deep.

I wrap my arms around myself. Their voices rise louder and louder, some shouting, some wailing, some speaking in tongues, all blending into a confusion that drowns out every thought in my mind. It would be so nice, so easy, to float away on it. But I don't. I look up, but there are too many hands above me to see anything. The air is thin inside this bubble, and it is so hot.

I sink to the floor. As I do I hear them swell to bursting. They think I've been slain in the Spirit. Maybe they're right. Maybe I'm finally experiencing it for real this time. Maybe God feels like drowning.

CHAPTER FIFTY-FOUR

THERE'S A KNOCK ON my door at six the next morning, then it opens. It's my dad.

"Wake up. Time for school," he says. This isn't something he usually does. It's my mom who wakes me every morning. He starts to leave, and I stop him.

"Dad?" I ask. "Please don't make me go to school today. Please." I can't handle it today. Not after church yesterday. Not after the video. I can't handle all their eyes on me, hating me. And besides, shouldn't I be expelled by now? If it hasn't happened yet, it will happen today. Why even go?

"I'm not going to allow you to hide from the repercussions of your actions, Emma. School is non-negotiable." His face is grim, stony. "I expect you to be ready to leave in forty minutes." He walks out.

I dress quickly and stuff my school books into my backpack, feeling sick at the thought of walking down those halls.

Breakfast is a lesson in being seen and not heard. I eat quietly and quickly, sneaking glances over to my mother, who's at the dining room table buried in her Bible. I want to beg her to let me stay home, but there's no way I'm interrupting her devotional this morning. It wouldn't matter. She won't defy my dad, and he has his mind made up.

I put my dishes directly in the dishwasher and even wipe down the kitchen counter. By the time forty minutes have passed, I'm waiting for them in the family room, ready to go.

They drop me off in front of the school. As I'm walking away, I hear the window of the passenger side come down.

"Emma?" It's my mom.

I turn back. "Yeah?" I ask, my eyes wary but hopeful.

"I love you," she says, and grabs my hand. Tears spring to my eyes. Maybe there's still a chance to fix all this. I don't know how, but maybe. Maybe she's still on my side.

I rush forward and hug her through the open window. "I love you too," I say.

No one says a word to me as I make my way toward my locker, and I'm thankful for it. I open it up, put my schoolbooks inside. Then I hear someone behind me. I turn around. It's Paige. She has a look of determination on her face, the hard focus she gets in tennis before she goes in for the kill.

"Hey," I say. "What's up?" The words feel too normal, too wrong.

"Everyone says I shouldn't talk to you at all, Emma, but I think you deserve to at least hear this from me."

"What?"

"We can't be friends anymore. You're not the person I thought you were."

I've dreaded this moment for months—the moment when she finally realizes that the gulf between us is too great. But still, hearing her say it is so much more painful than I ever imagined. It feels like my air has been cut off, like I'm sinking into the deep of the ocean. I can see the light sparkling above me, and the blue sky, and birds, but it's too far, and I'm too heavy.

"Paige, please."

"It's like I never knew the real you at all. You lied about so much, Emma." Her voice starts to break. "Why would you do that? I thought we were friends. No. I thought we were something bigger than that. Something better. I thought we could trust each other. Do you know what it's like to feel like you can't trust your best friend anymore? I've never felt so lonely in my whole life."

"You can trust me. Let's just sit down and talk, okay?"

"All you had to do was say you were sorry and tell me the truth. You know that, right? I would have—I don't know, I would have at least tried to understand."

"I'm so sorry. I—"

244

"Too late. I know God says we're supposed to forgive, but I don't know how to do that right now. I'm sorry."

She turns and walks away. Down the hall, a group of girls—Ruth, Naomi, and Katie—surround her and squeeze her tight. I want to die. The part of my heart that's always been her is gone.

There's a jolt from behind. Not hard, but a surprise. I stumble, fly forward, land on my face. There's a scuffle of feet near my eyes.

"Back off, man, she's not worth it." I look up to see Mike holding Nicolas back. Nicolas. From me. Chuck and Ben are there too.

"Is it true?" Nicolas asks.

"What?" I say from the floor, pushing myself up to a seated position, shocked into tears.

"Come on, guys. Let's go," Chuck says.

"Did you do it?" Nicolas asks. "Because of me?"

"Nicolas," I plead. How could he think that? He knows me. He might have even loved me once. Maybe not real love. Maybe just a baby sort of love, but still. "No. I—no."

"How am I supposed to believe that? You're a liar, Emma. A total liar."

Chuck tugs Nicolas away. The boys shuffle off, consoling Nicolas. As they go, Mike puts a fist to his mouth and fake-coughs, "Slut." Some of the other guys snicker. Only Chuck looks back with any sort of remorse on his face. My cheeks are wet and hot.

I hate that he made me cry. I hate that they all watched me break. It's so stupid. I feel so stupid.

Then Miss Hope walks up and offers her hand to me on the floor. "Come on. Get up."

"Go away," I plead. "Please just leave me alone."

"I can't do that, Emma. I think you need to talk to someone about all this."

"I don't want to talk, especially not to you," I say. I sound like a child who just dropped their ice cream cone. I can't help it. I want to hit her, just for looking at me.

She kneels down on her heels and crosses her arms over her chest, exasperated.

"What did you think was going to happen, Emma?"

I wrap my arms around my legs and bury my face in my knees.

"Huh? Did you think you could go on deceiving everyone and get away with it?" she asks, "Yeah. I saw that video too. And let me tell you, I was very disappointed. Very disappointed. How could you do something like that? I thought you knew better. I thought you were a good example that I could tell other girls about."

Fuck her. Fuck her and her high horse and her stupid fish mouth. I'm not going to sit here and listen to this. I stand up and swipe the tears away from my eyes.

"Well you were wrong. I'm not good. I'm bad. I'm everything everyone says, so go ahead and do whatever you're going to do to me because I just don't care anymore."

I stalk away, and she grabs my arm.

"You still have a chance. "For all have sinned and fall short of the glory of God.""

"Oh, fuck off!" I tear my arm away from her and race down the hallway. I don't know where I'm going. I can't go to class. I can't leave, or I'll lose the little favor I have left with my parents. I have nowhere to go.

I dart outside and head over to the football stadium. I just need a minute to collect myself. Just a minute. Then I'll know what to do. There's a gym class running laps on the track, and another group playing soccer, but no one seems to notice as I climb the bleachers on the far side of the field.

I sit down and take in air until my breaths are slow and even again. What should I do? Where should I go?

There really is only one thing to do. I have to find my parents and beg. Maybe they'll let me homeschool until the end of the year. Other students have done it. Cassidy Long did it when she got knocked up. Maybe if I leave for a while this will all blow over and everyone will forget about me.

I stand up and walk down the bleachers. I'll go to my mom's office right now, ask her to call in my dad.

I'm just about to the bottom when I see something strange. Three big, muscular men dressed in black and accompanied by Principal Hendricks. They're walking straight toward me. I see Principal Hendricks point to me and say something to them. The men pick up their pace. I stop.

Something in my gut tingles. I have a sense, a fleeting second of awareness that I should run. But I force it away as irrational. Principal Hendricks is there, my parents are across the street; what could happen? The men reach me.

"Emma Grant?" one of them asks. He looks like a white-trash version of The Rock—scraggly goatee hiding a weak chin, and muscles that stretch the arms of his T-shirt to their breaking point.

The runners on the track have stopped to watch. The soccer game is on pause. Everyone stares in my direction.

"Yes?" I say. My instincts tell me to deny it, but it would be worthless. I wonder why they even ask. They must already know.

Before I can ask what they want, he grabs me, whips me around, and squeezes my wrists between one of his hands. I scream.

"You're coming with us," the man says.

CHAPTER FIFTY-FIVE

THE OTHER TWO MEN descend and each takes one of my arms away from him. They yank my backpack off my shoulder and toss it onto the track. My pencils and pens spill out on the red rubber surface. My notebooks flap open and flutter their pages in the wind.

My arms are pulled behind me, and something cold clicks into place on my wrists. Handcuffs. But these men aren't wearing uniforms, so they can't be police.

Which means they must be, they must—oh God.

"No!" I scream. I should have run. I should have run. I should have run.

I scream and kick at them, flailing my legs while one of them grabs me by the arm and lifts me off the ground. It's like kicking a concrete wall. The entire force of my blows is absorbed in a meaty thigh, a trunk-like chest. I am nothing against them.

"Calm down," somebody says.

Whoever I kicked grabs both of my legs and secures my ankles under his arm. I fight against it but am reduced to a squiggling worm. One man holds my arms, the other my legs. The third brings out a roll of duct tape and wraps it around my ankles.

"You can do this the easy way or the hard way," somebody says.

"Either way, it's gonna happen," somebody else says.

Principal Hendricks is just standing there. He doesn't even look concerned. He's doing nothing as they attack me. Surely they're not allowed to do this.

I try to speak, but the words won't come out. Instead I scream. I scream and writhe and flail against them.

My eye catches another girl's on the field. Erica. She's holding a soccer ball, frozen, watching me. I beg her with my eyes, with my screams, to help. But I can't make words, and she couldn't help even if she tried. Her eyes are the last thing I see.

"Guess it's gonna be the hard way," somebody says.

A dark hood slides over my head. There's something cold pressed to my back, under my shirt.

A jolt of electricity tears through my body. It is fire in my veins. And ice too. I feel my body go rigid, though every instinct is to run away. But I can't move. I'm paralyzed by the force of it.

My chin dives into my neck as my body shakes violently. I feel bile rise in my throat and burning, burning, burning. My skin crackles. I suck in burlap with a hard breath, and everything goes black.

CHAPTER FIFTY-SIX

I WAKE TO JOSTLING and stifle the urge to scream. I'm lying on my side. My body bounces up and down on something soft. I can't see anything. There's country music playing, some twangy something I don't recognize. It smells like stale French fries and cigarette smoke. I can hear the whirr of pavement beneath me and feel the slick of leather against my hands. I'm being moved somewhere. How long have I been out?

My feet and ankles are still bound, and there's something else around my waist, holding me to the seat. The seatbelt? I wiggle my body toward where I think the buckle will be, but my feet thunk against what must be a door.

"We got a live one," somebody says.

The hood is yanked off my head, and I scream.

"Keep it down."

I stare into the face of a red-faced white guy with a shaved head. He's holding what I can only assume is the Taser they used on me.

"Please," I say. "I haven't done anything wrong. You can't just do this to me. I—"

"Quiet," the guy says.

"I'm gonna be eighteen soon."

"Did you like getting buzzed before, kid?"

No. Not again. Please. I shake my head.

"'Cause that's exactly what's going to happen if you say one more word. Just one. Got it?"

I nod, my face sloppy with tears.

"Good girl. Now I'm gonna let you sit up."

He pulls at my shoulders until I'm upright. I'm in the back seat of a large SUV. There are two single seats between me and the driver's row. The one on the left is empty. That's where baldy must have been sitting. Now he sits beside me on the long back seat. Goatee man from before sits in the seat on the right. Up front the third guy, big with a mop of thick black hair, drives. There's the shoulder of someone else in the passenger seat. It's smaller, maybe a woman's, but I can't make out anything else from where I sit.

The windows are tinted dark, but I can see the shape of things through them. The mountains are to my left, which means we're headed north. We're not in the city, we're out on the prairie somewhere. It reminds me of the landscape on the way to the Limon Correctional Facility, and I feel a lump rise in my throat. Everything from Denver to Montana looks like this. Where are we?

The landscape makes me almost long for the prison, for a chance to try my case, to at least know where I'm going. Am I even still in Colorado? I was never formally charged by the police. Is it illegal to go out of state when you're a suspect? Would they look for me if I disappeared? Or do they already know where I'm going? I could be headed anywhere.

"Here's how this is gonna work, Emma. You're going to do everything we tell you to do. You're going to do it right away. And you're going to do it without questions."

I nod. I shift in my seat, trying to slip my sore wrists out of the handcuffs, but they're too tight.

Baldy continues. "We told you before that things can happen the easy way or the hard way, remember?"

I nod.

"You chose the hard way before. It's up to you whether you choose it again," he says. "So which do you think you'd like to choose? You may answer."

"The easy way," I choke out.

"The easy way what?" he asks. At first I don't know what he means, then I realize.

"The easy way, sir," I say.

"Good girl. That wasn't so hard, was it?"

I shake my head.

"Sit tight. Won't be long now." He settles in next to me. I try not to think about what "Won't be long now" means.

We drive for what feels like forever. Eventually, my hands go numb. I try to move them but I can't tell if my fingers are wiggling or not. I peer out the window and try to recognize anything on the landscape. There's nothing. No mile markers, no signs for towns, no businesses. We are on some back highway somewhere. The speed limit is sixty-five, and I haven't seen another car. It wouldn't matter if I did.

"Lean your head toward me."

Baldy's holding the hood again. We must be close to our destination.

I don't want to, but I do it. It's sick how quickly I've gone from fighting to total, complete obedience. What will they do to me if I don't do it? What will they do to me if I do?

The hood slides over my face, and it's dark again. I suck in a breath, and my mouth fills with canvas. I try not to cry.

A few more minutes of driving. The car turns right, the road gets bumpy. There's a jolt as the car stops. Someone grabs my shoulder.

"Time to move."

Outside the car, there's dirt under my feet. I want to ask where I am, but I don't dare. They wouldn't tell me anyway. I have a pretty good idea, and I'll know the specifics soon enough.

I hear a squeak and flinch. A door? The body next to me moves behind me and pushes me through. The darkness inside the hood grows darker. The surface under my feet changes too. Concrete? Tile? I hear a muffled gasp. I hear a whisper, but can't make out the words.

I'm shoved into a seat. It feels like a metal folding chair. Someone grabs both of my wrists. There's a click, and the handcuffs release. I want to rub my wrists, but I can't. In the moment it takes to wish for it, my hands are separated and cuffed to the poles that make up the chair's back. At least I can rest my back against it now. I do.

I hear something that sounds like whimpering. Who else is here? For a moment I imagine opening my eyes and seeing June, alive, kidnapped and being held here too. But I saw the bullet hole with my own eyes.

The hood is torn off my head. A couple hairs get ripped out with it, and I flinch with the sting. It takes a moment for my eyes to adjust. I'm in a dimly lit room. There are others here with me. Beyond the lights that shine directly above my head, I spot a familiar face that solidifies all my fears.

My mother.

CHAPTER FIFTY-SEVEN

THERE ARE OTHER FACES too. My dad. Pastor Pete. Mike. Paige. Paige and Mike's parents. They are in a semicircle, and I am at the center. It should make me feel safe to see them, but it doesn't. It just confirms every suspicion I've had since those men grabbed me at school. I'm at some reform school, some wilderness camp or something like it. There were rumors at church about different places like this, bad kids who left and never came back, but we never found out the details. I'm just as scared, if not more, than I was before.

I scan the room. It's simple. Mint green and baby pink tiles from the '50s checker the floor. The faded chintz curtains on the windows appear to be hand sewn. There's a neat stack of metal folding chairs against one wall, and a large bulletin board that takes up most of the space on the other. The bulletin board is like something out of a kindergarten classroom, with girl's names and hand-cut, fist-sized yellow stars next to them: Tabitha—eight stars, Brittany—two stars, Felicia—twelve stars, Amber—one star. There are at least a hundred names.

The three men who abducted me stand at the edges of the room, arms behind them like soldiers at the ready. There's also a woman sitting inside the semicircle. She looks familiar, but I can't tell why. I don't recognize her. Her dirty-blonde hair is tucked into a prim ponytail. She's wearing a floor-length khaki skirt, tennis shoes, and a loose plaid button-down that looks big enough to fit a man twice her size. Inside of it she is both trim and shapeless. She looks older than my mother, but something about her makes me realize she's not. Maybe it's her lack of makeup doing the aging. Without blush and lipstick her face looks flat and plain, not contoured and striking as it could be. Then I notice her perfect hands. They look baby smooth, almost childlike, and are perfectly manicured with a blush-pink polish. No one near my mother's age could have such perfect hands. This woman can't be more than thirty.

The woman stands and speaks.

"Emma, I am Mrs. Hemple." Her voice is sweet and light. She folds her hands in her lap and crosses her ankles. "Your family, friends, and I have gathered here to have a serious discussion about your behavior."

My mother lets out a sniffle from my dad's shoulder. Mrs. Hemple gives her a sympathetic smile.

"Mom?" The word croaks out of my throat. "What is this?"

My mother wipes away tears and shakes her head.

"It's not your turn to speak, Emma. It's ours," Mrs. Hemple says. "It sounds like you've been saying plenty through your actions lately. Today it's time to listen."

"Mom, please don't let them do this to me," I say, motioning to my restraints. "I can't feel my hands."

"Can she at least be out of the cuffs?" my mom asks.

"Stop lying, Emma," Mrs. Hemple says, and casts a warning look to my mom. "No one is hurting you. You're in no danger whatsoever. Your restraints are merely a precaution against you trying to hurt yourself." It sounds like the repetition of something she's said many times before, to other kids, or their parents, or mine.

"Why would I want to hurt myself?" I ask, bewildered.

My dad coughs. "Perhaps for a little while," he says.

Mrs. Hemple sighs, displeased. "Derek?"

Baldy steps forward. Does he still have the Taser? I can't tell so I cower away from him. My mom looks confused, worried. But as soon as he reaches me, Derek kneels down and unlocks the cuffs.

"There. Is that better?" Mrs. Hemple asks. "This is how cooperation works. But when you ask something of me, I expect something in return. Do you understand?"

I nod and rub my wrists. Feeling rushes back in the form of pins and needles.

"Good. As long as you remain calm and stay in your seat, you may have the privilege of having your arms free."

"I don't need this, whatever this is," I say.

"I think you do," says Mrs. Hemple. "And so does your family. That's why they had me bring you here. They asked me to kidnap you from your self-destructive life the same way the devil has kidnapped your mind. Each person in this room has traveled here to tell you something to aid you in your treatment. I expect you to listen." Her eyes are as black-brown and serious as a spider. "Miss Kent, why don't you begin?"

"I told her already. This morning. No one told me this was going to happen."

"Why don't you read the letter your parents had you write on the way here?" Mrs. Hemple says.

Paige turns and stares at me with watery eyes. She pulls a piece of paper out of her pocket and unfolds it. Then she folds it back up again, quick and decisive. "I'm sorry. I can't do this," she says.

She stands up to leave, but her father puts a hand on her arm and she sits down again, crying softly. Then Paige's mother takes the letter from her grip, clears her throat, and begins to read.

"Emma, you were my best friend, but you haven't been a friend to me in a long time. There are so many ways you've hurt me with your actions."

Paige burries her face in her palms.

The letter lists everything that I've done, and she knows more than I gave her credit for. The sex. My lack of faith in God. Me not even confiding in her that I'm a murder suspect. The plans to go to a different college. We were supposed to be roommates, but I never filled out the housing request forms. Of course she figured it out when she saw a stranger's name instead of mine. I should have anticipated that, but I was too wrapped up in myself to think about her. They want it to hurt me that I've hurt her, and it does.

Pastor Pete goes next. Like Paige, he takes out a letter to read to me.

"You've been struggling for a while. I didn't want to see it at first. I prayed that you'd figure things out on your own. I've worked with tough kids before. I've seen it a million times, but I never thought it would come to this with a girl like you. I can only pray that you'll take this for what it is. An opportunity to change your life for the better."

He looks into my eyes, and his gaze is caring and earnest. He's everything he's supposed to be, but it only makes me angrier. I don't need his generosity or his understanding.

"My life is fine," I say. It's not. But God certainly can't help.

"You may be done with God, but He's not done with you. Not yet." Pastor Pete reaches across Mike's lap to squeeze my mother's hand. "And neither are we."

When Mrs. Hemple calls on Mike, I protest.

"No," I say. "He doesn't get to talk. Not to me. Not about what I've done wrong."

"Is this about that story you told your principal?" Mrs. Hemple asks. "I've been working with girls like you for a long time, Emma. And you know what? They use stories like that to gain sympathy or to call attention away from their own actions. We call them TTs here for Tall Tales. It's time to stop the lies."

"You don't know anything about it," I say.

"I know everything, Emma, absolutely everything. Do you think Mister Kent would have come all the way down here if he didn't want to see you get the help you so desperately need?"

I shoot out of my seat. "I won't listen to it," I say. "Not from him."

The men are on me before I see them coming. They force me back into the chair and grab my wrists.

"No!" I scream, "let me go!" I struggle away from them, but they hold the chair still so I look like a child throwing a tantrum. Maybe I am.

I catch Mike's eyes as I writhe against the men. His face is the model of the concerned boyfriend, but his eyes are as happy as a cat who just caught a mouse. He wants to see me struggle, wants to hear me scream. The knowledge of it gives me the strength to calm myself. I won't give him the satisfaction.

The cuffs click onto my wrists, tighter than before.

"What did I tell you, Emma? Your freedom is a privilege here, not a right."

"Mom? Please tell them to take these off," I ask in as even a tone as I can manage.

"It's for the best, honey. I know it doesn't feel like that right now, but you'll see."

"Your mother is right. We're all here because we care about you. That includes Mister Kent. You will listen to him like all the others. Mr. Kent?"

Mike clears his throat, just like Paige. They have the same nervous tics, the same wrinkle between their brows. The difference is in the eyes. I steel myself for his words.

"Dear Emma."

I'm right here, asshole.

"You are a liar." It comes out angrier than he wants it to. He takes a deep breath. "You lied about loving me." He pieces his own words together like an early reader making them whole for the first time. "You lied about loving God. You lied about where you were after Winter Formal. You lied about wanting to stay a virgin. The Bible says to resist the Devil and he will flee. That's why I had to resist you. You are filled with the Devil."

I roll my eyes so hard it feels like they're going to pop out of my head. Mrs. Hemple notices.

"An open ear is an open heart, Emma."

I guess I have neither. I stop listening to him. I count tiles on the floor. I count spots on the tiles. I count roses on the curtains and stars on the bulletin board. I memorize the girls' names and how many stars they have. Annabel—zero stars, Lisa —fourteen stars, Jenny—four stars, Krista—seven stars, Bianca —nine stars, Chloe—twenty-two stars, Carrie—three stars, Selena—

"Emma?" I look up. Mrs. Hemple's brow is furrowed. "I asked you what you had to say to Mister Kent."

I snort. "Go fuck yourself."

This does not go over well. My father gasps, my mother sobs. Mrs. Hemple sends them out of the room to have a private "time out" session with me.

"I do not tolerate that kind of language here. You are in God's house, and you will use your words to honor Him. Chris?"

Goatee walks behind me, and I hear the shuffling of cupboards and something else. He returns with a Dixie cup. He hands it to Mrs. Hemple. She presses it to my lips.

"Drink," she says.

What's inside is blue. Right away I can smell it. It's liquid dish soap. I squeeze my lips tight.

"Derek?" He steps forward and puts his hands on my face. They smell like motor oil and cheap cologne. He clenches my jaw with one hand and squeezes my nose with the other.

I won't let them do this to me. I won't.

"The easy way or the hard way," Mrs. Hemple says. "Those are your choices. It's completely up to you. You can accept your situation and have it done with, or you can struggle and it will be worse."

I choose the latter. My face goes hot from the force of my resistance, from the absence of air. I don't care. I can hold my breath forever.

"Very well," Mrs. Hemple says. "Chris? Why don't you show Miss Grant what the hard way really looks like?"

Chris steps forward and karate-chops my windpipe. Not hard enough to break me, not that hard. Just hard enough to make me gasp. Once my jaw is open, Derek holds it tight. The third guy, the one I call Hairy, holds my head back against the chair. My arms strain as I fight against it, but it's no use.

Mrs. Hemple pours the liquid into my mouth. It's bitter and sour and awful. I choke against it. My throat churns the goo to bubbles. I want to spit it out, but I can't force my jaw together enough to do it. I scream instead. I gag.

"Your parents will not come for you," Mrs. Hemple says.

She's right. They don't.

The cup is full, and the liquid is slow as it drips down my throat. I can feel foam spilling past my lips, dribbling down my neck. *My cup runneth over.*

Mrs. Hemple doesn't stop until it's empty. Then she closes her eyes, puts a hand on my forehead and prays. "Cleanse this child with the blood of the Lamb. Cleanse her, oh Lord, that she may see Your glory and change her ways to please You. May we help her to create a life that glorifies You and not her own desires. Amen."

Mrs. Hemple takes a pitcher of water and pours it into my mouth. It gushes over my face and down my shirt. When it's gone I can still taste the soap, but I can't feel it anymore.

She leans down and looks into my eyes. "We love you, Emma. Each and every one of us." She kisses my forehead and walks away. I hate that I'm crying.

I hear a door open and close. And clearly, on the other side, I hear my mother say, "Can we see her now?"

Mrs. Hemple says, "Emma needs some time to consider her actions."

"Of course," my father says.

They heard me. They heard everything and didn't stop it.

After that there is nothing left in me to fight with. Derek releases his grip on my jaw, and I collapse into the chair. I am a small pile of something. Dirty laundry. Wilted petals. Fall leaves in the rain. My spirit goes dark.

When they finally bring everyone back inside my shirt is dry again, and I am dead eyed, slumped into the chair, head bobbing nearly to sleep.

My parents say their words, but I barely register them. They are not my parents. I have no parents anymore. I am an orphan.

"We love you," they say, as they leave me behind.

CHAPTER FIFTY-EIGHT

AFTER THEY'RE GONE, MRS. Hemple calls someone else into the room. The girl is blonde and sturdy, what a German masseuse might look like at fifteen. She wears a floor-length khaki skirt and a loose pink T-shirt that says, *New Mercy Ranch for Troubled Girls*. So hell has a name.

"This is Chloe," Mrs. Hemple says. Chloe, twenty-two stars, the most on the board. "She will be your companion during your transition here. You will do everything she says and model your behavior after hers."

The cuffs come off. I'm too tired to tell who helps me to my feet.

"Chloe, please show Emma to the dormitory."

We walk out into the night. The area is barren and dusty. I can see buildings dotting the landscape that look like big metal barns, like the buildings on a chicken farm. A chain-link fence surrounds it all. It looks about ten feet tall.

"Where are we?" I ask.

"Do not ask questions and do not speak unless spoken to," Chloe says. She calmly grabs a whistle around her neck and shows it to me. "All I have to do is whistle to let them know you're being a bad girl, so don't try it."

"Fine," I say.

"Do not speak unless spoken to," she repeats, irritated this time.

"Okay, sorry," I say.

She glares at me and lifts the whistle to her mouth. I lift my hands in surrender and shake my head. I give up. Even being with this mini-Hemple is better than the real thing. She calms down and turns sincere.

"Good girls follow orders. Dirty girls do not. From now on you'll be a good girl, right?"

I nod and try not to laugh at the painfully earnest look on her face. I feel like I just stepped into bizarro-land.

"Good. Follow me."

She leads me down a dirt path toward a building that's labeled *Dormitory—Stage One.*

"This is where you'll sleep. I'll sleep here too until you and Tessa move on to stage two, which is five stars." Tessa, zero stars. "That's when I can graduate. So you better get them quick because I don't want to spend any more time in here than I have to."

I nod. When we get inside I can see why she doesn't want to sleep here. The room is small and cramped. The beds are wooden with thin mattresses and bunked three high with barely enough room to fit between them, enough to sleep maybe twenty girls. There are no sheets, only thin wool blankets. Some of the girls turn to stare at me with empty eyes, but none of them makes a sound. The whole scene reminds me of *Schindler's List*, which everyone has to watch in ninth grade even though there's a part with nudity they fast forward through. I wonder if they built them like that on purpose.

"The dorms get nicer after you move up stages," Chloe says. She's not reassuring me. She's reassuring herself.

We walk to the back wall of what must be our bunk. There's a girl already lying on the middle bunk who must be zero-star-Tessa. She glares at us with bright-green eyes. Her red tresses fan out across the pillow, long and blazing and glorious. Her beauty is stunning and frightening all at once.

"I sleep on the bottom, you sleep on the top. We'll hear it if you try to get down. Won't we, Tessa?" Tessa just rolls her eyes and turns over toward the wall so her back is to us. Chloe seems irritated by it, but she doesn't speak up. Something about Chloe makes me think of the homeschooled girls at church, the ones who look at groups of girlfriends like a dog kept away from a steak. I wonder what she did to get here.

Then I look up to the top bunk. A shelf juts out on the end, the same as the other girls' bunks, one shelf for each bed.

There's a small red suitcase on it. My red suitcase, which my mother must have packed days ago. It unnerves me how little I saw this coming. I think about my chances for escape. About my car parked snugly in the garage at home. How far am I from home? I have no idea.

"Change into your sleep dress in there, then brush your teeth," Chloe motions toward a door that must be a bathroom, then looks at her watch. "You have seven minutes. Then it's lights out."

I stare at her for a moment. I usually sleep in my yoga pants and a tank top. I don't even know what a sleep dress is, much less own one. Looking around the room, I see girls in old-timey white nightgowns. They're buttoned up to the neck, full-sleeved, and down to the floor. No flowers, no frills.

Chloe interrupts my observation. "You have to be ready for lineup after that so you better hurry up."

I climb into the top bunk and unzip my suitcase. I'm desperate to brush my teeth. There's a note on top of my things in my mother's handwriting. I can't read it right now. I shove it deeper inside, resisting the urge to tear it to pieces. I find my toothbrush and my bath robe and a long granny nightgown I didn't own before. I scramble down and head to the bathroom. Chloe follows. I expect she'll be my shadow for a while.

The bathroom only has two stalls, and girls are lined up to use them. Two stalls for twenty girls? I'm glad I don't have to pee. I start to undress, but Chloe slaps my hand. The line of girls turns to look at me.

"Don't be indecent. Undress only behind the curtain." She points to another doorway, and we go through it. Inside the second room is a line of empty stalls with curtains on rope as dividers. I enter one of them and pull it shut, glad to be alone for the first time since I left my house this morning.

It occurs to me that the undressing rule must exist for the girls who got sent here for liking other girls. The thought makes me almost mad enough to walk out among them naked in protest. Almost. But if soap is the punishment for swearing I don't want to think about what the punishment for that would be.

A soft tone rings from a speaker above my head.

"Hurry up!" Chloe says. "That's the three-minute warning."

I pull the nightgown over my head and bundle my dirty clothes under my arm. I exit and make a beeline for the sink.

"No time," Chloe says, and yanks me away.

My mouth is still sour from the soap. I want to pull away from her, but the frantic look in her eyes convinces me not to.

When we step out into the main room, all the girls are lined up against their bunks. Chloe starts to run, my arm in her grasp.

We make it to our bunk. Tessa is standing there, hands clasped behind her back like everyone else. She's tamed her wild tresses into two neat French braids.

Chloe grabs my things and shoves them into my suitcase, then smoothes the pillow and the covers. Tessa gives me a glance. I smile at her. I want her to like me. I want to have a friend here. She doesn't smile back.

"Her hair," Tessa says. At first, Chloe seems ready to yell at her for talking. Then the words register.

"Shoot," she says, fully panicked now. "Shoot!"

Chloe yanks my hair. "Ow!" I say.

"Stay still," she says to me, then turns to Tessa. "Don't just stand there. Help me."

Tessa steps behind my back. I can feel Chloe dividing my hair down my skull with her fingernails, then handing half to Tessa. They pull at the sections fast and hard and sloppy. My scalp stings.

"Careful," I say, but they're not more careful. If anything, they yank harder. I look around the room and notice every other girl in tight French braids, just like Tessa's, two down each side of their head. All except the girls with short hair. Those girls wear elastic headbands. Everyone is staring at us, anxious.

There's another soft tone from the speakers, and Chloe drops my hair and lines up next to me. She yanks at Tessa to stop braiding, but she won't. Tessa finishes her side, then switches to the left, which Chloe only managed to braid to the top of my ear. I hear the click of the front door opening, and Tessa drops my hair like it's on fire and snaps to her position in the lineup.

"I'm sorry," she whispers. There's pain in her voice. She didn't finish. The last third flows loose down my front. I glance at Chloe, but she won't look at me. There are tears in her eyes. I reach to finish the braid myself, but she slaps at my hand. I toss the unfinished braid behind my back, hoping to hide it.

Mrs. Hemple walks in with Hairy and Baldy, who stand by the door. She walks slowly past every girl, examining each one. No one makes eye contact with her. No one says a word. They stare at the opposite wall or at their toes. There are no words from Mrs. Hemple either. The room is devoid of any noise except the soft thud of her tennis shoes. She looks like she should have a riding crop in her hand, but she doesn't.

As she reaches one girl, a mousy brunette near the front, the girl sucks in a sharp breath, then holds it until Mrs. Hemple passes.

Thud. Thud. Thud.

We're near the back of the room. She's walking so slow it takes a full five minutes for her to reach us. I think I hold my breath the entire time too.

She stops in front of me and immediately reaches for my hair. I've fooled no one.

"What happened here, Chloe?" she asks.

"Tessa didn't finish the task I assigned her," Chloe says. There's fear in her eyes. I glance at Tessa, and her mouth hardens into a firm line, but she says nothing. Why would Chloe lie? We ran out of time. So what?

"Is that so?" Mrs. Hemple asks.

"Yes, ma'am," Chloe says. I don't understand why she's doing this.

"No," I say. Their eyes snap to my face. I spot the fear in Chloe's eyes. She's all but begging me to shut up. "It's my fault." I won't have Tessa take the blame for something she didn't do, and Chloe will only lie like she already has. Mrs. Hemple looks to Chloe.

"It was both of them," Chloe says, trying to cover for her lie. "Tessa dawdled and Emma resisted. But it's Emma's first night. Tessa should know better."

"It's kind of you to show compassion, Chloe, but it's not up to you to decide who is guilty and who is not," Mrs. Hemple says. She reaches for something inside her deep pockets and pulls it out. It's a large pair of scissors.

"Please don't," Tessa says. "It was Chloe. She forgot."

In a flash, Mrs. Hemple grabs Tessa's left braid, the same side that's unfinished on me, and cuts it off close to her scalp.

"No!" I scream. "She didn't do anything!"

Mrs. Hemple turns to me and swiftly grabs my left braid too. I hear the swoosh of the scissors and watch as Mrs. Hemple pulls my braid free. More than a foot of hair, my hair, dangles from her hand.

I reach up and feel the absence of what once was a source of pride. I loved my hair. I loved playing with it and styling it and shoving it into buns and ponytails. Now half of it is gone. The surface is nearly bare, just a quarter inch of stubble pokes out at the center of the cut. At least a foot of hair. Two years of hair. Gone. It doesn't seem real.

"Those who cannot take care of what God has given them do not deserve to have it. These will be sent to Locks of Love and made into wigs for people who do deserve it," Mrs. Hemple says. "Perhaps you will remember not to be so careless in the future."

Tessa is crying. Chloe looks half mad, half relieved. I am speechless.

Mrs. Hemple turns on her heel. "Evening prayer," she says.

Immediately, everyone in the dorm drops to their knees and folds their hands. I follow their lead, still in shock. In unison, they recite:

"Now the light has gone away;
Savior listen while I pray.
Asking Thee to watch and keep
And to send me quiet sleep.

Jesus, Savior, wash away
All that has been wrong to-day;
Help me every day to be
Good and gentle, more like Thee.

Let my near and dear ones be
Always near and dear to Thee.
O bring me and all I love
To Thy happy home above."

Mrs. Hemple walks to the door. The lights go out, and we

climb into our beds. It sounds like a hundred mice scampering to their holes.

"May Jesus bless your dreams and wake you with new energy to be more like Him day by day," Mrs. Hemple says. The door closes, and there's a click as a lock turns.

It's the darkest darkness I've ever experienced. There are no windows. My eyes fight to adjust, but it's too dark to see anything. Someone is crying below me. I think it's Chloe, but I can't be sure. I wish she'd stop.

I've never heard the words of that prayer before, but they haunt me. *Now the light has gone away. Now the light has gone away. Now the light has gone away.* It has.

I won't stay here. I can't.

CHAPTER FIFTY-NINE

SOMEONE BANGS ON THE door early in the morning, so early it feels like I haven't slept at all. It takes me a moment to remember where I am. When the realization hits, I dig back under my thin blanket, wishing for the pleasant ignorance of sleep. But soon there's a harsh tug on my elbow.

"Get down!" Chloe says, her pug face staring up at me. "Now."

I notice everyone scampering out of their beds and kneeling on the floor in front of their bunks. Reluctantly, I get down too.

Mrs. Hemple comes in, and there is another short prayer, then Chloe informs me that we have a mere ten minutes to get ready for the day. The other girls are rushing around like madwomen, so I follow suit. I brush my teeth, pee, put on my standard-issue long khaki skirt, tennis shoes, and a loose pink T-shirt that has the New Mercy Ranch logo printed in the upper right hand corner. Even my bra has to change. Instead of my regular underwire (a weapon!) I'm now shoving myself into a shapeless sports bra with a neckline almost as high as the T-shirt.

When I catch a glimpse of my hair in the mirror, I nearly lose it. I try to catch Tessa's eye, but she has her back to me, and no one is talking so I'm guessing it's a rule.

"Hurry up!" Chloe barks at me.

"What am I supposed to do with this?" I ask, pointing to my lopsided locks.

"Clean up the braid and use this for the other side," she says, shoving an elastic headband at me that she grabbed from a basket of them on the counter. I'm guessing I'm not the first to face Mrs. Hemple's shears. I do what Chloe says to my hair, and I look ridiculous.

Next we file out of the dorm (prison bunk) and into the cafeteria. Some girls have eggs and pancakes with syrup, but when I get to the front, I'm handed a solitary bowl of tepid oatmeal. Much like the bunkers, there's a caste system with the food too: you don't get real food until you earn it.

The sight of the lumpy, cooling mass turns my stomach, so I shove it forward and lean back in my chair.

"If you don't eat it all, you get locked in the Grace Tank," Tessa whispers to me across the table without even looking up. I don't know what the Grace Tank is, and I don't want to find out. I stare at the bowl, trying to muster the courage to eat.

"Is God's provision not good enough for you, Miss Grant?" this is another adult. I don't know her name, but I assume she's another enforcer under Mrs. Hemple.

"No, ma'am," I say, and force myself to take a bite. It's everything I can do to stuff the rest down my throat before yet another bell rings and everyone at my table stands with their dirty dishes and walks toward the kitchen.

I realize after a moment that it's only my table who's standing up. The other girls, the ones in levels above me, continue to eat, some tables even allowed to chat. I open my mouth to ask Chloe what's going on, but she interrupts me before I can.

"Level Ones do the dishes," she says, then sits on the counter in the kitchen to supervise. She doesn't lift a finger until we're done.

As it turns out, Level Ones don't just do the dishes—they do all the cleaning. For the girls' side, and the boys' camp too, which is on the opposite side of the property from ours, past what looks like a training pen for horses. I only know it's the boy's side because Tessa tells me. While we're cleaning, there's no sign of them.

I can tell the direction by where the mountains are. We couldn't have been driving long enough to cross over them, so they must still be to the west. But beyond that, I can't tell much. Even as a Denver native, I don't know the Rocky Mountain Range well enough to tell which peaks are which, or where I am in relation to them. Tessa doesn't know where we are either.

The rest of the morning is spent on our hands and knees, scrubbing tiled floors with rough steel wool. Cleaning toilets and washing windows until my fingers pucker. By the time lunch rolls around, I'm so tired and hungry I take what they give me and devour it: a stiff bologna sandwich (one slice on stale white bread) and a glass of milk. And after we're done eating, the dishes again.

Finally, after doing the dishes, we're allowed to sit down. Chloe leads us into the "community room," which turns out to be the same room they took me to when I arrived.

The chairs are arranged in a tight circle. Mrs. Hemple is sitting in one of them, studying her Bible. We all sit down, and she raises her gaze.

"Bow your heads," she says, and all of us obey. "Dear Jesus, I ask You to be with us right now. Let Your light shine on our darkness until it is exposed and cleansed with Your love. Amen."

Everyone raises their heads. I notice that they're all sitting perfectly still, knees together, hands clasped on their laps. I do the same. Today is about watching, learning, finding a hole.

"Chloe, begin please."

"My name is Chloe, and I am asking Jesus's forgiveness for the sin of rebellion." What that could mean, I have no idea. I wonder who Chloe's parents could be—Puritan-level Christians who tolerate no disobedience? Or lazy people who ship off their daughter so they don't have to deal with any sort of disagreements at all?

"And why are you here, Chloe?" Mrs. Hemple asks.

"I'm here because I am a willful and disobedient child who needs the love of Christ to change my bad attitude."

This continues around the circle.

"My name is Rebecca, and I am asking Jesus's forgiveness for the sins of lust and murder." Jesus.

"And why are you here, Rebecca?"

"I am here because I gave away my purity before marriage, then killed the child God gave me in His grace." Well that explains things. Abortion, the worst sin of them all.

"My name is Zoe, and I am asking Jesus's forgiveness for the sin of wrath."

"And why are you here, Zoe?"

"I am here because I punched a boy at my school and broke my dad's nose with a hammer." She doesn't look like a particularly violent girl. She looks tiny, weak. It makes me wonder what her dad did.

"My name is Cassandra, and I am asking Jesus's forgiveness for the sin of coveting."

"And why are you here, Cassandra?"

"I am here because I stole a pair of jeans from the mall." Oh, come on. This is just ridiculous. I'm not saying she should go around stealing things, but to send her here for something like that? It seems totally insane.

I have no idea what I'll say when the circle comes around to me. Is this something I was supposed to be considering? Everyone else seems to be reciting the words from memory.

As I'm thinking, I hear Tessa's voice.

"My name is Tessa, and I'm asking Jesus's forgiveness for the sin of unnatural love."

"And why are you here, Tessa?"

"I'm here for falling in love," she says. Oh, Tessa. My heart breaks for her. Of all the reasons people are here, this one seems the cruelest.

"You know the rules, Miss Smythe. And you know what happens if you break them. Why don't you try again?"

"I'm here because I committed unnatural sexual acts with another female." I hate that she's forced to tell the room this.

"That's better."

The circle comes around to me. Everyone's staring, and I don't know what I'm supposed to say.

"Miss Grant?" Mrs. Hemple says, her eyes intent on me. She knows I couldn't possibly know what to say. Does she just want to make me squirm?

"Yes?" I say.

"Please share with the group what you are seeking forgiveness for."

"I'm not seeking forgiveness for anything." There's no reason to lie. What else could they possibly do to me that's worse than being here?

"So you're perfect then?" Mrs. Hemple asks.

"I didn't say that."

"'For all have sinned and fall short of the glory of God,' Miss Grant. I imagine you're familiar with that one?"

"Yes."

"Then what is it you're seeking forgiveness for?"

"Nothing," I say. "I don't need to be forgiven for anything."

"What do you think, girls? Do you think Emma is as flawless as she says?"

"No, ma'am," they all say in unison.

"Lie down on the ground Emma," Mrs. Hemple says.

"What?"

"You heard me. Right in the center here."

I roll my eyes, but follow her directions. If she wants to publicly humiliate me, I don't care. But I will not lie.

"Stretch your arms out and close your eyes," Mrs. Hemple says. I see her yank a dark cloth from her pocket. Whatever is coming, she planned it. She knew what I would say, and what she would do when I said it.

I let my arms extend along the cold linoleum, like a snow angel. I close my eyes, and as soon as I do I feel Mrs. Hemple's sour breath over my face, feel her hands and the cloth around my eyes, feel her lift my head and tug the cloth into a tight knot, feel her drop my head back to the ground with no efforts to soften the landing.

"Open the chest, Chloe."

I breathe deeply, shut it all out. I don't care, I don't care, I don't care. I'm on top of the Empire State Building. The wind in my hair. The sun on my skin. And Jackson. Jackson.

"Girls," Mrs. Hemple says.

I hear the shuffle of feet, then feel hands. Hands gripping my wrists, my ankles. Panic rises inside my belly, but I push it back down. What can she do to me? She can't kill me. I can handle everything else.

Then there's a heave and something heavy, really heavy, thuds onto my chest. It feels like a sack of dirt, the kind you buy from the hardware store to fill flowerbeds, but there's no smell of earth. The weight of it presses on my belly, on my lungs. Then there's another thud and the weight doubles.

I struggle against the grip of the other girls, but they're holding on tight.

"Be still," Mrs. Hemple says.

"Take it off. I can't breathe," I say.

"It hurts, doesn't it, Miss Grant?" Mrs. Hemple asks.

"Yes."

"Just like the weight of your sins. They hurt just as much, if not more. We are literally buried under the weight of all that pain. Only Jesus can take away our burdens."

Then another thud and another and another. My feet. My hands. My arms. My toes are angled foreword, pressing my ankles and feet into a dancer's pointe. My hands and arms are pinned to the ground.

"Please take it off," I say. Every breath is an effort.

"Who are you asking?"

"You," I say.

"Wrong," she says. "Another."

Another thud, and the weight on my lungs grows again.

"Please."

"Please who?"

I know what she wants me to say, but I won't do it. She wants me to break, to beg Jesus for help.

I stay silent.

"Very well, Miss Grant. Have it your way."

I hear the footsteps of the girls, walking around my head. Then another bag lands on my face, smothering and heavy and hard. I feel my face purpling, feel the pressure build behind my eyes.

"Is this how you want to meet the Lord, Emma? Buried in your own sins? Pray over her, ladies. Pray that her pride doesn't get in the way of her eternal salvation."

I feel the tiny pressure of hands laid upon me, then voices raised in prayer, then the faintest whisper, "Just say it." It's Tessa. "It's not worth it."

My air is nearly gone. And she's right. It's not worth the fight. It's not worth my life. I know what I believe. A few words can't change that.

"Jesus! Jesus! Jesus! Jesus!"

Immediately, the bags are pulled off me and the other girls are hoisting me upright. Mrs. Hemple starts singing.

"Amazing grace. How sweet the sound. That saved a wretch like me."

The other girls join her.

"I once was lost but now am found. Was blind, but now I see."

Mrs. Hemple pulls the blindfold off my eyes. There's a pile of sacks, big rice sacks, stacked inside the circle.

"Isn't that better, Emma? Isn't that easier than fighting? All you have to do is accept Christ's love, and He immediately takes away the burden of our sins."

Her face is so earnest, so joyful that, for a second, I want to believe her. I want to think that all I have to do is ask Jesus for help and all of this, all my problems, will go away. But then I remember the last two years of struggle and prayer and asking. There was no help then, and there will be no help now. I glare at her with every dagger in my eyes.

"What do you have to say for yourself? Are you ready to accept Christ's love?"

"Oh please," I say. "This is all bullshit."

Everyone gasps, but out of the corner of my eye, I think I see Tessa smile.

"It sounds like Emma needs some time to pray."

Mrs. Hemple grabs my arm and drags me out of the room, down the hallway, and into a room that must be her office.

She swings open a closet door and shoves me inside. Everything is black. I hear the door lock and feel around in the dark.

"Ow!"

My finger comes back with a splinter. Plywood, on all sides. The floor so small there's not enough room to stretch my legs out all the way.

Then there's a crackle from above. Speakers. Music. "Amazing Grace."

It's a chorus of girls, probably ones stuck here at some point, because it sounds folks-y, not professional. The volume spikes, so high I have to shove my fingers in my ears to avoid the sting. This must be the Grace Tank.

I spend the entire song hoping for just an inch of silence, but when it ends, it plays again. And again. And again. By the tenth repetition, I know I'll be in here for a while.

CHAPTER SIXTY

TIME MOVES SLOWLY. AFTER a while I lose track of how many times the song plays. Eventually, my ears grow numb to the sound, and I risk pulling my fingers out of my ears. But it's still so loud it's uncomfortable.

I take off my T-shirt and rip out the neckline, then stuff the fabric in my ears. The sound dulls to a manageable level. My head clears, and I decide to find a way out of this place. I don't know how yet. But I will find a way.

I wad up the T-shirt and stuff it behind my neck, leaning against the wall. I try to sleep, but my head is churning with so many thoughts it makes it impossible. I think about Jackson, about what to say to him the next time I see him, about what I've decided about us after being here.

Most of my thoughts are about June, though. And about me too. Theories dance around, twisting and untwisting until everything is tangled together in an unmanageable heap. I decide to think through things from the beginning again. I sort people by motives. I sort people by opportunity. I sort people by whether or not they had something against June. I sort them by whether or not they had something against me. I lay out the timelines of that night, of my past, of June's.

That's when something, a little tiny something that might be nothing at all, clicks. Two thousand and five. Jay Peterson died in 2005. What if Lee was right? What if…?

It's a long shot, really long. But it's not impossible, is it? No. It's not.

There's no way to know without proof, and I'm stuck here.

Which makes it even more important that I find a way to escape.

Eventually, my mind running itself into the ground with the idea, I fall asleep.

I don't know how long I'm sleeping, but my dreams are dark twisted things. Guns and blood and chests torn apart by bullets. And June, her face twisting away from me on a wisp of smoke.

I'm awoken by light. Streaming through the doorway, cutting my pupils into painful slivers.

"Have you had the time you need to pray?"

I have. There's been no praying, but I've thought a lot. I put on my best Christian-zombie face: eyes blank, mouth slack, and say, "Yes, ma'am."

"And what have you learned?"

"To ask Jesus for forgiveness for my sins."

"Which sins?"

"Lying and doubt and fornication." I say it like a mantra, without feeling, without meaning. Even though I know it's a lie, even though I know it's just a means to an end, saying it out loud hurts.

"Good. Put your shirt on and have a seat."

She motions toward the chair across from her desk, and I climb out of my hole and into bright daylight that beams through the slats in her window blinds. I look around the room. Sparse, mission-style furniture, simple but expensive. She's probably making a load off this little brat camp of hers. A bookshelf with Christian-themed books about raising youth to follow God. Pictures of her family—a husband and three toddlers. The clock on the wall reads 7:40 a.m. I've been in there for over fifteen hours.

I sit in the chair, stretching my neck and my legs. Everything is cramped and tight. I daydream about a massage, a pedicure, and especially Jackson's touch—anything to make my body stop hurting. Mrs. Hemple's voice breaks into my mind.

"I know the punishments here seem harsh, but I truly believe they are effective. By the end of your time here, I hope you'll be able to call me a friend."

She believes this shit. She really does.

Mrs. Hemple gets out her scissors and walks toward me. I try not to flinch as she cuts the other side of my hair.

"There. A reward for your attitude. See? I can be fair, can't I? My daddy named me Mercy for a reason."

"Your name is Mercy?"

"That's right. Pretty, isn't it?"

Well, at least I know whose idea it was to send me here now.

"So your sister is Miss Hope?" I ask, though I'm fairly certain of the answer. She and my parents must have been whispering it outside the door after we talked, which means this little plan has been in the works for at least a week, before they even saw the video. If only I had seen it coming. I would have run away.

"Yes. I thought you knew. She was very concerned about you. Called me personally to discuss your case and convinced me to take you on. I'm very selective about the girls I accept here, Emma. I only choose the ones I know I can help. And I believe that about you. I truly do."

I bet she does.

I reach up to touch the short spot on my scalp and feel only uneven chunks. I can't imagine what I must look like now.

"Hair can grow back, Emma, but we only have one chance to lead a life worthy of God's grace. I know it seems hard right now, but God puts obstacles in our path to make us stronger. That's what my daddy always said. And he was right. You will come through to the other side of all of this."

Mrs. Hemple lets me join the rest of the girls in the bunks as they prepare for the day. I wash my face and hands, trying to avoid the mirror so I don't have to look at what Mrs. Hemple has done to me, to my hair. But it's inevitable. It looks like I've been attacked by a weed whacker. I brush it and put on one of the elastic hair bands the girls with short hair are allowed to use.

When I'm done, I line up at the door, ready to go to breakfast, but Chloe yanks me out of line.

"Change your shirt, Emma, or you're going to get me in trouble," she says.

I look down and realize that I'm still wearing the shirt I tore up in the Grace Tank. Apparently, deconstructed fashion hasn't hit the halls of New Mercy Ranch quite yet.

I go back to my bunk and climb up on the side rails to change. I unzip my suitcase. Then I stop.

I hear something strange, see a movement beneath my

clothes. Is it a trick of the light?

Gently, I pull back my nightgown.

The tail of the rattler stands straight up.

It bears its jaws and hisses as angry venom drips from its fangs.

CHAPTER SIXTY-ONE

I SCREAM, REAR BACK, and tumble off the bed frame onto the floor.

The other girls run over to see what happened, and soon I'm not the only one screaming. The sound is like a fire alarm.

I get up and race toward the door, but it's still locked for the morning. Some girls climb on top of the bunks across the room and huddle together. A brave soul named Stephanie whips the blanket off her own bed and throws it over the snake.

The rattler snaps at the blanket, twisting out of its cover and falling hard to the floor, where it slithers under Chloe's bottom bunk. It moves so quickly and smoothly into the darkness that it's hard to tell what direction it was headed. Will it stay under there or come out somewhere else? I was scared when I saw the snake. I'm even more terrified not seeing it.

I bang on the door, "Help! Help! Let us out!"

Baldy opens the door, and we rush to get out, but his broad body blocks us from leaving.

"Hey! Back inside!"

"Please, there's a—"

"What's going on in here?" Mrs. Hemple asks, appearing behind him. "What is all this ruckus about?"

"Snake!" Me and several other girls shout. "Rattlesnake!"

"Are you sure?"

"Yes,"

"That's odd. Long way from their nest. Where'd you see it?" she asks.

279

"Under Chloe's bed," I say, pointing to the last place I saw it.

"Just the one?" she asks.

"Yes."

Mrs. Hemple charges forward. She grabs a broom from where it's resting against the wall and hands it to Chloe.

"You. Go to the other side and poke the broom under. I'll be waiting at the other end."

"But Mrs. Hemple—," Chloe says.

"Do as I say. Right now."

We all hold our breath as Chloe creeps toward the bed, the broom held in front of her like a weapon. She stands a few feet away, too scared to move.

"For goodness sake, girl, do it now," Mrs. Hemple says.

Chloe timidly stretches the broom out in front of her. Then, in a rush of fear, she thrusts the brush end under the bed. There's a hiss, but sure enough, the snake races out the other end toward Mrs. Hemple.

Everyone screams as it rushes past her and bolts toward the door.

Straight toward me.

But just as I think it's going to bite, Mrs. Hemple snatches the thing by the neck, behind its jaw.

She holds it into the air, squirming and hissing and terrifying. The grin on her face is triumphant. I doubt anyone has seen her happier.

"There's a reason the devil takes the form of a snake in the Bible, girls. Snakes are runners. They don't confront their problems. They're weak." She turns to Derrick, whose mouth is as wide open as the rest of ours. "Don't just stand there. Fetch me a potato sack."

Derrick races out of the room.

"Better get on to breakfast before it gets cold," Mrs. Hemple says.

We file out past her, the snake hissing as each of us passes.

I eat my gruel in a daze, thinking, my thoughts churning to peaks of anger, making my stomach roil with anxiety and fear. That was no accident.

Miss Hemple said it herself. How did a snake make it into my suitcase? There's no food up there. And with all the cleaning we've done, I can't imagine the property attracts mice. Not to mention how difficult it would be to even get into the room in the first place with only one door and one window.

If it did get in, why would it skip a lower, quieter area, like under a bed, and go up into a top bunk? And then my suitcase?

There's no way that was an accident. Someone just tried to kill me. Here.

I wanted to leave the moment I arrived. Now I have to. I'm a sitting duck.

The ever-present question pokes me relentlessly. Who? Who? Who? My mind lists the people who know where I am: my parents, Miss Hope, Pastor Pete, Mike, Paige, their parents. And who else? It wasn't exactly a private display, their taking me. The word likely spread to the entire school before lunch. And my parents had to have told other people at church too.

My gut is telling me something, but I need more information before I'll know for sure. And to get it, I'll have to get out of here.

The rest of the day goes by slow and cloudy. I move through my chores and meals mechanically, watching, plotting, waiting for my chance. When we go into our dorm for the night, everyone triple checks every nook and cranny for snakes. No one finds anything.

And then it's time for lights out, and I wait.

Eventually, the room goes soft with sleep. Quietly, the rhythmic breathing of twenty girls blends into a gentle hum, like the constant pull of the wind only without the ebb and flow that marks its arrival and departure. I listen, wide awake, until I can clearly hear Chloe's droning snore, then sit up and reach for the suitcase at my feet.

The zipper is plastic, and I'm thankful for its quiet buzz as I gently pull it open. My eyes have finally adjusted to the almost total blackness, but still I can barely make out my dirty clothes smashed on top of everything else. I pull them out and feel around to see if there's anything else useful inside the suitcase. I wish for a knife or scissors or a hanger or anything I could use to help me escape, but all I find is a nail clipper inside a small toiletry bag. There isn't much in there, just the basics: shampoo, toothbrush, toothpaste, tampons, hair ties, a compact brush. But it could be useful. It would be easy to carry, and who knows how long I might be on my own? I set it aside.

I keep digging. There's a Bible and a notebook and a new metal water bottle. There's also fresh underwear, socks, my fluffy bathrobe, and some other clothes I can't identify as my own. They feel stiff and new, unworn. More khaki skirts. I don't need them. I set aside the water bottle, the toiletry bag, and a fresh set of undergarments. Everything else is useless to me.

I strip off my nightgown as quietly as I can and dress. Each swish of fabric over my skin feels like the echo of a gun. Out of habit, I grab a ponytail holder and reach to wrap my hair into a bun. The shock of the short hair hits me again. It's jarring to reach up and feel nothing. It spurs me on. I have to get out of here.

I dig in the suitcase for my shoes, but don't feel them. My hands hit something else—my mother's note. I don't take it with me. I don't care what's in there. Nothing my parents can say will ever make up for this.

I look for shoes, then remember that they're nestled at the foot of the bed, right by Chloe's head, another measure against me trying to run. Dammit. There's no way I'll get anywhere barefooted.

As quietly as I can I climb over the edge of the bed, then I think of something. I scramble back up and pull the nightgown over my head and roll up my jeans. The nightgown is big and billowy enough to conceal my real clothes. I grab my bathrobe too, and stuff my small stash into the giant pockets, then slip it on as an added layer of concealment, even though it's way too warm for a robe in here. The room is stuffy, airless. My temperature shoots up, but the robe will help if anyone sees me. I can ditch it later.

I slip my legs over the edge of the bunk, using every muscle in my body to make my movements slow and controlled. Chloe and Tessa cannot wake up. They just can't.

Finally, I feel the floor beneath my feet and ease myself down. My shoes sit right under the bed, directly beneath Chloe's gaping, drooling mouth. I tiptoe lightly over. One step, then another, until I'm close enough to crouch down. I reach for them, my face level with Chloe's, my eyes only inches away from hers. I hold my breath and feel my hands close around my sneakers.

Then I feel a hand on my shoulder.

CHAPTER SIXTY-TWO

IT TAKES EVERYTHING IN me to stop the scream before it reaches my throat. My head snaps up. Staring at me, from the bunk above Chloe's, is Tessa. Her green eyes nearly glow out from the darkness. Her brow is furrowed. Her hair, at some point, has been cut on the other side too, just like mine. A reward for good behavior.

"I'm going with you," she whispers. Then adds for good measure, "Please."

I don't know what to say. I don't want to say anything at all, for fear of waking Chloe. Can I trust Tessa? Will she hold me back?

It doesn't really feel like I have a choice, though. If I tell her no she'll wake Chloe, I'm certain of it. I nod my head yes and motion her to hurry. Tessa shoots up to a seated position, her eyes wild, excited. Chloe stirs. I whip my fingers to my lips, motioning Tessa to be quiet. She stills, and I can see the wildness behind her eyes retreat. Chloe smacks her lips and breathes deep, then rolls over and tugs the pillow under her head. Her snoring resumes.

I motion to Tessa to come down. Carefully, she swings out of bed and grabs her entire suitcase. I shake my head violently. She can't take the whole thing with her. We need to be fast. She lifts one finger, motioning for me to wait, then points to the bathroom. She's right. It will be quieter to gather what she needs in there. I grab her shoes for her, and we make our way to the bathroom.

Once inside, Tessa carefully closes the door behind us.

"Thank you," she says. "I can't stand being here even one more day. You don't even know."

"I know enough," I whisper. "Hurry up. We need to go before anyone needs a midnight pee break."

Tessa drops her bag to the floor and starts to unzip it.

"Not in here," I say. "Someone might see you. Use one of the stalls in the dressing room."

"Good idea."

We make our way into the dressing room, which also happens to be the only room in this whole place with an actual window. Tessa digs into her bag and starts to change.

"How are we getting out? Did you nab a key or something?"

"The window."

She stares at me blankly, stops buttoning her top. Her face looks like someone just stole her puppy.

"What's the matter?" I ask.

"Go out the window? That's your big plan? I thought you were smarter than that." She reaches for her nightgown. "That window leads to a central courtyard where all the dorms meet. They've got a guard out there all the time. Last week Shania tried to get out that way, and they put her in the Grace Tank. She was in there for three days. It's basically a trap to figure out who the bad ones are right away. Otherwise don't you think they'd put bars on it or something? They want you to run, but on their terms so they can fuck you over, just like everything else around here."

"Do you know of any other exits? Any ways out besides the front door?"

"That's it. The front door and the window. Unless you've got something strong enough to bore through concrete blocks we're stuck."

Shit.

Tessa pulls the nightgown back down over her head, giving up on escape, giving up on me. "God help them if there's ever a fire," she says.

A fire? God help them indeed.

"What if there was a fire? They must have a plan for that sort of thing. They seem to have something planned for everything else. They'd have to evacuate us, right? It'd be easy to disappear in the confusion."

"You want to start a fire?" Her voice is harsh, skeptical, but she's stopped herself from taking off her jeans mid-leg. "Haven't you read the rules? No matches allowed. Lighters either."

My memory tries to grasp at something, something that seemed stupid at the time, silly. A movie? A joke? Then Tessa's eyes light up again, and whatever it is I was thinking of slips away.

"We could wait until tomorrow. I bet there's some matches in the shed by the outdoor chapel. We've only been there during the day so far, but there's a fire pit out there. I think they use it for graduation."

I remember what it was that my mind was grasping at.

Tessa continues. "They have to have a way to light it, and it's kind of far from the rest of campus so maybe—"

"We don't have to wait until tomorrow. I know how we can start a fire tonight."

It was a couple summers ago, at Youth Council Retreat. The summer was nearly over. After the sun goes down up in the mountains, August feels like October. We all thought it would be fun to build a bonfire. That's what made me think of it. The fire pit. The bonfire.

The boys were showing off. They wanted us to see how strong and smart and wilderness-y they were. Only in the church crowd would guys think the way to impress a girl was a bragging about the survival skills they learned in Brothers In Christ. As if any of them had ever been more than a couple miles from somewhere that could sell them a Coke, or ever would be the rest of their lives. But to their credit, they did know what they were doing. There were plenty of matches, but they didn't use them.

I remember Nicolas's hands guiding mine, remember the spark as it started, the glow of it in the night.

Tessa is staring at me, her face tentative but hopeful.

"Get dressed," I say.

She obeys, tugging her jeans back on, gathering her things. She can sense the excitement behind my words, hear the sureness in my voice. I leave her on her own and race into the bathroom.

There's got to be some in here, we've been using them for all our chores. I slide open the cabinet under the sink, and sure enough, it's right there with all the other cleaning supplies. Steel wool, the cheap scratchy kind that gnaws at your fingers with every scrub. Of course Mrs. Hemple wouldn't spring for the gentle plastic ones. I wonder, not for the first time, what my parents are paying for me to have the privilege to scrub toilets with steel wool.

It doesn't matter. Only escape matters now. I grab the steel wool and a roll of single-ply toilet paper for tinder and head back into the dressing room. Tessa is almost ready.

Whatever these buildings were originally built for, it wasn't to house teenage girls. There are no electrical plugs for curling irons or hairdryers anywhere. The only electricity piped into the place is for a single overhead light in each room. But the dressing stalls are against the wall, away from the center, and would be dark without extra light. And no good comes from girls left to their own devices in the dark. What easier way to illuminate them than mounting a battery operated tap light in each stall?

I go to one of them and twist it until the housing pops off of the base. The tab slides off easily, and I pop out exactly what I need: a 9-volt battery.

I hold my breath and rub the nub end of the battery against the steel wool. A tiny, orange spark lights into the air. It's not a lot, but it's something. Tessa stares at it, at me, in amazement.

"How'd you know to do that?" she asks.

"Long story. You ready?"

She nods yes. Her robe pockets bulge just like mine, but she's been smart. She's only taking what she can carry, no more. I notice her Bible on top of her suitcase. It didn't make the cut.

I imagine that places like this turn you into two types of people. The first are people like Chloe who will never trust themselves again and cling to the church even harder once they leave, praying for guidance on every decision in their lives from college to which peanut butter to buy. She's the kind of girl who believes every bad thing anyone in authority ever says about her, or anyone else for that matter.

The second are people like me and Tessa, people who may have been on the fence about God before coming here, or at least close to it. We're the kind of people who can trust no one but ourselves afterward, especially not the church. Especially not God.

Please let this work, I say to the great someone or no one at all. Please let this work.

I scan the room again. I don't want to hurt anyone. All we need is a few minutes of chaos to escape out the window while everyone else is racing out the door. I lug an old metal waste basket directly under the smoke detector that's closest to the entrance of the dressing room.

"Open the window just a crack," I say to Tessa. It's covered with some type of frosted plastic to obscure the view. "See if the guard's out there."

She scurries over and eases the window up slowly, then peeks out. She looks back at me and nods. There's a guard.

"Keep watch," I whisper. "Signal when he leaves."

I fish some papers out of the trash, letters home that have been discarded as either not good enough or too useless to send. Quietly, I pull a curtain down from one of the stalls and stuff it into the waste basket. I rip the toilet paper off the roll and place it on top of the curtain, then stuff the cardboard tube with the letters.

"Here goes nothing," I say. Tessa is crossing her fingers. She may not totally believe in a higher power either, but we need as much luck as we can muster right now.

I rub the battery against the steel wool, holding it right above the cardboard TP tube.

Nothing.

I try again. Just a tiny spark this time, that fizzles out to black before it lands on the tube without any heat.

I ball the steel wool up tighter and strike it against the battery as hard as I can. This time it catches, and hard. Before I know what's happening the entire wad of steel wool sparks to flame in my hand. I drop it into the can, but miss the tube. It's not hot enough to light the TP yet. I need the flame to grow from the cardboard and paper, and the wool is burning out fast.

I nudge the tube toward the flame with my bare fingers. It smokes for a moment, almost goes out. I blow at the embers gently, evenly. They glow with my breath, then simmer down. I blow again then, whoosh! The cardboard tube lights up.

It spreads to the toilet paper, and the curtain underneath.

The smoke is billowing now, riding high up into the ceiling.

BEEP! BEEP! BEEP! BEEP!

The smoke alarm blares to life. I hear the shuffling sound of girls waking and peek my head out into the room, concealing myself in the shadow of the doorway. They're all awake, looking around, trying to figure out where the noise is coming from, not thinking for a second that there could actually be a—

"Fire! Fire!" a girl screams. She's pointing toward the bathroom, to the smoke now billowing out the doorway.

"Everybody out!" another girl demands.

Girls scream and cry. They jump out of their beds and panic as they remember that the door is locked. Somebody races to the front door and pounds on it, but it doesn't open. More girls join her. A crowd surges against the door, banging on it to open.

"Help! Help!"

"Let us out!"

"Please! We're trapped!"

Smoke is filling the air, and I resist the urge to cough. I look back to the window, to Tessa. She's motioning for me to come. Come now! The guard must be gone. But I have to be sure the others can escape.

The front door whooshes open, and a flood of girls races through it. All sense of orderliness is gone. I race back to the window and hoist Tessa up to the sill. She sits on it and pulls me up. I glance back. The fire has died down to almost nothing now. Its flames barely lick the edges of the waste basket. It's the last thing I see as I jump out into the cool night air.

CHAPTER SIXTY-THREE

As SOON AS I hit the ground I feel Tessa grab my hand and lurch me forward. It's the first time I realize that without her, I'd have no idea where to go to get out of here. All I've seen are the buildings that need cleaning. She's been here longer. I don't know the place well enough yet. And it won't take long for somebody to figure out what's happened. We have seconds —not minutes—to disappear.

I run, holding Tessa's hand tight as she dodges between buildings and into the darkness. I'm thankful for my sneakers and my lungs, conditioned from years of track and cheerleading and soccer. Tessa is heaving, but she doesn't stop. After a few minutes I have to slow down so she can keep up, but she pumps along at my side, not allowing herself to quit.

We run for what seems like forever. Through buildings and a field filled with rusting farm equipment. We run past the last buildings and out into the fields. We run past what must be the outdoor chapel she talked about, past the shed that might contain matches. We run and we run and we run.

It's so open out here. The landscape is low, scratchy brush and dust and dirt. There are no trees to obscure our presence. The moon and stars are so bright it almost feels like morning. There's no point in trying to hide. We are completely exposed. All we can do is put as much space between them and us before anyone notices we're gone.

We climb a hill, and when we crest it I see a fence. It's at least ten feet tall. There's barbed wire on top of it too, as though this was a real jail, not just an overpriced time-out corner. Tessa's pace is barely running anymore. I yank on her hand and pull her toward the fence, but she breaks away from me, leans over and sucks air.

"Come on. We're almost there."

Beyond the fence there are trees, real trees, which means there has to be a source of water nearby too. Maybe a lake, or maybe even a river we could get in and let carry us off to somewhere. I wonder if Tessa knows how to swim.

She stands back up, and I tug her toward the fence. I climb up first, but Tessa's not far after me. The barbed wire looks sharp, but I'm not staying on this side just to avoid getting cut. Just as I'm about to reach for the top, Tessa speaks up. "Your robe! Throw it over the barbed wire!" She struggles up until she's next to me and helps me out of it, then I help her do the same. We toss the contents of our pockets over the fence, then double-layer the bathrobes over the sharp barbs.

I go first. As I swing my leg up and over the fence, I hear something that turns my blood cold. Voices. Shouting.

"Go! Come on!" Tessa says.

I launch myself over and climb down. Tessa makes it across, then gently pulls our robes off the fence before climbing down herself. She's smart. I would have left them, signaling to whoever is looking for us exactly where we escaped.

We barely make it to the trees before we see the bounce of flashlights crest the hill just before the fence. Tessa and I scramble behind a huge trunk just in time. A giant beam scans the area beyond the fence. The light is slow, searching.

"Check the entire perimeter," I hear someone say.

Someone else says, "They couldn't have made it far yet."

I hold my breath, which is impossible with my chest pounding, my blood pumped so full of adrenaline. Gasps of air leak out and betray me, and I know, just know, that someone must hear us, must see us, must be climbing over the fence right now.

But miraculously, the voices and the flashlights pass on, scanning out even farther, heading away from us. I barely register it when Tessa takes my hand again and guides me farther into the trees. I follow her lead.

Dawn is moving into full-on morning by the time we hear the

cars and nearly stumble right onto the highway. We ditch the robes and nightgowns, pat our choppy hair down as best we can, and stick out our thumbs. It doesn't take long. Even two dog-faced girls our age could hitch a ride in no time. But with Tessa? It doesn't take long at all.

A grungy-looking guy in his late twenties picks us up. I have to shove fast food bags off the backseat in order to find a place to sit down. Tessa insists on sitting in back with me. The guy seems disappointed. Once again, I'm glad she's here with me. One of us, he could drive anywhere he wanted. But two of us together? He may think about it, but he knows it wouldn't work. Tessa grabs my hand and squeezes it tight for support. I don't miss seeing the guy lick his lips in the rearview mirror, churning up who knows what kind of gross fantasies.

"You guys girlfriends or something?"

"No," I say. I let go of Tessa's hand. Why do some people have to turn something perfectly innocent into something gross? Even though I'm not into girls, I wouldn't care if somebody thought I was gay, at least not anymore. But this guy?

"It's cool if you are, you know. No judgment here."

"We're not," Tessa says firmly.

"Okay, okay. Just sayin'. Where you girls headed?"

Tessa looks over to me, and I realize she has nowhere to go. I hadn't even asked. I just assumed that she was escaping to get to a girlfriend or a cousin or something. But her look tells me that's not the case.

"Denver," I say. "Where are we now?"

"Wyoming, just outside of Powell. I can get you as far as Cheyenne," he says.

"Thanks."

He mostly leaves us alone after that. We drive all morning, him chatting away, us trying to play along like we give a shit what he's chatting away about. Once we hit Casper he buys us some lunch at a diner and offers to get us a hotel room. He backs down after we tell him no, but just to be safe we sneak to the bathroom and go out the back and hitch another ride.

The next guy is older, a cowboy, probably sixty-five. We slide into his pickup cab, and he doesn't say a word. I hated the last guy's chatter, but it's scarier, this guy not talking. I'm in the middle seat and expecting his hand on my thigh at any second, but he never does. He just drives, eyes on the road and the sun cutting a line across his face where the visor hits. Tessa grips my hand the whole time. He gets us to Cheyenne. As we're leaving, he forces a wad of cash into my palm.

"I don't know what you two are doing out here on your own, but the road's no place for two young ladies like yourselves. Why don't you catch a bus the rest of the way?"

We thank him and wave as he drives off, but I'm in too big of a hurry to catch a bus and it's too risky besides. They could already have police out looking for us, or e-mailed our pictures around or something. In this case, a stranger is safer.

We get lucky on the next car. It's a woman, middle aged. She tells us she sells pharmaceuticals and talks about girl power and tries to get us to tell her all our hopes and dreams. I think she thinks we're prostitutes. She probably imagines getting an "all-because-of-you" letter ten years from now with pictures of us super-successful at our non-slutty careers. But whatever. I put on my pastor's daughter smile and keep the lady talking the whole time, making up a story that we got lost camping and just need to get home. It's only a couple hours between Cheyenne and Denver, and she takes us straight to my neighborhood. She seems confused by the area when we get there. It doesn't match what she thought about us. With our awful hair and dirty clothes we can't seem like we belong.

Eventually, though, we thank her, and she drives off and we're standing at the end of my block. The sense of relief that washes over me is physical. But I don't feel stronger; I feel suddenly weaker. I can see it in Tessa too, a shift, as though she's just grown smaller. We've been up almost a solid twenty-four hours now, and it's the first time we haven't had to put on a show. We need sleep. We need food. We need shelter. We have none of it. And I have questions that need answers fast.

I tell her to wait there, then walk toward my house. It's just after one in the afternoon on a Friday. My parents should be at church. Should be. But with everything that's happened lately, who knows? Maybe they'll finally take a day off. I peek through the tall windows on the garage door and see that mine's the only car inside. Good.

I use the electronic keypad on the garage door to get in.

Inside, I throw a couple things into a duffle bag. Two sleeping bags. Some food from the fridge. Clothes for me and Tessa. A couple of mementos I can't bear to leave behind: a photo of me and Paige at camp last year, the Statue of Liberty figurine Jackson gave me. I look for money from my parent's dresser, but there is none, and I have to go before anyone figures out I'm here.

I get in my car and pick Tessa up on the corner. We drive. She's asleep as soon as the car starts moving. I want to sleep too, but there's too much to figure out. I have no idea where to go from here. I know Jackson would help if I asked, but what if the police are watching him? It's too risky. There are no friends left, no family to call, nothing. All we have for money is $40 the guy gave us for bus tickets, not even enough for a hotel room tonight.

It makes me think of June, alone out in the world, broke, nowhere to go. I always thought of her as fragile, weak, but you have to be some kind of strong to survive that kind of life. Am I? I don't know.

Eventually, I decide it's wasting gas to drive around. I only have a half tank, and I don't want to spend what little money we have on filling it up. I drive to City Park, the place Jackson and I used to meet. It's one of the biggest parks in Denver and has a golf course and a zoo and three lakes. I park near the biggest of them, Ferril Lake. It's warm, and the fountain in the center is going. There are runners out, moms with strollers, teenagers from East High School across the street, eating lunch on the long green lawns.

Tessa stirs, stretches awake. "Hey. What's up?"

"I'm gonna take a walk. Want to come?"

"Okay."

We lock up the car and head to the lake path. I need to think things through, figure out what to do next. She probably does too. We make it halfway around the lake before either of us says anything.

"I love this place," Tessa says.

"You're from Denver?"

"Yeah."

"But you don't want to go back to your family?"

"No. They hate me. There's no place for me there anymore."

"Any ideas of where else we could go?"

She shakes her head. Whatever happened to her has made her just as alone as I am. She pulls out a pack of cigarettes from her hoodie pocket, cigarettes she picked up at a truck stop in Wyoming. Taps one out. Searches her pockets for something.

"You don't have my lighter do you?" she asks.

"No."

"Must have left it in the car."

We turn around to go back for it, and see, racing through the five-mile-per-hour park streets, four police cars, lights flaring.

They come to a screeching stop next to my car, and the shape of a person I recognize gets out: Detective Boyer.

CHAPTER SIXTY-FOUR

I YANK TESSA BACK around, and head the opposite direction. We have to get out of here. Fast.

"What's going on?" she says.

"The police found my car."

"How?"

"I don't know." Could they have put a tracer on it? Back when they were following me everywhere? I can't rule it out.

"Why are they after you?"

"I don't know," I say. I really don't. Why would Detective Boyer go to all that trouble? Four police cars, all those lights, for a runaway teen? I turn eighteen in two weeks. It doesn't make any sense. "I need to get to a phone."

We book it out of the park, jaywalking across four busy lanes on 17th Street, toward East High School, hoping to blend in with the lunch crowd. As we walk toward the school, we hear three more police cars zoom by behind us, sirens blaring. No. This can't be for a runaway teen.

We walk past the school, out on to Colfax Avenue, and I spot a 7-Eleven on the corner. We go inside, looking for a pay phone, but there are none. I spend ten of our precious dollars on a prepaid cell phone, then realize I have no idea what the number is. I'm so used to having everything programmed in. I'm going to need a computer too.

Tessa and I catch a bus, the 16L, down Colfax toward downtown. It drops us a couple blocks from the Denver Public Library, a building that looks like a bunch of multicolored blocks stacked haphazardly, but still manages to be one of the most interesting buildings in Denver. We go inside, and I use one of their computers to log in to my iCloud account. I transfer a few numbers to the prepaid phone, log out, and we go. I have no idea if the police can trace me from this account. Are they even looking? Can they tell what computer I'm on if they are? It's safer to go.

On the street, I make a call.

"Emma, where are you? You're parents are very worried," Mr. Graham says.

"Why are the police looking for me?"

"Just tell me where you are, and I'll send a car to pick you up."

"Tell me why."

"They have a warrant for your arrest. For June's murder. You need to come to my office—"

"I don't understand. I haven't done anything."

"They found the murder weapon, Emma. It was in a Sunday school room at church, one of the church guns. Stolen from the security office. The police have been keeping that detail out of the papers."

The church guns. Of course. There's cabinet full of them in the security office that the Security Team carries during services just in case. Not that the guns did any good when there was an actual emergency.

"So what does that have to do with me?"

"They found your fingerprint. On a bullet inside the gun."

"They made a mistake," I say. "That's not possible."

"It is to them. You could have used your dad's key to get access to the cabinet and—"

"I'm telling you it's not possible."

"Look, just come down to my office, okay? They already have that Jackson Thomas boy in custody."

"Jackson's been arrested?"

"Brought him in an hour ago. With your record, it's pretty clear who masterminded this whole thing. If you come in right now, I think we still have a chance to—"

I hang up the phone.

Jackson is in jail, not juvie this time, actual jail. And it's all because of me. I lean against a concrete block wall, the feel of it cool on my back as I sink to the ground.

And the other thing too. My fingerprint on a bullet. How?

"So?" Tessa says. "What did he say?"

"Give me a second. I need to think."

My fingerprint on a bullet. There's no way.

Tessa spots someone smoking on the corner and walks up to them. "Got a light?"

"Yeah, sure," the guy says.

My fingerprint on a bullet.

Out of the corner of my eye I spot the flame shoot out of the lighter, ignite the cigarette. Smoke curls from Tessa's mouth.

Then it hits me. Lighter to fire to steel wool to batteries.

Batteries.

The cool metallic feel of them on my fingertips. Me blindfolded and clueless. But in a moment so inconsequential that they crossed my fingertips for just a few seconds, then slipped my mind. Nearly forever. If it hadn't been for that video, I wouldn't even remember it.

The moment it clicks into place other things do too. My missing earring, the few people who knew for certain I would be out of the room at the time of the murder, even that little detail must have been planned ahead.

And something else, Lee Stuckey right about trusting people, just like I thought. Only now, everything feels flipped. But what other reason could there be?

Connections form and join until I can see it all in front of me, like sheet music, each note perfectly in place, playing a melody I've never heard before.

I know who did it. I know exactly who did it.

CHAPTER SIXTY-FIVE

"TESSA, IT MIGHT NOT be safe for us to stay together. They're looking for me, and if they find me, they'll find you too." Tessa is a senior in high school like me, but she's only seventeen, won't be eighteen until August. They'd send her right back to her parents, who would send her right back to that place.

"Are you sure? I don't like the idea of you being alone."

I don't like the idea of it either, but I can't risk her life too.

"I'm sure. It's safer this way." If what I think happened actually happened, I'll need proof. And it could be dangerous.

We find a scrap of paper and borrow a pen. I give her my phone number at home, my address, my e-mail. I give her a note to give to my parents in case something happens to me. We split up the rest of the money and make a plan to meet at the boat house in City Park in a few days.

She gives me a big hug, then heads toward the 16th Street Mall. I stand at the bus stop and watch her disappear into the crowd, wondering if I'll ever see her again.

Then I make a call.

"Hey, Chuck. I need to ask you something."

A few bus rides and a short walk later, I'm standing in front of Pastor Pete's house. He lives in a small split-level not far from the church. It's made of red brick and looks like it was built in the '80's.

I knock on the door, but there's no answer. What time is it? Three something? He wouldn't be home. He'd be in his office at church. Good.

I try the handle, but it's locked, so I go around to the back. That door is locked too, so is the side door to the garage. I test all the windows I can reach, but they don't budge. On the upper floor, there's a window open, but there's no way to get to it. I'll have to break a window or something.

I spot a storage shed under a tree in the back yard, and go inside to look for something heavy. But I find something even better: a ladder.

I pull it out and prop it against the house, underneath the open window, and climb up. The screen pops out of its frame so easily I realize how simple it would have been for the killer to get into my bedroom when they planted the gun.

It's a little bit of a reach to get myself through the opening. I have to launch myself off the ladder toward the window, and I accidentally kick the ladder away from the house in the process. There's a loud clatter as it hits the ground. My stomach hits the sill hard, nearly knocking the breath out of me. But soon I'm tumbling through into Pastor Pete's bedroom.

It's sparse, not many pieces of furniture: a king-sized bed, a small dresser, what looks like a chair from an old dining set I've never seen in the house. I paw through the dresser, and look under the bed and mattress, but what I'm looking for isn't in here.

I search the top floor and find nothing, not a file cabinet in sight. There are only two bedrooms, and all the other one has in it is a small glass desk, no drawers, and an empty closet. It looks like he never even comes in here.

I go down the stairs onto the middle level. I scour the cabinets in the kitchen. Nothing. I go into the living room and pull up couch cushions, search the hall closet. Nothing.

I go down into the garden level basement, and through a short hall with a door that leads into the garage.

Much like Jesus, Pastor Pete fancies himself a carpenter. There's a workbench and tools, and a half-finished project that looks like it will be a headboard. Probably a wedding present. I search the drawers of the workbench, search behind it, on shelves holding sports equipment, in a box labeled simply, *Stuff.* But that turns out to be random parts of electronic equipment, and after scouring the rest of the garage, I find nothing, so I head back inside.

Even at just two bedrooms, the house seems big for a bachelor, but he told us he chose it for the basement. It's big enough to hold thirty of us on a good night. I've spent so many nights in this room—summer barbecues with the youth council, organizing agendas with other school captains for Prayer at the Pole, or sometimes nights with just Mike and Paige for what we called PK night at PP's. Pastor's Kids. Pastor Pete's. We'd watch movies, eat cereal—he's not exactly a cook, but it didn't matter. They were nights we all looked forward to, a chance to get away from the responsibilities of church. Pastor Pete seemed to understand that we needed them from time to time and opened his home to us. The memory of them makes everything so much more confusing.

The room is wide open, but unlike the bedrooms, this space is packed with things. There's a collection of mismatched couches lining the room, each of them Goodwill bargains hauled back here in his pickup truck and carried in by willing youth-group boys. There's a collection of artistically crafted crosses on one wall and posters of Christian bands on the others. Built-in bookshelves line the fireplace at the far end of the room.

I go through it all and find nothing. Could I be wrong about this?

I put my hands on my hips and give the room one last scan. My eyes land on the bookshelves. I have an idea. There are no yearbooks, like what my parents have taking up space on our shelves. But sure enough, there's a small, tattered-looking photo album on the bottom shelf. I leaf through.

When I find it, it's in an odd place, stuffed behind a photo of Pastor Pete on the pulpit at Bethany Bible College. It's a picture of a woman with shiny black hair and olive skin, smiling broadly in a green wool dress from the '70's. She's holding a baby boy. They're standing against a clearly fake backdrop of fall foliage, the picture tinted yellow with age. I flip it over. In scrawled, looped handwriting, the back reads:

Mommy and T.J., 6 months old, 1976.

T.J. Not Peter, not Pete, not even Petey.

And stuffed in right behind the photo? Tattered and stained, its edges mangled by years of being hidden away, is a birth certificate.

CHAPTER SIXTY-SIX

Pastor Pete is Jay Peterson. Lee Stuckey was right. He did trust the wrong person. And I'm pretty sure that person turned against him, turned him in with everyone else. I realized it when I compared the dates. Jay Peterson died in 2005. Pastor Pete, with no real history to show for himself even though he was already twenty-four years old, started college the same year.

I pocket the birth certificate and photo and head toward the front door. It's the evidence I need, but only half. There's still more to do before I go to the police.

Then there's a metallic click that makes my heart stop. I look for a place to hide, but there's nowhere, no time.

The door swings open just as I'm turning to go upstairs.

Pastor Pete stands in the doorway, his arms laden with a suit bag from the dry cleaners and shopping bags from the mall. His face is startled at first, then confused.

"Emma? What are you doing here? How did you get in?"

I had hoped I wouldn't have to do this. Not yet at least. "We need to talk," I say, and his face falls. He walks past me into the kitchen, as though me breaking into his house, a person charged with murder, is no big deal at all.

"All right. Whatever you need. Let me just put this stuff down."

I follow him inside, watch him hang the suit bag on the stair railing. It's only then I realize what's inside: his tuxedo. What day is it? Friday? Saturday? No, it must be Friday. His wedding is tomorrow.

"What's your real name?" I ask. "Because I know it's not

Peter Jakeman."

His body stiffens, but he says nothing.

"Did the police cut you a deal? In exchange for identifying the others?" I wasn't sure about this. But after I knew, when I was trying to figure out why, it made perfect sense.

He turns to face me, and his face is ashen.

"You can't tell anyone," he says. "Please, Emma. It means my life."

"Because you still have the money?"

"The money? No. No. The police have it."

He sinks into a chair at the kitchen table and buries his hands in his hair. "That was the deal. The money and the rest of them, and I'd go free. They agreed not to make it public so the others wouldn't know it was me. I don't have a single dollar of it, I swear."

His eyes beg me to believe him.

"Doesn't matter as far as Stuckey and his crew are concerned, though. They'll kill me themselves if they don't send someone else to do it before they get out."

"From the way he made it sound, it seemed like it was you who was in charge."

He looks away from me, out the window. "I never told them to bring guns. That wasn't supposed to happen. None of that was supposed to happen."

"June knew it was you, didn't she? She recognized you. She remembered your face."

He nods.

"When did you figure it out?"

"Her testimony."

Then it clicks. Her story. He wouldn't have known about it unless he was there. "It was you. You're the one who saved her as a kid."

He nods. "We were all supposed to be at that birthday party. We were supposed to meet there to divide the cash, but I had already talked to the police by then. The other guys were getting arrested, or already had been. I'm the one who sat down next to her on that ride. I didn't know she was too little for it. That experience…it changed everything for me."

He looks up at me then, his eyes bloodshot and his face flushed. It's odd to see him this way, so weak and powerless.

303

Our roles have switched. He's the child now.

"Afterward, she gave me the pig to say thank you. Her little heart, even at that age, was so generous. I saved it to remind me." He takes a deep breath, "To remind me to do something good with my life. To make up for that little baby and his mom."

He reaches out for my hand and grips it with both of his, the way I'd imagine him gripping the hem of Christ's robe. "I know how it looks, but I had nothing to do with her death. Absolutely nothing. I promise to you in the name of our Lord and Savior Jesus Christ."

I look him straight in the eye, "I know you didn't."

CHAPTER SIXTY-SEVEN

"You do?" Pastor Pete asks.

"But you told somebody else about it, didn't you?"

The look on his face breaks my heart. I can see the connections forming in his mind, the impossibility of it becoming possible, the weight of it crashing down on him. How his very presence caused her death, even if it wasn't his fault.

"No," he says. "I can't believe that."

"You have to tell the police," I say. "There's an innocent man in jail right now, and I'm not far behind. You have to tell them everything."

"But—"

There's a knock on his door.

"Are you expecting anyone right now?" I ask, my heart thudding in my chest.

"No, I—" he stands up. "You should hide."

I shuffle farther into the kitchen, past the view of the door. I hear the creak of it open.

"Hey, Pastor Pete," her voice says, happy and singsongy, and the sound of it makes me want to race out from hiding and hug her. "Could you come out and help me with something in the yard, please?"

I'd know that voice anywhere. It's Paige. Somehow hearing her voice is a sign that this will work out.

"I'm sorry, I'm sort of busy right now," Pastor Pete says.

"Come on," she says, "it'll only take a couple of minutes."

"I really wish I could, but I have so much to do. I still have to

305

pack for the honeymoon, and my house is a mess. I haven't done dishes in ages."

I hear her footsteps charge inside, past him. "Just go outside, okay? You kinda have to. I'll do the dishes for you."

"Paige, wait—"

I see him grab her arm, but it's too late.

"Em-bot? Is that—? What are you doing here? What happened to your hair? How did—? Oh, Emma, I'm so sorry." She races toward me and pulls me into a hug. "Are you okay? I was so worried about you after I left that place. I didn't know they were gonna do that to you, I promise."

"I'm fine. It's okay. Listen, you can't tell anyone I'm here, okay? Can you promise—"

"Oh, Em, they're all here. Outside."

"Who's outside?" Pastor Pete asks.

"A bunch of kids from youth group," she says to Pastor Pete. "They're gonna sing you this song they made up and spray you with shaving cream. It was supposed to be a surprise, for the wedding, but—"

"Paige," Pastor Pete says, "Do you have a car with you?"

"Yes," she says.

"Okay. I'll go outside and get rid of them. I need you to get Emma out of here. There's a walking trail right outside the back gate that empties out to Vine Street. Can you pick her up there?"

Paige nods. "Yeah, of course."

"Meet me at the police station in an hour," he says, then shoves me out the back door.

Paige sneaks out to her car while everyone is busy playing the prank on Pastor Pete. She picks me up exactly where he told her, and we drive toward the police station.

"I'm so sorry, Emma. Really, I am," she says after I tell her the whole story. "I should have given you a chance."

"I'm the one who should be sorry," I say. "You're my best friend; I should have trusted you with the truth."

"You don't have to be sorry about that," she says, going quiet. She stares straight ahead of her, and has that face on again, the one that tells me she's made a decision about something. From the look of it, it's something big. "You're not the only one with secrets. I know it's not the right time right now, but there's a lot I have to tell you too."

"Okay," I say.

When we get a block away from the station, I make her stop to drop me off.

"I'm not leaving you alone here," she says.

"You have to, Paiger. Just in case I'm wrong. I'm a fugitive. They can't know you helped."

"No way," she says.

"Look, I need you to do something for me, okay?"

Her face is skeptical. "What?"

I pull the birth certificate out of my pocket. The photo too. "I need you to keep these. Just in case they lock me up right away, okay? If it doesn't happen the way I said, don't wait. Go to the police and show them this."

She takes them. "I don't like leaving you here."

"It's almost over," I say. "Tomorrow, everything will be different."

Paige drives away, and I find a place to hide across the street until he shows up. Is Jackson in there right now, getting questioned again? Or have they already put him in a cell? I can't think about it. I have to stay focused, or there's no chance to save him, to save us.

The hour goes by, and still no Pastor Pete. I try not to worry. It may have taken him longer to get rid of everyone than he thought.

But after another forty minutes, I really start to panic. The sun is dipping close to the horizon, and it's starting to get cold out here. Where is he?

After two hours have passed, there's a sinking feeling in my gut and I realize I've made a big mistake.

I leave the station, catch a bus across town, back toward Pastor Pete's house.

I see it the moment I turn onto his block: his garage, standing wide open and empty.

CHAPTER SIXTY-EIGHT

ALL HIS TOOLS ARE gone, his bike too. The unfinished headboard is abandoned against the wall, forever unfinished.

I walk up to the interior door, just to make sure. It's standing slightly ajar. No need to lock up when you're fleeing in the middle of the night, I guess.

The crosses on the wall are gone, a few of the posters too. The bookshelves look picked over. I know before I look that the photo album is gone. He doesn't know I have the photo. He doesn't know I have his birth certificate. I almost feel bad. It might be the only thing he has left from his childhood.

I walk through the living room toward the kitchen. The counters are strewn with the leftovers of a quick move: pots and pans, cups and utensils lying around haphazard in the moonlight streaming through the back window. He wouldn't have had room for much in the bed of his truck, just the essentials. And her things too, of course.

He must have started right after I left, right after he got rid of the other kids. I gave him so much time, trusting that he would do the right thing. He seemed so beaten up, so repentant. How could he have done this to me? To June?

Now I have nothing to take to the police but an old birth certificate that only tells part of the story, a part the police may have known already, if I'm honest with myself. June's killer is gone. And without anyone else to prosecute, everyone will think it's me. Maybe I should run. Now, before the police track me down.

I'm so lost in my sadness that I almost miss the sound. A

soft whine, a whimper, coming from upstairs.

CHAPTER SIXTY-NINE

I GO TOWARD THE stairs, following the sound. Someone is here. Someone is crying.

Pastor Pete? Could he be hurt?

I start to run, but stop myself. What if it's someone else?

Gently, slowly, I place a foot on the stairs. Then another. And another.

I creep down the hall, the carpet making the softest of shifts against my sneakers. The shadows of the dark house play tricks on my eyes. As I get closer, I can hear that the sound is coming from Pastor Pete's bedroom. Could it be? Is there still a chance?

I press my back against the wall of the hallway, debating what to do next. Go in? Leave and call the police?

"Baby? Is that you?" her voice calls. "Petey?"

I step into the doorway. There's not much left in the room. The dresser. The bed. An abandoned baseball bat. A few hangers scattered around. On the bed, Miss Hope is curled up on top of the covers, crying. She's clutching a piece of paper in her hand.

"Emma?" she sits up, swipes at her eyes, irritated at my presence, irritated at me seeing her like this. "What are you doing here?"

"I came to see Pastor Pete."

She stands up, crosses her arms over her chest. "I should call the police. They've been looking for you. You're going to be in a lot of trouble once they find you."

"I know," I say, trying to think. "Where is he?"

All of a sudden, she lunges forward, pulling me into a hug.

"He's gone, sweetie. He's gone."

She's gripping me so hard, digging her fingers into the flesh in my back. This was a mistake. I have to get out of here.

I have the phone. All I need is a minute alone. One minute to call Boyer or Paige and let them know I'm here. One minute to crawl out a window and run.

I don't get any time at all.

"You ruined my life," she whispers, digging her nails even farther in. "You ruined everything."

She pushes me to the ground.

I feel something heavy and hard hit my head. Everything goes dark.

CHAPTER SEVENTY

WHEN I COME TO I'm lying naked in a bathtub. My head is swimming, but I'm still alive. Water pours from the faucet, filling the tub millimeters at a time. I try to lift myself out of the water, but my body is heavy and the water makes it even heavier. I heave myself up to a sitting position, then force my torso over the edge and spill out onto the floor like a seal. I feel so weak—dizzy, disoriented.

Before I can sit up, the door opens, and she comes inside, wearing her white wedding dress, the satin swishing around her ankles, me lying on the floor at her feet.

"Please let me go. I won't tell anyone. I promise."

She says nothing, just lifts me back into the bathtub, averting her eyes from my nakedness, my wet body spreading a stain across the front of her dress. She doesn't seem to notice. She doesn't seem to care.

"You don't have to do this. We can forget all about it right now. No one has to know. I won't tell anyone."

She looks at me with a pitying crease between her brows. "Of course you will." Her voice is empty, deadpan, her face as lifeless as a zombie.

She turns away and reaches into the medicine cabinet for something. "You had a chance to live, you know. If you'd just accepted things, this wouldn't be happening. But you couldn't submit to God's will, could you? You had to keep digging. I knew it the moment you asked about June getting baptized. After that, framing you wouldn't be enough. It was just a matter of time before you, too, had to die."

I don't know what to do, so I try to keep her talking.

"She was going to tell everyone, wasn't she? Tell everyone who he was?"

"She thought it would make him a hero, but she was wrong. He'd just have to run again. But you took care of that, didn't you?"

I would never have thought of it if he hadn't been for Paige's video from the night of the lock in. The blind-feely game. Miss Hope planned the game and handed me the box herself, but it wasn't batteries inside, it was bullets. That's how she got my fingerprints on them. She was the last person on my mind before I knew.

Then it all came together. She was the one who was mentoring June. She was the one who stole my earring and planted it under June's body. She was the one who asked me to go upstairs for the soda that night, to get me out of the room. She was the one who killed June after leaving Pastor Pete and Chuck to talk alone.

She was the one who used Pastor Pete's key to get into the gun cabinet, even bought a silencer so no one would hear her do it, then broke into my house to plant the gun. She tried to run me over with that car after I got too close to the truth. And she sent me to New Mercy Ranch.

"You could have gone with him," I say. "You could have run together. Maybe you can still catch him if you try."

"God called me to be a pastor's wife," she says, turning around, pushing something behind her back. "And he's not going to be a pastor anymore, is he?"

"He still could be. You could start over."

"Don't be foolish, child." She slaps me hard, across the face. It stings, but it also sharpens my senses. "There was so much good we were going to do together, but he wasn't strong enough."

She kneels on the cold tile floor, leans over the bathtub edge.

"Because God blessed me with a kind heart, I will give you one last chance to repent your sins before you meet Him and go to God with a clear conscious. Give me your hands. Let's pray."

I shake my head. But she grabs one of my hands in hers.

"It's your last chance, Emma. Do you really want to meet

Jesus with a dirty soul?"

"You can still have a clear conscience too."

She meets my eyes then, surprised. Surprised and angry. "Don't you dare accuse me," she says. "God knows my heart. He knows I did what I had to do to fulfill His higher purpose for me. He knows there's so much more good I can do. Even if that means…"

Her voice trails off, but I know what she's saying. Even if that means killing June, and killing me too.

"So repent now. Or don't. It makes no difference to me. I've never understood the mercy of the Lord. Some people deserve to burn in Hell for their sins."

"I have nothing to be ashamed of," I say.

She squeezes my hand in hers, so tight it feels like my bones could snap.

"You think I don't know about you, but I do. I know everything. I saw you with that boy months ago, in the park, throwing yourself at him, bold as daylight."

She saw me? She knew about Jackson all along?

"I've had my eye on you ever since. I've seen you drift away from Christ, harden your heart to Him, and it's made me sick. You standing up in front of everyone, pretending to love our Savior when you're really whoring around in the shadows? You're a wolf in sheep's clothing, Emma. Those children will be better off without you to lead them astray."

She grips my wrist even tighter, and something slices across it. I scream as pain shoots through me.

She's holding an old-fashioned straight razor, the flip-out kind with a long blade. I recoil against the wall, trying to hold my wound closed, but the blood dribbles down my arm, drips into the bathtub.

Suicide. She's trying to make it look like I committed suicide.

"How are you going to explain this to the police?"

Blood pumps cloudy trails through the water. It turns my stomach to see it.

"A sad affair between an over-sexed teen and a lascivious pastor. You killed June when she saw you, and you killed yourself when he left town."

"No, please. There's still—"

"Quiet!"

She forces my body down under the surface. She's strong, so much stronger than I imagined.

I writhe against her grip, kicking, fighting. She may be strong, but I want to live.

I launch myself out of the bathtub and land on top of her. She throws me off, onto the cold tile. I slide, then I see it. The razor, spinning across the floor. She lost it.

I reach for it and grab it. She's on me, behind me, binding my arms to my body, preventing me from hurting her. Her grip is suffocating. I grip the blade so tight it cuts deep into my palm.

"It's your destiny, Emma. Don't fight it. Go to God."

She's right. I should stop fighting her. I can't win this way. I let my body go limp in her arms. I let my tears turn into desperate sobs.

"Okay," I say. "I beg your mercy. I beg God's mercy. He sent you here to guide my path, but I was blinded by my own pride. I didn't listen to you. I didn't listen."

She loosens her grip. "Give me the razor."

"Let me do it. If it's really God's plan, then let me do it myself."

She switches her grip to my wrists and tugs my back toward the tub, taking the razor out of my hand.

"Please let me do it myself," I beg. "It just scared me is all, your doing it so fast."

I go back into the tub of my own free will, sit down in the water, watch my blood curl into its depths. I lie back. I close my eyes.

"Dear Jesus," I say, "please forgive me for all I've done. I come to You a broken and helpless lamb. Let the glory of Your light shine upon me and heal my aching heart as I meet You in Your glory."

I feel her hand on mine, squeezing. "Was that so hard?" She slips the razor into my hand.

I launch upright and swipe her eyes, missing one, but slicing a line across the other.

She screams, reels back.

I tumble out of the tub, fighting the sway in my head that swirls my vision to mud, but I don't make it.

She lurches forward, blind, blood dripping down her face, and finds my neck with her hands. Suddenly there's no more air in my lungs. I open my mouth to gulp, but nothing makes it down my throat.

The razor. I still have the razor. I slash madly, furiously, and make contact.

The gurgle of blood rips across her throat, deep and dark.

It's the last hit I make.

She squeezes harder, but has to pull one hand away to hold it to her throat.

I struggle out of her grasp just as she falls backward, gripping her neck with both hands, a fountain of red spilling against the pure white of her gown.

I stand and slip, slide my way across the tiles.

I reach for the doorknob and feel her fingers wisp past my ankles as I stumble out.

The air as I leave the house, a blanket wrapped around my shoulders, police lights blaring toward me, the stars kissing my fingertips as I reach up for them, is the sweetest I've ever breathed.

I find my phone and call Boyer.

"I'm at Pastor Pete's. With the killer," I say.

Sitting on the steps as they carry Miss Hope out on a gurney, paramedics racing her still-breathing body to the hospital, I think about June.

I think about June's life cut too short, how she was one of the few people who deserved kindness. Deserved it and never got it.

I think about June free. I think about June as a star in the sky.

I think about what she believed, about heaven and God and angels singing at the pearly gates to welcome the faithful. I hope, for her sake, heaven is real.

CHAPTER SEVENTY-ONE

PAIGE FINDS ME IN the hospital. My parents too, but I scream them out of the room. I don't want to speak to them. I may never want to speak to them again.

So it's Paige, not them, that sits by my side through the night, holding my hand when the nightmares hit and promising everything will be okay.

She's the one who goes to meet Tessa in the park, to tell her where I am and help find her a place to stay.

She's the one who finds a hairstylist who does hospital visits to transform my chopped locks into a pixie cut.

She's the one who tells me it was the IP address of Miss Hope's computer that the police finally hunted down from the e-mail she sent to all my friends. She's the one who tells me they found my acceptance letter to NYU at her apartment, and my money too. I won't get it back anytime soon, but when I do, it's all going to Tessa.

Paige is the one who lets me know they've officially released Jackson, and dials his number for me so I can apologize. But when his parents answer, they say he doesn't want to talk to me.

She's the one who dries my tears. I guess I don't blame him, but it still hurts, thinking about all he's had to suffer because of me. Thinking about not being his anymore.

When I'm about to be released from the hospital, Paige is the one who goes to my house and packs a bag for me, telling my parents how things are going to be from now on.

She's the one who takes me to the airport to put me on a plane to my Grandma Wellington's in Maine, where I'll stay until college starts in the fall, the school having agreed to just give me my damned diploma after everything I've been through.

We sit in a coffee shop and watch the foot traffic at Denver International Airport, me still looking like I just got released from the loony bin with bandages around my wrists, and her trying to be as cheerful as she can, but knowing this is goodbye for what may be a very long time. We haven't been separated for more than a couple weeks since we were babies. And this goodbye is coming three months faster than either of us expected.

"Before, you said you had something to tell me," I say. "But you never said what it was."

"Maybe later," she says, stirring her coffee with a spoon. "Another time."

"When's that gonna be?"

"You know I'm gonna come out and visit. As soon as I can."

"Just tell me."

"Okay," she says warily. "Promise you won't freak out?"

"There's basically nothing that could shock me at this point."

"Okay. Okay, okay, okay." She's talking fast, like she does when she gets nervous. "I…"

"What?"

She takes a deep breath. "I don't like boys," she says.

"You what?" Maybe I was wrong when I said I couldn't be shocked. My eyes go doe wide.

Wait. She's not saying? Oh god.

"Not you, stupid. Don't make it weird. We're like…*sisters*."

"Okay. That's—good for you."

"Oh boy. You're making it weird. I knew you were gonna make it weird."

"No. No! It's fine. It's totally, totally fine. I'm just surprised is all."

"See? Weird. Super weird. I shouldn't have said anything."

"I'm glad you told me. I swear. I am. When did you—? How did you know?"

"I don't know. That time I kissed Ben our freshman year? There was, like, no spark. So then I kissed Ryan, and Greg, and Clark, and remember that boy at summer camp, Martin something? Who was really good looking?"

"Yeah?"

"Still nothing."

"Well, at least you were thorough," I say with a grin.

"Shut up."

"Sorry. Really, though, Paiger, it's not a big deal. I mean, it's a big deal, but not a big deal."

"I kinda figured you'd be cool with it, what with all your recent revelations and everything."

We sit there in silence for a moment. She's giving me space, but I can tell it's her personal mission to bring me back into the fold. It's sweet of her, and I know why she's doing it. A year ago I might have done it too if our places had been switched, even after everything that's happened. Maybe especially after everything that's happened. But today, the odds aren't exactly in her favor.

"I'm still, you know…I still believe in God. I know you don't, but I do. I want to change things for other kids like me." She sits up tall in her seat. "I want to be a pastor someday."

This blows me over almost as much as the other thing. I don't know which will be harder for her. Being gay in a fundamentalist church, or trying to be a female pastor. But either way? I know she's gonna be just fine. She's still the strongest person I know.

"I'm sure you'll be amazing at it," I say, tugging the ratty edges of my old T-shirt—one of my favorites from a mission trip we took together to Costa Rica a few years ago, well worn and so much more comfortable for it.

She smiles, softens. "Thanks."

Paige checks her watch. The moments are ticking away, and we both know it.

"So how about you? Are you ready for this?" she says.

I think about everything that's happened to me in the last few weeks. About love and about suffering. About faith and about trust and how the two are so different. Faith is believing without evidence. Trust is seeing evidence over and over, and still believing, even in the little moments when the evidence doesn't look like it's there anymore. Trust is something I can get behind. Faith, not so much.

I'm standing on this threshold to a new beginning, and don't know the answer to her question. I don't know the answer to any of the questions. Am I ready for everything to change? So fast? Will I ever speak to my parents again? How will I keep myself from falling apart if I see Jackson on campus in just a few short months? I don't know. But I'm okay with the not knowing. I trust Paige, and I trust myself. For now, that's enough. I, too, will be just fine.

"I think so," I say.

It's time. She stands, and I stand, and we hug like it's the last time we'll ever see each other. It won't be, but it sort of feels that way right now. I can't imagine not having her a few blocks away. I can't even think about her being on an opposite coast by the fall. There are phones, and airplanes, but that's not the same. It's one of the hardest things I've ever done to let go of her, but eventually, I do.

"Text me every day, okay?" she says.

"I will."

"I'm gonna be so pissed if you don't."

"I will."

She hugs me again, then yanks herself away. "Okay. You better go before I lose it and chain you up in my basement."

"Love you, Paigers," I say.

"Love you too, Embot," she says. "Everything's gonna be good from now on. I promise."

I squeeze her hand then walk toward security, turning back to look at my best friend, her face shiny with tears, biting her cheek like she used to do when she was a little girl, and still my best friend after all this, after knowing everything there is to know about me, about each other.

By the time I get to the plane, it's already boarding. I'm one of the last to arrive, which is exactly how I wanted it. Fewer people to stare. I scan the aisle numbers, looking for my seat.

That's when I see him, in the seat next to my empty one. He's looking right at me, no doubt in his eyes, no shock at the mess I must be. Just steady, strong. What he's always been really.

Something that was broken inside me seals back together, melted wax reshaped around a fresh wick, ready to burn again.

"Jackson?" I say, my throat tight.

He stands, the height of him bowed against the overhead compartment, making a cave of the two of us together. His face is so close to mine. So close.

320

"I'm going to kiss you a lot of places, Emma Grant," he says, his voice hushed, just for me. He reaches out, slides his hand against my cheek. "But first I'm going to kiss you right here."

And he does.

And we fly.

About the Author

When she's not hanging out with her ginger husband and two stinky basset hounds, Livia Harper writes modern thrillers and mysteries in the vein of Megan Abbott's *Dare Me* or Gillian Flynn's *Gone Girl.* She's a film lover who graduated with a degree in Writing & Directing from Colorado Film school, then went on to study even more about storytelling at UCLA's Professional Program in Screenwriting. For a long time, she made her living as a photographer, and even spent some years doing marketing for a real estate firm. But today she's happy to call writing her occupation. She's overjoyed to be sharing her first book with you, and plans on many more to come.

Continue on for a sneak peak at Livia's next work: *BOYFRIEND GLASSES*, the first book in a trilogy of psychological thrillers coming soon.

Here's sneak peak at Livia Harper's upcoming novel…

BOYFRIEND GLASSES

Livia Harper

TODAY, 7:52 PM

Some people say there's no such thing as love at first sight. They're wrong.

The first time I saw Blake... well, it was like his heart was a magnet and mine was molten nickel. I could feel the fire of it singe my skin as it left my body. I could see its hot cord twining orange out of my chest, melting its way directly toward his. When our hearts met, they fused. Mine wrapped around his, holding him forever.

I knew it was love because the first time I saw him, the very first time, Blake did something no one else had ever done before. Blake made me forget all about Johnny.

We were at a geeks/greeks party at the Sigma Phi Upsilon house, before I knew to call it SigUp. It was the first real party of many that night, the first party night of the year. We were drunk on freedom and electric with high expectations for our future. Walking in there with Amber, like we belonged, like it was no big deal, like they threw parties just so girls like us would come, made me feel wild and alive for the first time since Johnny. It was everything I hoped college would be. It was everything high school wasn't.

Blake was... all Blake. There's no other way to say it, no other way to define all the little parts that add up to him being him—his confident smile, his body tall and statuesque as a Michelangelo, the absolute command he had of the whole room. Dark hair and tan skin and eyes like peridot: green and shimmering and endless. He was all Blake.

Every single girl in the room was looking at him. Every single one. Why wouldn't they? He was perfect.

But Blake didn't pay attention to any of them. He knew what he wanted and he knew he would get it. And what he wanted was me. Right from the beginning. He could feel me there, in that room, feel our connection just like I could.

But he saw Amber first. And he got confused.

He walked right up to her, like I wasn't even there. He didn't say a word, just held her eyes and took her hand and led her into a corner. Everyone stared as he took his fake black glasses off and put them on her and kissed her. They looked like the perfect couple. But we would have been better, so much better.

Amber wore those glasses all night, a trophy of his love. Her cornsilk eyelashes brushed against them, every flutter reminding her that she was his choice. His.

I wanted to rip those glasses off her face, just to touch something he'd touched.

But I don't want to anymore. I don't have to. I'm wearing them right now.

And Amber is dead.

WANT TO READ NEXT three chapters? Sign up now at:

www.LiviaHarper.com/BOYFRIENDGLASSES

You'll get the chapters for free **AND** be the first to know when the book comes out.

Thanks for reading!

Acknowledgements

Thank you to Dave, my amazing husband. It's a hard job being married to a writer, but it's a role he's always filled with the utmost care and support. My forever love and gratitude for every minute of every day.

Thank you to Sara and Jolene, without who's encouragement it would be difficult to imagine completing this book.

Thank you to the many individuals who read and re-read *SLAIN* and helped me shape it into something people might actually be able to look at. Their fine writing inspires me to be a better writer every day. Specifically: Jennifer K., Jennifer C.P., Alex S., Sara S., Kelly C., Cassi C., Josh V., and all the wonderful people at writer's group.

Thank you to my family, both biological and the one I was gifted through marriage, who are kindly supporting both me and this book, despite their beliefs.

Thank you to my editor, Jason Whited (www.Jason-Whited.com)for sweating over the capitalizations of God/god in this book almost as much as I did.

And finally, thank you to my readers for taking the time to read my work. It was truly a labor of love to create this book, and I'm so pleased to have been able to share it with you.

Dear Reader,

I hope you've enjoyed reading my debut novel, SLAIN.

While the book contains a lot of controversial subject matter, my rule-of-thumb was to deal with it in a way that was true to Emma's character. Parts of this reflect my own beliefs, and parts do not. I have a great respect for many people of faith, my own family included, and my hope is that the book sparks thoughtful discussion instead of ire on both sides of the issue. I'm not naive enough to believe that my hopes always translate into reality, but please take that sentiment to heart.

Lastly, I love to hear from my readers. Love/hate it? Have questions? I'm dying to know. Feel free to drop me a line at Livia@LiviaHarper.com.

Thank you again for taking the time to read a book from a first-time, independent author. It means so much that you did.

Sincerely,

P.S. If you have a moment, please take a second to leave an honest review wherever you purchased this book. It really helps other readers find me, and know what to expect from the book. Thank you!